Nicole Helm grew up with her nose in a book and the dream of one day becoming a writer. Luckily, after a few failed career choices, she gets to follow that dream—writing down-to-earth contemporary romance and romantic suspense. From farmers to cowboys, Midwest to the West, Nicole writes stories about people finding themselves and finding love in the process. She lives in Missouri with her husband and two sons and dreams of someday owning a barn.

K.D. Richards is a native of the Washington, DC, area, who now lives outside Toronto with her husband and two sons. You can find her at kdrichardsbooks.com

HUNTING
A KILLER

NICOLE HELM

PURSUIT OF
THE TRUTH

K.D. RICHARDS

MILLS & BOON

First Published in Great Britain 2021
by Mills & Boon, an imprint of HarperCollins*Publishers*
1 London Bridge Street, London, SE1 9GF

Hunting a Killer © 2021 Harlequin Books S.A.
Pursuit of the Truth © 2021 Kia Dennis

Special thanks and acknowledgement are given to Nicole Helm for
her contribution to the *Tactical Crime Division: Traverse City* series.

ISBN: 978-0-263-28320-4

0121

MIX
Paper from
responsible sources
FSC™ C007454

This book is produced from independently certified FSC™
paper to ensure responsible forest management.

For more information visit: www.harpercollins.co.uk/green

Printed and bound in Spain
by CPI, Barcelona

HUNTING A KILLER

NICOLE HELM

For all those happily-ever-afters
that started as workplace romances.

Prologue

The tears leaked out of Kay Duvall's eyes, even as she tried to focus on what she had to do. *Had* to do to bring Ben home safe.

She fumbled with her ID and punched in the code that would open the side door, usually only used by a guard taking a smoke break. It would be easy for the men behind her to escape from this side of the prison.

It went against everything she was supposed to do. Everything she considered right and good.

A quiet sob escaped her lips. They had her son. How could she not help them escape? Nothing mattered beyond her son's life.

"Would you stop already?" one of the prisoners muttered. He'd made her give him her gun, which he now jabbed into her back. "Crying isn't going to change anything. So just shut up."

She didn't care so much about her own life, or if she'd be fired. She didn't care what happened to her as long as they let her son go. So she swallowed down the sobs and blinked out as many tears as she could, hoping to stem the tide of them.

She got the door open and slid out first—because the man holding the gun pushed it into her back until she moved forward.

They moved out the door behind her, dressed in the clothes she'd stolen from the locker room and Lost and Found. Anything warm she could get her hands on to help them escape into the frigid February night.

Help them escape. Help three dangerous men escape prison. When she was supposed to keep them inside.

It didn't matter anymore. She just wanted them gone. If they were gone, they'd let her baby go. They had to let her baby go.

Kay forced her legs to move, one foot in front of the other, toward the gate she could unlock without setting off any alarms. She unlocked it, steadier this time if only because she kept thinking once they were gone she could get in contact with Ben.

She flung open the gate and gestured them out into the parking lot. "Stay out of the safety lights and no one should bug you."

"You better hope not," one of the men growled.

"The minute you sound that alarm, your kid is dead. You got it?" This one was the ringleader. The one who'd been in for murder. Who else would he kill out there in the world?

Guilt pooled in Kay's belly, but she had to ignore it. She had to live with it. Whatever guilt she'd felt would be survivable. Living without her son wouldn't be. Besides, she had to believe they'd be caught. They'd do something else terrible and be caught.

As long as her son was alive, she didn't care.

The three men disappeared into the night, wearing the clothes she'd stolen for them. She hoped they froze to death. She hoped every bad thing befell them. As soon as her baby was safe, she'd help the authorities in whatever way she could.

She slammed the gate closed and locked it. She was

sick with anger and terror, and her hands shook as she fumbled for her phone. She dialed her mother. Just because she couldn't sound the alarm didn't mean she couldn't make sure Mom was all right. Had they hurt her when they'd kidnapped Ben? Was she terrified too?

Or worse, dead? Mom definitely would have fought off anyone trying to take Ben, even if it ended her life.

Another sob escaped Kay's mouth, followed by a bigger, louder one when her mother answered sounding perfectly calm and cheerful. "Hi, honey."

She could only gasp for breath. Relief but new fears bubbling up inside her.

"What on Earth is wrong?" her mother asked, worry and confusion seeping into her tone. *New* worry. *New* confusion.

Kay blinked, taken aback by how calm her mom sounded. Did she not know? Had Ben been kidnapped without Mom even realizing? How could that happen?

"Ben..." she managed to croak.

"Shoveling in his mac and cheese like usual. We really need to work on getting this boy some vegetables. I know you don't want to give him a complex, but he can't subsist on cheese and pasta alone. Are you okay?"

"I'm fine. Mom... Everything is okay there? You're sure."

"Of course I'm sure. Ben's right here. Did you want to talk to him? Ben, here's your mom."

She closed her eyes, tears pouring over her cheeks. She heard her baby's voice, safe as could be, chattering about something in the background. She swallowed down the sinking, horrible realization she was a stupid, utter failure. "No, Mom," she croaked. "I have to go. I may be home late."

Her mother's words were little more than a buzz as she hung up the phone and slid it back into her pocket.

There was only one thing to do now—sound the alarm, own up to her mistake and pray she didn't end up an inmate herself.

Chapter One

Selena Lopez yawned as she filed into the meeting room of the Tactical Crime Division—a specialized FBI team made up of experts from several active divisions in one small group.

Selena's specialization was currently back home asleep in her crate. Lucky dog. Of course, if Selena was deployed into the field, she'd be waking her German shepherd and taking her out to track regardless of the time.

She yawned again. She was used to middle-of-the-night calls, going on little to no sleep, but her neighbors had been having one hell of a party. *Again.*

She was really getting tired of apartment living.

In the boardroom, half the team were in various states of disarray already situated around the large table. Sleep-tumbled hair, casual clothes and desperate looks at the cups of coffee in front of them were all typical signs of a middle of the night call.

Selena knew once their director walked into the room, they'd all sharpen into the tools they were. But for a few more minutes they could be human.

Axel Morrow walked in behind her. He looked like he'd somehow had the time to take a shower, comb his hair and get dressed in fresh clothes without a wrinkle in sight. Casual though the jeans and long-sleeved tee were, he could have walked in at two in the afternoon looking like that. His blond hair didn't appear sleep-tousled at all, and his green eyes were perfectly alert.

How did he look perfect at two o'clock in the morning? When she knew he'd driven in farther than everyone else, since he lived on an old nonoperating farm outside town.

She frowned at him when he took the seat next to her. God, he smelled good. And when he flashed her a smile, that obnoxious fluttering she got whenever she saw him spread deeper and flirted way too close with serious attraction.

Which was *not* allowed.

She knew exactly where those kind of thoughts led. To poor choices and embarrassing breakups. The TCD team was pretty tight-knit, and she wouldn't jeopardize her good standing here over attraction. Not when everyone liked her.

She glanced at her sister across the table. Okay, maybe not everyone. Opaline had been here longer. She hadn't exactly been hostile toward Selena joining the group, but she hadn't been welcoming either. Their continued standoff remained as it always was.

Tense and mostly silent. But they worked together when they had to.

Selena had hoped coming here might help bridge the gap between them, but she'd yet to figure out *how.* They were so different. What they believed and how they felt about their family… How could it not keep them at odds?

Dr. Carly Welsh entered the room and sat down on the other side of her. "You look rough."

Selena slid her friend a look. "You try living in party city. I bet they aren't even allowed to have parties in your swank place, and I'm guessing Noah's isn't prone to loud raves into the night."

Carly rolled her eyes, but the smile she always got when anyone mentioned her fiancé spread across her face. "You could live somewhere nicer," she pointed out.

"Who's got the time to find a nice place when we're getting called in at two in the morning?"

Carly didn't answer because Alana Suzuki walked in. Director of TCD, she looked put together in her smart suit. It didn't matter that it was the middle of the night. She carried a folder, and her face was grim.

Which made Selena fidget. Alana was *all* business, and while their business was serious, there was something…discomfiting about the way Alana specifically looked at her.

Then Opaline.

"Selena, Opaline, could I see you outside for a moment?"

The discomfort settled into full-on dread in her gut, but she got to her feet and walked out of the boardroom with Opaline.

Alana stopped in the hallway and looked at both of them with some sympathy. "I wish we had more time so that I could put this delicately."

"No need," Selena replied, careful to keep her voice even and calm. "Lay it on us."

She heard her sister huff, but Selena couldn't look at her just now. She had to keep it together. Doing her job required being able to compartmentalize. Opaline had never understood the fine art of pushing things away, let alone dealing with things at appropriate moments. She always reacted. Oftentimes when it got both of them in more trouble.

"I'm afraid you have a personal connection to this assignment," Alana began.

Selena closed her eyes. She knew she couldn't outwardly react, but in this moment, just the three of them, she gave herself a moment to breathe. "Peter."

When Selena opened her eyes, Alana's expression was empathetic. "Yes, your brother has escaped prison with two other convicts. We need to stop them before they cross the Canadian border."

Alana was a good boss, an excellent director. The perfect mix of personal and business. She knew how to take care of her people. Selena appreciated that beyond measure.

Which meant she wouldn't let Peter jeopardize her job here. She'd do whatever she had to do to complete the mission that involved her half brother. She'd bring him to justice, no matter what it took.

"We'll go over the details inside, but before we head in there, I wanted to give you both a chance to bow out. We can replace either or both of you for this mission if you feel your relationship with Peter would keep you from being able to do your job. Conversely, you can take some time to think about—"

"I don't need any time," Selena said, keeping her voice devoid of any and all emotion, no matter how it battered at her on the inside. "If we're tracking, you need me and Blanca."

Alana nodded, then turned to Selena's sister. "Opaline?"

Selena finally glanced at her. Opaline looked at her like she was some kind of monster. She'd never understood you couldn't save people who didn't want to be saved. And seemed to blame Selena for the fact their half brother did not want to be saved.

"I can handle it," Opaline said, glaring daggers at Selena. Her voice was rough, and her eyes were bright with unshed tears.

For a half brother they hardly knew, who'd refused help, again and again. Whose very existence had caused such a rift in their family, it still hadn't healed.

Selena would never understand it or Opaline. She turned on a heel and walked back into the boardroom. No one looked directly at her, but she could feel their consideration all the same.

She slid into her chair, keeping her expression neutral. Carly was friend enough not to say anything, but of course Axel would be obnoxious.

"You okay?" Axel asked.

Selena raised her chin, keeping her gaze on where Alana was taking her place at the head of the boardroom table. "Just fine."

SELENA WAS DEFINITELY not just fine, but as Alana walked back into the boardroom, Axel Morrow had to focus on the task at hand. TCD business, and the challenge Alana Suzuki would lay out before them.

"Team, I appreciate you all coming in at such an hour, but we need to get started as soon as possible. Opaline?"

Where Selena was completely blank, Opaline was outwardly shaken by whatever Alana had told them. It didn't take a special agent to deduce whatever the mission was involved the sisters on some kind of personal level.

Still, Opaline went to the front of the room and took over the computer. As the tech specialist for TCD, it was always her job to run through the slideshow.

"Three inmates have escaped a maximum-security federal prison this evening. Because of the nature of their crimes, the way they've escaped and where we think they're going, TCD has been tasked with stopping them and bringing them back before they cross the border to Canada. Police have set up roadblocks on routes to the border since they likely stole a car, but so far, no sightings to give us an idea of their route." Alana nodded at Opaline, who brought up a mug shot on the screen at the front of the room.

"Leonard Koch is the presumed leader of this little trio. He's in for life for the murder of a family, among a litany of other charges."

Alana didn't look directly at Axel, but he felt the consideration all the same. Murder was part and parcel with his job as special agent, even in his supervisory role. He still considered himself part of the team more than some kind of leader.

But the murder of a family was…well, it hit close to home. Families being murdered was why he was here. As an FBI agent, as the person he was today. To stop men like Leonard Koch before he hurt any more people.

Alana nodded at the screen, and the mug shot changed to the next slide, which included a list of charges.

Max McRay, special agent and explosives expert, let out a low whistle next to him. "That's quite a rap sheet. How'd this guy get out?"

"He and his cohorts convinced a prison guard they had her son. Unfortunately, since they had a lot of personal information and were threatening her son's life, she fell for it. On the bright side, the child is fine. So, right now we're just focused on apprehension." Alana pointed at Opaline to bring up the next slide.

"Steve Jenson is our number two. A history of battery, assault, but he's in for his role in an armed burglary that went south when a security guard was killed in the resulting shootout. Though we don't have any concrete idea of what kind of access they have to supplies, we're considering them both armed and extremely dangerous."

"And the third?" Aria Calletti asked. She was the newest member of TCD, but she'd proven herself extraordinarily capable last year when she'd been instrumental in bringing down a murderous smuggling ring. Axel had been with her when she'd gotten their best lead to talk. She was a go-getter, that was for sure.

But Axel wished she hadn't pressed so quickly when it clearly upset Opaline. The woman let out a shaky sigh before she brought up the next picture.

"The third escapee is Peter Lopez," Alana said with more gravity than she'd used to announce the other two.

As it was a group of highly trained FBI agents, no one immediately looked to Selena or Opaline, but that didn't mean everyone in the room wasn't paying attention to the reactions to the two women who shared a last name with the third man.

Opaline wiped at her eyes and shook her head. Meanwhile, a surreptitious look at Selena showed a woman with no reaction at all.

"Peter is Opaline and Selena's brother, and they've both been briefed in advance and given the option to remove themselves if they felt like they couldn't do their jobs, but both agreed to stay on."

"We're not close," Selena said, her voice even. "He's our half brother, the product of an affair our father had. Don't feel like you have to walk on eggshells around me. We might share some genetic material, but I don't know the guy."

Alana nodded, and Opaline glared daggers at her sister, but she didn't argue with the assessment.

Axel found he wasn't sure which reaction made more sense. The complete lack of emotion had to be hiding *something*, but if they were so removed from the man, why was Opaline so upset?

Something he'd get to the bottom of before the day was out, but for now, they had to decide on a course of action.

"Opaline, would you bring up the map?"

The screen changed from Peter's mug shot to a topographical map of the area between the prison in northern Michigan and the Canadian border.

"We have reason to believe they're heading for Canada. We want to catch them before they do, and before they hurt anyone. The first wave of that will fall to Selena."

Selena nodded. "I'll take Blanca up to the prison and we'll start from there. Unless we have new known whereabouts?"

"Rihanna will keep in close touch with local authorities," Alana said, referring to TCD's police and press liaison. "If we get any updates on location, that will be relayed to you and Axel."

Selena straightened next to him. "Axel?"

"He'll partner with you on this. No one works alone. Aria and Carly will work together as well, and we'll bring in Scott Fletcher from the FBI to pair with Max to keep things even. We'll station the teams of two along the Canadian border. While Selena and Axel track, you'll set up a perimeter where hopefully if they don't catch up to the trio, you guys can stop them. You'll want to stay in close contact, and adjust as necessary. Axel will be lead on this."

He nodded at Alana before sliding Selena a look. She continued to show absolutely no reaction. She was a statue.

"We might be in charge of tracking," Alana said, "but the local police will be helpful resources, especially if the escapees cause any trouble in some of the smaller towns or more remote areas. This is a true team effort.

The six of you tracking, Opaline working on tech—she'll get you all the maps you'll want to download onto your phones. Rihanna is working with local authorities in case we catch wind of them somewhere. No one acts alone."

"And we bring them all in before anyone else is killed," Axel added. Maybe it didn't need to be said, but there was an urgency that had to be heeded. He stood as Selena did.

"I'll follow you to your apartment in the Jeep. We'll go from there."

She didn't say anything, just gave the slightest nod and then walked out the door. Axel looked back at Alana, but her expression was neutral.

This wouldn't be as simple as bringing three fugitives to justice, that much was for sure.

Chapter Two

Selena pulled her personal car into the parking space of her apartment complex. The partiers seemed to have finally dispersed—since it was nearing four in the morning at this point.

She trudged up the stairs to her top-floor apartment and thought about Carly saying she could move if she didn't like where she was. Selena was sure there wasn't time, nor did she have the energy to look for a new place. But she realized she'd been doing this for four years now. Saying she didn't have time. Saying she didn't have the energy.

Was she going to settle into this crappy apartment complex forever and just exist? She put a lot into her work at TCD, and enjoyed it, but that didn't mean the rest of her life had to be…this.

She shook her head as she unlocked her door and then the dead bolt she'd installed herself. There really *wasn't* time to deal with her living quarters right now—but she promised herself when this assignment was over, she'd really start looking into a more permanent living space.

For now, the focus had to be getting her dog and tracking the three escapees.

One of whom you know.

Didn't matter. She hadn't lied to her team and friends.

She'd had limited contact with Peter. She'd tried to help him over the years. Not because she'd wanted to, but because her father had insisted her position in law enforcement made her the perfect person to reach his son.

His son. With a woman who had not been his wife at the time. Yet he'd expected Selena to step in and…

Selena couldn't let herself go down these messy emotional paths. She'd attended Peter's trial in some silly attempt to understand how a man related to her could go so wrong, and what she'd realized sitting there watching him answer questions belligerently was that she couldn't allow herself to take responsibility for her father's mistakes. Or Peter's.

She'd been in the midst of her own stupid personal drama, surprised at all the ways she could screw up her own life. All the ways she could fail.

Then and there she'd promised herself to stop letting other people run her life. She wouldn't feel guilty about Peter, she wouldn't keep helping her father when she didn't want to and she certainly wouldn't let herself get so wrapped up in a man that her entire career could be threatened.

No, she'd come to a lot of conclusions in that courtroom. Her life was her own. Peter being involved in this latest suspect apprehension was irrelevant. Partnering with Axel Morrow? Irrelevant.

Selena walked into her bedroom. Blanca raised her head with a huff.

"Sorry to disturb, queen of the manor, but we've got work to do." Selena opened her closet and grabbed the backpack she always had ready to go should she be called off on a mission.

At the word *work*, Blanca slowly got to her feet, stretched and then shook her head. She padded out of the room, and while Selena gathered the rest of her stuff, she could hear Blanca lapping up some water.

Satisfied she had as much as was reasonable to take, Selena headed to the kitchen and grabbed herself a water bottle and a protein bar. There wouldn't be time for breakfast.

Blanca waited by the door. Selena took a moment to pause, to pull herself together. Axel was…a problem, but she could hardly let him know that. She knelt next to her dog.

"This isn't going to be an easy one." She scratched Blanca behind the ears and glanced out the window that looked out over the parking lot. Axel was pulling the Jeep into a parking space next to her car. She sighed. "And we've got help."

She couldn't be bitter about it. Working alone was rarely part and parcel with this kind of mission. She might have preferred Carly's company, or even Aria, rookie though she was.

Okay, in her apartment she could be honest with herself. She'd prefer anyone over Axel. Even her sister, probably. She might get in a fight with her sister, but she wouldn't have to deal with…attraction.

Even when they didn't have a mission to complete, she didn't want to think about that enduring problem with Axel Morrow. "So aren't you lucky you have more important things to concern yourself with?" she muttered to herself.

She stood and grabbed the duffel by the door that had all Blanca's supplies. Axel was waiting at the Jeep, which she appreciated. Selena let Blanca out then focused on locking up the apartment. When she made her way down the stairs, Blanca was sniffing around the grass while Axel stood next to the Jeep.

Watching her, not the dog.

She didn't let the jolt inside her show on the outside. It was still dark. The only light illuminating him was from the parking lot light. Still, his gaze on her felt electric.

She let out a slow breath, being careful to keep her expression neutral as she approached. "Gassed up?"

"All ready to head out to the prison," Axel confirmed.

Selena tossed her bags into the back of the Jeep, next to Axel's bag. A beat-up military pack. She whistled for Blanca, who trotted up to Axel.

He offered the dog a pat, then opened the back door for her. Blanca jumped in. At six, she was a veteran and a pro. She knew her job, and she did it well. She'd acclimated to TCD quicker than Selena herself had, but four years later, it often felt like they'd always worked with TCD.

"I'll drive."

As if she had any doubt Mr. Second in Command would drive and call the shots. Much as she respected Axel on a professional level, she was going to have to bite her tongue to keep from knee-jerk sniping at him on a personal one.

Hardly his fault she thought he was hot. Definitely not his fault she'd already learned her lesson in that department. She moved into the passenger seat without a word.

He climbed into the driver's seat and turned the key in the ignition. Blanca had already settled herself into the back—specially designed for tactical dogs, so Blanca wouldn't be too jostled by any off-terrain driving.

"No word on any new sightings?" Selena asked, pulling out her phone and bringing up the map of the area Opaline had sent all members of the team. By the time they got to the prison, the escapees would have a significant head start. They could head toward the prison, but what they really needed was someone to report seeing the fugitives.

"Afraid not," Axel said pulling out of her apartment complex's parking lot.

"I don't know how we're going to catch up with them at this rate."

"I imagine they'll hang low during the day. They won't want to be spotted—not before they cross the border. That should give us a few hours to minimize the distance. There's only so many ways to get to Canada, and the prison guard was sure that's where they were headed."

Selena wasn't so sure. There wasn't much in terms of towns or people between the prison and the Canadian border. Lots and lots of wilderness and lakes, though. The kind it was easy to disappear into. Even crossing by water could be done with the right amount of money. They might not have had any leading the prison, but that didn't mean some wasn't waiting for them.

They drove for a while. Selena was grateful Axel didn't try to fill the silence with chatter. He was good at knowing when to do that and when not to. He read people well.

It was one of the many reasons she avoided being alone with him. The last thing she needed was him *reading* all that went on in her head when she looked at him.

Axel's phone rang, and he used the Jeep's Bluetooth system to answer it. "Morrow."

"Hey, guys," Rihanna's voice greeted them. "I just got off the phone with local police in Winston. There's been an incident, and it looks to be our guys."

"What happened?" Axel demanded. With a glance at the lane next to him, he moved over to get off at the exit, immediately altering their course to head toward Winston instead of the prison.

Selena studied her map, but Rihanna's pause on the other end had her gut clenching in dread as she calculated their new driving distance and how much of a head start the escapees had.

"Local wildlife officers found two poachers who'd been shot," Rihanna said at last. "One was capable of telling local law enforcement a little about who'd shot him. They'd stumbled upon three men, who fired without pause. They left our witness for dead after stealing guns and money. His description of them matches our escapees."

Axel's grip on the steering wheel tightened. "You said one was capable of talking to law enforcement," he said, his voice abnormally cold. "What about the other poacher?"

Again, Rihanna paused, and Selena watched Axel's expression get harder…and harder. She wasn't sure why he cared about the other poacher. Another set of eyes? Two stories instead of one? More witnesses meant more information and—

"He was dead when the wildlife officers arrived."

The coldness in his voice spread into his gaze on the road. The clear *fury* pumping off him was an emotional response Selena wouldn't have expected from him. He was always so controlled. So *cool* under pressure.

"Get us the location," he said, the words having a sharp bite. "We'll meet local law enforcement there."

"I'll make sure they know you're coming." Rihanna hung up.

Axel increased the speed of the Jeep. The roads were mostly empty this early in the morning, but he was taking exits too fast, and curves even faster, to the point Selena was actually afraid they'd wreck before they got where they needed to be.

"Getting there faster won't change the fact the man is dead," Selena said, gripping the handle of the door as tight as she could.

"But it might stop another innocent man from being killed."

THOUGH IT GRATED, Axel slowed down. It was possible he was pushing things just a little too hard. Yes, it was a failure a man had been killed. A failure he felt deep in his bones. But if he did something foolish because of that feeling of failure, that would also be his fault.

And if it hurt Selena or Blanca...well, no. He had to get a hold of himself. They'd get to Winston soon enough.

"I don't like being too late," he muttered, the closest to an apology he was going to get.

"Who does?" Selena replied, too flippantly for his tastes. "But I can't blame myself for every criminal who does the wrong thing. I'd never get out of bed in the morning."

Axel knew he had to control his emotions, knew he couldn't compare this to all those years ago, but his temper strained at how unaffected she was. "Even your own brother's wrong thing? Because I think that'd mean *something* to you."

She whipped her gaze toward him. There was fury in her dark eyes, but she'd paled a bit. Like he'd landed a blow.

Hell. He'd screwed up. He could blame it on lack of sleep or what have you, but the bottom line was he should handle loss of life better. He had to. "I'm sorry. That was uncalled for."

She slowly looked away from him, her eyes on the road before them. The sun was flirting with the horizon, and she said nothing. Not that it was okay. Not that she accepted his apology. Not even telling him where he could shove his apology.

Which was somehow worse. He squeezed the steering wheel, then forced himself to loosen his grip. "Look. It bothers me."

More silence, because it bothering him was hardly an excuse for being a jerk.

"Which isn't an excuse. I can't excuse it. I shouldn't have said it. I shouldn't have let the emotional response take over. But I've been the survivor in that situation, so there *is* an emotional response. Better to get it out now rather than let it bubble up later." Or so he'd tell himself for the time being so he could focus on getting the job done.

Selena's eyebrows drew together. "I don't remember hearing anything about that."

"Not on duty. Not... I was a kid."

Her silence in response made his skin feel too tight. While there were members of the team who knew about his past, he didn't trot it out to discuss for fun. If people knew, fine, but he'd rather not have to get into it too often.

Still, he'd been the jerk. This was his penance.

"My family was killed when I was seven. The FBI had been after the guy for months and were closing in, but they didn't make it in time. He killed my parents, my brother. He shot me, but by that time they'd surrounded the house. I was transported in enough time to save my life. I got into this so some kid didn't have to be the one with the murdered family members, and yeah, I can't save everyone. But I don't like to lose a life on an active case I'm on, knowing if we hadn't sat around in a briefing meeting we might have gotten there."

"I don't know what to say," Selena said softly. "I guess there really isn't anything to say."

Most people said they were sorry, which he hated. Or went on and on about how awful it must have been. How brave he was to survive it. To go into the FBI. He appreciated the fact she knew there wasn't anything that would actually help.

"Except briefing is necessary to know who, how and what. We could have been on the road to the prison sooner, but it wouldn't have saved that guy's life."

Axel pushed out a breath. "I guess not."

"There's enough hard stuff in this job without heaping guilt and blame on yourself or your team that doesn't belong there. You start questioning—"

"I'm not questioning. I have the utmost confidence in our team."

"Okay, well…" Both their phones pinged at the same time. He let Selena deal with the information.

"We're meeting the local police force at a cabin near where the incident took place," Selena said, tapping a few keys on her phone. "GPS isn't going to be much help once we go off-road, so I'll navigate once we're in Winston."

Axel nodded wordlessly. He was glad they were moving on. They had a job to do, not pasts to obsess over.

"Is that why you have a scar on your jaw?"

He slid Selena a look. Her gaze was on the road in front of them, but the scar was faint these days. Hardly noticeable. Unless someone had been looking.

Which of course, he knew she had. Four years they'd worked in the same department. He was aware there was…chemistry. It was why he kept his distance. Clearly he had enough of his own baggage, he didn't need to add the complication of romantic entanglements.

Still, he wasn't *unaffected* that she looked.

"Yeah. The guy shot me, but mostly missed. Didn't have time to check I was dead before he ran."

"And they caught him? The FBI?"

"Before he'd even gotten out of the neighborhood."

"That's rough." She shifted in the seat and slid her arm back to give Blanca a pet, all the while keeping her gaze on the road. "Turn here," she instructed. "We want to go in on the west side of town."

Axel only nodded and took the turn she instructed him to make.

"I got into law enforcement because of family too. Because of Peter, to be specific. Some part of me thought if I became a cop, I'd be able to talk him out of being hell-bent on destroying his own life."

"I thought you didn't have a relationship."

"We don't. Doesn't mean I wasn't aware what was going on with him. Mom complaining about Dad's dead-beat son. Dad washing his hands of any kind of trouble because heaven forbid he try to help his own kid." She shrugged jerkily. "Point is, we've all got our stuff, right? Sometimes it pops up and gets the best of us for a minute or two, but we're pros. I've never seen you falter when it mattered. I haven't either."

She was saying it so he didn't think too much about the moment before. That was obvious, but he thought she was saying it a bit for herself too. She might act unaffected, but Peter meant something to her. They both had their baggage that might affect them as they went through the assignment.

But in the end, regardless of feelings of failure or brotherly attachment, they'd both do their jobs.

They had to.

Chapter Three

Early morning light filtered through the trees as Selena followed Axel toward the flashing lights of a police car and the low hum of conversation. She held Blanca on her leash, keeping her close.

The air was frigid, and Selena was grateful for the thick tactical boots she wore as they hiked through the snow. It was packed down from many sets of footprints. Were any of them her brother's?

It didn't matter. She couldn't think of Peter like her brother. She had to think about what he really was: a stranger she was tasked with bringing to justice. She didn't know him. And he most certainly didn't know her.

So, he was a stranger. She would work with Axel to apprehend him, because regardless of what genes they shared, he was responsible for killing a man. Maybe he hadn't pulled the trigger on the poor poacher who'd come across the wrong men at the wrong time.

But maybe he had.

Axel's strides were long, and she didn't bother trying to keep up. Blanca sniffed the snow and trees and oriented herself to her new surroundings—in order for her to be ready to track, she needed that time. Selena refused to admit she was giving the time to herself, as well.

She needed a little distance from Axel Morrow. She

hadn't gotten into the FBI and this special unit by being soft, by showing compassion and empathy for her partner. There wasn't time for that. A teammate had to be understanding and forgive their partner's mistakes, or you'd never keep moving forward.

But that wasn't what she'd done. She'd given him a piece of herself. When he'd apologized for snapping at her and using her brother to do it, she should have accepted it. The end.

But *no*. She'd had to tell him she'd gotten into law enforcement because of Peter. She'd *shared*, when she knew that was professional suicide as a woman in a tough field. Oh, she'd worked with Axel long enough to know he wasn't one of those guys who used every weakness a woman showed against her, but that didn't change the fact she was on dangerous ground.

Dangerous ground she'd walked on before, and lost far too much of herself in the process.

By the time she caught up with Axel, he was already deep in conversation with the local police officer.

"I think they'd planned to stay at this cabin for the day," the officer was saying. He gave Selena and Blanca a brief nod. "But the poachers came in and... Well, you can read the statement."

"I'd like to talk to the survivor first, if you don't mind."

Again, the officer nodded. "We've got him in the car. We've already taken his statement, and we'll drive him home once things are good on your end."

The officer started walking toward the police cruiser, but Selena stopped Axel with a light touch of the arm. It would be impossible to get through this mission without touching him like this—lightly, casually—but that didn't mean she had to like it.

"I'm going to search the cabin," she said, maybe a little bit sharper and more authoritatively than she needed to.

His expression was flat. She'd worked with him for four years, and she'd learned—whether she wanted to or not—to read Axel's moods on a case. The murder bothered him, plain and simple, and now she knew why.

She wished she didn't.

"Cops said they left everything as is," Axel said quietly, his green eyes searching the woods around them. "Blanca should be able to pick up something. We'll track from here with her."

"We shouldn't take too much time. The snow will make tracking harder, and they've already got a head start."

"Yeah, but this poacher might have overheard something. Search the house while I talk to him. We'll head out from there as soon as we can."

They parted in silent agreement, and Selena urged Blanca to the cabin. Since she had winter gloves on, she opened the door and stepped inside. There was no electricity, and very few windows, so the interior lighting was dim at best. She pulled the flashlight off her utility belt and began to search.

"Stay," she ordered the dog. Blanca settled into a seated position by the door while Selena moved forward.

They couldn't have been here long, and Selena had to wonder why they'd rest at night. Wouldn't they want to get as far away from the jail as possible? On foot, they hadn't gotten more than twenty miles from the prison. Which meant they hadn't stolen a car.

Yet.

It had been cold last night. Temperatures dipping well below zero. Even if they'd stolen some supplies, they wouldn't be well equipped for a trek across the northern

Michigan wilderness in February. Maybe they hadn't stopped because they'd wanted to, but because they simply hadn't been prepared for what lay in front of them.

But the escape had been so well planned, executed perfectly. Why had they decided to escape in the dead of winter? What more was at stake here aside from simply freedom?

Too many questions. It wasn't her job to imagine answers. It was her job to find facts to bring them to answers. Or if not answers, the men themselves.

Selena let her flashlight roam the area of the small, rustic cabin. It was sparse. Clearly a space used simply as a base for hunting or fishing in the wilderness rather than any kind of cozy vacation home. There were quite a lot of these types of cabins in the area the police had been searching. Hunting spaces, or the nicer lake houses probably closed up for the winter, family cabins. If they knew where to look, the escapees would be able to find shelter here and there. Most of it empty in the middle of February.

But this one hadn't been. On first sweep, she saw nothing in the main area. There was a couch, a table and a fireplace to one side, and then a kitchenette to the other. There was one door besides the front door, which Selena assumed was a bathroom. If anyone slept here, they likely slept on the couch or on the floor.

Selena wrinkled her nose at the floor. It was hard planks of wood, no carpet or rugs to soften anything up. This wouldn't be the place she'd want to spend some free hours.

The windows had thick curtains that looked like they'd been collecting dust for years. She approached the fireplace. Though there was no fire, not even a glow of embers, she could smell the trace of smoke in the air. When she squatted to hold her hand over the blackened wood, the air was warmer than it had been closer to the door.

They'd come in here. Made themselves comfortable, then been surprised into moving again.

Selena glanced back at the door. Blanca still sat dutifully, waiting for the order. But if Selena didn't find anything that might have a good scent on it, there wouldn't be much for Blanca to go on. They'd have to get a look at the tracks outside and make a decision from there.

Selena got back to her feet, and as she stood she noticed something slightly different colored than the blackened wood in the hearth. A gray fabric. She leaned closer. It looked like a glove.

There was no way to tell whether it belonged to one of the men they were searching for, or the owner of the cabin, or another passerby altogether. But it was *something*.

"Blanca. Come."

AXEL PRIDED HIMSELF on the fine art of compartmentalizing. Senseless murder always tested that ability, but he muscled through because that was what this job required of him.

He loved his job. The structure. The clear goal. Sometimes cases dealt more in the gray area, but when it came to murder, the task was clear—stop the murderer before he could do any more damage.

Axel frowned at the surviving poacher. There was more to his story he wasn't telling. Axel slid a look at the cop next to him. From what Axel could tell, he was a good one. But tired and ready for this to be over.

Axel couldn't blame him. Even with the sun inching up in the sky, it was bitterly cold. The snow was fairly deep, and despite waterproof clothing, the chill of having your feet surrounded by snow wasn't for the faint of heart.

The poacher sat in the back seat of the cruiser with the door open. He looked at his hands. When he answered Axel's questions, questions the cop had already asked him before they'd gotten here, he mumbled.

Axel nodded away from the cruiser, and the officer followed him. "I want five minutes alone with him."

The officer scratched his cheek and sighed. "Poor guy's friend is dead and he's been out here for hours. Let me take him in."

"He's got more information than he's letting on. Come on. You know he's afraid of the poaching repercussions."

"I've told him—"

"Just give me five minutes alone. That's all."

The officer sighed but gave a short nod and then moved stiffly away. Axel turned back to the poacher. He'd said he didn't know which way the escapees had gone. That they hadn't taken anything.

"What aren't you telling us?"

The man looked up, noted the cop had moved away. Still, he shrugged. "Nothing I can think of."

"Your buddy is dead, and it's my job to stop these guys from killing anyone else. The local's gone. Anything you tell me? Stays between us. Whatever illegal hunting you were doing? I don't care about it. I want these guys. So, tell me. What are you leaving out?"

The man looked at the cop, then back at Axel. He blinked and looked down at his hands. "Earl didn't deserve to die."

"I'm sure he didn't. So, why don't you help me get Earl a little justice."

"Justice," the man repeated. Then he sighed. "They took some stuff."

"What kind of stuff?" Axel demanded.

The guy fidgeted and shook his head. He scowled out the back window of the car. "Guns," he finally muttered. "Cash."

Axel didn't allow himself to swear, though that's what he wanted to do. "And why didn't you tell him?" Axel said, jamming a finger toward the officer. "Or any other law enforcement."

"The guns aren't registered to us, and I didn't tell my father-in-law I took them. The cash?" The poacher licked his lips, and his eyes darted back and forth.

The man was not good at lying. Likely the cash was from some underhanded dealings. Ones Axel didn't have time to care about. "That all?"

The man scrunched his face up. "They made me give them my car keys. It's not parked here, but I told them where it's parked a few miles out."

"A car? They stole your car and you're just now telling us?" Axel knew his voice was a little too sharp when this man had just lost his friend, but he couldn't bring himself to care.

"Just the keys. They'd have to get to it first. I... The car is my wife's, and she's going to leave me if she finds out I got caught poaching again."

"I want the make and model of the car," Axel bit out. "License plate number. You don't know it? You're going to be breaking the bad news to your wife a lot sooner than you'd like. Then you tell me exactly where you left it."

The poacher rattled off the information, still staring at his hands. Axel noted everything down in his phone and sent a quick text message to Opaline, Rihanna and Alana. Between the three of them, the information would get out to all the necessary authorities.

The difficult part was that the men were now confirmed as armed. They'd killed together, which meant they would kill again, given the chance. Authorities had to be extra careful.

Axel had to hope no one did anything stupid before he and Selena could track them down. Axel glanced back at the cabin. Selena was still inside with Blanca. If she'd found anything, they should head out.

He gave one last look at the poacher, who appeared as miserable as possible. Axel didn't think there was any information left to get from him, so he turned to walk away. It was time to move.

"You're going to bring those SOBs in?" the man asked.

Axel stopped and glanced at the poacher over his shoulder. The shock he'd been under when Axel had first arrived had worn off and shifted into anger. Axel understood. "That's my job."

The man nodded. "Good. Well, I'd cooperate in whatever it took to get them behind bars. Earl didn't deserve to die. He wasn't perfect, but he didn't deserve to die. Not like this."

Not like this. Yeah, Axel knew that feeling all too well.

He headed for the cabin, instructing the local cop that he could take the poacher into the station. He opened the door. Selena was crouched by a rudimentary fireplace, Blanca sniffing something.

He rubbed his hands together. "A little warmer in here than out there," he offered by way of greeting.

"A little. Looks like they had a fire going. There's a glove left behind, but who knows if it belonged to the guys we're looking for." Selena pointed to the glove Blanca was sniffing.

"We know they're in the area," Axel said. "We know they were in here, and the poacher said this cabin was his friend's and they hadn't been up here in a month or so because of the snow. His buddy was shot before they entered, so I think the likelihood of it belonging to or at least used by one of the escapees is high."

"Agreed," Selena said, standing up from her crouched position.

"Stole a car, guns and cash."

Selena swore.

"My thoughts exactly. Poacher said the car was a few miles out. They took his keys. I imagine that's what they headed for."

Selena nodded, motioning for Blanca to follow her to the door.

"Why don't you drive? We'll track, make sure the glove is one of theirs. I'll keep in touch and meet you at where this car was parked."

Axel studied her. She was dead serious. And out of her mind. "Nice try."

She puffed out a breath, her distractingly full mouth curving slightly. "It was worth a shot," she offered.

"Was it?" he returned, working hard to keep his voice light and even. Close quarters with Selena Lopez was not high on his list of ways to torture himself. "You know you're not going to work alone."

"I'm not alone. I have Blanca."

Axel looked up at the dog, waiting patiently by the door. Then at her again. He raised an eyebrow.

She rolled her eyes. "Yeah, yeah. We're in pairs for this one. So, you want to drive to where the car was?"

Axel nodded. "I've gotten the information out, so hopefully someone will catch sight of them in the car."

Selena frowned. "If not, Blanca isn't going to be able to track a car. Certainly not in time to stop them from crossing the border."

Axel nodded. "They won't stay in the car long. They'll

assume it'll be tagged. My guess is they find some place to stay, then get a new car. But they're going to want to stay as rural as possible to avoid detection. At some point, they might even camp."

Selena looked out the open door dubiously. "You couldn't pay me to camp in the dead of February." Her expression went thoughtful. "You know, I was thinking about that. Why plan this escape in February? Why not wait till April or May when you might have more survivable weather?"

Axel considered. He'd been focused on the poachers and hadn't thought about the time of year. Selena was right. If it was just about escape, they would have waited for a better time of year.

"So, there's more to it."

"Has to be. Don't you think?"

Axel nodded. "Come on. Let's get to the Jeep and see if we find anything where they took the car."

"Got it, boss," Selena said, stepping outside, Blanca at her heels.

"Don't call me that," he muttered, following her.

"What?" she said, grinning over her shoulder at him. "Boss?"

He didn't scowl, didn't allow himself to. He kept his expression as neutral as possible. "Yes."

"But are you not, technically, my boss?"

"I'm not—"

"Your title is *supervisory* special agent, right? That seems to imply, or perhaps even straight out say, you are something of a *supervisor*."

Axel didn't say anything to that. Though it *was* his official position title, it was more about seniority and the chain of command than wanting to place himself above anyone in the team. They had to be a *team*. Not boss-employee. As full supervisor, Alana felt the same way. It was why they were a successful FBI division. They'd worked hard to foster a community of teamwork and equality, to avoid any politicking or grandstanding to get positions over each other.

And mostly, he didn't want Selena thinking of him as her *boss*. It made his shoulders tense in a way he didn't want to analyze too deeply.

"That's what I thought," she said with a sultry chuckle. She sauntered off toward the Jeep, and Axel tried *very* hard not to watch her.

Chapter Four

Selena watched the forest pass as Axel drove to where the poacher had said his car would be. Sun glinted off the snow, glittery, white and beautiful. She wasn't sure how long they'd have the luxury of heat blasting from the vents, so she tried to soak up all that she could.

Finding the escapees in a car was going to be more difficult, especially with their head start, but she didn't mind avoiding a hike through the woods. No matter how the sun shone, the air was *cold*.

More to it. Why would three men escape prison in the midst of this? Why would that be the plan? "Do we know if they have any connections in Canada? Maybe it's not the final destination. Maybe it's stop one."

"Maybe. Maybe it was just a…chance. Happenstance. They saw a moment of weakness to escape and they used it."

Selena shook her head. "No. It was too coordinated. And the three of them… There has to be something they have in common. The briefing didn't say anything about them knowing each other on the outside."

"No. They didn't, as far as we know."

"There's a piece we're missing."

Axel nodded grimly. "I agree. But right now our job isn't the pieces, it's tracking them down."

Selena didn't say anything to that. She wasn't so sure they shouldn't be trying to figure out the puzzle. Sure, some of the people back at headquarters were doing that, and as an agent she specialized in tracking and suspect apprehension, not investigation, but that didn't mean investigating wouldn't get them closer to apprehension.

Axel slowed the car, squinting into the midmorning sun. "It's still there."

"You're sure that's the car?" She could only see a flash of silver—not enough to make out the model yet.

"Silver sedan. In the exact place he said." Axel came to a complete stop. "If it's still there, they might be too."

Selena studied their surroundings, as Axel did. She didn't see a sign of anyone, but that didn't mean they weren't out there. Waiting.

"I'll get Blanca out and we'll track using the glove. You search the car."

She waited for Axel to argue. To say they should stick together. With the potential for attack, they couldn't split up.

"Vests," was all he said.

They had their tactical gear in the rear cargo space, so when Axel slid out of the car, Selena did the same. They moved quickly and silently, watching and bracing themselves for a surprise attack.

But they met at the trunk with no hint that anyone else was near them. Axel held out her vest, and she took it. They both shed their jackets, pulled the Kevlar vests on, tightened the straps and shrugged back into their coats.

Then, in nonverbal agreement, they went completely still and silent, listening to their surroundings.

The wind whistled through the trees, and snow blew so hard it sounded like pebbles being tossed in the wind. Any slight noises made by anyone else would be lost.

There would be no way to *hear* if anyone else was around, though the wind might have also drowned out the sound of their car approaching, depending on how close the men were to the silver sedan. Maybe she and Axel would have a chance to sneak up on them.

Selena nodded toward the car, a signal she was going to let Blanca out and begin to track.

Axel nodded his head, green eyes cool and assessing. He had many sides to him. This was the man back in the car this morning who'd driven too fast to stop a murder that had already happened.

They both crouched behind the car, guns drawn and ready, and Selena knew she had to say…something to keep his focus on the task at hand, not the life they'd lost.

"We take all three in alive, they'll fold on each other. They'll go back to jail for a very long time."

His gaze met hers, green and cold. She might have shivered, but there was something about Axel. She didn't know what it was, didn't *want* to know what it was, only that it always had things shifting around in her chest. A flutter. A sense of…not just wanting. Something far more complicated than that.

The worst part was, she got the impression he felt it too. The way their gazes held just a little too long in moments like this. When they should be moving forward. Acting.

And where did you end up the last time you thought a guy felt the same thing you did?

She held his gaze out of her own warped sense of spite, but she struggled to find her equilibrium here, in the depth of green that reminded her of a spring forest rather than the winter white they were surrounded by.

"Got it," he said.

She'd forgotten what point she'd made, but she wouldn't

dwell on that. She gave Blanca a quick pet, then held out the glove. Blanca sniffed. Moved ahead a few feet, came back to sniff again.

Selena kept her gun drawn, her eyes scanning the area around Blanca. Blanca did her job, sniffing and inching forward. She was struggling to find the scent. Selena knew they had to get closer to the car, but she wanted Axel to clear the area before she moved Blanca in.

"Clear," Axel called after a few minutes.

Surprised, Selena jogged over to the car.

"They were stuck," Axel said, pointing to where the tires were lodged deep in the snow and, below that, mud. "Ran the car till the gas tank was empty, probably trying to get out. Engine is still hot, but they're gone."

"If they did that, I can't imagine they're too far ahead of us."

"No, they can't be. We'll grab our packs and follow Blanca. I imagine the car should give her a good scent to go on."

Selena nodded. "You get the packs. I'll search the interior."

Axel nodded, and Selena jerked the driver's side door open. There was the smallest hint of warmth still in the interior, but it dissipated quickly as Selena leaned inside. She wanted clothing, preferably. Nothing in the front seat, but as she moved to look into the back, something on the floorboard caught her eye.

She was already wearing gloves, so she reached down and picked it up. It was a prisoner ID card.

Peter Lopez.

She looked at the face of a man she didn't know. One her father had expected her to save. How had he gotten tangled up with murderers and batterers? He'd been arrested during a drug deal that had gone wrong, but his sentence was shorter because in the trial it had been proven he hadn't been carrying a weapon.

He was still responsible for fleeing the scene of a murder, and for dealing, but if there was anything Selena had ever comforted herself with—and likely why Opaline still thought Peter could be saved, and expected Selena to *help* save him, just like Dad did—it was that he wasn't in prison for a violent crime.

Or hadn't been. Maybe he'd been the one to pull the trigger on the innocent poacher back there. Maybe this was the end of the line for Peter. And there was no doubt in her mind that Dad *and* Opaline would blame her for that.

"Selena?"

Selena didn't startle—she was too well trained—but she closed her eyes and immediately chastised herself. She'd told Alana she could handle this case without her personal feelings getting in the way, and she *had* to make certain not to make a liar out of herself.

"Prison ID left behind," she said, reaching backward to show Axel, who stood outside the car behind her. "You were right, they were definitely in the car."

Axel took the ID. "Anything Blanca can track?"

Without moving and giving away the fact she hadn't fully searched the car yet, Selena looked into the back seat out of the corner of her eye.

"Clothes in the back. But even if they sat in here, this isn't their car. Too many competing smells. Give me a few minutes to use the glove around here to see if she gets a trail scent."

Selena scooted out of the car and stood, Axel way too

close for comfort. Luckily he wasn't looking at her. He was frowning into the woods.

"They got guns, a car and cash from the poacher. The car is stuck."

Selena worked with Blanca while Axel mused aloud.

"They warm up, then take off again. There has to be a plan to get supplies. They can't make it to Canada on foot without food and water."

Selena held the car open while Blanca sniffed the back seat. "Plenty of hunting cabins and the like scattered around. Could be they expect to find shelter and food as they hike along."

Axel's frown deepened as he pulled his phone out of his pocket. "I wonder if Opaline could get us an idea of where the cabins on the route to Canada are."

"Maybe, but how would they have anything like that? As far as we know from the prison, they got clothes and the security guard's gun. That's it." Selena looked at the winter landscape around them. "Unless they had more help than that."

Axel's expression was grim. "That's what I'm afraid of."

Blanca moved forward, gave one bark, then sat and waited for further instruction. "She's got a scent. We can pack up and follow?"

Axel nodded. "I'll update the team."

Selena waited by Blanca. The dog would wait for the signal to search, though she all but vibrated sitting there in the snow. It was a good sign. She had a good scent on at least one of the fugitives, but Selena worried about the snow. It wouldn't stop Blanca from tracking, but melting snow could hinder their progress.

"I guess I have to be grateful it's so darn cold," Selena muttered.

Axel brought their packs to where Blanca waited to search. A cold, isolated landscape.

Selena was right. There were a few threads that didn't make sense, and Axel knew their priority had to be this search. But when there was a mystery, a puzzle, what he really wanted to do was sit down and sort through it.

"We've got teams of two moving in from the Canadian border," he told her. "Local police notified of the information we have. It'd take some serious planning and skill to evade capture." Or help from a bigger, stronger threat.

Selena secured her pack on. "Ready?"

Axel nodded and she gave Blanca the *search* command.

Blanca immediately moved forward. There were some footprints, but the wind had blown snow over them so they were just little indentations in the snow. Likely they'd be completely gone before they followed the dog for a mile.

They walked in silence for a while, pausing when Blanca paused, then following behind her again when she moved forward. "I'm not sure how much of a head start they've got, but she'd be moving faster or signaling if they were close. She does either of those two things, we'll want to pause and draw our weapons."

Axel nodded. He'd never worked this closely with Selena and Blanca before. While he prided himself on being a team player who didn't use the "supervisory" part of his title to take over any assignment, it was an odd sensation to be completely beholden to how Selena decided to use her dog.

Axel watched the time as they walked, routinely checked to see if there were any updates from the team and mostly tried not to think about the subzero wind chill.

"Let's take a water break," Selena suggested, and it

took Axel a moment to realize she meant for the dog. "Pause."

Blanca immediately stopped. Selena shrugged off her pack and got out a water bottle and a dish. The dog eagerly lapped up the water, and Selena took her own swig. When their gazes locked, Axel didn't look away.

He should. He knew he should. They didn't need to constantly be staring at each other a little too long when there was work to be done. But he wouldn't be the one who looked away first. She was the one who'd always avoided this...*thing* between them. Not that he pressed the issue, but she'd set the precedent to ignore it.

And now was *not* the time to play these mind games with himself.

Selena looked down at her pack, dug around until she came up with a dog treat. She tossed the Milk-Bone at him, Blanca's eyes following the treat even as she stood completely still.

"She's still not sure about you," Selena said casually.

Axel frowned at Selena, then at the dog, whose focus was on the treat in his hand. "Excuse me?"

"She likes you, but she's not sure about you. Just in case you need to give her commands, you need to suck up to her a little."

"I need to suck up to your dog?"

Selena nodded. There was humor in her eyes, but her expression was serious. And Axel wasn't comfortable with the serious nature of the reasoning. "Why wouldn't you be able to give her commands?"

Selena shrugged. "We're law enforcement, Axel. Don't pretend like you don't know what could happen."

No, it was never far out of his mind, but there was something about the dog that added a weird weight to all the things that could go wrong in their profession.

He shook his head and crouched, holding out the treat. "Come."

Blanca trotted over and took the treat from his fingers, then she stood in front of him and let him scratch her behind the ears. "There's a girl. I miss having a dog," he murmured, more to himself and the dog than Selena.

"You don't have one out on that farm of yours?" Selena replied, packing the supplies away. "What's the point in space if you don't have a dog?"

"I'm gone too much, so I've had to settle for animals that don't need constant care. Chickens. Cows. I was thinking about getting a goat."

She laughed. It wasn't something she did a lot around him. Sometimes he'd hear her talking to Carly, and she'd laugh like that. It hit him a little too hard out here in the snowy wilderness, just the two of them.

"A goat?" she said, somewhat disbelieving as she adjusted the pack back on her shoulders.

Axel shrugged, trying to keep a casual grin on his face. "Sure. They're good at keeping a lawn tidy."

She shook her head, her mouth curved into a smile. She seemed relaxed enough, and he'd never gotten much of that with Selena. "Search," she commanded Blanca.

They set out again, and Axel couldn't help wanting to let the moment stretch out a bit. "You know, I was reading this article about a former NHL player who raises llamas. Maybe that's what I'll do in my retirement."

He got another husky laugh out of her. "Llamas. You've lost it, Morrow. Besides. You? Retire?"

"Sure. We all have to sometime."

"I don't know. You seem like one of those guys who'd just transition into the guy in charge. Not retire and putter around at your farm."

"Lots to putter around with on a farm, no matter how

old or small. It's peaceful. It's home. Sometimes I look
forward to it."

"And the other times?"

"I'm glad I have a challenging job that keeps my mind
occupied." Though the older he got the more he wondered
if keeping his mind occupied kept him from fully dealing with things he'd have to face eventually. Or maybe
he wouldn't. Maybe he'd let the loss of his family define
him and keep him from ever building new, deep bonds
that went beyond work friendships. It didn't seem so bad
when he was working.

Only when he was home on his farm. Alone.

"Now, keeping a mind occupied I understand," Selena
said, stifling a yawn. "I don't think we're going to catch
up to them at this pace."

"No, but we'll stay close. And unless they've magically found supplies somewhere, we should be able to
keep going longer than they do."

But that *unless* hung between them, because they both
thought there might be more to it. Help somewhere. A
plan TCD hadn't figured out yet.

"Tell me about Peter."

She clammed up immediately. The easy curve of her
mouth gone, any light in her eyes vanishing in a second.
He might have regretted focusing back on the task at
hand, but the tightening in his gut wasn't at all appropriate for the situation. Better to focus on what they should,
even if it made her uncomfortable.

"I've told you all there is to tell," she said, her voice
as cold as the world around them.

"So, why was Opaline so upset?"

"Opaline's…emotional. I know you guys see the
happy, bubbly side of her, but there's the other side of
that. She feels things…deeply. It's just who she is."

"And you aren't emotional?"

"I'm an FBI agent, Axel. That's what I am."

"Last time I checked, FBI agents got to be human."

She snorted derisively. "You can say that because you're a man."

"Fair enough. The point I'm trying to make, though, is... You get to have some feelings about this. Even if once we catch up to them, you push them aside and do the job."

"Or I can handle it my way. Thanks all the same."

"It might help the case, Selena."

She whipped her head around to stare daggers at him. "I'm not sure how my father and Opaline thinking I should be able to save Peter, convince him to follow the straight and narrow, has anything to do with the case. I don't know the kid. I've been responsible for him for half my life and I don't *know* the guy. I don't know his friends. I don't know what he's capable of, and if you think Opaline might, that's a laugh and a half, because she thinks she can save anyone if she forgives and forgets. Well, I don't believe in forgiving and forgetting betrayal, and I don't believe in ignoring that people have their own free will. Peter made his choices. I don't know how or why. I only know I'll make sure he pays for them. And if that makes me a crappy person? So damn be it. Because my *job* is what I care about. It's who I am. The end."

Axel didn't say anything to that. She wouldn't listen anyway. Still, it was hardly *the end*. That was a lesson he'd had to learn the hard way, and no doubt she was in the midst of learning it.

She wouldn't appreciate his understanding, so he kept it to himself. Just like attraction. His own doubts and conflicting emotions about the assignment. *Keep it to yourself. Bury it down deep.*

And hope the dam that kept it all inside never broke.

Chapter Five

Selena didn't mind losing her temper when the situation called for it, but this was not that situation. She'd been… hurt. God, she was an idiot. But they'd been talking. She'd actually been enjoying his company without being too worried about the whole attraction thing.

Then he'd asked her about Peter. Like sharing genetic material made him *her* responsibility.

Why did everyone in her life want to make Peter her responsibility?

She blew out a breath slowly, willing her anger to cool, her heartbeat to calm. She'd spewed all that at Axel, and that had been a mistake. She knew this was going to be an assignment fraught with them. She would deal with that by promising herself those mistakes would only be here, in these quiet moments.

When they had to act, really act, all of this conflicting, ancient history garbage would be shoved aside to do her job. If she lost her temper in the *waiting* that was so much of her job, well, she'd forgive herself. She *was* human.

So was he.

"I don't know him," Selena said calmly. "I don't have some secret understanding of who he is as a person, who he might be connected to. Fair or not, everyone in my life has expected me to in a variety of ways. I'm not here because Peter Lopez is my estranged half brother. I'm here because Blanca and I make a good team apprehending suspects. I need you to understand that."

Axel was quiet as they walked. When he finally spoke, she got the feeling he'd really *thought* about what she'd said. "Understood," he offered.

She thought he might…actually do just that. An odd feeling when she'd felt misunderstood and maligned for a really, *really* long time. First with her family and their insistent need for her to be the one who handled *everything*, and then at her last department when…

Well, it didn't do to dwell on all the ways she'd been humiliated and embarrassed. She snuck a glance at Axel. Maybe it was good to remember that sleeping with a coworker, especially in law enforcement, never ended well for the woman.

Blanca paused, scenting the air, her body vibrating in a way that spoke to an excitement. Either they were close, or the scent trail was clear enough she wanted to take off. But Selena had a feeling they were quickly catching up to the escapees.

Who were armed and dangerous.

Selena held up her hand and drew her weapon. Axel did the same. Instinctually, they moved so they were almost back to back, protecting themselves from being surprised. A unit that could see in both directions.

"Close?" Axel asked quietly.

"Within shooting distance," Selena murmured, eyeing the trees around them. Blanca's positioning meant the three men were not all in one direction. Were they fanning out to surround them?

"We're easy pickings right here. We need cover," Axel said. "See anything?"

Selena scanned the area in front of her. "Some dead

trees. We'll have to lie in the snow, but they'd give us some cover." Not enough. Not from all sides. But that was the risk of the job.

"You go first. Then call Blanca. Then I'll follow."

"Got it." Selena moved slowly and carefully, on full alert. She studied the pile of logs, tried to adjust and re-arrange them in her mind to give themselves the best tactical advantage. They'd still have to lie in the snow, and dead trees weren't exactly bulletproof shields, but it was something. She crouched and said softly and force-fully, "Blanca. Come."

There was a moment of hesitation from the dog—she wanted to do her job, track—but she obeyed Sele-na's command. Selena pointed to the spot she wanted Blanca—behind both the tree cover and Selena herself. If they had anyone sneak up from behind, Blanca would sound the alarm.

"Clear," Selena said to Axel.

He started moving toward her, and almost immedi-ately a shot rang through the quiet air. Selena flinched, and Axel dived to the ground. Selena felt her heart leap to her throat.

"Hit?" she called out, hoping her voice didn't sound as panicked as she'd felt.

"No," Axel replied through gritted teeth. He was army crawling through the thick snow, which couldn't be com-fortable.

Selena couldn't see anything. Wherever they were was either too far away or too well camouflaged. Another shot rang out. She ducked. When she peeked her head over the dead tree, Axel still had his head in the snow.

"Morrow," she barked.

He shook his head and started crawling again. Each

inch seemed to take forever, and she had to fight back the need to jump out and pull him into the makeshift cover.

He was fine. Not shot. Just trying to avoid it. He was a skilled agent. They might be a team, but it wasn't her job to *protect* him, just to have his back. The fact that *protect* seemed to be an instinctual need inside her was perplexing.

Luckily, she didn't have time to think about it. After what felt like hours and was maybe minutes, Axel crawled over the logs and laid himself next to her. He faced the same direction she did.

"Two shooters in front of us," he said, his voice low but not a whisper. Too deep and authoritative to be called a whisper. "If there's a third, he hasn't fired yet."

"How do you know it's two shooters?"

"Sound of the gun. Angle of the shot." Axel lifted his own gun and rested it on the log in front of him.

"What about the third? Coming from behind?"

Axel glanced over his shoulder. "Blanca will warn us, don't you think?"

"I know. She'll bark, once, the minute anyone's within forty feet of us."

"Good. So, they're still a ways off."

Another shot rang out, and they both ducked again. Selena couldn't tell where the shots were hitting.

"Bad aim?" she asked.

Axel shook his head. "They're just too far away to get a good shot. They're trying to keep us far away, though. Don't get me wrong, they get the chance, they'll kill us, but right now these are warning shots."

"Why not come and kill us?"

Axel was quiet for a moment, clearly considering. "I suppose the risk they'd get shot in the process. They're more worried about escape than adding more crimes to their rap sheet?"

"Escaping prison isn't going to do them any favors. And they already added another murder to their rap sheet. Axel, there has to be something more they're trying to do than escape. I can't imagine all this is just to be free."

"Men have done far less just to be free."

But it didn't set right. These were career criminals. Her brother had been in trouble with the law since he'd turned thirteen. A prison sentence was hardly unexpected. It was a risk he was well aware of—a path he'd chosen to go down knowing full well what the consequences might be.

Another shot, but Axel and Selena had their heads below the logs so there was no ducking this time.

"They're retreating," Axel noted.

"How can you tell?"

"Sound of the gun. The direction they're coming from isn't so spread out. They'll keep shooting, even out of range, in the hopes the sound of the gunfire will keep us off their tails. Only two are shooting—which leads me to believe one is doing everything he can to hide their tracks."

"They can't hide from Blanca's nose."

Axel nodded.

"We shouldn't fall for it. We've got vests and we're trained FBI agents. Sitting here being scared of a little gunfire doesn't complete the mission."

"They're heading right toward the rest of our team. All we have to do is keep behind them like this, make sure they don't slip through any cracks. Eventually we'll have a tight enough circle to bring them in without a dangerous shootout."

Selena didn't particularly care for the slow, patient approach. It meant more days out in the wilderness alone with Axel. But she knew his plan was one that would be best to safeguard the team.

Trying not to scowl, Selena settled into the cold snow around her. "How long?"

"Until we don't hear the gunshots any longer."

IT TOOK FAR too long. Axel was doing everything to keep his teeth from chattering. Even in layers of tactical gear, lying in the snow was cold, uncomfortable business. Once they'd gone a good ten minutes without hearing a gunshot, Axel motioned for Selena to sit up.

"How's Blanca in this cold?" he asked. The dog had remained alert and still the entire time.

"She'll need a break eventually, but she's good for a few more hours yet."

"Good. I think we're safe to get up out of the snow now, but let's call in."

"And give them more of a head start? Let's get going and call on the way."

She was too impatient. It wasn't her usual MO, so Axel had to wonder what was driving it. The cold? Her brother's connection? The same things that bothered him about being out in the expansive wilderness with only her and her dog?

Best not to think too much on it. Focus on what needed to be done. What he'd really like to do was find somewhere warm to change into dry clothes, but that wasn't an option.

He settled himself on the log, Selena beside him. Blanca would warn them if the escapee trio doubled back. Axel pulled out his phone and started a conference call with Aria and Max.

They popped on, seated next to their respective partners. Both screens showed two people, perfectly warm and indoors.

"I hate you all right now," Selena said grimly.

Aria grinned from the screen. "Got a nice fire going. Some hot chocolate ready for marshmallows. It's actually so warm I might have to take off my sweater. What do you think, Carly?"

Selena snorted in disgust as Carly smiled ruefully next to Aria on the screen.

"You're going to have to move out of the cozy digs," Axel offered, not above a little jealousy himself. "We want a tighter circle."

"Something happen?" Max asked.

"We got too close, and they took a few shots," Selena said with a shrug. "Too far away to do any damage."

Carly frowned, and Aria's humorous expression got very serious.

"Do you have the map of cabins in the area Opaline sent?" Axel asked.

They all had the partner not holding the phone pull up the maps on their phones.

"Right now we've got a triangle of sorts, with our trio right in the middle," Axel confirmed. "We need to make our triangle smaller, keeping them in the middle. They're armed and they're going to shoot, so we want to be slow, steady and careful."

"There has to be something more to this," Selena said, hugging her arms around herself. "It's miserable out here. No one *plans* to escape prison in the middle of February unless they've got to accomplish something in the here and now. In whatever downtime you guys have, see what you can come up with."

"But first, we want everyone moving in closer," Axel said.

Selena tapped the interactive map on her phone as Axel looked over at her screen. There were three cabins they could use to try and surround the fugitives.

"Axel and I will move to the one I've marked three." Selena said, glancing at him for agreement.

He gave a nod.

"Aria and Carly, you'll take cabin two. Max and Scott, you'll base at one. Our escapees are currently closest to three, but heading toward one and two. As Axel and I head for three, we'll be following them toward one and two. Think of your cabins as bases. You'll want to take turns patrolling the area in between. We've got Blanca, which means we'll be able to stop any backtracks. Our main concern is them taking a longer route to the east or west rather than the straight shot toward the border."

"We'll call Rihanna and see if there are some local law enforcement who we could get stationed in the east and west," Max said, all business. "Small departments in these parts, if any, but maybe we can get a county to lend some manpower beyond the APB."

"Good idea," Axel agreed. "I think they'll take the straight shot, but we can't be too careful. Armed. Dangerous. I want everyone to understand that. Leonard Koch has already killed someone. Cold-blooded. We have to assume anyone associating with him has the same capability. We want these guys, but we want to be smart and safe."

"They can't do much damage in the middle of nowhere, upper Michigan, can they?" Aria offered. "I haven't seen a soul around this cabin."

"One man is already dead," Axel replied flatly, trying not to sound too much like a superior dressing down a subordinate. Aria was a rookie, but she was good at her job. Still, lives had already been lost, and they all needed to remember that. "A man who had nothing to do with any of this. Keep that in mind."

They all nodded their assent, then closed the call. Axel could *feel* Selena's steady gaze on him. He didn't look toward it. He put his phone away.

"Will it bother you forever?" she asked quietly.

Axel frowned, turning to glance at her. "What?"

"That a man died. A man you didn't know, that you had no responsibility to. It bothers you now. I'm just curious if that sticks with you forever." She was too close, her dark eyes too discerning.

Axel wasn't sure he was comfortable with the question, and he definitely wasn't comfortable with the answer. Especially when she kept talking, right here sitting hip to hip on the log.

"Innocent people have died during assignments I've been on," she said, her gaze never leaving his. "I've never felt responsible. They don't haunt me. So, I'm just wondering if I'm cold-blooded, or if you get over it."

"You're not cold-blooded," Axel muttered.

"How do you know?"

"You care about your brother, that much is clear." Her expression shuttered, and she looked away. Which, yeah, he'd been going for. "You care about Opaline. You hide it all, compartmentalize it all, but you've got family issues up to the hilt, Selena, and you wouldn't if you didn't care. If you were cold."

She stood abruptly, adjusting her pack and ignoring him completely.

He blew out a breath. He should let it go at that. Keep his mouth shut. But she'd asked him a question, and he felt some…*need* to answer her. To try to make her understand what he felt.

"It's not the individual deaths that haunt me. It's the feeling of being too late. When you lose your family the way I did, when you survive, you start to realize that timing is everything. And it's the one thing beyond your control. You can be the best damn FBI agent out there, and you might still be two seconds too late."

"So why be an FBI agent at all, knowing that you'll be faced with the uncontrollable timing part of things?"

"Because if you never face the things that haunt you, Selena, they eat you alive."

She stared down at him a moment, something that looked a lot like shell shock in her expression. She frowned, shook it away and then held out a gloved hand.

It was an offer of teamwork. Help him up off the log though he didn't need it. But it put them back on equal, mission footing.

Or it was supposed to. Even though they both wore gloves, fitting his hand into hers, letting her help pull him to his feet, it ignited a dangerous warmth that spread through him. He should have immediately let her hand go once on his feet, but he didn't.

He held on, stood far too close and looked down at her face. Dark eyes, cheeks and nose pink with cold. She was a complicated woman with a complicated past, and they were on a *very* complicated mission. Everything was dangerous and required a delicate balance.

But here they were, in this side moment, separate from everything else. Touching hands. Looking at each other, and he thought, most dangerous of all, *understanding* each other.

She didn't pull away. He didn't let her go. They didn't speak, and they didn't move. They simply looked at each other, breathing in time with one another. He could imagine what it would be like if he did. If he stepped closer, if he pulled her to him, if he fitted his mouth to hers.

It was like a mirage in front of him, one he wanted to lean into.

Her phone buzzed in her pocket, breaking the moment. *Thank God.*

Chapter Six

It took a moment for the buzzing to break through the odd static in Selena's brain. A static she didn't understand. She'd been made stupid by lust and inexperience once. This was neither. It was something far…bigger.

Far scarier.

But the phone buzzed incessantly in her pocket, and she finally thought to drop Axel's hand and dig out her device. It was her sister calling.

There were so many reasons she didn't want to deal with Opaline right now, but it very well could be about the task at hand. The task at hand being searching for and apprehending criminals, *not* having weird out-of-body experiences with Axel.

And, wow, what would an in-*body experience with Axel feel like?*

"Hello," she greeted too harshly, trying to get the image of *anything* with Axel out of her mind.

"Selena. You were shot at?" Opaline demanded. Her voice reminded Selena of their childhood. Opaline was older. She'd taken that role seriously, but something about their parents' divorce had seemed to flip their roles. Opaline had turned emotional and needy and at sea. She'd thrown herself at people, men in particular, always looking for safety. For shore. Selena had to take over being the one who could handle anything and everything their mother and father threw at them.

Selena had gotten away from that as soon as she'd been able.

But this sounded like concern, with a hint of scolding, which was far more big sistery than Opaline had acted in over a decade. It made Selena's heart twist uncomfortably with a hope she thought she'd eradicated a long time ago.

"Shot at is probably an exaggeration. There was shooting, but it was far away." She couldn't help but try to soothe. After Dad had ruined everything, Selena had been the one to pick up the pieces. But maybe they were adult enough now that they could find a way to bridge the gaps in their relationship.

"Do you think Peter was the one shooting?" Opaline asked in a hushed whisper.

The bubble of hope burst in an instant. It was always that. Always about Peter. Never about her. Why did that still hurt? She'd kept herself separate and away, and still Opaline could cut her in two. Over their *half* brother. "I don't know," Selena said flatly.

"I hate that you're out there as enemies."

"His choice, Opaline. Did you call about something in particular?"

"He's our brother."

"I'm your sister."

There was a silence, charged with hurt. But how was that fair? "You don't need my help, my support. You never did," Opaline said softly—the opposite of her usual loud demeanor. "But Peter did."

Selena didn't know what to do with that, even less so when she could practically *feel* Axel watching her, listening to her side of the conversation. Picking it apart.

No doubt thinking of all the ways she should be responsible for Peter.

"You gave up on him," Opaline said, sounding more like herself. Overemotional. Laying the blame on Selena's blameless shoulders.

Or does she just sound like Mom?

Selena was in the middle of an important assignment. She couldn't cry. She couldn't indulge in self-pity. She had to set this aside and move on. Ignoring all the feelings it churned up. "I'm sorry you feel that way," Selena said robotically. It was how she talked to her mother too. "Maybe at some point you'll understand that while you were all so busy trying to save Peter, some of us needed help and support too." She tried to hold her tongue, ice out the emotions, but those words…

You gave up on him.

It hurt because it was true. She had given up on Peter. She didn't know how to keep believing in someone so dedicated to ruining their own life.

And when she'd needed her sister, when everything had blown up at her last job, Opaline had been so obsessed with Peter's trial and him going to jail, she hadn't bothered to ask Selena if she was all right. If *she* needed anything. Peter was her project. Selena was on her own.

They both were still on the line, in a weighted silence neither knew how to fill. Maybe Selena should just accept they never would.

"You never let me help," Opaline said, hushed and pained.

"When did you ever try?"

"When did you ever ask for any?"

Selena didn't know what to say to that. She was sure she'd asked, or at least hinted… Hadn't it been obvious to anyone after Tom had ruined her reputation that she needed someone to hold her hand—just for a little while? Someone who understood what it was like to feel betrayed by someone you'd loved, or thought you had.

"I have important work to do," Selena said. Her voice was so cold it matched the air around her. "And so do you."

"The difference, Selena, is I can care about both." The call ended with a click and echoing silence.

Why did she always handle things so badly when it came to Opaline? If she'd kept her feelings out of it—a lesson she'd been trying to impart to Opaline since their parents had started the divorce process—everything would be okay.

A lesson life had reinforced, over and over again. *So why are you still struggling?*

It was just Peter. Opaline. The perfect storm of things she didn't want to deal with. In a few more days, after they tracked him down and Peter was in jail, Selena could leave all this *feeling* behind.

Because if you never face the things that haunt you, Selena, they eat you alive.

Axel's past was a lot more haunted than hers, so she should ignore that he'd said that. That it had clamored around inside her like church bells, too close, too loud. *Too right.*

"Everything okay?" Axel asked gently.

"Just fine." Certainly none of his business.

"It's not unnoticeable, you know," Axel said softly, almost sympathetically. But she didn't want his softness or sympathy.

"What?"

"The tension between you two."

Which was the worst thing he could have said to her. She worked so hard not to let those feelings show. The cracks in her armor. She knew the people they worked with could tell they weren't close, but to have him stand there and say it was obvious…

She would have preferred a slap to the face.

"Yeah, I'm pretty well aware," she returned, wincing at the acidic note in her own voice. Which only made her angrier. At him. At Opaline. At Peter. But mostly just herself. "And Aria made sure to let me know the tension between *us* isn't exactly unnoticeable."

AXEL COULD ADMIT that she'd shocked him into silence. It wasn't the information that surprised him—Max, on occasion, had asked what on earth was up with them. Axel had always played it off, but he knew people…sensed it. Much like sensing issues between Selena and Opaline.

But for a good four years there'd been a tacit, silent agreement between him and Selena that they would not speak of that tension. If they ignored it, it wouldn't go away, but, well, they could avoid it.

Now she'd laid it out between them. He wasn't *opposed* to that exactly. Clearly ignoring it hadn't done them any favors. But the timing was less than ideal.

"We should move out."

She laughed. Bitterly. Though he got the sense her bitterness wasn't just aimed at him, but at everything. Hard to blame her.

They got their stuff together. Selena ordered Blanca to search, and they started moving forward again, following the trail of the escapees while keeping an eye on the map and the cabin they'd try to reach by nightfall.

It was a cold, quiet and mostly miserable hike. Occasionally Blanca would pause and they'd wait, weapons drawn, ready for the next round of gunfire.

Axel began to dwell on that, to turn it over. His job

right now was apprehension, but the puzzle pieces were irritating. "Why not stay and take us out?" he wondered aloud after they'd started again after another stop that yielded no gunfire.

"Oh, lots of reasons, I suppose," Selena said. All the emotions she'd had before and during Opaline's call were now wrapped up and hidden under the veneer of professional detachment. "If they kill us, there will be a bigger task force working to stop them. They might now know our numbers and don't want to risk the chance."

"Bottom line, it's clear their goal isn't just escaping to escape. It's bigger than that. Wouldn't you say?"

"I'd leave the profiling up to you," Selena replied. "That's your expertise."

It was, and Axel felt like he had a good picture of the men as individuals. It was the combination of the three men that didn't make any sense to him. Leonard Koch was a cold-blooded killer. Steve Jenson not quite as clever, but just as interested in violence. Motivated by it, in fact. Peter Lopez…he was the loose thread. The one that didn't tie in.

He glanced at Selena. Her gaze was on Blanca. They'd stopped to water the dog a few times, but Axel knew Selena wanted to get them to some shelter so the dog could rest in some warmth.

She didn't know Peter. Axel had to believe she wasn't holding anything back on that front. She cared too much about her job to thwart it. Alana had questioned Opaline herself after he and Selena had left, but the answers she'd passed along to Axel didn't help him any.

"Your brother was the getaway car driver in a murder."

"You could call him the escapee, the perp, the criminal, the suspect, et cetera, et cetera."

"Noted."

"So, he's weak. The weak link you pressure into doing something stupid."

"But what would they need him for? What does he bring to the trio?" Axel continued. Alana had sent the police report from the security guard who'd let them go, and Axel had reviewed it. Once they got to the cabin, he'd need to go over it again. Or even request new questioning for the security guard.

"It's the bigger thing we're missing. Career criminals don't escape from jail in the dead of winter unless something better is waiting for them," Selena said. "A sure deal. But there's no evidence the three men were connected in any way. They all were involved in different groups."

Axel glanced at the map, noticing how low the sun was in the sky. They should be getting close to the cabin. They were equipped to continue to hike through the night, but they'd need a rest for Blanca and a meal for him and Selena. He wanted to get to that base before true night descended.

"So, we need to look beyond the groups." But where? The problem with being on the tracking trail was he couldn't study the evidence the way he'd like.

"What about the victims?" Selena offered. "Maybe the victims of the crimes they committed connect in some way? Remember that case we had two years ago? The trafficking case that looked so similar, but we didn't find the thread until you connected the two missing people."

Axel nodded thoughtfully. "Once we get to the cabin, we'll talk to Alana. It's a good thread to pull."

"We should be getting close."

Axel nodded. They kept walking. Axel tried to work through all the angles of the case that he knew. Leonard had murdered someone. Steve had been part of a group of thugs who'd beaten another man to death. Peter had been the driver in fleeing a murder scene. They were different crimes, but all involved a dead person one way or another.

Would the three dead people connect?

Blanca stopped, barked twice.

Selena frowned. "That's not one of our signals."

Which was when Axel's nose began to burn. "Do you smell that?" he murmured. The world was dusky, the sun setting somewhere behind the trees. The faint hint of…

"Smoke," Selena said. "Surely they didn't start a fire knowing they've got a trail."

"Maybe they're trying to draw us out."

Selena crouched next to Blanca, running her hands over the dog's furry coat. She murmured encouraging words to the dog, scanning the trees herself. "What do you think, Axel?"

He really didn't know what to think. "How's Blanca holding up?"

"She'll keep going if we need to."

Axel considered that. In the dark, they could sneak up on the trio if they really were just…sitting around a fire. But he couldn't ignore the possibility it was a trap. The men had shot at them—they knew they were being tailed.

"Why doesn't any of this add up?" Axel muttered. He frowned at the eastern horizon. Something flickered. "Do you see that?"

Selena looked to where he pointed. "That's no campfire."

No, it wasn't. So what was the fire? A diversion? An attempt to hurt them? Something else altogether?

"Blanca, follow," Selena commanded her dog. When Axel fell into step next to her, she spoke quietly and started moving toward the fire, weapon drawn. Same as him.

"I think we should see what's going on. If she follows rather than leads, she'll alert us to any ambush from behind."

Axel nodded, and they crept forward. The smoke in the air got thicker and thicker, the flickering light in the distance bigger and bigger. Until they both stopped in their tracks.

A cabin was ablaze. The cabin on their map that they'd been hoping to find for a rest.

"Why on earth would they do that?" Selena asked.

But Axel didn't have an answer for her.

Chapter Seven

Selena lifted her sleeve over her mouth. The air was choked with smoke. They hadn't just set fire to the cabin. They had to have used something for it to be completely engulfed in flame like this.

"I'll get Max on the phone."

Selena nodded. Max was their explosives expert. He'd have a better idea what could have caused the fire. She didn't know what he'd be able to tell them over the phone, or if it mattered, but it was a reasonable next step. At some point the information they gathered had to lead them to some answers.

"We've got a situation," Axel said into his phone. "The cabin we were headed for is on fire. Not just a little fire. It's completely engulfed in flames."

Selena stared at the blaze, frowning as she thought back over the past few minutes. "We didn't hear anything. Everything has been quiet," Selena said more to herself than to Axel, since he was on the phone.

But he turned to face her. "You're right," he said, then relayed the information to Max on the line.

Axel held the phone to his ear so Selena couldn't hear Max's reply. While Axel conferred with Max on the phone, Selena studied the flames. They were on every side of the cabin. The chilly wind seemed to feed the blaze, and even with the snow Selena didn't foresee the fire going out any time soon.

What on earth could be the point of this?

"Max says if we didn't hear anything, explosives are unlikely," Axel said, sliding his phone back into his pocket. "The advanced blaze could have more to do with the use of accelerant, but he'd have to discuss it with someone with more expertise in fire over explosives."

"What's the point?" Selena said. "This doesn't stop us following them. In fact, it slows them down. It had to have taken time. We can't be that far behind now. We could catch them and—"

"And they could shoot us both dead. We have to be more careful than that."

Selena knew he was right, but it tested her patience. Though, that's why they did this kind of thing in pairs. To balance each other out. To work through the problems with a plan. She was trained specifically in search and apprehension, and she was very well aware of the necessary role of caution.

But I want this over.

She took a moment to breathe—though she couldn't allow herself a deep inhalation when there was so much smoke in the air. Still, she needed to remember her calm, remember her center. Her job over feelings. Her assignment over herself.

"Why did they burn it down, Axel? We can keep following them, we can even apprehend them, but there's something to that. They did it for a reason, and I think it's important we figure out what it is."

Axel studied the burning cabin grimly. "You're right."

"That's two 'you're rights' in under twenty. Should I be concerned?"

He gave her a sardonic smile, which produced an unnecessary and untimely flutter in her chest. She looked back at the blaze. "What about the owners of the cabin? Could they have a connection?"

"Opaline is on it."

She could feel his considering glance at that. She refused to fall for the bait. She kept her expression neutral. Because her sister was part of the assignment too, and she would do the work she needed to do while Selena did the work she needed to do. "Good. Now, what are we going to do about shelter? It's nearly dark."

"Wasn't there another cabin in the vicinity?"

Selena pulled out her phone and brought the map onto the screen. "Not confirmed as a cabin. A structure of some kind. No known owner."

"Some shelter is better than none, yeah?"

"Agreed. But let's follow our crew a bit beyond the fire. Make sure we've still got an idea of what direction they're heading in."

Axel nodded and shrugged off his pack. He pulled out a headlamp. Selena wrinkled her nose. "Those look ridiculous."

Axel chuckled. "It's dark, we're tracking three escapees and you're worried about your appearance?"

She didn't snap at him about not understanding. She preferred people think her vain when she talked about appearances rather than have to explain that being a woman meant things were different. You had to look the part too. If someone *knew* you were trying to look authoritative, it undercut the effect.

So she said nothing and pulled a flashlight out of her own pack. Even in the dark she didn't miss his eye roll.

That was fine. Let him. She knew what she was about.

"Blanca. Search."

It took longer than before because the odors of the fire

interfered with Blanca's sense of smell. Selena had to get out the glove and use it a few more times to ground Blanca in the search.

"Could they have set the fire to interfere with the dog?" Axel wondered aloud.

"A lot of work to go through for one search dog." They moved away from the fire, getting Blanca back into clearer air. Another sniff of the glove and she was moving at a better pace again.

Axel kept an eye on the map on his phone, determining if they were getting closer to their potential shelter or farther away.

Selena let out a sigh when Blanca lost the scent again. "It's too much. She needs a break."

"We could use one too," Axel said, clearly holding no blame for the dog, which soothed Selena some. "We'll head for the shelter. Food and rest for everyone. Our counterparts up north will keep the escapees from crossing the border. They'll likely have to stop too. They can't keep going on forever without food supplies."

But Selena wasn't convinced they didn't have access to *something*. They'd ventured out into the bleak winter. They'd burned down a building. Both things required supplies or the promise of supplies.

So many things didn't add up.

Still, they marched on through the dark and the cold and the snow. Axel navigated with his phone until they found the structure Opaline had dug up on some far-flung map.

Selena and Axel stopped in their tracks, his headlamp and her flashlight illuminating the…teeny, tiny shack. It'd be a tight squeeze for the three of them, and even with the close quarters, the gaps in the wood wouldn't give them much shelter. There was a roof with a crooked chimney, and if their shafts of light weren't creating an illusion, there appeared to be a foundation, which meant flooring without snow.

"It's better than nothing?" But Axel's voice was hardly one of certainty or relief.

"We might want to make sure there aren't bodies in there."

Axel snorted. "Allow me."

He moved forward. He didn't draw his weapon, but he kept his hand on the butt of it in its holster. He toed the door open with his foot. It creaked and groaned like it might fall off its rusty hinges at any moment.

He swept his beam of light inside, taking his time to examine the opening. So much time Selena eventually moved forward, pointing her own flashlight inside the doorway above Axel's shoulder.

There was a small, ancient stove in the corner of the rectangle of a building, connected to that crooked chimney she'd noticed on the roof. The floor was concrete and cracked, bits of ice and snow here and there, but that could be brushed off.

If anything it had maybe been some sort of rustic hunting shelter. For one. Not two and a dog.

But the stove was a potential for warmth. "Think that thing works?"

"Only one way to find out."

They both ducked into the shack. Axel went about examining the stove while Selena pulled some of Blanca's supplies out of her pack. A blanket that would be more comfortable to lie on than the icy, cracked concrete floor.

There wasn't much room to maneuver. Occasionally they bumped hips or elbows, and Selena focused on Blanca, ignoring that the person she kept jostling into was a very large, very attractive man, and eventually got the dog situated. She was curled up in the far corner, resting on the blanket Selena had brought. She'd drunk some water, eaten some kibble and now rested her head on her paws and watched the fire be slowly brought to life by Axel.

Selena didn't have much of a choice of what to watch, but she just knew it couldn't be Axel stoking a fire. She settled herself on the cold ground next to Blanca and distracted herself with getting the food out of her pack, a water bottle, arranging it all in her lap. By the time she'd arranged and rearranged and driven herself slowly insane, Axel had the fire glowing in the stove.

She could feel its warmth on her face, though her body remained cold. She had to focus very hard not to shiver or let her teeth chatter since Axel looked perfectly comfortable.

The jerk.

He settled himself into a seated position as far away from her as he could manage. It still meant she could reach out and touch him, but at least she knew better than to do that.

He got his own food supplies out of his pack and began to eat. Selena tried to focus on the fire, but her gaze kept drifting to Axel.

"We shouldn't stay here too long," she offered. Not because she couldn't handle it, but because the escapees were moving forward.

"No. How long do you think Blanca needs?"

Selena looked at her dog resting next to her. "An hour. Maybe two."

Axel nodded, the flickering light of the fire giving his chiseled features a dangerous cast. Silly to let that flutter through her stomach. She knew better than to be attracted to danger.

"While Blanca rests, we can check in with various members of the team and do some of our own research about the victims, or what might connect these three and so on."

"Sounds good," Selena said. "What kind of research are we going to do from here, though?"

He turned his gaze to her, and she had to fight the tide of embarrassment from the knowledge that she'd been staring at him, not the fire.

"I know Peter is a sore spot."

Embarrassment gone, Selena turned her expression to stone. "Not sore," she replied. "Complicated."

"Use whatever words you like, but no matter how little interaction you've had with him, you know his past. You know what's shaped him, even if you don't know how. The other two men, I've only got rap sheets on. With Peter, I have a connection with you and Opaline, who know his whole background."

"Get to the point, Morrow."

"I want to know about Peter. Maybe if I do, I can make some connection to how he'd get wrapped up with these two much more violent characters. Their rap sheets don't add up. *They* don't add up. But maybe if I get a better picture of Peter, something will."

Selena stared at the flickering flame through the slats in the stove. What she knew about Peter wasn't much, but she believed Axel was right. As a gifted profiler, the more information he had, the more he could paint a picture and develop theories. Theories that could lead them to the answers they needed.

She just…didn't want to go here. Didn't want to re-member, rehash or share.

But it was her job. So she'd just have to suck it up.

TESTING THE WATERS, and what Axel knew of Selena, he shrugged. "I can ask Opaline if you'd prefer."

Her jaw tightened. "What kind of things do you want to know?"

He bit back a smile. She couldn't always be maneu-vered, but when she could it was a little too satisfying. "Everything. Just start from the beginning."

She clasped her gloved hands together, then rested one of them on the dog next to her. "We didn't find out about Peter until he was about two. His mom brought him to our mother to drop the bomb about their existence. I don't think Peter would remember that. He was a little thing."

Her expression was bland, but there was a hint at some emotion in her voice.

"Where was your father for that?"

She shrugged. "Work, I think. I don't remember the whole thing. Opaline and I walked in from school and Mom and this woman were yelling at each other and crying, and there was this little boy between them. He wasn't crying."

"So, he was used to emotional outbursts at that age?"

"I suppose. I don't know."

"How old were you?"

"Ten. Opaline was twelve."

Axel knew what it was like to have your life pulled out from under you at a young age. Sure, death was a little more traumatizing, especially when you'd been a wit-ness to it, but trauma was trauma, no matter the severity.

"After Mom divorced Dad, Peter and his mother lived with my dad for a while." She paused, picking at a thread on her coat. She took a deep breath. "Sometimes Dad would show up and take us to his house. Mom would tell him he couldn't. Dad would insist we had to. It was ugly, and the only reason I'm telling you that is because when we'd then go over to Dad and Mariane's, we were always…upset. Then Mariane would get upset."

"And Peter?"

"I never remember him crying. I never remember him doing much of anything except watching us." Her hand curled into a fist and then released. "I wasn't very nice to him."

"How so?"

Selena shrugged jerkily. "Opaline always played with him, read him stories. I kept my distance. Rebuffed him if he tried to play with me. At that age, I didn't understand he wasn't to blame for what my father had done. I'd only known Peter had showed up, and my life had changed irrevocably."

"You were young." Too much for a young girl to try to sort through.

"Yeah, I was. It went on like that for years. When Peter was about eight, Mariane was diagnosed with cancer. Dad got clean—I didn't realize until that point he'd been an alcoholic. Maybe drugs too. I didn't really get it until he stopped."

"Mariane died, right?"

Selena nodded. "When Peter was ten. I was in the police academy at that point. Dad did okay for a while, but I'd say by the time Peter was thirteen, Dad was drinking again. Peter was getting into trouble. Opaline was married to her first mistake in a line of many. I was working on the road, taking classes for K-9 handling, and once Dad started drinking again, I cut him off. Which cut Peter off too."

"You feel guilty." It surprised him. She'd imparted how much they weren't connected, and he'd believed they really had been separate, but there was a heavy, sad guilt in her voice that couldn't be ignored.

"He had his mother's family. He preferred them. When Dad begged that I help Peter, I tried a few times. Peter rebuffed me at every turn. I did what I could. He wouldn't have it. That's Peter. That's the thing you need to know."

But there was guilt there, whether it was warranted or not. Still, Peter was his target, not her. So, he should focus more on the information she'd given him. A few extra details to what he'd already known about the criminal.

"How was his relationship with your father?"

Selena's expression was grim. "Volatile."

"Violent?"

She took a moment, eyebrows drawing together as if she was deep in thought. "I guess not. A lot of yelling. Throwing things. But they never got into a fistfight or anything like that. At least, not that I ever saw or heard about."

"That's the part that's stumping me. There's nothing violent in Peter's record. Everything he's been in for has been mostly aiding and abetting."

"And don't forget, selling drugs."

"Sure, but Leonard and Steve have a violent bent. Where does Peter fit in?"

"We need to know who owned that cabin. There has to be a clue in there."

She was right. Still, Axel brought up the file on Peter he had on his phone. "Gangs. Peter was involved in a lot of gang stuff. So was Steve. But not Leonard Koch."

Selena's expression went thoughtful. She looked…gentler in the firelight. Softer. He was under no illusions she was either, but he had to wonder if there was this side to her, just hidden deep down under the professional, put-together facade she seemed to need.

"No ties to gangs at all?" she asked.

"No. Leonard Koch's misdeeds were almost always done on his own. He's not a man who works with a team, but he has one now."

Selena tapped her own phone, frowning over something. "The security guard's statement, did you read it?"

"Yeah. She says Leonard was the ringleader in the escape, in threatening her."

Selena tapped her fingers on her knee and Axel brought up his Leonard Koch profile while snacking on the nuts he'd pulled out of his pack.

"There is one arrest on Leonard's record where he wasn't working alone, but the charges were dropped," Axel said as he skimmed the information.

"Who was he working with?" Selena asked.

Axel kept reading. "A man named Bernard McNally."

Selena tapped a few keys on her phone. "Bernard McNally." She let out a low whistle. "Well, he's clean as far as I can tell. Nothing since that incident."

Axel was already typing a text to Opaline and Alana. "We'll get a full background check from headquarters on him. See if something adds up. Connects." He grinned over at her. "See, a little rest did us good."

She grunted. "We'll see."

Chapter Eight

Selena dreaded leaving the shelter they'd found. It was uncomfortable, she was way too close to Axel Morrow and the subtle smell of his soap or cologne or something male and a little too enticing, but it was warm in these four walls.

Still, keeping up with their escapees was of the utmost importance. So, once they'd given Blanca an hour's rest, they started gathering their things again, Axel dousing the fire, Selena putting Blanca's supplies back in her pack.

She adjusted her hood on her head, and Axel placed the silly headlamp over his stocking cap. Why didn't it look silly on him? Something about the square jaw or sharp nose. *Or just the fact he's a hot guy.*

"How long do you think they can last out there without supplies?" Selena asked. Maybe the cold wouldn't be so bad. She wouldn't be tempted to study his face when the wind felt like knives against her exposed skin.

"We don't know what they might have taken from that cabin," Axel said, adjusting the pack on his back, then eyeing the shack to make sure they hadn't left anything behind.

"Could something have been *left* at the cabin for them?"

Axel was quiet as he opened the door and they stepped back out into the icy chill of a February night.

"Interesting thought," he said after a while. "I'm hoping the owner of the cabin gives us some clues as to that, but for now…"

"For now, we march."

"You know, some people do this for fun."

"Chase criminals through the arctic tundra?"

Axel chuckled, a low, grumbly sound that had no business making her stomach flutter helplessly. What *was* that? She was a sane woman. A sane woman who'd gone down this particularly stupid road before. She'd learned her lessons, sworn an oath to herself up and down, and she *loved* her job more than anything else.

So, why did it feel like Axel Morrow threatened all that?

"Winter night hikes. Full moon. Starlight. Some people find it exhilarating."

"Some people need their heads examined. It's *freezing*." She'd thought the cold would be bearable, but her feet felt like ice blocks, and when the wind blew just hard enough, it made her eyes water and her teeth want to chatter.

Pretty? Sure. The stars through the bare tree branches were something else—something she didn't see in town—and the dark of the forest was an eerie kind of moody that she got a kick out of. But she'd much rather be cozied up next to a fire looking at it all through a window with heat blasting over her feet.

Blanca sniffed the ground. It took a few tries for her to pick up the trail they'd left behind. With the snow and the wind and the dark, it was harder to keep track of. But the rest had done the dog some good, and though they had to pause and reset on occasion, they were continuously moving forward. Selena following Blanca, Axel behind her.

They were quiet as they walked, which Selena knew was for the best. They had to listen for potential danger, pay attention to Blanca's cues. But she wished she could talk to him if only to keep her mind off the cold.

It was a trick of the trade when it came to long, monotonous searches, stakeouts and waiting. So much waiting in this job. But she didn't usually have to be quite so cold.

Look it as a challenge, she ordered herself. She liked a challenge. Relished proving to herself she could do more than she thought. She could be silent, frozen and strong.

She listened to the whistle of the wind, Blanca's panting, the crunching sound of their feet on snow. "Do people really find this exhilarating?" she muttered.

Again that dark chuckle. "There's no accounting for what people find exhilarating."

He really had to stop saying that word. It made nerve endings she'd purposefully forgotten about spring to life, all crackling energy. Wanting to be *exhilarated*.

They stepped into a clearing, both slowing their pace and listening and watching with great caution. Clearings could be dangerous. Without discussing it, they each clicked off the lights they were carrying.

Selena heard nothing. Saw nothing as she turned in a slow circle. She was about to suggest they turn their lights back on.

"Wait," Axel said, so authoritatively she stopped moving immediately, and Blanca did too, even though Selena hadn't uttered the command.

"What is it?" Selena moved for her weapon, but Axel's large hand closed over her arm. "The northern lights."

She looked up at the fathomless sky to see the pale

greenish sparkle that seemed so otherworldly it took her breath away.

They were silent, still for a few moments.

"Haven't you ever seen them before?" he asked, standing way too close since she could feel his breath on her ear. Yet she couldn't pull her gaze from that rippling, colorful light in the middle of the night sky.

She shook her head. "I don't spend much time out of the city." Why not? Why didn't she get away from the buildings and the crowds every once in a while and just…breathe?

"I can see them from my farm sometimes," Axel said, his voice low and sensual in her ear. She could feel warmth emanating from him, which she knew meant he was too close, but she didn't move. She didn't say anything.

"Getting out of the city would do you some good, Lopez," he continued. "And *that* feeling you've got going on—the awe, the peace, the idea that the world is bigger and more amazing than you'd ever imagined—*that's* why people take a night hike through the frozen tundra or whatever you called it."

She didn't fully absorb his words—she was too busy looking at the sky and absorbing the feel of standing here watching this. With him.

"Is it like this all the time?" she wondered aloud before she could think to censor herself. "You just live out in the middle of nowhere and feel this awe?"

"A lot of the time. Other times it's just…quiet. There was a time in my life I didn't want the quiet. The noise, the push, it was better. But you get old enough…"

She scoffed, turning to look at him though he was only a shadow above her shoulder. "You're hardly ancient."

"I've lived a lot of years in thirty-four."

"Mmm." She knew he meant what he'd been through as a child, and she had to admit sometimes he *felt* more than three years older than her. It was the way he held himself. That supervisory part of his job. He was a man who'd either been born older or had come to it honestly after losing his family in such tragic circumstances.

The thought of a boy who'd had his family murdered around him, who'd somehow survived, living alone as a man out in the middle of nowhere on some nonfunctioning farm felt…wrong all of a sudden.

"You need a dog, Morrow. You make that quiet sound far too lonely."

Though she couldn't make out his face, she could sense he stared down at her. She could sense them measuring each other up, even in only shadow.

Maybe that was why she didn't move away. It was dark. She could pretend that this spiraling, *exhilarating* feeling inside her chest wasn't about him—a man she worked with. But instead just a shadow. Someone removed from TCD and the FBI.

"Maybe I need more than a dog," he murmured.

Her breath caught, and it felt like her heart mirrored the movement. A sharp beat followed by a holding moment where she thought about all the implications of what that might mean.

But she'd been here before. All those what-ifs used like promises. She couldn't believe them, no matter how different Axel felt. Older, wiser—she didn't make the same mistakes twice.

She just wished he'd *feel* like a mistake, instead of something she wanted.

"Selena."

His voice was a velvety promise, the northern lights all around them, Blanca waiting patiently in the dark.

Their work was hardly done, but it would hardly be ruined by one…

The vibrating buzz of a phone interrupted the quiet, and thank *God* it interrupted her break with sanity. Again.

"Saved by the bell. Twice," she muttered. Because both times his phone had gone off, interrupting these *moments*, she knew she'd been far too close to giving in. When she'd promised herself never to give in again.

"Morrow," Axel answered his phone, sounding terse and gritty.

It soothed her a *little* that he didn't sound his cool, collected self.

"Well, we've got our lead," Axel said after talking in low tones on the phone. "The cabin belonged to a shell company, but Opaline did some digging and found a connection to Bernard McNally."

"The guy Leonard was arrested with way back when?"

"One and the same. Now to figure out who and where Bernard is."

AXEL COULDN'T SAY what the hell was wrong with him. Working with Selena for four years had been a challenge at times, but it had never truly tested him. Granted, they'd never been quite so alone, so isolated.

He knew all sorts of things about her, but there was something intimate about watching a person see the northern lights for the first time.

Maybe he was delirious from smoke inhalation or some sort of brain hypothermia.

"Friend or enemy?" Selena said into the quiet.

They'd resumed their walking, following Blanca in a line through the clearing and toward another thicket of trees. Axel had to remind himself they were in the middle of an assignment and bring his mind back to what they'd been discussing.

Instead of how easy it was to forget what he was doing the more time he spent around her.

You make that quiet sound far too lonely. The soft, gentle way she'd said that seemed to infect him. He couldn't help but picture her…at his farm. Watching the stars come out on a pretty spring night.

Yeah, right.

"Axel?"

Get it together, man. "Yeah. No. I don't know. Foe seems more likely if they burned the guy's cabin to the ground."

"Why take the time? That's what I can't get over. We'll catch up by morning even with our break. They took time to burn that place down."

"Must have been important."

"To Leonard."

"Seems that way."

They fell into an easy silence, following Blanca through the woods. She seemed to have a good trail now, and he knew that Selena was listening to the world around them just as he was. How far back were they? How much longer would they chase, just out of reach, before they acted?

He checked his phone and the map. Both teams of TCD agents were still a good fifty miles away. The trio couldn't have made it that far yet. As long as they kept it up like this, they'd be able to surround, outnumber and take down the trio without anyone getting hurt.

He hoped for that outcome, even with all the questions about the case still bothering him. He could hope for easy.

Slowly, after hours of walking, a faint hint of light creeped into the woods around them. Selena had turned off her flashlight, and he'd taken off the headlamp and thrown it in his pack. It was still early, dawn just a pearly promise, but it gave them enough sight to walk.

This time it was Selena's phone that buzzed.

"Yeah?" There was a pause. "Opaline, calm down." The words were spoken with some impatience, but also a certain authority that was interesting to note. She was the younger sister, but she was the one more…in control of the situation.

He thought about what she'd said about everyone in her family wanting her to take responsibility for Peter. She was the rock there, and she didn't want to be. Still, when push came to shove, they all turned to her. No matter the bad blood, or the tension, Opaline was calling her with a problem.

Family. A bond even bad feelings couldn't erase. Did Peter have that? Axel knew he himself didn't. He'd watched people have that, wondered how his life might be different if he'd had a family. If he'd had that connection no matter what happened.

But Peter's family connections weren't simply lost by losing his mother. He still had family, but it had been fractured by his father's actions with another family. Gangs were notorious for attracting people who wanted a sense of family, community, purpose.

Had Peter simply fallen into this trio to belong? To feel a part of something? And if that was true, could he be convinced to do worse things than he'd done before? Or was there some breaking point for him?

"They don't know who?" Selena asked carefully, something a little bleak in her eyes, and if the light wasn't playing tricks on him, she'd paled. Quietly he commanded Blanca to stop so they could stop walking for a minute while Selena finished up the phone call.

She stood there, still as a statue, blinking at the ground. When she spoke, she had to clear her throat first. "They found a body in the fire."

Axel's mind flipped through a hundred different scenarios, but he kept his expression neutral. "And there's no ID?"

"Not yet."

She was trying to be strong, but they both knew the body could be Peter's. Unfortunately, the profile he had of Peter Lopez only supported the possibility. A man desperate for family, but not desperate enough to get violent. With two violent men, who'd likely leave him behind in a heartbeat if he didn't fall into line.

"It'll take some time to get the ID. We should keep walking," Selena said. She ordered Blanca to search and started following the dog without waiting for his response. Still, he followed, but he wasn't totally ready to let it drop.

She, on the other hand, was good at letting things drop, burying them under layers of professionalism and cynicism. But he'd seen underneath all that these past few hours more than he ever had.

"Was Opaline upset?" he asked, keeping the query casual.

"In Opaline's world everything is worth getting upset over. Every bad possibility is one to indulge. Instead of just waiting and seeing and dealing with the reality, she has to drama her way through it."

There was a simmering anger there, but Axel could see it was covering up Selena's own fear. A grief she didn't even know for sure she had to feel yet. So, he decided to help her. To focus on the things that made her angry. If Opaline was one of them, so be it.

"Four years you guys have worked together. And unless I'm mistaken, it was your choice to make the move."

"You *are* mistaken, hotshot."

"What? She forced you to take the job?"

"No, of course not. It's nothing to do with her or here. The last department I worked for…" She shrugged, her shoulders jerking restlessly. "Things were messy. Someone was making it messier. I had a choice, I guess. Take Alana's offer and work with my sister, or keep fighting a losing battle. Opaline won out."

"Messy how?"

Selena shrugged again.

"Romantic messy?"

She laughed, but it had a sharp edge of bitterness to it. "There was nothing romantic about it."

"What exactly does that mean?"

"It means I made a stupid mistake, slept with the wrong guy who then used that against me."

The thought of someone using something personal against her, in a professional situation, had his fingers curling into fists. Maybe when they got back after this assignment he'd do some digging into whatever waste of space thought messing with Selena was a good idea.

But for now, he had to focus on the task at hand. Keep Selena's mind off the body until they knew for sure whose it was. "Sounds romantic to me."

"Maybe it was all mean-spirited lust."

"Not for you, it wasn't."

She stopped following Blanca and whirled on him. "How do you know?"

"Because I've got a pretty good handle on you."

"Oh, have you made a little profile about me, Morrow?" she demanded, angling her chin and putting her hands on her hips. All the fear was gone. She was nothing but anger and irritation now.

He probably shouldn't find that attractive. "What's more," he said, ignoring her irritation and demand, "it wouldn't still bother you if there hadn't been feelings attached."

"It doesn't still bother me."

"Then you wouldn't be afraid to kiss me."

The noise she made was neither a laugh nor a shriek nor a grunt. It was some mixture of all three. "Afraid? To *kiss* you? You're accusing me of being afraid to kiss you while we're tracking three escaped criminals, one of whom happens to be my brother?"

He flashed a grin he knew would piss her off—and that would result in one of three things, she'd haul off and hit him. A potential he could live with, though he no doubt she packed a punch. Two, she might kiss him out of spite. He wouldn't complain. Three, she'd march off and they'd keep following Blanca. Not his favorite option, but he'd deal.

"If the shoe fits," he offered, and he decided to add insult to injury and follow Blanca himself, leaving Selena gaping behind him.

Chapter Nine

Selena wanted to strangle him with her bare hands. Or she wanted to kiss the living daylights out of him and saunter away completely and utterly unbothered.

She knew *that* wouldn't happen. No matter how much she prized her control, kissing Axel would be… Well, she'd prefer to consider her other options rather than risk losing herself to *that*.

She considered trying to murder him. Satisfying, but it would take too much time when they had an assignment in front of them.

So her only option and recourse was to find a way to be calm.

Which was part and parcel with her job that she loved. Remaining calm in high-pressure situations. His ridiculous statement was hardly high pressure, but everything surrounding them was.

Too bad it was a lot easier to ignore the barbs of a perp over a man who seemed to have been created *specifically* to torture her in any number of ways.

Because he wasn't like Tom. If she gave in to the buzz of electricity between them, no matter what happened, she *knew* he wouldn't use it against her like Tom had done. It wasn't who Axel was. Even when she tried to convince herself she'd ruin her career by letting any of the feelings she had for Axel come to the surface, she just…couldn't.

He wouldn't do that to her.

But that didn't make giving in to those feelings safe or right by any means. She didn't want to analyze too deeply all the ways she thought it would be far more dangerous than the disaster with Tom at her last department.

Maybe because your heart would be more involved than your pride this time?

Yeah, she was definitely not thinking about this right now.

So, she walked. She allowed herself some inward fuming, just as she allowed Axel to be the one to follow the closest behind Blanca. Focusing on anger had gotten her through a lot of tough situations. Anger could be controlled. Sadness, grief, worry…those things spiraled out of control.

With anger there was a clear line. She might say the wrong thing, even do the wrong thing, but as long as she wasn't using her fists on someone, she knew she hadn't gone too far. Anger was a safe box within which to act, up to a certain point.

You never knew when you'd gone too far with hurt. With hope. With loss. Life just came and shoved them in your face regardless. You couldn't predict it, fight it, control the tide of it. Which was why she did everything in her power to channel all of those things into *anger*.

She looked at the man hiking in front of her. His broad shoulders, strong back, the easy strides through the snow. He had his hat pulled low against the wind, and still he walked with a strength of purpose as if it wasn't freezing and miserable.

Kiss him? That was hardly all she wanted to do with the man. Which was why she held herself back. Under all that made him nice to look at, and the easy way he had with people wasn't the Napoleon complex, weak-willed, nasty streak that Tom had wallowed in once she'd broken things off.

She was terrified there'd be no breaking *anything* off when it came to Axel. Like loss and grief and hope, wanting someone completely was out of her control.

She wanted no part of it. Even while her body told her all the things she *did* want part of when it came to Axel Morrow.

So, no. No kissing. No more bringing up her past— Peter, Tom, who and whatever. No more looking at the northern lights and hearing that thread of loneliness in his voice and wanting to do something about it.

No. More.

His pace slowed, and Blanca stopped abruptly, a low growl emanating from within her. Selena came to stand next to Axel, ready to think about the real problem, not the stupid ones in her brain.

He pointed at the ground. "Tracks," he murmured.

Selena looked down at them. They weren't just following the scent anymore—they were close enough to see tracks not altered by the wind. It *wasn't* as windy today as it had been yesterday, but the clear indentations spoke to being right on the escapee's heels.

Selena crouched down. She studied the footprints, forced herself to think dispassionately about what she thought she saw. She got down, measured the different marks with her hands, squinted around to determine the wind's effects. She knew how to track people like this— Blanca made it easier, but Selena knew what she was doing even without her dog.

She looked up at Axel, doing everything in her power

to mask the relief and hope she felt swelling in her chest. "This is three different sets of footprints."

His eyebrows raised, but that was the only reaction. There was no doubt there, but she felt the need to prove to him she wasn't reaching anyway. Wasn't trying to prove Peter was still alive when that's what she desperately wanted to do.

"Look," she said, pointing out the three different sizes and treads. "One. Two. Three."

"We have to be close," Axel said, scanning the woods around them.

Selena nodded. "Very close." She wanted to rush forward. She wanted to take them down now. She wanted to find Peter and *demand* to know he didn't have anything to do with the body in the burned cabin.

And she hated herself for that very Opaline response. She wanted to let Peter go. He was an escaped convict. She didn't care about him. For years and years she'd tried to convince herself she'd done her part, he'd rebuffed it and she didn't care. She'd washed her hands of it and moved on.

But there always seemed to be a glimmer of that toddler, quiet and sad, standing between her mother and his, while they screamed at each other.

Because if you never face the things that haunt you, Selena, they eat you alive. She hated that Axel's words would come back to her now. That they'd make something shift inside her, a sad realization she'd been fighting for a long time now. She was too hard on Opaline, always, because she was trying to forget that little boy, and Opaline always wanted to bring him to the forefront. And while they fought those things they never addressed, never dealt with, it continued to haunt them both.

"Selena." Axel's voice was gentle, as was the hand he placed on her shoulder.

"I'm fine," she said, probably too sharply, getting to her feet. "It doesn't mean anything. Not really. He could be the murderer. Hell, it could still be him charred to a crisp and his friends picked someone else up along the way. I know it doesn't mean much. I just…" There was a lump forming in her throat. She'd never give in to tears, but she couldn't stop that lump from lodging there.

"It's okay," he said, his hand still on her shoulder, giving it a squeeze that infused her with a warmth she couldn't afford. Not here. Not now. Not with a damn lump in her throat.

She shrugged his hand off. "I don't want you to understand or absolve me," she said, because that was exactly what she wanted. Too much. For *someone* to understand, to tell her she wasn't…all the things she was so afraid she was. Cold. Mean. Wrong.

He shrugged, unbothered. "Too bad. I absolutely understand you, and I absolutely think it and you are *okay*." He looked around again. "Let's fall back a little bit and conference call with the team."

She opened her mouth to argue. *This* close to the escapees, to finding out if Peter was still alive, they should act, but his expression was stone. The kind even an FBI agent didn't get to argue with.

"Two people are already dead on this little path of destruction," he said in that cold voice from before, when the poacher had died. "I won't add either of us to the tally. Fall back."

It was an order. A sharp, decisive one. He could say he wasn't her boss all he wanted, but that was Mr. *Supervisor* right there.

She wished it bothered her more.

Blanca started following him back in the direction they'd come without Selena giving her the command. Selena frowned at both retreating figures.

But there was no recourse here. Much as she *wanted* to move forward, Axel was right. They had to employ caution. The men were armed. Dangerous. She and Axel might have vests and their own guns, but the trio—whoever they were—likely had a better vantage point and certainly knew they were being tracked.

They might not know people were waiting to stop them, so to keep following and lead them into that surprise would be best. Safest.

So all she could do was follow Axel.

AXEL BACKTRACKED UNTIL he found a tight grove of pine trees. He contorted his body, ducking his head against the sticky, snowy needles. "This'll work," he said. Inside the thicket there was a small space. It wasn't much protection, but it would keep them out of sight.

He heard Selena murmuring to Blanca before she shoved her way into the space. She wrinkled her nose. "Smells like Christmas," Selena commented. The haunted look she'd been sporting out there had dissipated back to professional stoicism. It was what the moment needed, but unfortunately it didn't eradicate his sympathy, his... very visceral need to make this okay for her.

"Blanca will guard," Selena added, nodding at the trees. "She won't bark if she senses something, she'll either come in here or let out a low growl depending on the level of threat."

"She's some dog."

Selena's mouth curved slightly in pride. "Yeah."

Axel got out his phone and set up the conference call. It took a while to get everyone connected. He'd patched in Opaline and Alana along with Carly and Aria, and Scott and Max.

"We're tight on their heels. Going to keep giving them space until we've made a good circle around them. Selena found something that we'll want to keep in mind."

"There are three separate tracks in the snow." She looked at the screen in Axel's hand, and Axel could tell she was staring at the little box that was Opaline. "Don't know what it means, of course, but there are still three of them. Whether it's our original three or a new one, we'll have to get close enough to find out."

Opaline let out a long breath. Clearly she wanted to believe the third track was Peter, and Axel found himself wanting to believe that too. For both sisters.

"After this call I want you to do just that," Alana said. "Don't act unless you have a surefire way of bringing them down without injury to yourself. Your purpose this morning is to get close enough to see who our new trio is, if it is new. The better idea we have of who we're dealing with, the better choices we'll make."

Axel nodded, though he didn't like the idea at all. Did it matter *who* was out there *now*, when they'd find out when they all met together? But you never knew what kind of advantage knowing who someone was could give you.

Still, he'd rather keep Selena safe and sound right here until they were ready to act. Which wasn't his job. His job was to be Selena's partner. Not her protector.

Why was that getting harder?

"I already marked our location on the map," Axel said. "Carly and Aria, Scott and Max, you'll want to adjust your locations accordingly and make sure there aren't any holes in the direction they're headed toward."

"I think we're good," Aria said, looking down at what

he assumed was the map. "If they keep heading in this same direction, we should be able to have a tight circle around them by…tomorrow morning?"

Axel nodded. "They've taken some breaks, but I'm not sure any of them have stopped to rest. They'll have to eventually."

"I imagine they got some kind of foodstuffs and possibly more weapons from the cabin they burned down," Selena said from beside him. "Enough food and water, they might be able to go on without sleep if they have a destination in mind and someone to meet."

"It's possible," Alana said, her voice cool and calm even over the phone. "From what Rihanna has relayed to me from local law enforcement and fire department, the cabin was well stocked. And purposefully burned to the ground."

"We're still looking into Bernard and what his connection might be to Leonard," Opaline said. Axel gave a sideways glance to Selena, since he could tell Opaline was searching the screen for signs of Selena being in distress.

Did Selena notice that? Did Opaline notice the heartbreak in Selena's eyes? It seemed more and more wrong to him that these sisters would be so antagonistic toward each other when the things that had caused their rift were beyond their own control.

"When do you think we'll have an ID on the body?" Selena asked, and Axel knew she was doing everything in her power to sound robotic and unmoved about the potential answer.

"Hopefully soon," Alana said. "Rihanna will send out an alert to all of you the minute she's got the information. She's at the morgue now waiting. We'll want to reconvene and discuss the information, of course, but I'm hopeful the identity gives us a clue as to what we're dealing with." And if Axel knew his director, which he felt like he did, she knew Selena and Opaline needed to know right away without having to wait for a conference call.

"It doesn't make sense they took the time to burn the cabin," Selena said. "There has to be something more to it."

"I agree," Carly chimed in. "I've read the arson investigator's initial notes—not a formal report yet—but the time it would have taken them to burn that cabin in the way that they did, it's considerable. And seemingly pointless."

"So, there's a point," Max said. "What's the usual reason for arson?"

"Insurance money," Aria offered.

"Kill someone," Selena pointed out.

"Or," Max returned, "destroying something. Sometimes even evidence. Could be there was something there our escapees didn't want anyone to find."

The call went quiet for a few seconds. "Definite possibilities," Alana agreed. "We'll work on that on our end. Those of you in the field, let's concentrate on getting these three men without any injury to us. Axel, Selena, find out who we're dealing with, but don't act until you're close enough to the others for all six of you to move."

"Yes, ma'am," Axel and Selena murmured at the same time the others on the call did. They offered brief goodbyes, then the phone went dark. Axel shoved it back in his pocket.

He knew what he had to do. He knew Selena wouldn't like it. So, he had to figure out how to play it.

Ah, screw it. "You'll stay here with Blanca. I'll sneak close enough to see who we've got. Then I'll meet you back here." Then he walked out of the tree enclosure before she could argue.

When Blanca began to trot after him, he turned and held out a hand. "Stay. Guard." He had no idea what the actual commands were, and Selena seemed to act like Blanca would only listen to her, but the dog planted her rear in the snow. Looking just like what he needed her to be. A guard dog.

Now, he had to find out what trio they were dealing with. Weapon drawn, Axel moved for the tracks.

Chapter Ten

Selena could take an order. As a law enforcement agent over the years, she'd had to take her fair share of them. And Axel was her superior, no matter how much he didn't want to label it that way.

Still, his order was tough to swallow. He was doing a simple reconnaissance mission. It made sense only one of them went, and it made sense it was him since she should stay with Blanca.

Selena was frustrated, angry and trying to convince herself those were the only two feelings twisting her stomach in knots. But there was an anxiety over Axel's well-being underneath that. One she couldn't afford.

"What the hell *can* I afford these days?" she muttered to herself. And her own voice broke her out of her trance of worry enough to focus on the moment in front of her.

She was going to stand here and wait for Axel because that was his order, which he had given because Alana had ordered him to find the ID of their third man before they went any farther.

Chain of command. There was no getting around it.

Since she was waiting, Selena needed to use the time wisely—give Blanca a drink, a treat and maybe even a rest. She whistled for Blanca, who pushed through the tree branches. If the dog's expression was anything to go by, she wasn't too thrilled by her current circumstances.

Selena got out the waterproof blanket from her pack, the water, the treats. She set up a nice little rest area for Blanca in the middle of the circle of trees. Blanca circled the blanket, then plopped herself down in the middle.

She looked at Selena with the haughtiness of a queen—at least that was Selena's interpretation. Which gave her a smile and helped her keep her mind off how long Axel had been or would be gone.

Blanca drank, ate the treat, then scooted her body closer to Selena. Selena crouched down and scratched the dog's ears, looking into her dark eyes. "I don't know what I'm doing," she whispered to the dog. "Everything feels all jumbled up, and I don't have time for that. I have to keep it together."

Blanca gently licked Selena's face. Some of the tension inside her chest unwound. There was nothing quite like laying all your problems on a dog. Who couldn't talk back and couldn't hold anything against you either.

"I don't even know what to hope for," she murmured to her dog. At the end of the day, Blanca was her *best* friend. The dog was the only being in her life she was totally honest with. Even as close as Selena had become with Carly working together, she still held herself back.

She'd learned a long time ago the only way to survive was doing that—holding parts of yourself back. Hiding them away.

And what had it gotten her? A job she loved, sure. But a lonely apartment. Distance from every member of her family. Surface relationships.

Selena blew out a breath and plopped her butt onto the blanket next to Blanca. She had to fight the urge to go after Axel just to avoid all these thoughts and feelings.

Because if you never face the things that haunt you, Selena, they eat you alive.

She thought she'd been strong. Tough. She'd withstood a lot of challenges and setbacks and considered that enough.

But no matter how strong her outer shell, she had the sinking realization those things she'd pushed away and never really dealt with *had* eaten her alive. Everything in her life outside TCD was a shell.

Blanca whined, not in communication but in commiseration as she laid her head on Selena's lap.

Selena felt shaky, but she was on a job. She couldn't indulge in tears. She didn't have time for personal epiphanies.

Do you ever?

"I don't want it to be Peter," she found herself saying. No one was here except her and Blanca. Maybe there could be something cathartic in laying it all out for her dog. Who wouldn't judge or ask for more. Who would just sit there and absorb. "I don't want him to be dead in that awful way. I don't want him to be a part of any of these murders. I want to go back in time and *force* him to take my help. But you can't do that. You can't force your help on someone, no matter what Opaline or Dad think."

She blew out a breath. She still had a lot of guilt when it came to Peter. She hadn't always been nice or loving like Opaline had been, but she *had* tried. Selena knew in her heart she'd tried. And Opaline had tried in her way.

So maybe she needed to let it go. Peter. Guilt. Expectation. Hope. Maybe when it came to her arguments with Dad and Opaline about Peter, she needed to accept... She'd done everything she could. It was up to Dad and Opaline to accept it.

It wasn't that easy, of course. She stroked Blanca's

ears. She couldn't just *accept* it or she already would have. But there was something about…thinking it over, speaking the words out loud even if Blanca had no response, that made the problems take shape.

And with a shape, there was the need to actually solve them. Not just avoid them.

"I want my sister to stop blaming me for Peter. I want her to…care about me as more than just the guardian of things." She thought of what Opaline had said on the phone. Wondering if she'd ever asked for help.

No, Selena wouldn't. Asking for help was like baring your soul. It was admitting you couldn't do it on your own.

She didn't believe she was the sole cause of this problem, but she shared some responsibility. She'd never told Dad or Opaline how she'd felt. She'd either been too angry, or more likely too upset and wanting to lean into anger, or she hadn't wanted to feel…vulnerable.

She never wanted to feel like she had the afternoon she'd walked into her normal childhood and seen her mother screaming at another woman, a little baby with her father's eyes between them. She'd never wanted all that *emotion* choking the room.

Emotion. Betrayal. Hurt. She'd found it anyway. She'd gotten involved with Tom because he was charming and because, she realized uncomfortably, she'd thought he was the kind of guy who couldn't hurt her.

In some ways, he hadn't hurt her heart. But he had hurt her pride. Which very unfortunately led her brain to think about Axel.

"And Axel." She looked out through the tree branches. "I don't want this feeling, but it's there." She nuzzled her cheek against the top of Blanca's head. "Why couldn't he be an accountant or something? Why couldn't we have met at the gym? At a bar?" Not that she spent much time at either—rarely bars, only the gym at work. Maybe if she did she'd find some other person who'd make her feel…

Right. This feeling had persisted for four years because it was ordinary, forgettable, and someone else could inspire it.

It just wasn't an option. Surely Axel thought so too, considering he'd kept his hands relentlessly to himself. Sure, he'd made that crack about her being afraid to kiss him, but it hadn't been so much a dare as…

As…

He'd been trying to keep her mind off Peter. Off her personal connection.

Her heart fluttered obnoxiously in her chest even as her stomach twisted at the thought he knew her, understood her *that* well. And cared enough to use that knowledge and understanding to help her get through the harder parts of this assignment.

Selena swore into Blanca's fur. "I am so screwed," she muttered.

AXEL HEARD THE raised voices after he'd been walking maybe ten minutes. There was some relief to that, that he wasn't spending hours distanced from Selena. They should stick together, but this was a one-person job.

All he had to do was make the ID. That was it. So he paused and listened to the murmurings. Carefully, he moved toward the sounds. He kept himself calm, present, focusing on getting closer to the voices without being heard himself.

He thought of nothing else. Not what it would mean when he identified the trio, not what he might do if caught. Not even the cold that seemed to seep into his bones. He could only let his brain focus on the mission and completing it.

Eventually he eased close to a line of trees. He thought he saw movement but got the impression the men were carefully dressed in camouflage. He stopped behind a tree thick enough to hide him, then carefully peered around the side.

He could make out three men now. They stood close together, making it harder to distinguish between them. Still, Axel was sure they were the fugitives.

"Would you shut up?" one voice demanded in a censoring command. "We know they can't be far behind. And with that damn dog. I don't want to stand here arguing when that dog is on our heels."

"It's a search dog, not an attack dog," a bored voice said. "Calm down."

There was incoherent grumbling. Axel stayed exactly where he was. It would be imperative to observe them without being detected. All three men were likely armed, and though he could probably pick all three off without a problem, that wasn't his assignment. Nor his duty.

As a law enforcement agent, his job was to *enforce* the law, not take it into his own hands. Or take the easiest way out. Apprehension was the goal here. Using his weapon to cause injury was a last resort.

When dealing with murderers, he sometimes had to take the moment to remind himself of that. He didn't believe in rehabilitation when it came to cold-blooded murder, but his job wasn't about his belief. It was about following the law.

He drew his weapon for his own safety and then crouched low. He moved toward the voices, keeping himself as hidden behind tree trunks as he could. He just needed one good visual, then he could retreat and head back for Selena.

Axel was beginning to make out the shape of them. The exact location. He crept closer still, keeping his breath soft and even. It puffed out in front of him, but he finally found a good vantage point behind another tree. Not as thick as the last, but if Axel kept his body angled, it was still good cover.

They were indeed dressed in camouflage, including stocking caps in the same pattern. These weren't the clothes they'd left the prison in. Which meant somewhere along the way they'd had help. Or they'd found clothes at the cabin they'd burned down? Something to file away to think about later.

"Why not kill them?" one of the men said. "Why bother with this chasing game? It's cold and miserable. Kill them. Bad enough we had to mess around with that fire, now—"

"You can't kill them," another voice interrupted, sounding panicked. When he spoke again, he was calmer. "Right now we're just escapees. You kill federal agents, they won't rest until they hunt you down. We just have to evade. Then we really can just…disappear. That's what we want, yeah?"

"You got that info from your sister yet?" the bored-sounding one asked. But he wasn't bored anymore. He was sharp. A leader demanding info from a subordinate.

Axel sucked in a breath, heart ramming against his chest in surprise. *Sister.*

"She's working on it," the voice said. There was a defensiveness to his tone, but that didn't do anything to put Axel at ease.

"What does that mean? It's been too long. She was supposed to give us the intel so we'd know where to go and more important, not go, after we escaped. You're the one who told me that." The angry one. Could that be Steve Jenson?

"That's the whole reason you're here even though I doubted your…mettle." Bored. Leonard Koch?

"She's just in computers, man. Besides, it's going to take her some time to make sure it doesn't come back on her."

Computers. Sister. Opaline?

"I don't care if it comes back on her."

"You should. I have someone in the FBI in my pocket. You should care she stays there." It had to be Peter Lopez. Who else had FBI connections?

"What about the other one?" This was the voice who'd expressed concern over the dog, and who Axel was moderately sure was Steve.

There was a cold silence. Axel couldn't see their faces, though he could see the three of them standing in a circle.

"What's this?" the leader said, his voice deceptively amused. "Secrets? Shame on you, Peter."

Axel had his confirmation. Peter was one of the men here. Sisters and the name weren't a coincidence. He couldn't make out the faces of the other two, but talking about escape, plus the heights matching the descriptions he'd been given, made it clear that these were the original three. Whoever was dead back in that cabin was someone else entirely.

"Pete's been keeping an ace in the hole," the taller man said. Steve Jenson. "He doesn't just have one sister in the FBI. The other one's an actual agent. She's not as easy a mark as the computer one, but I bet we can make her talk."

"And you both kept this from me because why?" The question was calm, even pleasant, but no one—neither the two men standing there nor Axel himself—seemed fooled by the tone. Yeah, this man was clearly the leader. Which meant he was Leonard Koch.

The man Axel assumed was Peter sputtered and stuttered but didn't actually say anything to defend himself.

"Hey, we all need an ace in the hole," Steve said with a shrug. He had a gun in his hand. Leonard had one in each hand. Both of their fingers were on the trigger.

They didn't trust each other. That was good. A fractured team didn't always make the best decisions. Information Axel could use. Or maybe they'd just kill each other right here and end it.

Guilt swept in. Selena could say Peter didn't mean anything to her, but Axel knew the kid did. If he got killed in all this, she'd blame herself. Maybe her family would even unfairly blame her. Axel couldn't hope for it to end in a hail of bullets. He had to work to make sure cooler heads prevailed.

"I could kill you right here, right now for lying to me," Leonard said. Then he jerked his chin toward Peter. "Keep him alive because he's the one with the connections."

Steven paused, seeming to consider Leonard's threat. "Come on, man. I convinced you to bring the kid, didn't I? Because I knew he'd be of some use. Yeah, I didn't give the whole story, but have you given us the whole story about your brother?"

Brother. Axel frowned. There hadn't been any information about Leonard Koch having a brother.

"So, these sisters." Leonard turned slightly toward Peter. His fingers remained poised on the triggers, even if the guns still pointed at the ground. "One is helping you?"

Axel felt shock, true, utter shock slam through him.

Helping him? No, Opaline was just talking to Peter. Not *helping* him. Had to be.

"Yeah, yeah. She, uh, she's trying to get their game plan. But she's just like a computer geek, you know? It takes her time to get the information."

"Time's up. Call her. Get the info now. From her. Or the other one. I don't care. I want to know exactly where the feds are—not these morons following us, but the one's they've no doubt got set up at the border. You don't get me that in ten minutes, you're dead."

Axel stayed where he was as Peter fumbled with a phone.

It couldn't be true. Surely Opaline wasn't helping Peter. She'd been with TCD for five years. She was...

Peter's sister.

Axel let out a careful breath. He had to push away any emotions he had about the possibility of Opaline betraying them, about making sure Selena's brother didn't end up dead at Leonard's hands. Bottom line, they didn't know where the FBI agents were, so it was possible Opaline was just pretending she was going to get him the info, setting a trap. Maybe Alana even knew about it.

God, he hoped.

"Well?" Leonard demanded when Peter pulled the phone from his ear.

"She didn't answer," he said, sounding...scared.

Axel refused to feel sympathy for him. Maybe he was young, but a man knew the difference between right and wrong.

And Opaline?

He couldn't think about it.

"Try the other sister."

"I don't know her number. I don't remember it. This

isn't my phone, you know." There was a mix of whining and anger in his tone.

Leonard shrugged. "Then I guess you're of no use to me. Steven? Take care of him."

Steven stepped forward, lifting his gun to point at Peter. Axel lifted his own. He couldn't let this man kill Selena's brother.

So he pulled his own trigger before Steven could.

Chapter Eleven

The gunshot was a clear, decisive sound in the otherwise quiet landscape. Selena jerked, and Blanca jumped to her feet.

Immediately, Selena grabbed her weapon. She left the pack. There was no time. She was out of the tree shelter in seconds flat, but she skidded to a halt as she realized Blanca was at her heels.

Whatever was going on, it was no place for a search dog. Swallowing down the fear and nerves, Selena had to find her authoritative and commanding tone. She crouched down and grasped Blanca's collar with a definitive hold.

"Stay," she said clearly, without any waver or shake. "Stay," she repeated. She would have given the command one more time just to be clear, but she knew her voice wouldn't hold.

Another gunshot rang out, quickly followed by another. Selena's heart lurched and she ran toward the sound.

The cold was like needles against her lungs, but it helped center her. It helped all that training she'd had kick into gear. This wasn't about Axel. It was about getting to and defusing the situation. It was about doing her job. Which involved helping people. Saving people.

Making sure Axel is okay.

He was wearing his vest. He was an excellent agent. If there'd been shooting, it had been...

He wouldn't have shot first. That wasn't the assignment. An agent like Axel being caught? It seemed impossible.

But things happened. Not just mistakes. Bad timing. Wrong place, wrong time. Not enough information to make the right choice.

And she knew the three trying to reach the Canadian border wouldn't hesitate to kill a man. Not when they'd already killed two. Not when freedom lay on the other side. And a Kevlar vest didn't make someone invincible.

A sob tried to fight its way through her throat, but she refused to let it win. She would get to him. Everything would be okay. She was a damn FBI agent—she would make sure of it.

But only if she thought rationally, calmly. She slowed her pace, though it killed her. But going half-cocked into the situation wouldn't help anyone.

She'd run toward the shots, but she hadn't *thought*. She slowed to a walk, surveying the world around her. Trees and white snow. She could see her tracks behind her. Axel should have left some too. She should have followed them.

She could backtrack, but there wasn't time. She sucked in a slow breath of the icy air. She moved forward, because this was the right direction. She kept her pace at a walk, but quick. She slowed her ragged breathing so she could listen.

But the world had gone quiet again. Three gunshots and now quiet.

Selena squeezed the handle of the gun. No use think-

ing about all the might-have-happends. She had to take
this one step at a time.

She slowed, paused, frowned. Were those…footsteps?
She looked in the direction she thought she heard the
sound. Crouched, and had her gun ready to aim and fire.

But the figure that materialized was solitary. Dressed
in black. Tall. Broad.

Axel.

He was running, but not crazed like she had been.
He wasn't exactly moving at a leisurely jog, but hardly
a life-or-death run.

When he saw her, he didn't stop until he'd moved
next to her, crouched in a similar position that she was
in and scanned the world in front of them. "No sign of
them?" he asked.

But she could only stare at him. Relief might have
swamped her, but there was a streak of blood across his
cheek, dripping gruesomely down his jaw. His right hand
was in much the same shape. Torn-open skin, dripping
blood, and he was holding his gun with his left—not his
dominant hand.

"You're bleeding." It was perhaps the stupidest thing
she could have said in the moment, but it made her heart
twist. He was hurt. Maybe not dead, but he was still hurt.

"I'm on my own two feet," he said, his voice calm. Re-
assuring. But blood was dripping *off* him. "I took one of
them down, and the other two took off after getting a few
shots on me. I could have followed, but they had a better
vantage point. Would have been too easy to pick me off."

"The other…" But she couldn't make sense of that
when he was crouching next to her, breathing hard and
bleeding. "Your face. Your hand."

He finally turned to look at her. "I'm alive, Selena.
And so is Peter."

She wasn't sure what she felt at that news. Relief wasn't the right word, but disappointment wasn't either. Besides, feelings didn't matter. Not when Axel was bleeding.

She stood to her full height, scanning the woods around them. "Shelter. We need shelter."

"If we follow—"

"No." Her heart hammered in her ribs, her pulse a painful throb in her neck, but the word was authoritative and calm. "We have to assess your injuries before we move forward."

"Selena—"

"It's protocol and you know it," she snapped. Though she managed to keep her voice steady, her hand shook as she pulled the phone out of her pocket. There had to be a cabin around here somewhere.

"Selena, I shot one of them. Took him down. We need to update the team and then get back to the scene." He moved to put his hand on her, she was pretty sure, but he seemed to realize it was torn up and bloody and stopped himself. "You can't tell them about my injuries."

"Axel—"

"They'll pull me. You know they will. All I need is a few bandages and I'll be fine."

"Your shooting hand… Axel, you could have some serious damage."

"Do I sound like I'm in agonizing pain?"

She didn't say anything, because she didn't *want* to admit he *seemed* fine, even when she could see he most assuredly wasn't.

"We'll go back and get the packs and Blanca. You'll call Alana while we do. We'll update them, see if they can get local law enforcement out in case the one I shot needs medical attention. I imagine we'll still get there before they do."

"Axel…" She didn't know what to say. She didn't think he should be hiking around with blood dripping off him, but he was right about acting like it was just…scratches at most.

Still, when Axel started walking back toward the way Selena had come, Selena had to follow.

"Tell me what happened."

There was nothing but silence as they walked, following Selena's hurried footsteps in the snow.

"Axel. Tell me what happened."

"A lot," he muttered. "Call Alana. Don't mention my injuries. Tell her we had a run-in. I shot one of their men—"

"Axel, she's going to want that information from you."

"Then we'll wait until I can slap a bandage on my face," he muttered, still striding purposefully through the snow.

She grabbed his arm, making sure it was his left, and whirled him around to face her. "You need to get bandaged up. You need to tell me what happened."

His expression was… Well, not as in control as she'd thought. Something had rattled him back there, and she didn't think it was shooting one of the men.

He gestured helplessly. *Helplessly.* It made her heart twist and dread sink like a rock in her stomach. "What is it, Axel?"

"Peter's been in contact with Opaline."

Selena blinked at the ragged note in Axel's voice. "In contact… Since…?"

Axel nodded. "At least that's what he made it sound like. They were using him because he had connection to people who worked with the FBI. They expected him to call Opaline and get information on where we were located so they could avoid us."

Selena couldn't wrap her head around the words. "She wouldn't…"

"No, she wouldn't," Axel agreed. But neither of them sounded convinced.

"We need…" She had to push away all the uncertainty, all the fear and worry. The gruesome look of Axel's bloody hand. There was only thing that could matter right now.

The assignment.

THEY WALKED IN silence from then on out. When they reached where Selena had left their packs, Blanca was waiting patiently. After Selena motioned, giving her the permission to move, she bounded toward Axel. She pressed her furry body against his legs and whined.

Axel could only stare down at the dog. Expressing some kind of sympathy or concern…for him.

Selena disappeared into the trees, then returned with both their packs. She was already rummaging around in one, likely for the first aid kit. When she pulled it out, she still didn't look at him.

He tried not to think too deeply at how much his minor injuries seemed to bother her. What that might mean. In the moment, it couldn't mean anything.

"Patch up my face so we can call in," he said gruffly.

She frowned and gestured at his throbbing hand. "Your hand—"

"Patch up my face so we can call in," he repeated. "We'll go from there." The damage was painful, and he'd likely need some professional medical attention eventually, but he could deal for a few days. He had to.

"I want you to walk me through it. Step by step," she

said, opening the kit and getting out what she would need. When she had everything, she stepped toward him and then hesitated.

"You're too tall."

His mouth curved. "Not a complaint I usually get."

It got an eye roll out of her, which was nice.

"Get on your knees. Put that hurt hand in the snow. I don't know if that'll help any, but the cold can't hurt."

He did as he was told, kneeling before her and plunging the injured hand into the icy cold of the snow. He sucked in a breath and tried to enjoy the interesting position of kneeling in front of Selena Lopez.

But she touched his face with a disinfectant wipe and the burning pain was the only thing he could pay attention to. Since he didn't want to embarrass himself by cursing up a blue streak or wincing away from what had to be done, he focused on his breathing. On the blue of the sky above them.

He told her what happened in quick, succinct summary.

"This might need stitches," she said, unwrapping a bandage with hands that weren't quite steady. "You were shot in the *face*."

"The bullet *grazed* my face. And, hey, it's not the first time. I'm old hat at this."

She paused, then instead of smoothing the bandage over his wound, gently touched her hand to his good cheek. Her expression went heartbreakingly sad. Not just sympathy or pity—that he could have ignored, shrugged away.

This was care. It tightened his chest, and for a few seconds the radiating pain in his body seemed to dissipate.

"Ax…" She squeezed her eyes shut, pulling her hand

away. She swallowed, wiping at the cut again. "Why would you take a risk like that?"

"I don't plan on witnessing any more cold-blooded murders in my life, Selena."

"You didn't have to—"

He reached up and curled his fingers around her wrist, needing her to understand that this didn't lie on her shoulders. Not the way she was thinking. "It would have been wrong to let them kill Peter. No matter the circumstances, it would have been wrong. It's what I had to do."

She let out a shaky breath, then nodded. He released her hand, and she smoothed the bandage over his cheek. It hurt all over again, but he'd survived worse. He'd survived a hell of a lot worse.

"Now—"

But he was silenced by her mouth on his. Her lips were soft, her hands cupping his face softer. This wasn't the sexual attraction that often crackled between them that they were so good at ignoring. The kiss spoke of fear and relief, care and…

He would have said hope, but she ended the kiss abruptly, stepping back and away from him. Her usual wariness was back in her expression, even as his body struggled to catch up.

Selena Lopez had *kissed* him, and not in the sort of way he'd rarely allowed himself to fantasize about. No explosion. No argument that led to the bedroom. She'd cleaned him up and kissed him like he mattered to her.

Then she shut it all away, assessing him coolly. "Well, your face is bandaged up. I don't know what to do about your hand. We need to call it in and then get you to some shelter."

His heart was beating so loudly in his ears it was a miracle he heard her at all. But since he did, some of that emotion and reaction faded quickly. He got to his feet. "I don't need—"

"We need to get your hand seriously bandaged. I can't do it out here." She handed him some gauze. "Try to hold that to the worst of the bleeding. We need shelter, and you need a meal and some rest. That's final, or when we call in, I tell them to medevac you out."

His eyes narrowed. "You're not in charge."

She cocked her head, fisting her hands on her hips. Her eyes flashed with temper and something else he couldn't pinpoint. "I didn't think you were either."

"Touché."

She shrugged her pack on, then held his out for him. When he tried to take it from her, she shook her head.

"You don't need to help me with my pack."

"Have you seen your mangled hand?"

Muttering irritation to himself, he turned around and let her help slide the pack onto his shoulders without jostling his, yes, big, mangled hand.

He moved to get his phone out of his pocket, but he reached with the right hand and hissed out a breath. Nothing was going to be easy without his dominant hand.

"I'll call. I'll say Blanca needs a break and we need the closest cabin they can find. Then I'll hand the phone over to you and you can report what happened." She already had the phone out.

He wanted to argue, to put himself back into the lead in this, but he also needed to keep his injuries as much a secret as he could. He wouldn't be pulled off this case. Not now.

Selena marched, following their footprints, back to the scene of the shooting. Blanca stayed close to Axel.

"Alana, hi. A few updates. First, Blanca needs a rest. A couple hours of real rest. Axel overheard them fighting, and we know that they know we're on their tail. Let's give them a chance to make their own mistakes. Can you get Opaline to track our GPS and tell us the closest available shelter?"

Whatever Alana said in response, Axel couldn't hear. Axel didn't bring up they couldn't trust Opaline. He wasn't any more ready to deal with it than Selena. But, he'd discuss it with Alana once it was his turn to talk.

"I'll hand it over to him to give you a heads-up on what he found." She handed the phone back to him without looking at him. Her jaw was set, her expression fierce.

She was going to march him to a cabin if she had to force one to materialize out of her own sheer will.

"Alana," Axel greeted. He launched into an explanation of what he'd seen, heard and done, leaving out only the fact he'd been shot and the conversation about Opaline. He made sure to emphasize there was dissent among the ranks. No one was following Leonard blindly, and there was a lot of mistrust among the three. They could use that in their favor.

"You're hurt," Alana said flatly.

Axel was taken aback that she had somehow ascertained that. But he couldn't let his surprise show or she might figure out just how much. "It's just a scratch. And it's worth it for the information I got. Alana, I'd like to speak with just you on the line. Just you."

There was a pause. "All right. Hold on." The line went dead for a few minutes, and Axel continued to tromp after Selena.

"All right. I'm in my office. No one else is on the line. What's so important and private you can't tell the team?"

Axel explained everything he'd heard about Peter and Opaline's potential involvement. It was hard to get the words out. Hard to fight for objectivity.

"It's possible Peter was lying," Alana said. She masked her reaction quite well, but there was something about the careful way she spoke Axel knew was a reaction in and of itself. And she certainly wasn't aware Opaline had been in contact with Peter. "To seem useful or valuable to the other two?"

"It's possible," Axel agreed.

Alana sighed. "But less probable."

"They didn't seem to know where we were. Peter acted like Opaline was low on the totem pole and didn't know anything, when we know that isn't true. It's possible Opaline has talked to him but downplayed what she knew."

"It's possible. But she didn't inform me."

Axel slid a look at Selena. Her gaze was on the terrain in front of them. He knew she was bothered, concerned, hurt and a whole slew of other things, but her expression was mostly stoic.

But that couldn't matter. "There's more. Steve mentioned Leonard had a brother. We don't have any intel on that, do we?"

"No. I'll put Opaline…" Alana trailed off. Though she didn't sigh into the line, there was a pregnant pause. "I'll have Amanda look into it," Alana finally said, speaking of her assistant. "And I'm going to sit down and have a conversation with Opaline, but until the situation with her is satisfactorily handled, no one moves on this group. We keep them in our sights, but absolutely *no one* moves. Got it?"

It was like a series of blows that kept landing. That one of their team might be working against them, and now they had to take precautions for that over finishing the mission. Still, there was no other choice when the safety of the team was at stake. "Yes, ma'am."

"Axel… If Opaline tells you where this cabin is, we don't know for sure you and Selena will be safe there. Nothing is for sure until we get to the bottom of this possibility."

Axel eyed Selena's back, so straight even as she struggled to walk through the deep snow.

"We'll take that chance. Can you get local law enforcement to check out…" Axel trailed off as they came to the clearing where the trio had been. There was a body, seated against a tree. He didn't move, and his open eyes saw nothing.

"You'll want to mark our location and send out a medical examiner," Axel said flatly. "The man I shot is dead."

Chapter Twelve

"You shot him in the head?" Selena said, blinking at the man in the snow. She'd seen her fair share of dead bodies, but she couldn't believe...

"No. I shot him in the leg." Axel pointed at the man's leg, where there was indeed another wound. "Leonard must have executed him."

"But why..." Of course she knew the reasons why. She just couldn't wrap her brain around them in these first moments.

"Couldn't keep up with them with a bullet in his leg," Axel said, his voice devoid of any emotion or inflection. "His use didn't outweigh his holding them back." Axel frowned, turning in a slow circle and scanning the trees around them. "They ran away when I shot. They were shooting at me, sure, but they were retreating. Why come back?"

It was Selena's turn to verbalize the answer they both already knew. "He'd talk. He knew their plans. They had to come back and make sure he couldn't."

Axel nodded grimly.

"It's not your fault."

"No, it isn't," he agreed, but his agreement didn't *feel* like one.

"So why do you look like you're blaming yourself?"

"Have you ever taken a life, Selena?"

She inhaled sharply, the words hitting their intended target. "No. But you didn't either. Leonard or Peter killed him. Not you."

Axel shrugged. "I think it could be argued that I started the chain of events that led to it. Justified or not, it has an effect. It's a part of it."

"A mangled hand also has an effect," she said crisply. She wouldn't let him linger on this. They had to move, or he might as well have been medically removed from the assignment. "There's nothing we can do here. Alana will send in the ME. Come on. Amanda sent me coordinates for a nearby cabin. She said half-hour walk, tops." Which Selena knew meant Alana hadn't trusted Opaline enough to handle finding them potential shelter.

Selena looked at Axel's hand. She didn't know what to do about it. He needed...stitches for sure. At the *very* least. There was no way to effectively field dress it to stop the bleeding. "You're losing a lot of blood."

He looked down at the bloody gauze he clutched in his hand. "Some of it's stopped."

She didn't believe him, at all, but they had to get away from the lifeless body of Steve Jenson. So, she looked at her phone and the map Amanda had programmed into the GPS for her. Instead of Opaline.

Opaline. She didn't want to think about her sister. So she focused on each step. She glanced back at Axel. Blanca was walking by his side as if she was protecting him. Some doggie sense that he was hurt.

It was easy not to think about kissing him back there. There were dead men, the possibility her sister was *helping* Peter, and even if she wasn't expressly helping him the very real possibility Opaline would lose her job over whatever she *had* done and kept to herself. Then there was Axel's hand. And the interminable walk to shelter.

So, no, whenever her mind drifted back to that ridiculous, *intimate* touch of lips that she'd initiated in some fit of…softhearted stupidity, it was easily shoved away again.

No matter how much she worried about Axel's hand, she couldn't imagine partnering with anyone else at this point. There was too much… He understood. The shock of Opaline being involved. The thorny connections between her, Opaline *and* Peter. Besides, he'd heard everything the men had said. Infighting and Leonard having a brother. It all added up to someone who was in the thick of things, who'd know how to proceed.

She kept herself from looking back at him. Examining his still-injured hand wouldn't change anything. They had to keep moving forward. It was the only way to end this.

They were silent as they hiked. Selena followed the directions on her phone, Blanca kept close to Axel's side and there were no sounds in the snow-covered forest except the occasional rustle of animal or bird.

It was almost meditative. Like the sun and trees worked together to make her breathe easier. Like the physical exertion outside had some special element she'd never find in the gym. She could breathe…deeper than she had in a long time. Despite the danger, frustration and worry around them, she felt more in control. As though she'd been granted new clarity.

When the cabin on the map came into view, Selena stopped short.

"Whoa," Axel said beside her.

This was no rustic hunting cabin, but a pristine, gleaming two-story *getaway*. The wood was a rich reddish hue against the bright white of the snow around it. The shutters were green, and they matched the door. There was a wraparound porch, liberally covered in snow. So, despite its gorgeousness, it wasn't being used right now.

"I think I'm afraid to go in." But that was silly, of course. They had a job to do, and if it meant commandeering this cabin, so be it. Her phone chimed, and she read the message on her screen aloud.

"Owners notified. Okay to break in. Our office will cover damages and cleanup."

"Know how to jimmy a lock?" Axel asked as they moved up onto the porch.

"I'm not going to waste my time with that," Selena muttered. If TCD was footing the bill, she'd get inside the quickest way possible. She eyed the door, then gave it her best skilled kick. Something splintered, but it took another two kicks to get the door swinging open.

"That was hot."

She snorted out a laugh, which loosened the tightening vise in her chest. Everything was a mess, but at least they could still laugh. "You're twisted, Morrow."

He shrugged, and they entered the cabin. Selena immediately slipped off her pack while Axel moved into the dim interior and turned on a lamp. Blanca padded inside after them.

"First things first. We need to get your hand washed up and sanitized." She looked around. The layout was open, and she immediately found the expansive kitchen and nodded him toward it.

Axel let out a low whistle as they passed a giant stone fireplace and hearth. "This makes my house look like a shack."

"It makes my apartment look like a prison." Selena turned on the tap, flipping it toward hot. She'd half expected the water or electricity or *something* to be shut off, but everything was working. "Must be nice to be loaded, huh?"

Axel didn't respond to that. He was eyeing the water dubiously. "How hot are you going to make that?"

"Hot as it can be. Scared?"

"Survived worse," he muttered, but he clearly wasn't too excited about surviving this.

"Stay put," she ordered, waiting for the water to get a little hotter. She searched the lower level of the cabin, found a nice mudroom off to the side. There was even a dog bed in it. A little small for Blanca, but it would do for now. "Blanca." The dog padded over, and Selena pointed to the bed. "Lie down."

The dog obeyed, and Selena knew she'd take a good doze for as long as Selena let her. When she woke up, or when they needed to leave, Selena would feed and water her again. Ideally the rest would do them *all* some good.

She returned to Axel in the kitchen. "Lose the bandage."

"Sure, Nurse Ratched."

She batted her eyelashes at him. "I'm a lot prettier."

"Yeah, you're all right," he grumbled, unraveling the makeshift dressing. He winced as he pulled it completely off.

Selena ignored the lurching of her stomach at the sight. The bullet had passed through the pad of his palm, ripping the flesh open and leaving a gruesome sight of blood, tissue and perhaps the hint of bone. She didn't look close enough to ascertain for sure.

She lowered the pressure on the water, then gingerly took his wrist and moved it under the slow, gentle stream.

"I'm not even sure how you managed to only get shot on the pad of your hand and a graze on your cheek. That's some luck."

"Yeah, some invisible force field of luck since the day I was born."

Her heart pinched at that. She couldn't possibly begin to imagine what he'd been through, and at such a young age. Still, she knew he wouldn't want her to *express* that. He'd survived close to thirty years since, and she imagined he had a handle on his own ghosts.

But that didn't mean she could just turn off the compassion she felt toward him because of it. Because of who he'd become in spite of it.

She blew out a breath and studied the hand, now that the water had washed away a lot of the dried blood. She held his wrist and forearm gently, trying to work out how to wrap the bandage, and lifted her gaze to his. "You know you need medical attention on this," she said, all joking aside. "Lucky or not, been shot and survived before or not, you need serious medical attention."

He held her gaze, a steely glint of determination in the green depths. "And I'll survive a few more days without it."

She pursed her lips. "Can you shoot with your left?"

"Can. Wouldn't risk a sniper situation or anything, but I do all right. Besides, we keep a tight enough circle, if we need that kind of help, Max is the best shot out of all of us."

His hand now disinfected and dried, Selena began bandaging it from the wrist up. She was as gentle as she could manage. Every time he hissed out a breath, she strove to be even more careful. She wrapped layer after layer, wanting not only to stop the bleeding but to make as much padding as she could so he wasn't constantly making the wound worse.

"I look like a mummy," he complained, the first signs of fatigue and grumpiness edging into his voice.

"You want me to kiss it and make it better?" She grinned up at him, hoping to lighten the mood.

But his gaze was serious. "I wouldn't say no."

Her heart bumped unsteadily against her ribs. Because she wanted to. Just like the moment before when she'd let down her guard because emotion had swamped all rational thought. She'd just wanted that…thing she'd been holding herself back from.

It couldn't be now. Maybe…she could think about it after the assignment was done, but it couldn't be now. She finished with the bandage and gently let his hand go.

"We need to conference call. Then we can grab a meal and some rest." Maybe if she stalled here enough, the other two teams could apprehend Leonard and Peter. She'd never once shirked her duty, or hoped someone else had to do the hard parts, but with Axel hurt…

"Don't get soft on me, Lopez."

Irritated he'd seen right through her, she lifted her chin and glared at him. "I wouldn't dare." She jerked her phone out of her pocket and pulled up the app to video-conference with the two teams to the north.

AXEL ACHED INSIDE and out. Bullet wounds. Heart. Other… places. Everything hurt or throbbed or wanted with something he couldn't have…or at least right now. The mission came first.

Max came on the screen, followed by Carly and Aria in their little box. Selena held the phone so Axel himself was out of frame. Clearly she knew he had to keep the extent of his injures as much on the down low as possible.

Max let out a low whistle. "Where the heck are you two?"

"Finally lucked out," Selena said, and despite the fact Axel could see her knuckles were white from the tension in them, she spoke lightly and easily. "You all talk to Alana?"

"Yeah. Told us to stay put unless we make a visual, and even then to only approach if necessary. You guys got an idea what the holdup is?"

Axel could only see Selena's profile, but she didn't seem to give anything away. "We found one of the men dead and left behind. I think Alana wants to get the body taken care of and a verified ID before we move forward. This just proves how dangerous they are. Not just to us, or passersby, but to each other."

"Right. But what's all this about filtering all info requests through Amanda instead of Opaline?"

This time Selena betrayed *something*, though Axel wasn't sure anyone would be able to notice the minuscule wince on the tiny conference-call video screens. "Opaline was a little overwrought about Peter's involvement and thinking he might be dead. She just needs a break. Have you guys seen anything?"

"Scott's out patrolling the gap we've got between us. He hasn't seen anything."

"By my calculations, they shouldn't be close to us until tomorrow," Aria said. "I'm not sure I understand why you guys don't just take them down now. Down a man. Surely you two could handle it."

"Alana wants to be more safe than sorry," Axel said decisively. "Leonard has already left a trail of bodies."

"Why are you creeping around out of screen, Morrow?" Carly asked with some suspicion.

Selena gave him a questioning look. Axel sighed. He'd keep his hand behind his back, but there'd be no hiding the bandage on his face. It didn't *look* as bad as it probably was, so that was something.

He gave Selena a little nod and scooted closer to her as she angled the phone to get them both in frame.

"What happened to you?" Max demanded of Axel.

"A scratch. Our focus now is on two things. One, tracking down Bernard McNally. And two, figuring out this mysterious brother of Leonard's that I found out about when they were arguing."

"Funny you bring that up," Carly said calmly, and though she studied Axel through the screen, she didn't let Max or Aria butt in with any questions about his injury. "I was doing a little digging on Leonard while Opaline researched Bernard, then Alana mentioned the brother angle. I dug at the potential connection between the two. I'm still working on irrefutable proof, but so far all evidence points to Bernard McNally being Leonard Koch's brother. Not sure if it's a half brother, stepbrother or just foster situation, but they're connected through family. Somehow. Brother would fit."

Selena shared a look with Axel. Even without proof, it did fit. But even knowing the relationship still didn't help them figure out what Leonard was trying to accomplish.

"And do we have anything on Bernard McNally or the body found in his cabin?"

"No body ID yet, and not a lot on Bernard. We think there are aliases, but tracking them down has been difficult. Opaline's been working on that arm. I suppose Amanda is now."

"Let's all work on it," Axel said. "There's no way they get to the border by nightfall. Even if they hike through the night, it's unlikely. If they go off course, we'll use Blanca in the morning."

"Resting like this seems…" Aria trailed off.

"Necessary. Smart. For the good and safety for all of

us," Axel said, bringing out his rarely used authoritative, brook-no-questioning voice.

Aria looked a bit chagrined, but Max didn't appear convinced. "Something is pretty off here," he said.

Axel didn't want to lie to his friend, wouldn't lie to his colleagues, so he could only give them reassurance, not fact. "Everything is as it needs to be. We'll plan to sit tight tonight unless Alana directs otherwise. Agreed?"

"Agreed," Carly said quickly. Max and Aria were a little more hesitant but eventually concurred.

At some point they might need to know about Opaline, but Alana would want to handle that herself. So, Axel would let her.

If that helped Selena out, so be it.

"Bernard McNally is our primary focus right now. I want to know all aliases, who he is, who he pretends to be. I want us completely armed with everything we can by morning. The more we know, the better chance we have of stopping this before Leonard kills anyone else."

He didn't usually bark out orders like this, but he supposed there wasn't anything *usual* going on right now. "Understood?"

Everyone agreed, and then gave half-hearted goodbyes as they cut off the call. Selena shoved the phone in her pocket. Her brows were furrowed, and she seemed to be deep in thought.

"Penny for your thoughts," he offered.

She lifted her gaze to his. Sad and serious. "I want to approach Peter. Alone. Just me and him."

Chapter Thirteen

He didn't laugh. She half expected him to. It was not the smartest plan she'd ever concocted.

But it was *something*.

Axel held her gaze, but he didn't say anything, and it felt like he could see right through her. Like he *knew* this didn't have anything to do with the mission and everything to do with the fact Peter was her brother and she wanted to save him.

Even now.

Are you any better than Opaline?

She couldn't hold his gaze after that popped into her head. She turned to the mess they'd left in bandaging him up. She threw away trash, found a dish towel to wipe the wet counters and desperately tried to find some way to get her professional shell back.

But he'd dissolved it, back there, when he'd let her kiss him as if they hadn't been avoiding it for *years*.

"How do you propose we go about letting that happen?" Axel asked.

She wasn't fooled by his even tone. His eyes said everything his voice didn't. *No way in hell.*

"You have good reason to rest. And do all those things you were talking about with the team. I'll take Blanca and—"

He held up his bandaged hand. "This is what happened the last time we split up."

She wanted to say it wasn't the same, but of course it was the same. Splitting up left them far more vulnerable, especially when her plan was just…personal. She could pretend it was about the assignment—that somehow getting a message to Peter would allow him to escape Leonard's clutches, or bring Leonard down and somehow redeem himself—but deep down she knew she was just grasping at the same old straws. Drowning under the weight of other people's expectations.

"You said they were all fighting. That they didn't trust each other. If we can use that—"

"I get what you're saying, but why not just keep closing in the circle until the six of us can apprehend them without anyone getting hurt?"

Anyone else, she wanted to say, looking at the bandages on his hand and face.

"We might get more information about this Bernard McNally and what he has planned. I've been saying from the beginning, escaping prison in February when you're in northern Michigan just doesn't make sense."

"And you don't think we'll get that information if we apprehend them?"

Selena wanted to present a calm, decisive front. The stoic agent who didn't care—that woman she'd been back at the offices. But Opaline being involved, Axel getting shot…it was poking holes in all her defenses. In all the ways she usually kept her feelings buried and to herself.

"You said Leonard was going to kill Peter. Because he didn't have a use," Selena managed to choke out. "If Opaline was his use…"

Axel scrubbed a hand over his face. "Listen. If Leonard was going to kill Peter, he would have done it then and there with Steve. He escaped *with* men, when it likely would have been easier to orchestrate alone, for a reason. Just like they broke out now for a reason. I'm not saying he won't kill Peter if it helps whatever his end goal is, I'm just saying I don't think it fits with Leonard's goal right now."

Selena tried to let that ease her worry. Axel wasn't the type of agent to say something simply to mollify her. It had to be the truth. The problem was the truth wasn't *certainty*.

Axel reached out, his hand touched her face. She didn't spend much time dwelling on how much larger her male coworkers were than her. She focused on herself, on being strong and capable regardless of size. But now... His hand was big, and he was so much taller with those broad shoulders and...

She was a federal agent. Not a woman. Not here. Not now.

But his fingers brushed her cheek with the gentleness of a...a... She was afraid to let her brain finish that sentence. Like thoughts would materialize in the ether and she wouldn't be able to fight for herself anymore.

"If you really feel like you need to do this," he said, his fingers on her cheek, his words low and serious. "If you take some time and really work through how and what you hope to accomplish, I go with you. Nonnegotiable."

She blinked. *With her.* That was most definitely not what she expected from him, and she didn't know how to... She didn't know...

"But for the next few hours, we take the time to eat and rest. You come up with a plan and we'll go from there."

She swallowed, but it didn't dissolve the lump in her throat. He sighed, fingers sliding off her cheek and then very carefully reaching around her and pulling her toward him. Carefully, gently.

A genuine, friendly, sympathetic, comforting *hug*.

He was warm, steady and still smelled like the fire they'd had in the shack last night. She couldn't seem to hold herself stiff like she knew she should.

When was the last time she'd let someone just hold her, comfort her with nothing more than the shelter of their arms?

She didn't have a clue, and it brought the sting of tears to her eyes. She wouldn't let them *fall*, but it was impossible to fight them completely off. She left her hands at her sides, afraid of what they might do of their own volition if she brought them up to touch. He had the palm of one big hand on the small of her back. He rested his chin on her head, and that had a breath shuddering out of her, sounding far too loud in the quiet room. But she didn't stiffen or pull away. She felt like the warmth of his body was some kind of drug lulling her into complacency, and in that complacency, she rested her head on his shoulder.

She didn't know how long they stood like that. She was half convinced they both dozed off, there on their feet, for a few minutes anyway. In that hazy place, she'd somehow raised her arms to wrap around him, to hold him tight and close as though she could hide away from all that needed to be done.

"You need to rest," she said, not sure why her voice was so thready, why she felt…shaky.

Oh, you know why.

She lifted her head up and dropped her arms. She tried to step away, but his hand remained on her back, a strong, steady pressure keeping her exactly where she was—leaned against him.

"Then we both need to rest," Axel said, his voice a rusty rumble that had her nerve endings tingling to life.

She looked up at him, convinced she would lecture, not get lost in the green of his eyes and the stubble now dotting his jaw. "I wasn't shot," she said, managing—just barely—not to sound like a breathy fool.

"We haven't slept in a long time."

Why did that sound like some kind of sensual invitation when it wasn't? It *wasn't*.

They needed a meal, sleep, and she needed to figure out a way to get to Peter. To hand him a lifeline. If he didn't take it, well, that was his choice. She just…had to offer it. And if Axel was by her side…

She sucked in a breath. It shouldn't feel good. It shouldn't feel necessary. He was her partner on this assignment. She knew how to work with a partner, but that didn't mean she had to depend on them to make her feel like she had a handle on things.

She'd only ever been able to depend on herself for that. Which felt sad with Axel's big hand on her back, holding her so close to him she wanted to give in and lean against him again.

But if she did, she'd lose. She'd lose everything. If she gave in…

What could you gain?

She couldn't listen to that voice. It was the voice that always got her in trouble. That had her trusting people. That had her offering Peter help against her better judgment. That had her moving to TCD thinking she and Opaline might have some sisterly relationship again.

It was the voice that broke her heart, again and again.

So when Axel touched her face again, she shook it off. She couldn't let it linger like some half-reached promise. "I'm not going to pretend we aren't attracted to each other. We've been dancing around that for years, but—"

"I'm not going to pretend attraction is all it is."

She sucked in a breath, and then another. Panic, she convinced herself, was all that she felt. The warmth around her heart, squeezing her chest painfully and beautifully at the same time, was just *panic*.

Not hope.

Even if he felt what she did, that didn't mean it could… mean anything. Go anywhere. She wasn't suited to any of that. She was bad at communicating. She was hard, mean.

Unlovable.

But this wasn't about love. It couldn't be.

And still she didn't move away from his hand on her back, or the soft look in his eyes, or all that *yearning* welling up inside her.

THEY SHOULDN'T BE doing this here. Now. But he was to blame, and Axel didn't know how to stop it.

They had been ordered to stand down, and yes, his hand and cheek throbbed in a mind-numbing kind of pain that was perhaps exacerbating his lack of control.

So damn be it.

"There's more here between us. You know it. I know it. We've pretended there isn't for a long time, but it doesn't go away." He'd kept thinking it would, so much that it had become a habit. Just keep assuming they'd hit some magical point where it didn't feel like some invisible cord tethered them together. "It doesn't go away, Selena. So maybe we address that in the here and now."

She let out one of those shuddery breaths that seriously tested what little control he had left. She was a strong, poised, controlled woman who had almost never showed any signs of weakness in the four years he'd known her.

To see it now sent a powerful bolt of need through him, to match all the other needs tangled up inside him.

"I don't know what you expect to *address* about it." She even tried to lift her chin, do one of those go-to-hell looks she was so good at unleashing on the world. But it fell flat. The only thing it served to do was crack his leash on control.

"This." He hooked his good hand around her neck and pulled her up to meet his mouth. This kiss wasn't soft as hers had been. It spoke more of frustrated attraction than *care*, and any of the many reasons he'd held himself back for *years* dissolved. Into heat. Into need.

Into the strangest, most disorientating sensation that this was exactly what he'd been waiting for, when he hadn't known he'd been *waiting* for anything. Exactly what he needed when he prided himself on being quite self-sufficient. But they were locks clicking into place. Bodies made to fit together. Her and him. Just them.

She didn't resist. That wall was gone. No doubt she'd fought to keep it erected, but some things were meant to be destroyed, and some people were meant to do the destroying. Which was okay. He'd be careful, he promised himself that. No matter what happened, he wouldn't be what her ex had been. *No matter what.*

Her hands came up to his shoulders, her fingers digging into the tense muscles there, as she lifted to her toes and kissed him back with the same need and frustration he'd initiated the kiss with.

It wasn't possible to think about anything else except the feel of her mouth on his, her body pressed up against his. She was soft and sweet, underneath that outer shell of strength and steel. It was the combination, both twined into one woman, that made it feel like this was…unavoidable.

At *some* point the dam was going to break, no matter what they did. It just so happened, the time was now.

He slid his hand down the sexy curve of her back, urged her closer, as if there was any space left to be closer.

Even if one of their phones rang at this point, he didn't think they'd hear it. He certainly wouldn't care. Not when the taste of her melted through him, rearranged something inside him.

He gentled the kiss, not sure he could have articulated *why*, only that he wanted more than just heat and need. Something softer. More lasting. His hand traveled back up the length of her spine to rest on her neck once more. Light. He kissed her with a gentleness he hadn't known himself capable of, his fingers trailing up and down the side of her neck.

His entire body was heat and tension, twined with a pleasure so big and different, he was almost afraid of what came next. Not afraid enough to stop. No, he wanted to wade into this new *thing* and explore it until it was his whole existence.

But that was clearly a mistake, since she pulled her mouth away from his. He could feel the war inside her, because her fingers still dug into his shoulders. She'd found some semblance of reason, but it was fleeting.

He wanted to eradicate *all* sense of reason. Here. Now.

"This is a mistake," she breathed. She kept her gaze averted, her breath coming in uneven puffs. But she held on, and he held on to that.

He wished he could agree with her, make things easy on either of them, but the word *mistake* landed all wrong. A discordant note in a strange new world that was all harmonies. Her in his arms, kissing him with all she was… He could find no mistake in there. Maybe someday he would, but for now, it was only everything. "Selena." He gave her neck a gentle squeeze, trying to get her to look up at him. But she refused.

He pressed a kiss to her temple. "What part of this feels like a mistake?"

Her gaze whipped up to his, arrested. She opened her mouth as if she had an answer, and he braced himself for it.

But none came.

Chapter Fourteen

Selena searched for an answer. An excuse. Anything she could throw at him, or convince herself to let go of him. Anything to douse the curling need inside her.

She tried to think about their assignment, about Opaline, about Peter, but nothing took hold. There was only this man who'd given her some understanding.

"It isn't a mistake," he said, his voice low and grave, like he was delivering bad news. And it *was* bad news. Terrible news. But he kissed her temple again, then her cheek, and no matter how she tried to hold on to the thought that it was bad, feelings crowded thoughts away.

It felt good. It felt right. He was right. Always had been.

She shook her head, trying to remind herself of all the ways this would end badly for her. "We shouldn't. Not here. Not now."

"Probably not," he agreed equitably, but his mouth touched her neck, trailed down the slope of it, and all those protests and reasons and rational thought slid through her mind like smoke.

Her hands were still on his shoulders, holding tight, as she tilted her head to give his mouth better access to her neck. She'd never felt this... It wasn't just that haze of lust, or the want of companionship, touch. There was something deeper.

It scared the hell out of her, and had for a very long time, but he was carefully kissing his way through all her defenses, all her fears. When his mouth returned to hers, she was shaking. She'd have been embarrassed by that show of weakness if she could think straight. But his kisses were like a drug, his hand traveling her body a spell.

It hit her that this wasn't—couldn't be—Axel's norm. He was an agent who prided himself on control and professionalism, and he was shoving that to the side. For her. Because of her. With her.

In that realization, something cracked for her. And then him. The kiss became frenzied. The soft touches were gone, replaced by desperation. They pulled off each other's vests and tumbled to the floor. She tried to be careful of his injuries, but even with only one good hand, it seemed he touched her everywhere, stoking fires, driving this insanity to a fever pitch.

She managed to get his shirt off, then had to help him get hers off. They kicked off their pants, neither quite caring if they were fully divested as long as skin touched skin, body met body.

When they came together, a tangle of clothes and limbs, they both stilled.

"Finally," he murmured into her ear.

Finally. Finally. It echoed in her brain like a chant while he moved inside her, driving her to a waving crest of pleasure she would have thought impossible. But it pulsed through her like light. Like *right*.

She rolled on top of him, seeking more.

They found that more, that release, together.

Selena tried to roll off him, but he only rolled with

her, not letting her go. She didn't know how to fight the need to cuddle into him, to hold on to this. She'd been fighting it for so long. *So* long. It had happened. What was the point of still fighting?

His breathing was heavy and steady, and while his arms were still tight around her, as though he hadn't fully drifted into sleep yet, she knew he was getting close. And if she let him fall asleep, she'd give in to the need to fall asleep. Tempting, but tangled in a mix of their clothes, half-naked on the floor of a stranger's cabin in the middle of an assignment, just wasn't going to work for her.

"Come on. You're dead on your feet. Let's get some rest." She wiggled out of his grasp and he finally let her.

He muttered something she couldn't understand, but she pulled her shirt and pants back on while he did the same. Then, with a hesitation that irritated her because it spoke to making this a bigger deal than it could be, she took his hand and led him to one of the bedrooms.

It was odd, using some other person's cabin as their own, but they both needed some food and some rest, and the strangers would be compensated. So, she had to get over her unease. She pulled the covers on the large bed back and gestured Axel to climb in.

He frowned at the bed, but she gave him a little push and he obeyed. He yawned, fumbling with his phone. "Half hour should be good, yeah?"

"Yeah," she agreed, slightly amused at how he fumbled to set his alarm. She stood there. Her body was still warm and lax and relaxed, but her brain was whirling.

Until he reached out and took her hand. He scooted over in the bed, then pulled her down next to him. "Get some sleep, huh?" he murmured, tucking her firmly against him.

It felt so *nice* and *normal*, she wanted to cry. Instead

she blinked back the tears and focused on keeping her breathing even. She thought about it—*in, out, slow, calm*—rather than all of the other emotions tumbling through her head.

Axel was asleep in seconds, each moment the tight hold he had on her loosening until it finally went lax. She slid out of his arms and off the bed, pausing to make sure he didn't stir.

He'd set his alarm for thirty minutes. She shook her head. That was hardly long enough after he'd been shot. She carefully took his phone and turned off the alarm. Then she slid out of the room.

She'd eat something, do a little work, then slide back into bed before Axel woke up. Maybe she'd catch a fifteen-minute nap. Let him think she'd slept longer.

Out in the kitchen, Selena poked through the cabinets. She didn't allow herself to think about what had transpired on the floor. It had been…stress relief. A blip. They'd go back to normal.

Her stomach flipped as she thought of the way he'd tucked her against him in bed. Why couldn't she have that with someone she didn't work with?

Because no one would do a very good job of understanding your job, or your strengths, without doing similar work.

"I really don't need that kind of clarity right now, self," she muttered. She found peanut butter and a frozen loaf of bread. She took a few slices out, used the toaster to thaw them, then went to work making peanut butter sandwiches.

When her phone buzzed, she pulled it out of her pocket and answered without looking at the caller. "Lopez," she said quietly so she didn't wake Axel. She licked peanut butter off her thumb as only silence greeted her.

"Selena," Opaline's voice finally ventured. It sounded scratchy and weak.

Selena blinked. She hadn't expected a call from her sister. She didn't know what to do with it when...

"I asked Alana to let me call you and tell you everything rather than you getting it from her," Opaline continued. Selena wasn't sure she'd ever heard her sister sound so...beaten down.

"All right," Selena managed, feeling as though her heart was in a vise.

"I wasn't helping Peter. I need you to know that up front. He thought I was, but I didn't give him any information. I wasn't going to. I just thought if he trusted me, he might tell me what was going on and I might be able to...make sure he didn't end up dead."

"But you didn't tell anyone."

Opaline let out a noisy breath. "No, I didn't. I didn't... I just thought it would be better if I handled it so..."

"So we didn't get involved and use him to end this?" Selena demanded, though she couldn't find her usual anger with her sister.

"I just wanted him to be safe," Opaline whispered.

Selena swallowed. The usual wave of frustration and anger didn't materialize. Selena wanted the same thing. She tried to pretend she didn't. Tried to be over Peter. Tried to blame Opaline for bringing up those feelings she wanted buried. But no matter how she tried, he was still that little boy to her, and she knew that was true for Opaline.

Opaline had been wrong, but she'd done it out of love and care. Love and care. Selena hadn't put much stock in those things in a very long time. Too often, they burned.

Axel's words had dug their way into her soul, though. *If you never face the things that haunt you, Selena, they eat you alive.* She didn't want to be eaten alive anymore. So it was time to stop burying, fighting, ignoring. Selena sucked in a breath. Being truthful, vulnerable with Opaline felt a bit like asking someone to shoot her in the face.

But maybe it was better to face the pain and the hurt, rather than to keep running from the things she couldn't outrun. "I don't blame you," Selena managed.

"You…don't?"

"You made a mistake. You shouldn't have done it. But I can't blame you. I know you want to help him and he's… He's our brother."

Opaline was quiet on the other end for a while. She clearly didn't know what to say to Selena's change of heart. "Alana's sending me home. I don't know what's going to happen. She said she has to think about it, but I'm not allowed back until she makes her decision."

Selena shouldn't feel sorry for Opaline. She'd made a very big mistake, but maybe instead of holding everything against her family, she could start…cutting them a break. No, not even that. Stop feeling guilty for *wanting* to cut them a break. Maybe she didn't need to hate herself for never fully being able to harden her heart to Peter and Opaline.

"We'll figure it out. We will." And Selena knew Opaline was their best chance to find something when it came to digging through digital files and information. "But while I'm finishing this, I need you to do me a favor. You can do all that tech stuff you usually do from home, can't you?"

"Not all of it, but some of it."

"Keep researching Bernard McNally. He's the key to all this."

"But what am I supposed to do if I find anything? Alana won't like me…butting my nose in."

"If the ends justify the means, she'll be hard-pressed to hold it against you. You find anything, you email it to *all* of us. Immediately. Okay?"

"O-okay. I guess. Okay. It'll help?"

"I think so."

"Okay. Yeah, I won't sleep till I find something."

Selena breathed out slowly. "And we'll get through this, Opaline. I promise." Because it was time to stop fighting her demons through her family members, and instead work on fighting them together.

"I am sorry, Selena. Really."

There was more to say, but now wasn't the time to say it. "I'm going to do everything I can, okay?" *For both of you.* She always had, but she'd kept it under wraps. Under a layer of blame and guilt. "And when this is all over, we should talk. Really talk."

"Then I guess you'll have to make sure you don't get yourself killed."

"I'll do my best."

"I know we…don't see eye to eye. I know… I've been blaming you, but we're both to blame."

"We are. I agree."

"I love you anyway," Opaline whispered fiercely.

Selena didn't think she would have been able to accept that even a day ago. But something inside her had changed today. "I love you anyway too. 'Bye, Opaline."

"'Bye."

Selena ended the call and closed her eyes, breathing carefully through all the emotional upheaval. When this was over, she'd give herself leave to cry, but for now, she had to stay in control. She had to get this done.

She forced herself to eat, though she didn't feel hungry. She hunted up a plate and put the other sandwich on it and returned to the bedroom Axel was sleeping in.

She put the plate next to his phone on the nightstand and stared down at him in the inky dark. He looked no less strong or big in sleep. In a stranger's bed. He looked more like a statue, something carved to bring out the best features of the subject.

Except his best feature was that good heart of his, and it was definitely going to get her into trouble.

She shook her head and pulled her phone out of her pocket, setting her own alarm for thirty minutes. It'd give him over an hour and her a quick, refreshing nap. Then it would be back to work.

She stared at the bed. Back to work. Except she'd broken all her personal rules with this man, and the way her heart was still all *fluttery*, it really was *all* her personal rules. But that would have to be dealt with later, on her own time. For now, she slid into a stranger's bed, next to Axel Morrow, and slept.

AXEL WOKE UP disoriented and starving. His hand and face throbbed, but it only took him a second or two for his brain to lurch into gear. to remember where he was. What had occurred.

He was in a stranger's bed and there was a woman beside him. She was curled away from him, her dark ponytail a tangled mess on the pillowcase. Her body rose and fell with the slow, steady rhythm of her breathing.

Axel rubbed a hand over his chest where a tight sensation seemed lodged. He'd crossed a few lines he'd never imagined he'd cross, and he didn't even know how to feel badly about it. It had built up too long.

Timing was a hell of a thing.

But it wasn't simple, that was for sure. He wasn't conceited enough to think she'd wake up ready and willing to just *be together*. No, that wasn't Selena's way. She might have given in for a moment, but she'd build that wall back.

And you'll just have to tear it down again.

There was a part of him that didn't want to. That wanted to let her build her barriers, and step back into his own walls. They were comfortable. He figured he was a little more aware of his than Selena was of hers if only because he'd had to deal with a lot of his stuff head-on and she'd clearly avoided, denied and compartmentalized her stuff. But awareness didn't mean a person didn't *like* the safety of their own walls.

But there was something here, something he didn't fully understand and didn't have the time to parse, that made returning to the way they'd been ignoring each other seem impossible.

She would not agree.

Carefully, he swung out of bed. He frowned at his phone. He'd set the alarm for… He glanced at the woman fast asleep next to him. She'd turned it off. He might have scowled, but he was more interested in the sandwich next to his cell. Peanut butter wouldn't have been his first pick, but it was better than the trail food he had in his pack.

He tucked his phone under his good arm, used his good hand to grab the sandwich and left the plate behind as he quietly moved out of the bedroom. He downed the sandwich, dumped his cell on the couch, then frowned.

She'd turned his alarm off so he could sleep longer. She'd clearly taken the time to make sandwiches, to clean up after herself. He'd bet money on her having done some work too.

"Two can play that game," he muttered. He went back into the room, careful that his footfall was silent and that he moved like a ghost. He picked up her phone from the nightstand on her side of the bed and typed in the department code. He turned off her alarm.

See how she liked it.

He didn't let himself linger. They would, at some point, hash this all out. Linger in some of the feelings they'd indulged, but this assignment needed to be finished first. He'd make sure it was soon.

Back in the living room, he decided to make himself comfortable and then do some of his own digging. They'd gotten some new information on all the players, and if Axel could take some time to really comb through it, he might be able to come up with deeper profiles of the three men who'd escaped. It wouldn't magically explain what the endgame was until they understood more about Bernard, but it would help predict Leonard and Peter's movements.

It wasn't too much later when Selena's alarm was supposed to go off, that he heard a quiet, irritable curse and grinned. He was smart enough to wipe the grin off his face as he heard her shuffling around, then walking out of the room. He looked down at his phone and pretended to be absorbed in the information on his screen.

"You turned off my alarm," she accused.

"You turned off mine first." He slowly looked up, and then wished he hadn't. She was…rumpled. Even on the trail she tried to look if not sleek, put together. Rumpled Selena made something painful in his chest catch.

They stayed there, regarding each other, both clearly grappling with emotions. He didn't think Selena was ready to let hers go, and maybe he wasn't either, because he didn't press the matter.

She swallowed hard. "Before we focus on work, we should clear the air."

"Clear the air?" Axel repeated blandly, though nothing inside him felt particularly *bland* at the way she was obviously trying to handle him. Put him into one of her neat little compartments.

I don't think so.

"You won't tell anyone about this."

He tried very hard not to be offended she was *ordering* him not to tell anyone, like he was some randy teenager who'd spread it across school after prom. Or worse, her ex, who'd used a relationship against her in her job.

"Look, I'm not saying you're going to be like my ex or anything," she said as if reading his mind. She even waved a flippant hand, but there was nothing flippant in her eyes. Anxiety and maybe even a little fear. Because some wounds certainly hadn't healed yet.

"I just don't think guys fully understand what it means for a woman. You tell the boys, and things change for me."

Maybe he should let her have her delusions, but surely she understood... "They're going to know, Selena. They're all going to know." She paled, so he hurried on. "Our *friends* are highly trained observers. They're going to see something between us changed."

"It was just once. There's nothing to—"

He stood then, because if he moved maybe he could control his reaction. "Like hell it was."

Chapter Fifteen

Selena's pulse pounded in her neck. Which was stupid, of course. She'd faced down men with guns and all manner of criminals. She wasn't afraid of Axel, of the feelings twirling inside her.

Of everything, some little voice in the back of her mind whispered.

No. She would not be afraid. "Look—"

"No, before you insult me, I want you to think about what you're saying."

"I have thought about what I'm saying," she snapped as he approached her. How could she think about anything else? When she was *supposed* to be thinking about everything else. And how could he want...

Me.

She swallowed at the lump in her throat. She wanted to tell him the truth. *All* her truths, but she couldn't do that and then turn it off and do her job. So, this just couldn't... It just...

Axel fitted his palm to her cheek, and his eyes were too much. She wasn't a coward, but she couldn't quite meet his gaze and stay...strong. She needed to be strong. She had a *job* to do.

"There's something here," he said quietly. "We could go back to ignoring it, but I don't think we'd last as long as we did the first time around. Not knowing how right it feels."

She felt absolutely lost at sea and hated that feeling, that weakness. His bandaged hand came to her other cheek, and it felt like an anchor. How could she let him be her anchor? Hadn't she learned she didn't get one of those?

"Maybe we both need some time to think about it," he said gently. "What it means. How it looks. What we want."

She nodded, a little too fervently, but God, she wanted time. *Needed* time. Away from him, and she wasn't going to get that any time soon.

His hands fell away from her face, and she didn't know why it made her feel downright bereft.

"I've been thinking about the three of them," Axel said, going back to the couch and his phone and his completely normal way of acting. "How they're connected. Why they'd have left together."

She would have been devastated that he could change channels so quickly, so easily, but he rubbed a hand over his chin, something he only ever did when he was agitated.

Thank God.

She let out a long breath, working to change gears too. Later. They would deal with them later. She didn't look forward to it, but at least it gave her the space to breathe.

"You have Leonard," he said, taking a seat on the couch. "A loner for all intents and purposes. Steve, a serial group criminal. He never did anything alone. Then you have Peter…"

"Who desperately wanted to be part of a group." She stood where she was, across the living room. Physical distance would be best for as long as she could manage it.

Axel nodded. "I think Steven and Peter were the group. Friends. Partners. Whatever. Leonard needs more than one guy—for reasons yet to be determined—so he goes to Steve, and Steve makes a case for Peter to go with them. Leonard needs men, so he says okay."

"Then why would Steve go through with killing Peter?"

"Because Leonard told him to. Leonard's the leader. Steve isn't a leader. He does what he's told. He *likes* doing what he's told. Or should I say, *wasn't* a leader, *liked* doing what he was told."

She heard the guilt in his tone. Even though he hadn't killed Steve, who was nothing but a criminal to Axel, he hadn't worked through the blame he felt. She didn't understand why he'd hold himself responsible. She wouldn't *let* him hold himself responsible. "You shouldn't feel guilty."

"Guilt's a tricky thing. I've learned how to deal with it, but it takes time. Luckily I've got about twenty-five plus years' worth of learning to take that time."

Twenty-five plus... Surely he didn't mean the murder of his family. But more than twenty-five would have put him at a child and... "But you couldn't possibly feel guilty about what happened to your family."

"Of course I did."

"You were seven."

"And I was there. I really have...moved on from that. It took a lot of therapy and maturing and whatnot, but... The thing about guilt is it allows you to think there was some way to make the world make sense, if you'd only moved through the right steps. Things wouldn't be this bad, you wouldn't have to feel this awful, but at some point you have to accept you had no power."

It shouldn't hit close to home. Not when he was talking

about his family being murdered around him and she'd just had to survive some family drama and betrayal, but something about his words made things in her chest shift, rearrange. Things that had been heavy and uncomfortable for a very long time.

"Sometimes the world is just...not fair for random reasons you couldn't have predicted or changed or fixed. No matter what you think about that situation, you have to live with the effects. There's no going back." He looked up at her. "I think you might understand the guilt thing a little more than you're willing to acknowledge."

She wanted to be something instead of more wrapped up in him. But he understood. Even though his childhood had been so much more tragic than hers, he didn't act like he won the bad childhood Olympics. He put them on the same level of understanding and didn't make her feel small.

He made her feel understood. She'd never wanted that. Still didn't. Or so she tried to convince herself.

"There's a lot of guilt involved for kids of broken homes," he said gently.

"Broken homes," she echoed. "It wasn't...broken."

"Your father had an affair that resulted in a child, which, once the news got out, caused your parents to divorce. You had two families, parents who used all three of you as pawns, death, uncertainty and emotional upheaval. No one looked out for you guys."

"We looked out for each other."

"Not good enough. Sorry. Kids aren't emotionally capable of handling all that with aplomb."

"I don't know what this has to do—"

"Peter is a part of that dysfunction. He's searching for the remedy. The thing that fills the holes it created. You went into law enforcement, and so did Opaline, in a way.

That didn't fit for him, or he didn't want it to. So, he's looking for the thing that balances the scales."

She didn't like him reading everything so easily. Putting her family into neat little packages. Especially since he was right. "I really don't like when you put on your profiler hat."

He smiled a little. "Noted."

"But if he's…searching," Selena said, thinking of her conversation with Opaline. "He can still be reached. He isn't a lost cause."

"No, I don't think Peter is." Axel tapped his fingers on his leg. "You want to talk to him."

Selena nodded. "A note? A text message? Something. If he knew… If he knew he had some place to belong, even if he had to go to jail for what he'd done…"

"I'd leave the last part out of it and go with the first part."

"So you agree?"

"Sort of," Axel said, pulling a face. "But I think— and you don't know how much I hate myself for thinking this—you need to do it face-to-face."

Undiluted shock crossed her expression before she blanked it out. "How do we manage that?" she asked, sounding like she'd put her agent hat back on.

"First, we have to catch up to them. Separate them somehow."

"You're really going to…" She didn't finish her sentence, just studied him with her eyebrows drawn so hard together her entire forehead puckered.

"It was your idea," he pointed out.

"Right, but to separate them, *we're* going to have to separate. Which, you know, you got shot up the last time we did that."

He frowned a little. "I'd hardly call it *shot up*."

"Well, whatever you'd call it, I'm having a hard time wrapping my head around you thinking it's a good idea."

"It's not. It's kind of terrible." He wished he could lie to her, pretend this wasn't *about* her, but there was no point wasting energy to lie. "I agree with you that Peter isn't a lost cause. And there aren't a lot of ways not to shove him into lost cause territory. So, we have to get him away from Leonard and into your orbit. I think we can do that without splitting up. If we come up with a good plan."

Selena seemed to mull that over. She looked around the room, then went over to the kitchen and grabbed something off the counter. She returned with a little pad of paper and a pen.

She drew some circles and some x's. "If we get close enough to everyone," she said, pointing at the circles, "we can use them to create a diversion to Leonard, while I approach Peter and you can be my backup," she said pointing to the x's.

Axel considered it as Blanca padded into the room. She sniffed Selena, then came over to him and rested her head on his leg. "Your dog loves me."

She grunted irritably. "My dog *pities* you and your mangled hand."

It was Axel's turn to grunt irritably. "The plan is solid," he said after working it around in his mind. "But we'll need to get back out there. I imagine they'll stop to rest at night, but we don't know for sure."

Selena nodded, but before they could begin to pack up and move out, both their phones vibrated.

"Alana," they both said together.

Selena blew out a breath and then took a seat next to

him. They both held up their phones for the videoconference that was about to happen.

The entire team popped onto their screens. Everyone except Opaline.

"I wanted to give everyone an update," Alana said without preamble. "And get any new information from the team, if there is any."

"I've done a deeper profile of the two remaining men we're dealing with," Axel said to the screen. "I'll be sending it over momentarily. Bottom line, Leonard is the leader of this whole organization, no doubt. Peter Lopez is a pawn at best. I don't think he's dangerous."

Alana's face was expressionless, but Axel felt a bit like an insect being sized up. "You're sure about this?"

And he realized Alana suspected, just a little, that Selena or his feelings for Selena might have impaired his judgment. It would have been insulting if he weren't a little worried about it himself. Still, he was a good profiler. A good agent. He'd connected the dots. "The facts support it, Alana."

When Alana said nothing, Axel continued with his theories. "My primary concern is why Leonard, someone who clearly prefers to work alone, took two men with him to escape prison. Being on his own would have been quicker and been easier to avoid detection. Especially in the wilderness."

"It has to connect to the brother," Selena told the team. "None of their choices make sense unless they're working for someone else, who's working toward a goal we don't understand."

"I agree," Carly said.

"Same," Aria chimed in. "Hiking through this weather is no joke, and I don't think they're stupid enough to think it would be."

"But we're hitting a brick wall on the brother," Max said, frustration simmering in his tone. "Unless Opaline's found something?"

"Opaline has been taken off the case until further notice," Alana said briskly. "Amanda is doing some digging while also finding someone who can replace Opaline for the time being."

A silence descended. No one asked why, but Axel slid a glance at Selena. She didn't look surprised, only a little sad. As if she'd already been informed that Opaline was off the case.

"Axel and I were discussing the need to move," Selena said, all business. "We've rested. Refueled. Blanca's ready to go. We tighten the circle, all of us. Instead of pushing them toward you guys, we all tighten."

"In the dark?" Carly questioned.

"Yeah, in the dark. We don't know what they're planning, or why they're doing this now. Let's not give them the chance to show us. How long do you think it will take if we all start moving in?"

"A couple hours," Max said.

"So, we move out now. In a couple hours, our circle is tight enough to apprehend both Leonard and Peter, and then one of them will surely be able to turn over on whatever this Bernard McNally is up to."

"They're armed and dangerous," Max pointed out. "We have to acknowledge the fact we may need to use deadly force, *especially* in the dark. In which case we wouldn't get any information."

Axel kept himself from looking for Selena's reaction out of sheer force of will. "Like I said, Leonard's armed and dangerous. Peter isn't. We'll try to split them up as Selena and I come up the rear. We'll want you guys to the north to see if you can get Leonard to follow one path, while we try to get Peter to come back to us."

There was a silence that spoke of dissension, or at least doubt, but no one voiced it. They were trusting Axel to make the call.

Anxiety tightened his chest, but he breathed it away. It *was* the right call. The facts supported the theories, and yeah, feelings were involved, but feelings weren't always the enemy.

"You all have your plan," Alana said, her voice cool and calm and authoritative, but Axel noted a hint of strain in her eyes and figured it had to do with Opaline's choices. "I agree the brother, Bernard, is the missing piece, and we're working on finding it. You'll all be notified immediately of what we find. Make sure you use the walkies once you're in range of each other. Communication is key. It goes without saying we want to avoid loss of life, but if we can't find anything on Bernard McNally on our end, apprehending Leonard Koch and Peter Lopez alive is going to be of the utmost importance to figure this mess out."

Selena let out a slow breath, clearly relieved Alana's orders prioritized keeping everyone alive.

"Let's get this done and get you all home," Alana said firmly.

Everyone agreed and hung up. Axel scratched Blanca's silky ears. "Back out into the cold," he murmured.

Chapter Sixteen

Back out in the cold was right. Night was falling and the temperature was dropping. After their few hours in the nice, heated cabin, in an actual bed, no less, it felt like a cruel slap to be back hiking through the snow.

Still, there was a clear plan now. An end in sight. God, Selena hoped.

They had to hike back to where they'd been when Axel had been shot, then hope Blanca could pick up a scent in the snow. Selena still had the glove from the very first cabin, but it'd be better if Blanca could pick up something new.

"You knew about Opaline," Axel said without preamble as they walked with only the light of his headlamp and her flashlight to guide them.

It didn't *sound* accusing, but she felt accused. Still, she tried to keep her response easy rather than defensive. She didn't have anything to be defensive about. "She called while you were sleeping. With Alana's permission."

"And you didn't think to mention it?"

Selena was glad to be in the dark, because she visibly winced. Maybe she should have told him, but her thoughts had been on ending this. "We were focusing on what was next. It didn't come up. I would have, but Alana mentioned it first."

"But didn't explain. And you'll note, no one asked her to."

"Yeah, because as you pointed out, we're all agents highly trained in observation. I'm guessing they knew it had to do with Peter. They didn't need to ask." And Selena couldn't help but wonder if they found Selena *herself* suspect now too, by association. Maybe the only thing keeping her on the case was being paired with Axel.

Maybe she'd been paired with Axel for *exactly* that reason. She couldn't be trusted with her half brother being one of the escapees no matter what Alana claimed.

"Your brain's working so hard, I can hear it," Axel said, not unkindly. "No one's blaming you, Selena. I doubt anyone's blaming Opaline. The thing about being in law enforcement is it isn't our job to be judge and jury. Your coworkers and friends are going to wait until they have the whole story."

Selena hoped that was true. She wanted to believe it was. She puffed a breath out into the cold. "I don't know what to do with these doubts," she muttered. "I feel like a rookie all over again."

"Dealing with a case that involves your family isn't exactly easy." Before she could be offended or doubt even harder, he continued, "That doesn't mean I think you don't belong here. It just means it's a more complicated situation, and that means it's going to have extra challenges. I happen to have all the faith in the world that you can meet them."

It shouldn't mean so much to her, but it did. His faith. His reassurance. Whether she'd been assigned with him as partner to make sure her association with Peter didn't affect her choices or not, she was glad she'd been partnered with him.

Sex aside, and it had been really good sex.

And it was really not the time to think about it.

"Now, what happened with Opaline?" he asked, gently.

She told him about her phone call with her sister. What Opaline had said. She thought about leaving out the part where she told Opaline to keep investigating Bernard, but then thought better of it. He was her partner out here. She had to trust him and…

She did. He understood her in a way she didn't think anyone in her life did. She cared about him, God help her. And she had to figure out a way to believe he cared about her too. Because Axel Morrow was not a careless man. He didn't do or say things he didn't *mean*.

He wasn't perfect, by any means, but he was a good man.

And once this was all over, maybe she'd figure out what that meant for her, but for right now, she had a job to do.

"Alana didn't fire her right away."

"I'm sure that's a process with a lot of red tape," Selena replied, trying not to let hope choke her.

"Sure, but she would have given Opaline some kind of notice. Just sending her home? I think she's hoping to find a way to just do a suspension or a write-up or something. Which would make sense. This was a specific set of circumstances. Ones that likely won't repeat themselves."

"God, I hope so."

He chuckled at that. They made their way to where he'd last seen the three men. It had been taped off by local authorities and Steve's body had been removed. She could see Axel staring at where Steve's body had been while she worked with Blanca to pick up the scent of their escapees.

She understood Axel too. That was the thing that

couldn't be ignored or shoved away no matter how much she tried.

Axel held himself responsible for things. He'd learned how to work through that, but it was a process for him. Of letting that responsibility go. She understood that, because she knew it was something she needed to do when it came to her family.

"He was a man who was going to get himself killed one way or another, Axel," Selena said quietly as she let Blanca sniff around the area, trying to find the right scent. "By his own choices. I know you know that, but I think it helps to hear someone else say it too."

"It does," he said, finally looking away from where Steve's body had been. He didn't look at her, she figured because his headlamp would blind her. But he came to stand next to her. They watched Blanca work, but as they did, his gloved hand slid into hers, their fingers curling together quite naturally.

It felt good and right, and yeah, a little scary, but Selena was used to fear and facing it on the job. Maybe it was time to start applying that to her personal life too.

"One step closer," Axel said quietly as Blanca sniffed a particular spot, and then another, in the way she did when she was getting ready to move. "Eventually, we'll have taken all the steps."

"And then what?" Selena asked.

Axel inhaled. She could tell he wasn't so sure and certain as he liked to pretend. But the pretending gave her some measure of comfort.

"I guess you should come over for dinner."

She wrinkled her nose. "Like…at your farm?"

"Yeah, like at my farm. A dinner, like a date. And maybe some advice on what kind of dog to get. You can bring Blanca and the wine. I'll handle the food."

"Are you seriously…asking me out on a date right here in the middle of the night on assignment?"

"Seems like. So?"

She wanted to laugh, and it felt good to want that. "So, I guess we have to take that one step and then another to get to that bridge."

Axel nodded, and in the faint glow of their lights, she could see his mouth curve. "I guess we should hurry up then."

This time Selena really did laugh. And though her toes were about frozen through, the rest of her felt warm, and it all centered on where Axel's hand held hers.

After a few more minutes, Blanca gave a short yip. "She's got the scent," Selena announced once Blanca gave the signal.

Axel nodded. "Then, let's move."

He dropped her hand, and that felt like a loss. Especially as they walked and walked and walked in silence, in the dark, and the cold dug deeper and deeper. They listened to the sounds of the night around them and just kept walking no matter how cold or dark it got.

She wasn't sure how many hours they'd walked when Axel held up a hand and pointed to his beam of light in the snow. Footprints. *Clear* footprints.

Selena gave Blanca a touch command to stop, then crouched down to study the footprints with her flashlight. Clear indentations with no sign of the wind softening the edges. The pair couldn't be too far ahead of them. She explained that to Axel, and he nodded.

"I wish we could wait for daylight," Axel muttered. "Too many things can go wrong in the dark."

"Thanks for the pep talk, boss," Selena returned in the same quiet voice.

He gave her a slight grin in the odd light of his headlamp. "Follow?"

She nodded. They couldn't wait for daylight. They simply couldn't wait. This had to end. Because the more it dragged on, the less chance of survival Peter had.

"We stay completely radio silent. I lead, then you and Blanca follow. If we caught up to them, that means they took a rest. By the way these footprints look, I'd say they're back on the move."

Axel pulled out his phone and typed in a message, likely telling the other agents what they'd found while also pinning it on the map, so they kept their circle around the right area. Once he was done, he nodded at her flashlight. "We stay close. We only need one light. Mine's hands-free."

"Mine's easier to turn off if we need to go dark. Plus, it makes a pretty darn good weapon in a fight. You turn yours off and follow me."

She could tell he didn't like that, but after an internal struggle, he clicked off his lamp. He got behind her. Selena gave Blanca the quiet orders to follow Axel rather than search. The footsteps would be all she needed for right now.

She felt the usual calm wash over her. This was her job. She was good at it. Peter aside, she knew what she was doing with a flashlight in one hand and a gun in the other tracking something. Dark or light, she knew how to come out on the other side of an assignment with all her goals achieved.

The calm led to confidence, and the confidence reminded her that she was a good agent. Maybe she'd been a crappy sister, and maybe she was an uncertain...*whatever* with Axel, but this was something she knew how to do.

She saw bobbing lights ahead and clicked off her flashlight.

"Walkies on," Axel whispered.

They both shrugged off their packs and pulled out the walkies and earpieces. If everyone was in range, they'd be able to move forward. Selena fastened hers to her vest so it was in easy reach. She had to help Axel with his since his right hand was incapacitated and his vest was under his coat.

She didn't let that shake her. He could still shoot with his left, and if everything went the way it should, there would be no shooting needed. Axel with only one good hand was still better than half the agents she knew with both hands in good shape.

They both turned their walkies on and kept their voices low enough not to echo across the quiet forest night.

"Team three in range," Axel said quietly into his comm unit.

"Team two in range," came the first reply.

"Team one in range."

"We want a split," Axel instructed. "Two different diversions. Bigger one from teams one and two. Smaller one from three, so ideally the two escapees split. Team one and two should be designed to attract Koch, and team three set to attract the smaller threat of Lopez."

"We'll turn on all our lights," Aria said. "Between the four of us, it should attract enough attention for them to move closer. Try to determine how many we've got."

"Good, and Selena and I will try to have a conversation that's overheard. We'll take our earpieces out, let the walkie static give us away."

Selena thought about what Axel had told her about Leonard ordering Steve to shoot Peter rather than do it himself. It might have had to do with Steve being the one to convince him to bring Peter, but Selena wondered if it had to do more with power. Or even not wanting to be the person accused of murder. "He'll send Peter toward the voices and tell him to take care of them, yeah?"

Axel nodded. "I think so. He might not come for the lights, but he's not going to come for the voices either. He'll send a subordinate. So, with your lights on, team one and two move in on Koch. We'll stay where we are and try to draw Lopez out."

"Clear," Max's voice said, the other team echoed his clear.

Axel nodded at Selena. They took their earpieces out and adjusted the walkie volume low, so the sound might also draw Peter without being loud enough for someone to make out the words unless they were very close.

"We'll want our conversation to be about Leonard," Axel said. "I think the more we talk about getting him, the more likely he'll be to send Peter to check it out."

"He wouldn't come himself?"

Axel shook his head. "Overhearing the conversation with Leonard, Steve and Peter was more enlightening than any profile could be. I could hear what he said and the way he said it. The way he interacted with the other men. He liked wielding his power. He wants to feel in charge. Like whoever is following him has to jump when he says jump."

Out in the woods, lights began to pop on. Flashlights, clearly carving out swaths of light. It was time to act. Axel started walking toward the center of the circle they'd determined on their maps, motioning Selena to follow. Blanca trotted behind them, still heeding Selena's earlier command to follow.

"I think it's interesting Leonard has clearly taken great

pains to distance himself from the brother," Axel said. He didn't shout it, didn't even sound particularly *loud*, but she could tell he was projecting.

"Are we supposed to be scared of this brother of his?" Selena improvised. "Seems like a penny-ante thief if you ask me. What was on his record? Like one arrest?"

Axel grinned at her. "Agree. My expert profiling skills tell me he's just another weak, ineffectual criminal. Not even sure he's worth the jail time or all this effort. But we might as well check it out while we're here."

She pretended to roll her eyes at his boast at expert profiling skills.

"I've got a visual through the night-vision device," Max's voice said from the walkie. "They're arguing. Leonard's pointing in your direction. Keep it up, whatever you're doing. I think he's going to send Peter your way."

THEY CONTINUED TO disparage Bernard, sometimes throwing in a few scathing remarks about Leonard's intelligence. The relationship between Bernard and Leonard beyond brothers of some sort was a mystery, but Axel threw in a few made-up criticisms of Bernard that wouldn't give away how little they knew about the mystery man.

From what Axel understood about Leonard, he wouldn't stand for it. But he'd want someone else to do the work. He wanted to be the head honcho, not the minion.

"Coming your way," Aria said over the walkie. "We're closing in on Leonard."

"Once you're in place, you'll wait for my signal," Axel ordered. They needed to play this carefully. So Peter didn't bolt, so Leonard didn't have a chance to call for reinforcements. But most importantly, so no one got hurt.

Selena made a hand motion that had Blanca sitting on her haunches in the snow. She leaned into him, whispered into his ear. "Listen."

Axel held himself still and did just that. The snap of a twig. A little sigh of breath. So, Peter wasn't carrying a flashlight or anything to help him move through the dark, but he was definitely coming for them.

"You should stay here," Selena said quietly, clearly not trying to be overhead now. "Out of sight with Blanca. So he thinks it's just me."

"He heard both of us."

"I know, but you said yourself I should talk to him alone. I'm not saying you should go away, just stay put. I'll keep my flashlight on, you'll keep us in sight."

"And what do you plan to do?"

"Just try to talk to him. Maybe I can get him to surrender without a fight. I take him, the team of four takes Leonard. Everyone's safe."

Axel hissed out a breath, realizing belatedly he'd curled his injured hand into a fist.

"If he didn't have anything to do with the string of murders…"

Selena trailed off and Axel knew he didn't have to remind her that it was a big *if*.

"Just stay here."

She said it like an order, but there was a question in the way she paused. Axel gave a slight nod. "No more than twenty yards, Lopez. No more."

She began to immediately move. Blanca whined next to Axel, and Axel felt a bit like doing the same. He just wasn't sure this was the right course of action, but he knew Selena needed it. She needed this chance, and she was a good enough agent to know that if it didn't work out, if Peter wasn't persuaded, she'd take him down.

Maybe not with as much force as she would have for a man who wasn't related to her, but she'd still do it. Axel had to believe she would.

Axel kept his eyes on the light, moving carefully in the dark of the woods. She took her time, which gave him some comfort. She wasn't hurrying in, guns blazing, trying to play hero to everyone. She was taking precautions.

His phone buzzed in his pocket, and Axel pulled it out, figuring it would be Alana with an important update on Bernard or even Leonard. He fumbled a bit trying to answer with his bandaged hand, but he wasn't about to put his gun down.

"Morrow."

"Didn't want to put this out over the walkie," Max's voice said, low and determined. "But I can get in place to take Peter out should the need arise. Just as a precaution."

Axel trusted Max's judgment, but it just didn't feel right. He wasn't one hundred percent happy with Selena over there meeting up with Peter, but a sniper in place felt all wrong. "We want them alive."

"We want us alive too."

"Six of us, two of them. We don't need a sniper."

"Selena is awfully close. It wouldn't take much for him to take her hostage, or worse."

"He's not going to hurt her."

"How do you know? I've seen family members do a lot worse than just hurt each other. Haven't you?"

"I've got a gun and I'm closer than you four. If Peter tries something, I can take care of it. That's why I'm here." Of course, he didn't have the night-vision devices the rest of the team had or his best hand available. Still, he trusted Selena to handle this. And if Leonard started toward them, the rest of the team would stop him.

"I'm just saying it wouldn't hurt—"

Axel cut him off. "Sometimes you listen to your gut, Max. A sniper in place is asking for trouble we don't want. Stick with the team and arrest Leonard."

There was a slight pause, as if Max was determining what exactly to say. When he finally spoke, Axel knew it was as a friend, not as a coworker. "*Is* it your gut? Or is it something else?"

It landed like the jab it was, though Axel knew it was concern not accusation. Axel couldn't help but entertain the doubt Max's words brought up. Was he letting something happen because of his feelings for Selena?

But he had to reject that thought. "If this was about that something else, I'd have her locked up in a room while I took care of everything. I'm not going to pretend I didn't have the urge, but we need information, and with Steve Jenson dead, Peter is going to be the best source of that. We can't just think about apprehension—we have to think about handling this in a way that creates an open-and-shut trial."

Max was silent for a few humming seconds again. "All right," he eventually acquiesced.

"Focus on Leonard. We know they were trying to get across the border. They had to be meeting someone there. We have to make sure whoever is waiting for them won't get antsy and come get them. And we have to make sure we can keep Leonard from taking Peter out if he thinks Peter's going to give us information."

"Got it," Max said. "Take care of yourself."

"You too."

Axel was about to shove his phone back in his pocket, but it buzzed again, a text from Opaline that read,

URGENT. Axel read the rest of the message, his stomach sinking as though it had turned to lead.

Bernard McNally. Think he's a serial cop killer. Emailing the evidence. BE CAREFUL.

He could see she'd sent the message to everyone. The entire team on the ground, Alana and Amanda, as well.

Axel didn't have time to read the email or the evidence. He looked up at Selena. Her light hadn't moved in a few minutes. He followed where it pointed, and though it didn't illuminate much from this distance, he thought he could make out a pair of shoes in the beam.

She'd found Peter and was talking to him.

"Lopez, we've got a situation," he said into his walkie.

"I thought Opaline was off the case," Carly said, her voice followed by a blast of static. "What's this text and email about? Should we really—"

"Someone tell me what the email says," Axel interrupted, keeping his gaze focused on Selena. Had she turned off her walkie? She certainly wasn't responding as she talked with Peter.

"Opaline tied each of his aliases she found with the murder of a police officer," Aria said, clearly skimming the email and giving the main points. "She says the cases have a pattern. He started with small-town, low-level sheriff's deputies, then moved up to bigger cities, higher ranks." Even over the walkie Axel caught Aria's harsh intake of breath. "The body in Bernard McNally's cabin was an ATF agent."

"No known whereabouts," Carly said. Her voice was hard, which meant she was rattled. "Which means he could be anywhere. Especially if that cabin was his."

"Clear," Axel muttered. This had just gotten a hell of

a lot more complicated. He had to believe Bernard was in Canada, that Leonard and Peter were trying to get there. But the fact the dead body in Bernard's cabin was a government agent…

It spoke of escalation, and it suddenly made Peter—who had two sisters who worked for the FBI—and his involvement with Leonard seem a lot more sinister.

Then, more sinister by far, Selena's light bobbled, jerked and went dark.

Axel stepped forward then forced himself to think before he acted. His light was off, and he'd keep it that way. Without light, he could only make out his team, not Selena or Peter.

Blanca whined from behind him, and Axel crouched next to the dog, focusing on the cool calm of a man on assignment. He couldn't afford to be anything else. "Blanca, I sure hope you're going to listen to orders from me, because you've got to find Selena. Now."

Chapter Seventeen

Selena approached Peter's antsy form. He looked like he was trying to sneak toward her, but he was too…fidgety. Everything a little too jerky to be smooth, undetectable movements.

She turned down the volume on her comm unit. It wasn't exactly standard operating procedure, but she needed to be able to focus on Peter. Besides, Axel would keep her in sight, and if something changed, he or the team would handle it.

She had to handle this. Everything would be fine. It had to be. And she had to give this one shot. If Peter refused, she'd let it go. She'd have to let it go, and the guilt with it. She'd arrest him herself if she had to. That was a promise—to herself, and to her team.

"Peter."

He came up short. She didn't know if he recognized her voice, was surprised to see her here or what. She could just barely make out his face, but surely he knew she'd be one of the people after him. Maybe he just hadn't expected her to catch up.

"Er, where's your dog?"

It wasn't the question she would have expected, and it made her wish she'd brought Blanca with her. She'd feel a bit like a safety net at the moment. Instead of out here in no-man's land alone with her brother, who was acting like they'd just happened to run into each other during a walk in the park.

Peter's gaze dropped to the gun in her hand. She lifted her flashlight so the beam would illuminate him and give her an idea if he was carrying a weapon.

"Did he really send you out here without a light or a gun?" she asked dubiously.

Peter didn't respond. He just looked around, still fidgety and...strange. She wasn't sure how she'd expected him to act, but she didn't understand this.

There was no time to. She moved a little bit closer. He didn't back away, just eyed her warily.

"Peter, I want to help you. I think you know Leonard would throw you under the bus the second he could. *If* you survive. Let me help."

His expression didn't quite curl into its normal sneer, but it was close. "You always say you want to help."

"So, why won't you let me?"

"I don't need your pity help. I'm taking care of things on my own."

She bit back the bitter laugh and tried to keep her tone moderate, without judgment. "Are you?"

He inhaled sharply at that, but he didn't answer or say anything else.

"You're going back to jail. For longer this time. You had to understand that when you escaped. You might be in there for the rest of your life. But if you come with me, if you give us what you know about Leonard, you've got a chance. A *real* chance to have a life."

"I don't have any chances," Peter said bitterly. But his expression went lax, almost...sad. "Steve was going to..." Peter trailed off, shaking his head. "He would have been fine if not for you guys."

"You mean if not for Leonard Koch. *He's* the one who killed Steve and you know it. Blame Leonard, not us."

Peter didn't shake that away. If anything, his expression kind of crumpled, like a little boy about ready to cry. But he didn't cry, and the sadness was quickly replaced by an edgy anger.

Selena didn't let it fester. She didn't have time to anyway. "Opaline got kicked out of the FBI because of what she did for you," Selena said. It was a slight exaggeration as Opaline hadn't been officially fired, but Selena figured she had reason to exaggerate a little. To try to reach Peter however she could, even through guilt.

Peter's expression shuttered. "She didn't even help me. She just pretended."

"Doesn't matter so much when you keep that pretending a secret from your boss. She's done nothing but try to be there for you. I've tried to help you." But that was anger and guilt talking, and she had to find something else, *hope* something else would get to him. "We're your family, Peter. We've all made mistakes, but I can help you now. If you let me."

"You don't want to help me."

"I am standing here, my team far away. It's just me and you. If I didn't want to help you, we'd all have surrounded you already and arrested you. We have more men than you. We know where you're headed. It's over for you and Leonard, but if you cooperate, Peter, I *can* help."

"You've got a gun," he said.

She didn't point out that she was a federal agent so of *course* she had a gun. This was dangerous, and God knew even if she let herself trust Peter, she wasn't going to trust Leonard. But this wasn't about her or reasonable action. This was about getting Peter to *listen*.

"You want me to put it down?" She started to crouch

to lay the gun down on the ground. Axel and the rest of the team would have her back, and she had to show Peter some evidence of trust. Besides, she could and would fight if she had to.

"No! No, don't do that," he hissed, surprising her so much she paused midcrouch. "You have to get out of here," Peter said. He was scowling, but there was fear under all that bravado. His eyes darted around the woods as if he thought anyone might jump out. Maybe he was afraid of being arrested, but Selena thought maybe…just maybe…he was afraid of Leonard.

"If you surrender yourself, come with me—"

Peter shook his head emphatically. "Too late for that. You have to get out of here. Now. Please."

Her eyebrows drew together as she stared at Peter. She didn't see the little boy she'd known right now. She saw a fidgety, scared guy who'd gotten into something *way* too deep. Who was begging her to get out of here. "Why?" she demanded.

"It's you they want."

He couldn't have said anything that would have confused her more. "Me?"

"Not you specifically, but—"

"That'll be enough, Peter."

Selena whirled at the voice, gun at the ready. But she didn't see anyone. Only darkness.

"D-don't hurt her," Peter said, his voice shaky and pleading. "She's… She won't… There's other ones out there. More important ones. You want an important one. The boss guy. That's who you said you really wanted."

Selena didn't understand what was going on, but she immediately clicked her flashlight off, plunging the entire world around them into darkness. Whoever was out there,

Leonard or someone else, was definitely going to kill her if they could. The light gave her away, but not now.

She'd have to disappear into the shadows, find her way back to Axel. *And leave Peter behind?*

And who was the voice? Leonard? But her team was supposed to have their sights on Leonard.

The boss guy. That was Axel. They wanted to kill Axel?

It didn't make sense, so she had to focus on what did. Getting away from that voice. Getting to Axel and warning him.

With everyone so close, everything so tense, she couldn't risk turning her walkie back up, but she had her earpiece in her pocket. If she could get far enough away that a few rustling noises and clicks wouldn't give away her exact location, she could get that situated.

She tried to give herself a second to orient. Peter had been in front of her, a few yards away. She hadn't been able to tell where the voice had come from. Neither direction nor vicinity to Peter or herself. It felt like it had come out of nowhere.

But thinking like that wasn't going to get her out of this situation. She could see where the rest of the team still had their lights on. Which meant she just had to slowly turn until she saw the slight beam of Axel's light.

If he'd turned it on. If she could get there without making too much noise. If—

Her phone buzzed. She bit back a curse, immediately moving as stealthily as she could in the direction she hoped would lead her to Axel. She pulled the phone out of her pocket, focusing more on those quiet, stealthy steps than the phone at first.

But it buzzed again, the screen brightening up. She fumbled with the switch to completely silence the damn thing, turn it off so it couldn't give off any light, but the message on the screen distracted her for one moment.

URGENT! Bernard McNally. Think he's a serial cop killer. Emailing the evidence. BE CAREFUL.

"You're going to want to heed that warning."

She couldn't bite back the scream that escaped her, or stop herself from fumbling her phone, which then thudded to the ground. She had to run, but the blow came out of nowhere instead and knocked her to the ground.

But she wouldn't go down that easily.

SELENA'S SCREAM MADE Axel's blood run cold.

"Move," Axel yelled into his comm unit. "All bets are off. Just get Selena out of there," he ordered into the walkie. He didn't listen for the answers. He immediately moved in the direction Selena had gone, Blanca at his heels.

Axel kept following Blanca, hoping to God the commands were right or at least enough for Blanca to lead him to Selena.

"Scott has Leonard. We're going dark." It was Aria's voice over the walkie. The lights went out, one by one, until the entire woods were pitched into darkness.

So Axel had to focus on the sounds of the dog moving, focus on following her in the complete and utter black.

Seconds turned into minutes, but Axel only focused on movement. On listening and following. He didn't let his brain go anywhere else. One thing at a time. One step at a time. They'd get to Selena. The dog would get to her owner, and then Axel would get her out of this mess.

He didn't let himself blame himself for allowing her to get into it in the first place. He'd save that for later, when they were both okay. Each next step would need to be assessed in the moment, so he kept his mind blank of everything except *this* step.

Blanca slowed and gave a slight growl. Axel gripped the gun harder in his left hand. He tried to squint through the dark, but it was no use. He thought of asking for an update from the team, but Blanca had stopped completely.

Surely they were close. To Selena. Or Peter.

Before Axel could decide on the next move, light flooded his surroundings in a blinding flash. Axel instinctually squeezed his eyes shut and flung his arm over his eyes before fighting back the reflex. Where was the light coming from?

Axel blinked through the painful brightness until his eyes adjusted. He frowned at the structure in front of him. Some kind of platform that looked newly constructed. Almost like a stage in the middle of the woods.

He raised his gaze to the figures on the stage, where four poles with bright stadium-esque lights blazed down, illuminating a large man standing at the center, Selena next to him.

"Drop your weapons," the man shouted. He had a gun pressed to Selena's temple. Her expression was furious and defiant, but her arms were behind her back and a trickle of blood dripped from her temple and her mouth.

She'd given him a fight, that was for sure. But her hands must be bound behind her back. Peter stood a few feet away, fidgeting. Axel couldn't see them, but he knew his team would be approaching, slowly. Tactically.

"You must be Bernard," Axel said, forcing his voice to sound calm. He didn't know this man or how to handle him, and if he got off on killing law enforcement, there'd be no *reasoning* with him. They just had to get Selena out of there, then take him out. Beginning and end of story.

"Axel Morrow, there you are!" he greeted jovially. "I'd drop the gun before I blow her brain matter everywhere."

That wasn't the example he wanted to set for the rest of the team. Still, it would buy him time. Slowly he crouched, making a show out of gently placing his gun on the ground as he spoke into his comm unit. "No matter what he says, at least one person keeps a gun on him. No matter what."

Slowly, Axel stood back up, and looked at Bernard, who was smirking.

"It's your lucky day, Axel Morrow, *supervisory* special agent. Why don't you come join us on the stage?"

"Suicide by cop," Aria said into the walkie. "This is about body count. Not survival *or* his brother. He knows we're out here. He knows even if he kills the both of you, he can't get out of here without going through us."

Axel agreed with the assessment. If he got up on stage, even if he put his weapon down, he'd have a chance to take Bernard down. But surely Bernard wasn't stupid enough to think two FBI agents couldn't stop him if given the chance.

He'd either shoot Axel before he got up on the stage, or there was more here. A bigger, far more dangerous plan.

Keeping the movement as discreet as possible, and his gaze firmly pinned on Bernard, Axel muttered into his comm unit, "Max, check for explosives." It would be a way to kill them all. If Bernard was already resolved to his fate, blowing up the whole area would be a way to kill a bunch of agents.

"Got it," Max said. "I'll check under the platform first."

Axel didn't say anything, but he figured Max was right. The platform could be hiding explosives. What other reason was there for it?

"Come on now," Bernard said, the gun still dug hard into Selena's temple. "Don't be shy. Let's get this show on the road. I've been planning for it. Thank you, all, for falling so perfectly into my plan."

Axel kept his expression bland, though fury bubbled under the surface. He wasn't sure how they could have possibly seen this coming, but he couldn't help wishing they'd taken some other tactic here.

But there were no do-overs. There was only now, and getting Selena and the rest of his team safe and sound. He couldn't order them to back off, even with the threat of explosives, until they got Selena out of there.

He took a careful step toward the stage, hoping Blanca would read and obey his "stay" hand command. For the first time, he let his gaze turn fully to Selena. The gun dug into her temple, and the blood was now dripping off her chin.

But when their gazes locked, she winked. *Winked.*

Axel didn't know what on earth to do with that.

Chapter Eighteen

Axel's shock at her winking was visible in his expression for approximately one second before he went back into FBI agent mode.

She couldn't verbalize to him that he was more of a target than she was. She was the bait. But she could give him at least a hint that she wasn't totally out of her element.

Not that Bernard wouldn't kill her. From what she could tell, murder was his only goal. Even if he died in the process. Maybe *especially* if he died in the process. As long as he took out a bunch of agents on his way.

Peter was the outlier. She didn't think he'd hurt her, not when he'd tried to warn her away. But he wasn't helping her either. He was too afraid. Too certain he had no hope.

Or maybe he just didn't care that the big psychopath had beaten up his sister. Maybe he'd even enjoyed it.

Didn't matter.

Selena had kept her head. Bernard had gotten a good few knocks in, but when he'd tied her hands behind her back, she'd managed to keep the bonds looser than they should be. It was taking time to wiggle her hands out because she had to make sure she didn't move any part of her body that he could see.

Once they were free enough, she could kick Bernard's

legs out from under him. As long as he didn't catch her wiggling her way out of the bonds.

Right now, Bernard's gaze was firmly on Axel slowly making his way onto the stage. In return, Axel eyed Bernard warily. He moved slowly, and Selena was grateful for it. It gave her more time to work at the bonds on her wrists.

She took a quick look around now that her eyes had adjusted to the light. She could make out Aria and Carly far off in the trees, guns drawn. She didn't see Max or Scott, but they were around somewhere. Probably with Leonard.

"Take all the time you want," Bernard said cheerfully, clearly talking about Axel's interminable approach. "It's not going to change the outcome. Nothing can change the outcome."

Selena fought off the shudder of dread. Her team was out there. They wouldn't shoot Bernard as long as he had a gun to her head. But with two team members missing, it meant they were somewhere out there getting into place. Unless Leonard was posing more of a problem than they'd anticipated.

But Selena wouldn't let herself think like that. Sometimes hope was all a girl had. She'd cling to it.

"Peter?" Bernard yelled, even though Peter was only a few feet away.

Peter shuffled in front of Bernard. He kept his gaze down, patently refusing to look at her. For the first time, Selena felt the true pain of betrayal. He was actually going to let this man kill her if she didn't get out of it herself.

"I tried to help you," she whispered. "You only have yourself to blame for whatever happens."

"Oh, shut up," Bernard muttered. "This boy knows

who really cares. Who's really going to help him. Cops and agents and the like just send people to jail. They don't care. They all deserve to die. Peter understands that. Don't you, Peter?"

Peter cleared his throat, still not looking at her. "Yeah, yeah. I do."

Selena couldn't give in to the tears that threatened. Too much was at stake. But it hurt. Even when she should be past it.

"Get the rest of the rope from the bag," Bernard ordered Peter. "Tie Axel Morrow up. You hear that, Axel Morrow? He's going to tie you up. You fight him off, she's dead. Right in front of you. Her blood on your hands, Axel Morrow."

"Why do you keep repeating his name like that?" Selena muttered. "Obsess much?"

Bernard laughed, which made her lungs contract in fear rather than resentment. She didn't think *amusing* him was a good thing in any way, shape or form.

"You and your kind are scum of the earth. This isn't obsession, it's *justice*. And you led me to it. You and your useless brother have given me exactly what I needed. How does that make you feel?"

Selena hid her revulsion, guilt, fear and every other negative emotion swirling inside her. She kept her expression carefully blank.

"Peter! Stop messing around and get it done!"

Selena winced against the sound of his bellow in her ear. Bernard's hand fisted in her hair roughly, keeping her head still so the gun dug into her temple. "Don't go moving on me. My trigger finger might slip and splatter you all over your friend over there."

His hand tightened, pulling at her hair until she saw stars. Still, she bit back the moan of pain. She'd withstand it. Find a way out of it. Six against one, basically. They had to find a way out of it.

"You know, I might enjoy that," Bernard said, contemplatively. "Watching his expression when it's your brain matter splattering all over him. Yeah, I think—"

"She untied her rope," Peter said, sounding small, but it interrupted Bernard's terrifying string of thoughts. His grip on her hair loosened for a second, but that did nothing to ease the pain.

Peter had just ratted her out. Selena felt the full blast of betrayal. Her one hope and Peter had taken it away from her? She would have glared at him, but she couldn't move her head with Bernard's hand in her hair.

"Untied her... You little..." He didn't let her go, but he didn't pull the trigger either. "No, we'll stick to the plan. Stick to the plan. You'll all die. All of you. Blaze of glory."

Bernard sounded insane, and Selena had to accept there was no reasoning with him. He wanted them dead. Not because of anything they'd done. Simply because of what they were. What they'd dedicated their lives to. Men like him didn't listen to reason.

And it very rarely ended well for the cops at their mercy.

Her only hope of escaping this was taking Bernard down and out. She was going to have to get his hands out of her hair. If she could do that, she had a chance. She could fight him. If he took her out, she could deal with that—if it saved her team.

"Should I tie them back up for you?" Peter asked Bernard, sounding fully subservient. "I think Morrow knows not to move, but she might try to fight you with her hands untied."

"Yes, good job, Peter. Fix her bonds. Then take care of Axel Morrow."

Peter scurried to do just that. He came up beside her, pulled her hands over to him. Which was weird. She didn't know why he wasn't standing directly behind her. This angle wouldn't allow him to tighten them enough.

Then he bent forward, his mouth practically on her ear. She would have headbutted him, but the gun was on the other side of her head and kept her from having any range of motion.

He fiddled with the rope, but he spoke into her ear, his voice an almost inaudible whisper. "I'm going to push you off."

Push her off? The shock slammed into her like a blow. Push her off the stage? *Save* her?

Hope she shouldn't entertain bubbled up inside her. If he pushed her off, that would be her chance to take Bernard out. If he pushed right, she could be close enough to Axel's gun to grab it and shoot Bernard first.

A risk, but a chance.

It would leave Axel vulnerable in the interim, though. When Peter pushed, who would Bernard target? She needed to communicate with Peter. Tell him which angle to push her out, tell him to give Axel some kind of signal.

Except she couldn't do any of that when Bernard was literally standing right next to them with a gun to her head. If Peter took much longer, Bernard would know Peter was talking to her or he might at least suspect something.

"I've got her," Peter said to Bernard. "Nice and tight now."

"Good," Bernard said. He seemed to pause and consider, then finally let go of her hair. "Good, Peter. You've been an undeniable asset in this. Forget Axel Morrow over there. Bring me the whole bag. It's time to begin."

"Yeah, okay," Peter mumbled, fumbling with Selena's rope as Bernard fully let her go. Though the gun was still pressed to her temple, if Peter gave her a good push, Bernard wouldn't be able to shoot in time. Not at first.

She felt the ropes loosen fully rather than tighten. Peter's mouth was still next to her ear, and he spoke once more.

"He's got a bomb. Run away from here."

A bomb. But she didn't have time to argue, to come up with a better plan that wouldn't get Peter *and* Axel blown up, because Peter gave her a hard shove that had her sailing off the stage and onto the hard, cold, snow-covered ground below.

AXEL WATCHED SELENA tumble off the stage, as if pushed. Pushed. Peter had purposefully pushed her off.

She landed on a tuck and roll, then was quickly up on her feet, holding out her hand. Axel realized she was warning Blanca off running to her.

Peter had pushed her off the stage to *help*. To save her life.

It gave Axel a surge of hope.

But in the next second Bernard's gun whirled on him and before Axel could act, the gun went off. Pain slammed into him and exploded across his chest as he fell backward and crashed onto the stage with enough force he heard some of the wood crack beneath him.

Head pounding, brain rattled, Axel struggled to get a breath in. The pain was excruciating, and he couldn't seem to suck in enough oxygen at first. He gasped and gasped for it before he could remind himself to calm down.

Calm down.

He wasn't dead. Thanks to the vest he wore. Because the bullet had hit him right in the Kevlar vest. He counted off breaths, doing everything to calm himself. He was alive, which meant there was still a chance to get out of this in relatively one piece.

Bernard must not know he was wearing a vest, or maybe was just a bad shot. Either way, it didn't make Axel invincible. He had to get out of here before Bernard shot him in a place that wasn't protected.

He barely heard the voices in his ear. They sounded far away, but his team was yelling words. He tried to make sense of them and move at the same time. Move and breathe. Listen and act.

Focus. Calm. Breathe in, one, two, three. Breathe out, one, two, three.

"No explosives under the stage that I can find." Max's voice.

"There's a bag on the stage," Aria's voice said. "Peter got the rope out of it. But it's big and there's more in there. He's dragging Peter to the bag now. I can't shoot without hitting Peter."

Axel could give no orders, no insight. He could only try to roll off the stage and away from Bernard. He had to get himself out of harm's way and make sure Selena was, as well.

Peter had saved her. Axel hadn't thought it in that moment he'd seen Selena tumbling into the snow, but it had only taken a few seconds—before the bullet had slammed into him—to realize Peter had been getting Selena out of Bernard's grip.

Though Axel was still in excruciating pain, the fog of the wind being knocked out of him started to lift. Someone was yelling. Raving.

Bernard.

"I'll kill them all! I'll kill you all. You'll all die. We'll all die!"

Cop killer. Suicide by cop. There was no getting out of this one without someone getting hurt. Axel would make sure it was Bernard.

"I've got the visual. He's got a bomb in that bag," Aria said. "Take him out. Someone take him out. I can't get an angle."

"Peter's in the way," Max said disgustedly. "From every angle. Bernard knows it, that's why he created that little corner on the stage to hide in. Peter is his body shield."

Axel knew they'd consider going through Peter. Why not? He was part of this after all, but he'd saved Selena. Hard to overlook that.

"I'll get Peter out of the way," Axel managed to rasp into the comm mic. He wouldn't let them consider taking out Peter too. Not when he was right here.

There was arguing, but Axel didn't have time for it. Maybe he wasn't one hundred percent, but he was the closest to Peter. If Max could take out Bernard in seconds, that was all Axel needed. He ripped the earpiece out of his ear and got to his knees.

Bernard was rummaging through the bag, holding Peter in front of him. Max was right. Bernard had built this stage just for this.

It was chilling, how well planned out this all was. How little they'd understood about what Leonard's trio was doing. Not trying to escape. No, they'd been a lure. Bait.

It explained everything Selena had questioned. Why February. Why let them catch up time and time again. Why kill Steve. Hard to lay a trap if someone informed the police about it.

But Axel couldn't dwell on that. They hadn't made

mistakes. They'd fought with the information they had. Now they had more. And now they would end this.

He glanced at Selena. She was crawling across the snow and toward the gun he'd left behind. Good. The more guns on Bernard, the better.

Axel got to his feet in a crouch. He moved to one side to get a better view of how Bernard was using Peter as a human shield. He had a gun to Peter's chest. Peter was still as death. Axel reminded himself that no matter how little Peter was fighting now, he'd saved Selena's life. At peril to his own.

And now Axel would do the same for Peter.

Chapter Nineteen

Selena got to Axel's gun and immediately grabbed and whirled, looking for Bernard. But all she saw was Peter, huddled over a corner. And Axel, a few yards away, looking like he was about to rush him.

Selena flipped on her radio. "Fill me in," she demanded to whoever was listening.

"Axel's going to get Peter out of the way so we can take Bernard out," came Carly's calm reply.

"Bernard's got explosives back there," Aria added.

"Some of the team should fall back," Max said authoritatively. "I've already got Scott taking Leonard to some backup agents, but we don't *all* need to be in the potential blast zone."

"We're a team," Carly said, sounding offended.

"We're not leaving Axel behind," Aria added forcefully.

"Damn straight," Selena said into her unit. Max was the one with sniper training, so if he didn't think there was an angle to get on Bernard, she'd believe it. "Morrow?"

"It's no use," Carly said disgustedly. "He pulled out his earpiece."

Selena cursed him silently, keeping her gun trained on the area where Peter was huddled. Bernard was behind him. She would take him out. She would damn well take him out given the chance.

Axel moved. A swift blur. How he managed to run across the stage making almost no noise was beyond her. Axel lunged, and both Axel and Peter crashed onto the stage, but they rolled—Selena couldn't tell who rolled who—nor could she watch them roll. She had to take out Bernard.

She fired, her gunshot echoing with at least one other. Bernard crumpled immediately.

Max's voice came out over the walkie. "I'm headed in to check the explosives. Someone follow and make sure Bernard is dead."

"I've got it," Axel said. His voice was rough. The man was hurt and still doing all the work. But he was closest to Bernard.

Selena dared look at him as he got up from Peter's still body. Axel stumbled a little, but he managed to push himself back up on the stage. As if he sensed the rising fear in Selena, he spoke as he checked Bernard's pulse.

"Peter's been shot," he said. "Fall knocked him out, I think, because the only wound I found was in his shoulder. He's going to need medical attention and a stretcher even if he does regain consciousness."

Selena moved forward carefully, gun still trained on Bernard, just in case. She couldn't think about Peter. She had to think about handling this the right way. So no more mistakes were made.

No more people shot. Hurt. No. This would be the end.

"Dead," Axel announced into the walkie.

Selena rushed forward and immediately searched Peter's body for the bullet wound. "Right in the shoulder," she muttered. But she didn't find any other wounds except a trickle of blood from his temple. Likely, as Axel had said, from the fall.

Bernard was dead, but there was no sense of relief. Peter was seriously injured, and there were explosives.

"Status of the explosives?" Axel demanded.

"There's a timer on these," Max said from where he was crouched over the bag of explosives. His voice gave away no hint of if he could handle that or not.

They weren't done yet, Selena thought grimly.

"Carly or Aria or someone with a pack? I need tools," Max said into the walkie.

Though Selena was close enough she could hear Axel and Max without the walkies, Selena barely registered their words. She did what she could, used what she could, to put pressure on Peter's wound. But his head was bleeding too. There wasn't anything she could do about that.

It was over, but it didn't feel over. Especially as Carly and Aria rushed forward. Aria dropped a pack next to Max, then crouched beside him taking orders to help stop the bombs.

Carly came up next to her. "Here's my first aid kit. What do you need?"

"I wish I knew," Selena muttered, but they worked together to patch Peter up. "What about you, Morrow?" Selena yelled at him. She was still bandaging Peter's shoulder, but she couldn't ignore Axel might have been hurt too.

"Fine," Axel gritted out.

"Liar," she returned. She took the brief moment to look over her shoulder at him. He sat on the stage, Blanca next to him. His face was bloody, both from his previous injury on his cheek and new ones. The bandage on his previously injured hand was a mess.

But Blanca sat next to him, and he rested his good hand on her furry head. Something in Selena's chest eased. Like maybe this was all over and going to be okay.

"Ambulance is on its way, but it's a ways out," Carly said quietly.

"He can hang on that long, don't you think?"

Carly nodded. "He's young and strong. He'll be okay."

Selena held on to that reassurance from her friend, even if that's all it was. She almost relaxed, but she couldn't ignore the fact there were explosives directly behind her. Max was an expert. He would—

But he stood abruptly and jumped away from the bag. "I can't stop this timer," Max said. He didn't bother with the comm unit now. He shouted. "We have to get out of here. As far away as you can get. Now. Move!"

Carly stumbled to her feet, but before she could help, Max grabbed her and was pulling her toward the woods, Blanca running after them, presumably on Axel's order.

Then Axel was on the opposite side of Peter. "Help me get him over my shoulder."

She might have argued that Axel was hurt and she should be the one to carry Peter, but Axel was bigger. He'd be able to move faster with Peter than she would.

Aria jumped next to them, lending a hand, even as Max yelled at all of them to move. They got Peter over Axel's shoulder and immediately began to head out. They ran as fast as they could into the woods, away from the impending explosion.

"You can run faster than this, Lopez," Axel said through gritted teeth, his pace hampered by the weight of another human.

"We're not separating," Selena replied, keeping her pace even with Axel's. If something happened, she... She just had to be here. With both of them.

"Take cover," Max yelled. "Find some cover!"

But before they could find any, the first explosion sounded.

THEY WEREN'T FAR enough away, that was all Axel could think as the explosion reverberated around them. Heat, the tinny sounds of metal falling all about them. The blast of air that had them all pitching forward and hard into the ground.

Peter's weight landed awkwardly on his own head, which was another rattle his brain certainly didn't need today. The biting cold was opposite to the heat on his back, and as much as he was aware of being alive, he couldn't seem to shift past that one and only thought.

"Cover your hard head, Morrow," Selena bit out.

He listened to her, folding his arms over the back of his head, but also lifted his head to see her pretty much bodily shielding her brother from the flying debris.

It didn't last long. Small bits and ash still floated in the air, but the thuds of large pieces of wood and other things hitting the ground had stopped.

Static blasted out of Axel's walkie, which must have somehow gotten turned up to max volume during his fall. Max's voice came out booming. "Everyone okay? Carly and I are good."

"I'm good," Aria's voice echoed.

Axel fumbled to roll over to turn the volume on his walkie down.

"Morrow and I are still breathing," Selena said next to him. Her voice was calm and cool and like some kind of balm. They were okay. They were all okay.

"Peter needs an ambulance stat," Selena said firmly.

"There's an ambulance waiting, but we've got to get to it," Aria responded. "Are we clear, Max?"

"Yeah. There were a series of explosives in the bag, but all set to go off at the same time. So, there shouldn't be another explosion unless he had more stashed elsewhere, but my bet's on that being it. Biggest concern now is falling debris, but we seem to be past the worst of it."

"We need help with Peter," Selena said. "He's still unconscious. We're not going to be able to carry him ourselves."

"I'm good," Axel insisted. He pushed out of the snow and onto his knees. The world spun, but he could breathe through that. He'd get used to it. He didn't feel pain. Everything was kind of numb, so surely he could get to his feet. But as he tried, the world didn't just spin, it seemed to tilt.

"You're really not," Selena said, grabbing onto him before he toppled over. "And I messed up my knee a bit. Can you guys find us? Blanca? Where's Blanca?"

"We've got her," Max said.

Selena let out a sharp whistle that felt as though it split his head in half. As if on cue, his entire body started throbbing in pain. Instead of letting Selena hold him up, Axel went ahead and lay back down on the ground.

Selena's face swam above him. "Don't you lose consciousness on me too," she demanded.

"Won't," Axel bit out, though it was a close thing. He could feel his vision graying, his body wanting to retreat from the pain. But he fought through it. Selena was here and they were all right. The team was all right. Somehow.

He heard panting, then felt the rough wet of Blanca's tongue moving across his face. He winced, which sent more sharp lances of pain through his body. But he was awake. Alive.

He reached out for the dog, and Blanca licked his face

again. "Not sure that's sanitary." But it was a nice reminder they'd all made it out okay.

"Up and at 'em." Max's voice, then Axel was being hefted to his feet. Things were still spinning, but Max held him upright. Then Carly stood next to him and wound her arm around his waist.

Aria was helping Selena, who limped. Max had moved over to Peter and was gingerly lifting him.

"Bit of a hike," Carly said next to him. "Just lean on me."

"I'm fine," Axel grumbled, but he ended up needing the support as they moved forward. He watched Selena in front of him, hobbling with the help of Aria, Blanca at their heels.

It *was* a hike, and all Axel wanted to do was lie down in the snow and go to sleep. But he kept moving and eventually the ambulance and a hive of paramedics and cops came into view. The medics rushed forward, immediately to Max, getting Peter onto a stretcher.

"Him too," Carly said, and Axel didn't realize she was referring to him until another paramedic came over. The man glanced at Selena. "You need medical attention too?" the paramedic asked.

Selena shook her head. "No. Just twisted my knee. I'll grab a ride in the cop car and get checked out without bogging down emergency. These two are the ones who need an ER."

Axel tried to argue with Selena, then the paramedic, but he was ushered into the ambulance and wasn't too pleased with himself that he didn't seem to have the strength to stop anything that happened. Somehow he was on a stretcher in an ambulance being rushed to the ER.

He didn't need an ER. He was conscious, wasn't he?

The pain was bad, the dizziness was almost worse, but he was *alive*.

Axel looked over to the opposite side of the ambulance where the paramedics worked quickly and efficiently on Peter, clearly the worse off between the two of them.

Axel tried to pay attention to what they were saying so he'd be able to assure Selena Peter was okay, but the words kind of jumbled and it took most of his concentration just to fight the gray fog that wanted to suck him under.

The paramedic leaned over him, studying his face. He lifted the bandage on his cheek, poked and prodded, then did something horribly painful to his hand.

"I'm all right," Axel grumbled, trying to roll away from the medic's attentions.

The paramedic shined the light in his eye and kept examining him as if he hadn't spoken at all. "Concussion. Your hand is a mess. You're in better shape than him, but it isn't getting you out of a trip to the emergency room. Good news is, you'll both survive."

Survive. Axel blew out a breath. Yeah, he had a lot more planned than just *survived*.

Chapter Twenty

Selena had lost all sense of time and place. She'd been right about her knee, though. She'd just twisted it, which was good. They'd given her a pair of crutches and told her to stay off it and to go home and rest. It had taken hours, and maybe she should have listened.

But she couldn't. She'd found her team in the ER waiting room. A bit banged up here and there, but mostly just waiting to make sure Axel was released.

Axel. She couldn't think about Axel yet. She had to deal with her family.

She found Opaline in the OR recovery waiting room. Opaline immediately jumped to her feet. "You should be home," she scolded, but she rushed over and nudged Selena into a chair. "You've got to rest that."

"I will. I just had to…"

"He's okay. He's okay. The doctor said I could even go back and see him in a few minutes. He'll recover just fine."

Selena nodded. She'd known as much, but it was good to hear hope and reassurance from Opaline. Then Opaline's arms wrapped around her. "I'm so glad you're okay."

For the first time in something like twenty years, Selena let herself feel comforted by her older sister's hug. She wrapped her own arms around Opaline and just sat like that for she didn't know how long.

"I need you to believe I really wasn't helping Peter," Opaline whispered fiercely. "I didn't even consider it. I just thought if he trusted me, if he thought I *would* help, I might be able to help everyone else." Opaline pulled back, though she kept her hands on Selena's shoulders. Her eyes were dripping with tears. "I need *you* to believe that, Selena, even if no one else does."

Selena took a deep breath. She'd done her fair share of trying to help Peter in this, in ways that wouldn't meet with Alana's full approval, that was for sure. But more... Peter had made mistakes. Mistakes he'd pay for, but at the end of the day he'd helped. He'd *saved* her when her team couldn't.

"I believe it. And what's more, I believe in Peter. He's going to have to go back to jail, no getting around that, but he tried to help all of us. He... He saved my life." And Axel had saved his. Selena couldn't dwell on that yet. "I'm going to fight for him."

Opaline gripped her hands. "We'll fight for him together."

"And you... You saved us too. Finding all that information about Bernard. We couldn't have handled it the way we did without your information. I'll fight for you too. With Alana or whoever else I need to." Selena sucked in a breath. There were so many old hurts, but at the end of the day, they were family. Family who'd try to save each other when they could.

They'd have a lot to work through, but instead of convincing themselves they were all uniquely misunderstood, maligned or not cared about enough, they had to try to save each other. Instead of doing everything they could to protect themselves from all the ways their parents had hurt them.

Selena stuck around long enough to see Peter. He was mostly out of it, but she got to thank him for saving her, and to promise to do better for all of them in the future. She thought he'd murmured his own promises, but it would take some time before he was lucid enough to fully deal with everything.

Dead on her feet, Selena still tried to argue with Opaline, who insisted she go home. But eventually Carly came in and ushered her outside against all Selena's protests.

Once there, Selena was surprised to find it daylight. She'd lost all sense of time. All sense of anything. But when she saw Blanca waiting patiently in Carly's back seat, Selena felt like maybe everything was going to be okay.

Selena crawled right back in there and cuddled with the dog while Carly drove.

"We'll have you both home in no time," Carly said. "I can stay with you if you need help."

"That's sweet," Selena said through a yawn. "But actually... Don't take me home, Carly. There's somewhere else I need to be."

"I REALLY DON'T like being chauffeured around," Axel grumbled.

"You don't say," Max replied blandly. "And here I thought being injured and fussed over was your favorite thing. You've been so gracious about it."

Axel glowered at Max. He knew he should be grateful he didn't have to spend the night at the hospital, but they'd given him those damn pain meds that made him feel fuzzy without *fully* eradicating the dull ache in his head and hand, insisted someone else drive him home, and left him with a list of instructions on how to care for his injuries a mile long.

He was in a filthy mood, and he wanted to be alone. "You're not staying."

Max chuckled. "Wasn't planning on it."

Axel eyed him suspiciously. He wasn't convinced his friend was truly going to let him be alone, at least for the first twenty-four hours, but Max didn't appear to be lying.

He stopped the car, didn't kill the engine, and let Axel step out. Axel frowned. The lights in the kitchen were on. He didn't leave lights on before he went onto an assignment. Weirder still, Max did not follow. Didn't turn off his engine. Just sat there and gave Axel a wave.

They were really going to let him be alone?

Then, breaking through the engine of Max's car in the quiet of a winter country late afternoon, there was a bark, and then Blanca bounded off the porch. Axel stopped midstep and just watched the dog run up to him, tongue lolling out of the side of her mouth.

She circled him, yipping and whining and wiggling happily.

"What on earth are you doing here?" he muttered at the dog, scratching her behind the ears before moving forward.

Max was driving away and Axel had no choice but to step forward. When he reached his front door, it was unlocked. So, he walked inside.

Selena was standing in his kitchen, fooling with something over the temperamental stove. Her hair was a little damp and piled on top of her head. She wore sweats—*his* sweats—and there were crutches leaning against his counter.

"Did you...break into my house? Are you wearing my clothes?"

She didn't even look over at him. "More or less," she replied cheerfully. She looked around the kitchen. "A little sparse, but I like it. It's…peaceful. Be a good place to recover."

"I…"

"I found the instructions you left the animal babysitter and followed them too."

Axel frowned. "He's a caretaker, not an animal *babysitter*."

"Right, well, all handled," she said with an easy shrug. "I liked the cows. The chickens, though? Mean as all getout. The horse is a sweetie. You'll have to tell me their names in the morning. But for now, all you have to do is sit down and eat." She put a plate—*his* plate—on the table—*his* table—with a flourish. Said *in the morning* like she belonged here.

It slammed into him, as hard as all the blows he'd received in the last few days, that this was exactly where he wanted her.

"Come on now. You have to be starving."

He didn't know what he was, but he managed to move forward and sit himself at the table. Blanca padded after him, then curled into a ball at his feet, resting her head on her paws.

The plate was filled with spaghetti. That she'd apparently made. In his kitchen. In his clothes. Was he hallucinating? But her crutches were right there.

Crutches. "You're the one who should be sitting down."

She waved that away, pouring milk into a glass. "Too antsy." She set the milk next to his plate, then stood there, all her weight on her good leg. She brushed fingers over the bandage on his cheek. "You got hospital paperwork? You once called me Nurse Ratched—well, just you wait."

She tried to move away, but he slid his arms around her and held her there. Just held her. God, they were both okay, and the relief hadn't fully washed over him until just now.

She stilled, rested her cheek on the top of his head. Then merely held on. "You saved Peter," she said, her voice cracking with emotion.

"He saved you."

She let out a shuddering breath. "He did. I didn't expect it."

He loosened his hold enough to look up at her. "You're not feeling guilty for that, after everything we went through?"

She looked down at him. Brown eyes swimming with emotion. "I don't know. I really don't know… I talked to Opaline. I visited with Peter. I think…things will be better between the three of us. That's good. I've needed that and was too…afraid, I guess, to try for it. Risk it." She shook her head, blinking back unshed tears. "You better eat before it gets cold. We can talk after—"

"I'm glad you're here. And not just for the food. I'm glad you're here. It feels like you belong here." She inhaled sharply. Then she shook her head, trying to pull away. But he held on tight. There was no more pulling away. No matter how tired or injured or hungry they were. "There's not going to be any more of that. We're going to deal, here and now, with this. With you and me."

She didn't struggle to get out of his grasp anymore, but she did keep shaking her head back and forth. "I don't know *how*," she said, sounding lost. "You think I understand this?"

"What 'this' are you referring to?"

"How I *feel*. I thought I'd come take care of you and

figure it out, but it just… I really don't know what to do about it."

He tugged her down and onto his lap. "I know what you can do about it."

"Oh, don't go thinking with your—"

"Stay, Selena. That's what you can do." He pressed his mouth to hers, just a gentle pressure. Just a promise. "Stay."

She searched his face, and he saw what she didn't want to feel. Fear, uncertainty and, yeah, that guilt they both needed to work through. Then she cupped her hands to his cheeks.

"You know you want to," he added, trying to sound cocksure, but it only came out serious. Hushed. "I know you're afraid. I'm not exactly steady on my feet here, but it's what we both want. What we both feel. You know it as well as I do. But we also came through life or death on the life side of things, so let's let the fear go, huh?"

She swallowed, still searching his eyes, still holding gently onto his face. She took a deep breath. "You're really afraid?"

"Of course I am. I know far more what to do with a gun in my face than I know what to do with a woman and a dog in my house. Doesn't mean I don't prefer the latter."

She smiled a little at that. "Okay," she said, in something no more than a whisper. "We'll stay," she said, giving a glance at Blanca, who sat on the floor, looking up at them with intelligent eyes. "That's where we'll start."

"She'd like it here," Axel said. "Room to run."

"You've got a home here. I've been…wanting a home for a long time. But—"

No, there wasn't going to be any buts. "I'm in love with you, Selena. I think I have been for a while now."

She nodded, those tears swimming back. He'd have

thought she'd fight them the way she always did, but instead one slipped over. He wiped it off her cheek. It meant more than words, that she'd finally let that wall down, no matter how reluctantly.

"I think I've been in love with you too," she whispered. "I'm not sure I'm going to be any good at that."

"Then let's agree to give each other a little bit of a learning curve, huh?"

She chuckled, but it was watery, then she leaned her head on his shoulder. And they sat there, in his little farmhouse, holding on to each other in the quiet stillness. In the warmth of love, no matter how much they had to learn.

He had no doubt they'd do just fine.

Epilogue

For the first time in Selena's memory, she didn't particularly look forward to the traditional TCD end-of-mission dinner. As glad as she was the mission was over, and Peter and Axel were recovering, and Opaline hadn't lost her job, she was nervous.

Downright *sick* with nerves.

All she could think about was what Axel had said to her back in that cabin, that the entire team would *know*. Arriving together with him and Blanca was hardly going to help matters.

Not that she wanted to change anything. The whole *love* thing had been surprisingly easy to slip into when they were at the farm. It was *here*, surrounded by the people she worked with day in and out, respected and cared about, that she felt strung tight as a drum.

"What do you think they're going to do? Kick you out?"

She gave Axel a look, not pleased how easily he read her. Or at least, she told herself she wasn't pleased, but the more she thought about it—really let herself think about it and not push away the uncomfortable feelings—the more she realized it was a great comfort to have someone who understood her when she couldn't verbalize the things churning around inside her.

It was the thing she'd wanted from her family that they'd never been able to give, but now that she had it in Axel, it seemed to help her find the words with her family.

They walked into the conference room, shoulder to shoulder, to find just about everyone already in the room, helping themselves to the spread of food and drinks laid out, likely by Alana's assistant, Amanda.

Selena wasn't sure what she'd expected. Speculative looks. Teasing. *Something.* But everyone just called out a greeting or smiled.

"All hail the conquering heroes," Max said, lifting his cup.

"Team effort, I'm pretty sure," Axel returned, taking the plate Amanda offered him and handing it to Selena.

"Sure, but we were talking," Max said, gesturing to Carly and Aria. "If you guys hadn't wanted to split Leonard and Peter up, we'd all be in pieces on the forest floor."

Aria nodded. "If we'd kept together, made the circle, Bernard would have been able to blow us all up."

Selena exchanged a look with Axel. They'd gone over and over that moment themselves, but neither had thought…

But Selena supposed it was true. She'd had guilt there, about letting her personal feelings interfere with a case, but in this strange instance… Max was right. It had actually helped.

Selena let out a whoosh of breath. She'd been harboring guilt or worry or *something.* She'd thought it would take time to work through, but in the end… Everything she'd chosen had actually *helped.*

The team chatted, discussed details of the case and Peter's prognosis and potential trial outcomes. Leonard's ranting that cops had ruined his life, much like his brother's same anger, had earned him a trip to the psychiatric hospital. He'd be carefully monitored for a very long time. The mission was well and truly over.

Still, no one stared or commented on Axel and Selena coming together. No one even gave a second glance when Axel absently ran his hand over her hair. Even as Selena blushed furiously, *nothing* happened.

Alana came into the room, and the chatter quieted as Opaline came in behind her. Alana took the silence as an opportunity to speak.

"While Opaline will be serving a two-week suspension, she was imperative in finding the information that led us to understand Bernard's motives. Which gives me full faith that when she returns, she'll continue to be a fine asset to the team."

The team cheered, and Opaline dabbed at her wet eyes. But her colleagues shoved a plate at her and drinks and…

Everything was going to be okay. Really okay.

A little while later, when Selena was filling her cup in the corner, Carly came up next to her, leaning against the wall.

Selena braced herself. Finally someone was going to say something.

"It's good to see you happy, Selena." Carly patted her shoulder. "Really good." And then she walked off, petting Blanca on her way back to the table.

Selena took a deep breath and turned. Everyone else was eating, chatting. No one acted differently. And they weren't going to. It was simply…accepted.

Because they were a team. Because they were friends.

"Enjoy your win here, team." Alana tapped on the table. "But be ready for the next assignment."

They'd all be ready for the next one. And in the meantime, she'd have a life. With a sister, a brother. With friends.

And with Axel.

Family, friendship and love. All things that had been within her grasp before, but she'd been too scared to reach for.

She wasn't scared anymore.

She was ready.

* * * * *

PURSUIT OF
THE TRUTH

K.D. RICHARDS

To Delria, who taught me I could do anything,
and to Neil, who makes anything possible.

Chapter One

Goose bumps tingled over Nadia Shelton's arms and neck as she exited her apartment building. She scanned the morning commuters looking for signs of someone watching her. And like every previous morning, all she saw were fellow New Yorkers hustling along the sidewalk, somewhat faster this morning than the morning before, as the gray clouds overhead pelted them with rain.

Nadia pulled her purse and briefcase closer to her body, hoping to shield them from the worst of the rain, and tightened her grip on her umbrella. The hairs on the back of her neck stood at attention as she entered the flow of bodies on the sidewalk. There was no time for paranoia. She was already ten minutes late getting to work. Granted, that was not typically a huge deal since she was her own boss, but this morning she had a meeting she did not want to be late for.

Should have thought of that while you were primping for a certain security specialist with sexy hazel eyes.

Nadia caught a glimpse of herself in the large front window of the corner bodega. She slowed and examined her reflection as she passed by. Her plum-colored sheath accentuated the curve of her hips and popped vibrantly against her dark skin. The dress showed just a hint of her ample cleavage—sexy, but still work-appropriate.

The off-white trench coat she'd slid into on her way out the door completed the look. She'd dressed to feel good about herself, and looking into the storefront window, she felt as if she'd succeeded.

Goodness knows she deserved some happiness. The last several months had been the most trying of her life.

She took a step away from the window, then jerked to a stop once again when the reflection of a man on the other side of the street caught her eye. He huddled under the awning of a bookstore, its interior lights still darkened.

Nadia strained to make out his features, but the window distorted his image, even as scores of people hurried by, making it even more difficult to get a clear view. She mentally noted the dark hoodie, navy jeans and black work boots before starting down the sidewalk again, her heart rate picking up its pace.

She shot a glance over her shoulder, but the man had moved from the doorway.

You're being paranoid. He was probably just taking a reprieve from the rain.

There was absolutely no reason for anyone to be watching her, and any other day, she probably wouldn't have even noticed the man. But this hadn't been the only odd occurrence lately. An image jumped into her head. Born and raised in New York, she'd seen her fair share of rats, even dead ones, but never mangled so horribly.

She shook her head to clear the memory of the rat from her mind. Her neighbor's cat had most likely left that little gift for her—it couldn't be anything more sinister than that.

And her keyed car and the late-night hang-ups? Was the cat behind those things too?

Stop.

It wasn't as if the garage she parked her rarely used

car in was Fort Knox. Teenagers had probably keyed the car. And the hang-ups could be teenagers too. Or tele-marketers. Or simply a wrong number. Repeated every night for the last two weeks?

She chewed her bottom lip as she hurried along the sidewalk, dodging open umbrellas. She was overreacting. The pressures of being thrust into the role of CEO of Shelton Hotels was making her jumpy. And anxious. And short-tempered.

Nadia drew in a breath and exhaled slowly, her thera-pist's advice not to be so hard on herself echoing in her mind. The last year had brought a lot of change, and it would take time to settle into a new normal.

For six years, she and her older brother, Nathan, had run Shelton Hotels, the company their father built from nothing into a small chain of boutique hotels in New York City. As vice president of operations, Nadia con-centrated on the day-to-day workings of the three hotels they owned, specifically their flagship hotel in Harlem where she kept her primary office. CEO Nate handled the big-picture stuff and was the face of the company.

That had all changed when Nate died in a car accident eleven months ago.

Nadia had inherited Shelton Hotels, lock, stock, and barrel. As the newly minted CEO, it was up to her alone to keep the family legacy intact. Not everybody believed she could pull it off.

She reached the corner a block from the hotel as the stoplight changed from green to yellow and the pedes-trian walk signal flashed a warning against crossing.

"Excuse me," a voice boomed in her ear, making her jump and gasp.

A tall man skirted around her, long coat flapping around his thighs, his briefcase held atop his head as a shield against the rain. Nadia frowned as the man dashed across the street without a backward glance.

Her frown deepened when her gaze fell on the bus shelter beside her. An advertisement for Aurora Hotels and Suites hung on the wall of the shelter. Aurora wasn't direct competition since it was consistently ranked in the luxury-hotel market, rather than the midscale market like Shelton. But she'd dated the president of Aurora briefly, and the whole affair had soured her on the man and the company he ran.

She tore her eyes from the offending advertisement and, following the lead of all the other commuters waiting for the light to change, pulled her phone from her coat pocket. She'd barely swiped the screen awake when big hands landed on her shoulder blades. She twisted to see who was behind her, but a shove sent her stumbling forward before she could lay eyes on the person.

Her knees and palms connected with the pavement, the impact sufficient to send waves of pain up and down her limbs and through her body.

Tires screeched, and Nadia turned her head to see a yellow cab bearing down on her as car horns blared nearby.

The cab screeched to a stop inches from her, the cab driver's ashen face and wide, terrified eyes clear through the windshield.

A man in an orange safety vest and tan boots ran to her side and knelt. A white hard hat was all the protection against the rain he wore. "You have a death wish, lady? Jumping in the street like that."

Nadia focused on the man in front of her, the shock of what had just happened, what could have happened, still wrapped around her. She pushed up from the ground, shaky as pain shot up her arms once again. She glanced down at herself, taking stock.

Angry red scrapes covered both palms, and blood trickled from a nasty-looking gash on her left leg. Thankfully, though, she didn't think there was any permanent damage. The same could not be said for her outfit. Dirt and grime covered her dress, and a cursory assessment made it clear that the formerly white coat would have to go in the trash bin as soon as possible.

"You trying to kill yourself or something?" the construction worker asked with a scowl.

Nadia recovered enough to scowl right back. "I didn't jump in the street. Someone pushed me."

The man eyed her with suspicion. "I didn't see anyone near you."

"Well, there was." Nadia scanned the sidewalk. Several people had slowed, some even stopping to gawk at the scene, but in true New York fashion, most walked by without a glance.

An angry car horn sounded.

"Get out of the street, will you?" the driver of the cab that had almost hit her yelled, seemingly recovered from the shock of almost running her down.

Nadia accepted her purse from a gray-haired lady who'd also stopped to help, smiling at the woman. Her umbrella was nowhere to be seen, not that the rain could do any more damage than had already been done. She limped across the street, on the arm of the construction worker, the heel of her left shoe broken. She declined the man's offer to escort her the rest of the way to work. It was only half a block to the hotel, and her appearance would draw enough attention.

She hobbled forward a few steps, then stopped. New Yorkers hurried by as usual. Anyone who'd been around to see her humiliating swan dive into the street had long since lost interest. Yet, the hairs on her neck stood at attention anew. She limped the rest of the way to the hotel, the feeling that someone was watching following her the entire time.

RYAN WEST DECLINED the coffee offered by Olivia Bennett, Nadia Shelton's administrative assistant, and took a seat in one of two armchairs in the office. His eyes roamed her ground-floor office, noting how much it reflected the woman that worked there.

Bookshelves lined the white walls to the left, while black-and-white photos of the Ponte Vecchio, the Millau Viaduct and the Brooklyn Bridge hung on the opposite wall. He sat facing a white L-shaped desk that sat atop a contemporary area rug, its blue-and-dark-gray hues adding color to the room. Fresh flowers graced a round meeting table tucked into the corner of the office. Feminine, elegant, yet professional, just like the woman who inhabited the space.

He checked his watch: 9:01. Nadia was officially late for their meeting. He moved his neck in a slow circle attempting to release some of the tension there. He'd sent his brother Shawn to get started on the security-system evaluation while he waited for Nadia. It was unusual for her to be late to one of their meetings, but that wasn't why he was irritated. What annoyed him was how much he looked forward to seeing Nadia Shelton.

"Get it together. She's a client."

He was determined to be nothing but professional when it came to Nadia, but a persistent whisper at the back of his mind challenged that determination. He may not have been as personable as his younger brother, Shawn, or as smart as his lawyer older brother Brandon, but he knew the security business. His blood, sweat and tears had grown West Security into one of the East Coast's go-to security and investigations firms.

As vice president of West Security and Investigations, he rarely handled quarterly meetings with clients. In fact, over the last eighteen months, he'd handled only one, Shelton Hotels. Last year their account executive for Shelton Hotels had gone on maternity leave, and he'd temporarily taken on the Shelton. Temporary had turned permanent the minute he met Nadia Shelton.

Their first meeting had taken place in this very office. The memory of her hand outstretched toward him, an intoxicating smile on her face, remained vivid. He wasn't dramatic or even a romantic, but an undeniable electricity had sizzled through his body when he'd touched his hand to hers.

His anxiousness about seeing her grew exponentially in the days leading up to each quarterly meeting. Which was why he was sitting in her office in his best suit, bent out of shape because she was—he glanced at his watch— six minutes late.

He had to turn the account over. He'd been down this road before, with disastrous results to his heart. He didn't even have the excuse of being young and dumb this time. He tortured himself, pining for a woman he couldn't have every time he walked into this office, and it had to stop. He wouldn't jeopardize the company's reputation, or his heart. Not again.

"Oh, my goodness."

The alarm in Olivia's voice had him rising. He crossed to the door but hesitated to open it, debating whether he should stay put or see if he could help. Olivia hadn't sounded like she was in any trouble, and whatever was happening wasn't really any of his business.

A soft voice responded, not Olivia's, but he couldn't make out who it was or what they said. Shadows passed the opaque glass in the office door.

"Should I call an ambulance?" Olivia asked, her voice fading as she passed by the door.

He pulled the door open and followed the sound of the voices to a small restroom at the back of the office suite.

Nadia leaned against the vanity, her dress splattered with mud, wisps of hair falling from her twisty updo. Olivia dabbed at a red gash along Nadia's calf.

A swear rumbled from his chest, drawing the women's attention to where he stood in the doorway. "Get the first aid kit," Ryan ordered, his tone harsher than he'd intended.

He knew they had one. West Security didn't just look out for the physical and cybersecurity of their clients. They made sure the basics that people often overlooked, such as fire extinguishers and first aid kits, were also properly stocked on-site.

Olivia glanced at Nadia with a question in her eyes.

A moment passed before Nadia nodded, and Olivia slipped past Ryan, disappearing down the hallway leading to the public areas of the hotel.

Ryan scanned Nadia from head to toe. In addition to the cut on her leg, she had abrasions on her hands and a wicked scrape along her right elbow. The heel of her left shoe literally hung on by a thread.

"What happened?" He went down on his haunches to examine the cut on her leg.

"I'm the most recent victim of the commuter wars. Someone shoved me into oncoming traffic."

Ryan tensed. "Did you see who did it?"

She shook her head, then winced.

He stood and examined her for bruises before looking

into her eyes. "Did you hit your head?" He gazed into her eyes, beautifully dark with flecks of gold. Scrapes marred the smooth umber skin on her arms and legs. Several chestnut curls had broken free from her updo.

"No," she said almost in a whisper, her eyes glued to his. After a long moment, she cleared her throat and looked away. "My hands took the brunt of the fall, but I think I might have jammed my shoulder."

"May I?"

She nodded.

He applied modest pressure along her shoulder and neck, keeping his touch gentle. An intense rush of desire nearly overwhelmed him at the feel of the silky skin of her shoulder. It took everything he had not to keep going when he got to the curve of her neck. He pulled his hand away before he did something stupid. "I don't think it's bad. Tell me exactly what happened."

Nadia pushed away from the vanity and started for the bathroom door. He grabbed her elbow, helping her balance on her broken heel. The scent of her jasmine perfume swirled around him as they walked back to her office, sending another wave of desire springing through him.

"It was probably an accident." Her halting tone belied the words.

"But you think it might not have been."

She didn't answer right away. Lowering herself into the chair he'd been sitting in, she looked up at him through long lashes. "It felt like someone pushed me."

Olivia hurried into the office with the first aid kit, cutting off his opportunity to follow up on what Nadia had just said.

"Thank you, Olivia. I'll be fine. You can get on with your work." Nadia smiled reassuringly.

Olivia shot a curious glance at Ryan. "If you're sure. I can catch up with the other Mr. West and see how he's doing with the security review."

Nadia's smile held steady. "That would be great. Thanks."

Ryan took the first aid kit from Olivia, who shot one more curious look at Nadia before leaving.

Ryan went to his knees in front of her, his six-foot-three height leaving him almost eye to eye with Nadia though she sat. He grabbed an antiseptic swab from the kit and began cleaning the wound on Nadia's knee. He raised his gaze to her face to find her eyes wide. "What are you doing?"

"Can you describe the people around you when you felt the push?" Ryan gently removed her broken shoe, the intimacy of their position sending his heart racing.

"I… I don't know. A construction worker helped me up. And there was an older lady that grabbed my purse for me."

She winced when he brushed the wipe over the wound on her leg, and his gut twisted.

"Sorry."

He wiped the wound again, this time blowing on it gently to minimize the chemical's sting. "Nadia? You okay?"

"Sure. Uh, yes, the construction worker and the lady. There was also the cabbie that almost hit me, but he couldn't have pushed me."

Ryan covered her bruise with a large bandage and moved to the abrasion on her arm. "Do you always take the same route to work?"

Nadia cocked her head to the side. "I live four blocks away. There aren't that many options."

Four blocks. That would put her apartment near Sentinel, the bar he and Shawn had recently purchased.

He finished bandaging her arm. It might be impossible to determine if she'd been purposely pushed or whether some inconsiderate commuter accidentally knocked her into the street, but every fiber in his body wanted to make sure she never suffered another bump or bruise to her beautiful silky skin.

He rose from the floor and stepped back. Nothing could ever happen between them, not only because she was a client, but also because she was way out of his league. That didn't mean he couldn't look and admire how perfectly she was built. Professional or not, he was a healthy thirty-six-year-old man.

His gaze finally landed on her face. For a brief moment, he thought he saw the desire he felt reflected in her brown eyes before she looked away.

Nadia stood and walked barefoot to the other side of her desk. "I need to call the boutique in the lobby and get a new outfit. Maybe you could catch up to Olivia and your brother, and we can talk later?"

He wanted to delve further into whatever had happened this morning, but it wasn't his place, and there wasn't anything he could do about it.

He stole a glance at Nadia as he left the office. She held the phone handset between her shoulder and ear, her fingers punching numbers on the keypad.

Her fall was probably just an accident, he told himself as he left the office. Yet, he couldn't stop the thought nagging at him in response.

But what if it wasn't?

Chapter Two

Lana's, the women's boutique in the hotel lobby, skewed toward women with fewer curves and less imaginative fashion sense than Nadia. Since she was in no position to be choosy, she bought a black suit, thankful that it not only fit but covered her bumps and bruises. Paired with an overpriced pair of black flats, she looked the part of a CEO once again.

Unfortunately, the morning's events had put her too far behind to meet with Ryan, leaving her with mixed feelings. She was willing to admit to herself, and only herself, that she anticipated their quarterly meetings with far more excitement than she mustered for any of the other hotel vendors.

Not that Ryan West would ever be interested in the dirty, bruised and disheveled woman that he'd played nursemaid to this morning. The picture of what she must have looked like flashed through her mind, sending a flush of embarrassment through her and heating her cheeks.

She needed to focus on work. She didn't have time for romance, and anyway, given her track record, swearing off men seemed the prudent course of action.

Nadia examined the spreadsheet her CFO had emailed the previous day. Last year's numbers were good, even better than the year before when Nate was in charge. Her father had loved Shelton Hotels, but he'd been slow to change with the industry. As deeply as she'd mourned his death six years ago, when she and Nate took over they'd both agreed that changes would have to be made if Shelton was to survive. Nate hadn't been sure about branding Shelton Hotels as an eco-friendly chain, but once she'd convinced him of the viability of the idea, he'd thrown himself into the rebranding just as she had.

She wanted to take Shelton beyond simply asking guests to reuse their towels and not requesting the bedsheets be laundered every day. They'd instituted a composting program, retrofitted every room in the hotel with automatic lights, changed their cleaning products and completely overhauled how they chose their vendors. It had been a huge and expensive undertaking, but they were paying off the loan right on time. The hotel's margins were tighter than she'd like, but conference season was just beginning, and they were booked solid for the next several months. The only thing missing was Nate.

They'd planned to take Shelton Hotels to the next level together, but now she was left to go it alone.

Nadia's desk phone rang, the caller ID showing Olivia's extension.

"I'm sorry to bother you," Olivia spoke as soon as Nadia connected the call. "But Michael Dexter is at the front desk asking to see you."

Nadia frowned and for a moment considered having Olivia say she wasn't in. Mike Dexter, president of Aurora Hotels and Suites, was not a man she wanted to deal with today. She'd made the mistake of dating Mike for a short period last year on the rebound from calling off her engagement. Mike hadn't been interested in her solely for her money like her ex-fiancé had been, but it had quickly become apparent his motives were no less selfish. It only took a few weeks of dating for her to realize that he wanted someone who would look good on his arm in public and would fawn over him in private.

That was so not her. Not that Mike had taken the time to get to know her while they'd dated. He'd been too busy trying to impress her and going on and on about how well suited they were for each other since they were both in the hospitality industry. He'd seemed genuinely surprised when Nadia had broken things off with him. The few times they'd run into each other at events afterward, he'd been borderline uncivil. She couldn't imagine why he'd show up at her office.

Today was not her day.

Curiosity won out, however. Minutes later Olivia escorted Mike into the office. With chiseled cheekbones and pale blue eyes, only his relatively short stature of five foot ten set him apart from the many male models that ran the streets of New York.

Nadia plastered a polite smile on her face, rising as Mike entered. "Mike, to what do I owe this visit?"

She didn't offer her hand or come around her desk to greet him. He was more of an interloper than a guest.

"Can't I just drop in to say hello to a friend?" Mike said.

She examined the man in front of her with open suspicion. The quarter-inch strip of pale skin at his hairline announced the bronzy glow on his face as store-bought, and his salt-and-pepper hair fell in waves that were a little too perfect to be natural.

There was no way in the world Mike had come all the way uptown to Harlem just to shoot the breeze. He was up to something, and she'd be wise to tread cautiously until she knew what that was. "I didn't know we were friends. Why are you here, Mike?"

Mike's smile tightened. "I forgot how focused you can be."

Nadia stared and waited.

"Fine." He let the smile drop from his face. "I have a business proposal for you. Aurora is a well-known luxury brand, but we're looking to expand into the midscale market. The board has authorized me to make you a very generous offer."

Nadia cocked her head, suspicion turning to confusion. "What kind of offer?"

Mike pulled a thin white envelope from the inside of his suit jacket and handed it over the desk, his mouth spread into a grin. "I'm sure you'll be pleased."

She took the offering, sliding the single sheet of paper from the unsealed sleeve. It was a letter, signed by the chairmen of the board of Aurora Hotels, offering a not-insignificant sum for the purchase of Shelton Hotels.

"Of course, the details will need to be worked out, but that's why we pay the lawyers, right?" A new smile slid across Mike's face. "The letter just deals with the important stuff—the money." Mike beamed.

Tension stiffened Nadia's back. She sat. Had Mike been in her office on a personal matter, this would be the point where she would have unceremoniously thrown him out, but professionalism kept her from doing so. "Shelton Hotels is not for sale."

"Why don't you take a close look at our offer before making any hasty decisions?" Mike unbuttoned his jacket and sat in the chair on the other side of Nadia's desk. Stretching his legs out in front of him, he leaned back in the chair, apparently confident that she'd see the light and accept the offer.

Her eyes never left Mike's. "There's no need. As I said, Shelton is not for sale."

Mike straightened in his chair. "I expected a savvy businesswoman like you to reject our first offer. So what will it take?"

Annoyance chased away her earlier inclination to-ward professional courtesy. "I don't know how to say it any more clearly. I'm not selling Shelton," she said icily.

"What if the deal included a position for you at Au-rora? It would be a significant step up."

His rudeness stunned her into a momentary silence which Mike apparently mistook for her considering his offer.

"How does vice president of operations sound?" He smiled a calculated, cocky grin.

"Like a step down from being CEO of my own hotel chain."

Mike guffawed. "Come on, now. Shelton is good for what it is, but it's a stretch to call it a chain. I mean you only have three properties, and they are all in New York. Don't you want more?"

"No." Her hands trembled with contained anger. She was tired of playing his game. And if she had to spend too much longer with Mike and his overinflated ego, she couldn't promise she wouldn't say or do something she couldn't take back. "But even if I wanted more, it would be here, at Shelton Hotels. The business my father built from nothing."

Mike held up his hands in a surrender pose. "I really didn't come here to argue. I went to bat for you with my board and convinced them that Shelton would be a good purchase. I thought I'd be helping you. Yet, the fact is I've now been tasked with acquiring Shelton, and I don't fail."

Anger surged, threatening to overtake reason. She

hadn't asked him to go to bat for her nor could she fathom why he'd think buying Shelton would help her.

Nadia stood. "It's time for you to leave, Mike."

He rose slowly, his mouth pulling so taut that lines appeared at either end. "Really? You want to play hardball with me?"

Nadia put her hands on her desk and leaned forward. "I'm not playing. Shelton is mine, and that's how it will remain. Now, get out."

Nadia rounded her desk and headed for the door.

Mike stepped in front of her, blocking her path. "Does your refusal have anything to do with our past personal relationship? I know that you might have hoped for something to develop between us, but…" Mike reached out and ran his thumb over her cheek "…sometimes these things just don't work out."

She stepped back out of his reach, her hands balled into fists. "Since I was the one who broke things off, I think I'll survive."

Mike's spine straightened. "I understand it can be difficult to see past sentimentality, but I wouldn't have expected this from you. It's a good offer."

He strode to the door, stopping at the threshold and turning back to her. "Think about it. We'll talk soon."

Nadia watched him disappear.

"Not if I can help it."

Chapter Three

Nadia's days were usually long, but this day had been longer than usual thanks to her late start and Mike's unwelcome visit. After her busy morning, she'd gotten a good start on closing out the file on the conference of local real estate agents from last week and began to prepare for the conference of freelance photographers that would start early next week. In doing so, she'd been able to avoid thinking about the embarrassment she'd felt with Ryan and the fury that had built from her encounter with Mike.

But as she made the short walk back to her apartment, her mind drifted back to the surprise she'd felt when Ryan had burst into the bathroom. As always, he showed up for their meeting impeccably dressed in what had to be a custom-tailored suit that did nothing to hide the well-muscled body beneath. And she'd been in a torn dress with dirty knees. Still, he'd been exceptionally gentle when he'd lifted her foot from her shoe. There'd been nothing inherently sensual about the act, but it had still been one of the sexiest things she'd ever experienced. And then he'd blown on her calf. It was a good thing she'd been sitting down because her legs—her whole body, to be honest—had instantly gone weak. The last thing she wanted Ryan West to know was that she'd been so attracted to him her knees had gone weak. Having him see her muddy and bruised was embarrassing enough for a lifetime. And a good reminder that she'd sworn off men.

Her choice left her lonely at times, but lonely was a far cry better than heartbroken when the people you loved and depended on left you.

She stood back from the curb while she waited for the lights to change and made it home without a mishap. After collecting the mail from her box in the alcove next to the building entrance, she rode the elevator to her fourth-floor apartment.

She was almost to her apartment door when she noticed it was cracked open.

She crept closer, stopping when a shadow crossed the opening between the door and the frame.

"Did you find anything?" a man whispered.

"There's nothing here," a different, deeper voice said.

"We'll wait for her, then," the first voice responded.

The shadow shifted, and a man in jeans and a black top crossed in front of the sliver of light emanating from the apartment.

She couldn't see a face, but she didn't miss the glint of the silver gun he held in his gloved hand.

Surprised, she let her purse and briefcase slip from her shoulder and land with a soft thud on the hallway carpet.

She crept back, away from her apartment, her keys still clutched in her hand.

Turning, she sprinted back the way she'd come. She couldn't risk waiting for the elevator. She headed straight for the stairs.

The sound of the bar across the door unlatching sounded like a firecracker as she hit it at a run.

Please don't let them have heard.

Nadia raced down the stairs, cringing at the sound of her footsteps pounding down the stairs. She'd made it to the third-floor landing when the firecracker sound came again, followed by thunderous footsteps on the stairs above.

Faster. Go! Go! Go!

She picked up her pace, unconcerned with the sound of her footsteps now and grateful for the expensive flats she'd purchased earlier in the day.

A sign on the door at the base of the stairs cautioned that an alarm would sound when the door opened. When she pushed through the door and into the alley behind the building, only the usual sound of traffic on nearby Fifth Avenue greeted her. There wasn't time to curse the negligent building management.

She ran for the entrance to the alley. She'd purchased her condo for its location and because of the quiet, tree-lined street on which the building stood. Populated primarily by professionals and young families, the neighborhood offered the serenity and peace she craved after hectic days dealing with hotel guests, vendors and conference-goers. But at ten o'clock at night, the streets were empty, making it impossible to blend in with or hide in a crowd.

You just have to make it to Fifth Avenue.

A major thoroughfare spanning a good portion of the length of Manhattan, Fifth Avenue was always heavily populated. There were several restaurants, bars and other venues that would be open at this time of night where she could borrow a phone to call the police.

She ran down the alley. The door she'd exited burst open just as she made it to the entrance to the narrow passage.

She slowed for a moment, glancing over her shoulder. A bald man, almost as wide as the doorway itself, stopped just outside the door. His gaze locked on hers, the ma-

levolence in his eyes visible even several feet away. She
attended yoga regularly, but with the fall earlier, her leg
muscles already ached and her lungs burned as much as
from the sudden exertion as fear. Still, she pushed herself to move faster.

Several people waited yards ahead for the pedestrian
walk signal at the corner of Fifth Avenue. Cars streamed
down the street.

"Help!"

A car horn sounded, drowning out her cry. The traffic signal changed to red, and the crowd swarmed into
the crosswalk, seemingly oblivious to her pounding footsteps behind them.

With a burst of speed, she made it to the corner, spar-
ing a second glance over her shoulder. The bald man
still advanced, joined now by another man equally broad
shouldered.

Nadia wove through the crowded street. She cursed
herself for dropping her purse in her apartment hallway.
She could ask to use the phone of a passerby, but stopping to explain the situation would eat up time she could
use to put distance between herself and the men after her.
Better to get somewhere safe first.

The stores on the block had already closed for the
day, but farther down, signs for restaurants and bars still
glowed. She kept moving, her eyes locking on a unique
sign, its letters illuminating one after the other above a
doorway until the name of the establishment glowed in
green. *Sentinel.*

It might have been comical in a movie or on television. At the moment it seemed like providence since a
guardian was exactly what she needed.

She hurried to the door, pausing at the entrance to see
if she was still being followed. The man whose eye she'd

caught at the end of the alley skirted around people on the sidewalk. He turned toward her, but she ducked into the bar praying he didn't see her.

Polished chocolate-brown wood covered the walls and climbed to the ceiling where matching beams ran the length of the space. Conversation competed with the pop music falling from the overhead speakers. Bottles of liquor in a rainbow of colors climbed the wall behind the long bar.

People milled throughout the bar, a decent showing for a Monday night, but still far too open to make for a good hiding spot.

The back wall opened up onto a hallway, the universal stick-figure sign for the restrooms hanging overhead. At the end of the hall, a door with the words *Emergency Exit* blocked out in silver lettering beckoned. If she could just get to that door, she could slip out the back and onto the adjacent street without the men chasing her any the wiser.

She weaved through the tables toward the exit, the soles of her flats adhering to the sticky floor.

The door to the bar opened, and her bald pursuer entered. She turned, stepping close to three laughing women headed toward the restrooms. The women shot her curious looks, but she laughed along, the sound brittle. The bald guy would look for a single woman. Nadia could only hope he wouldn't pay close attention to a group of women heading for the restroom.

Their merry band had almost made it to the hall when the door at its end swung open, letting in a chilly burst of air along with one of the men chasing her.

Nadia shifted, moving behind the tallest of the women. She only had seconds before the women turned into the bathroom, and there was no way she could go with them without being seen by the man coming down the hall. If she went in, she'd be trapped.

She glanced back at the front door. The bald man stood to the side, still scanning the crowd. He hadn't seen her, but it was only a matter of time before he did.

To her left, a corner booth packed with people celebrating something overflowed. Three large men stood around a table, all but masking it from the rest of the bar.

She slid between the two biggest guys and tucked herself in front of one using his body to hide her own.

"Hello." A deep baritone rolled against her back.

Nadia twisted to see the face of the man she was using as a shield, freezing when familiar hazel eyes met her own.

"What are you doing here?"

"I should be asking you that." Ryan cocked an eyebrow at her.

"I…" She stared up at the man she'd been crushing on for the last two years, unsure how to explain why she'd practically thrown her body onto his.

Through the sliver of space separating Ryan and the man standing next to him, she saw the bald man moving through the crowd, examining the women at the bar and at tables one by one.

"I know this is weird, but please don't move. Two guys followed me in here, and I need to hide until they're gone."

Ryan's face hardened. He already dwarfed her, but his body tensed at her words, his broad shoulders expanding.

Having overheard their conversation, the man standing next to Ryan stepped closer, making it harder for her to be seen.

She smiled her thanks.

"This is my colleague, Gideon Wainwright. Gideon, Nadia."

Gideon nodded.

The chatter in the bar was too loud for the other people at the table to have heard her declaration, but it didn't keep them from shooting curious glances at her. A thin man with a wispy blond goatee sitting on the far side of the booth leaned forward as if to direct a comment or question her way.

Ryan shook his head, and the man paused, his lips turning down in a frown, before sitting back in the booth and diving back into conversation with the woman next to him.

"Where are these guys that followed you?" Gideon asked with a Southern lilt that surprised her. With muscles on top of muscles, he looked more Arnold Schwarzenegger than Matthew McConaughey.

"One is a bald guy that followed me in the front door. The other guy came from the back hall."

Gideon angled his body away from Nadia and Ryan, his head turning slowly from one end of the space to the other. Nadia couldn't see the men who'd been chasing her, but based on the hard lines of Gideon's mouth, he did.

"Why are they following you?" Ryan rested his hands on her shoulders. She let herself rest against his warm body. She was still tense and afraid, but less so now that she wasn't alone.

She knew instinctively Ryan wouldn't let those guys get to her.

"I don't know. They were in my apartment when I got home tonight. The door wasn't closed all the way, and I heard them talking about grabbing me. I could see them a little through the crack in the door. One of them had a gun in his hand, so I ran."

Remembering their words and the sight of the gun sent a shudder down her spine.

Ryan kneaded her shoulders. "You did exactly the right thing. You got yourself to safety."

"They're leaving," Gideon said without looking at them. "I'm going to follow them." He walked away without waiting for Ryan's response.

The tension in her body melted away, leaving her feeling like overcooked spaghetti. She would have fallen if Ryan hadn't wrapped his arm around her waist.

He urged her toward the opposite end of the bar. As they moved away, he spoke to the table. "Keep the party going. We'll be back."

RYAN STOPPED BY the bar and asked his bartender, Stacey, to send a cup of hot tea to his office before steering Nadia through a door behind the bar. He'd have asked Stacey to send something stronger, but he wasn't sure if Nadia drank.

"Is it okay for you to be back here?" Nadia glanced back the way they'd come.

He waved her into a small office and moved a stack of papers from a black leather love seat before gently lowering her onto it.

"It's my office. I co-own the bar with Shawn."

He pulled his desk chair across the office to sit in front of Nadia.

Nadia's forehead scrunched. "I thought you worked at your father's security firm."

"We do. The bar is just..." He wasn't sure what the bar was. When the previous owner had decided it was time to retire to Arizona, he and Shawn hadn't wanted to let one of their favorite hangouts close. They'd bought it without a lot of forethought. Lucky for them Stacey wasn't just a great bartender, she was also an excellent manager. "Diversification. Now, tell me about the men that followed you in here."

Nadia crossed her arms over her chest, pushing her breasts together. *Focus.*

"I honestly don't know what they want from me. I've never seen them before."

A knock sounded on the door, and one of the newer waitresses carried in the cup of tea he'd asked Stacey to have sent to the office. He remained silent until the waitress backed out of the room.

"Start from the beginning."

Nadia let out a sigh and explained coming home to find the men in her apartment, being chased from the building through the neighborhood and ducking into the bar. It had been happenstance that he and Gideon had been standing close enough to act as a shield when she'd needed them.

Another knock sounded on the office door. Gideon and Shawn entered without waiting for an answer.

"We followed the guys to a parking garage on MLK Boulevard," Gideon said. "I thought it would be too conspicuous to follow them inside, but we waited awhile and got the tag of a black SUV that exited soon after the guys went in."

Ryan nodded. "Good. Run it. Let's see who the tag comes back to."

"Already done. Stolen out of Jersey five days ago," Shawn said.

Five days ago. That meant these guys either habitually rode in stolen vehicles or they stole this one in preparation for the break-in at Nadia's. Neither option was good for Nadia.

"Can you think of anyone who might have it in for you? Enemies? Ex-boyfriends?"

His stomach clenched involuntarily at the thought of her with another man.

Nadia rubbed her temples. "I don't have any enemies, and I haven't been on a date in over a year." Her fingers stilled, and her eyes squeezed shut. She clearly hadn't meant to say that last part.

He couldn't stop his lips from quirking up at the news. Shawn's gaze flicked from Ryan to Nadia and back, and Ryan quickly schooled his face.

"Who inherits the hotels if something happens to you?"

She opened her eyes and looked up at him. "It's just me and Uncle Erik, my dad's half brother, now. But there's no way my uncle would hurt me."

Ryan didn't bother telling her what families had done to each other in the pursuit of money. He'd look into Uncle Erik.

"Did you hear these guys specifically use your name when they were in your apartment?" Ryan asked, moving on.

"No, just that they were waiting for me to come home."

So the men might have had the wrong apartment. His gut didn't buy that, though.

Ryan turned to Shawn and Gideon. "Can you two check out Nadia's apartment?"

"No problem," Shawn said.

Nadia slid to the edge of the couch. "Hang on. I appreciate your help tonight, but I can't ask you to do any more. I'm sure my personal security isn't included in the contract you have with Shelton Hotels."

"Don't worry about it," Ryan said.

Shawn's lips curved up in a wisp of a smile.

Nadia rattled off her address and handed over the keys she'd miraculously held on to despite her mad dash through the streets of Harlem.

She stood as Shawn left and began pacing the small space. "Why do you want to check out my apartment?"

"We're not sure who was in the SUV. I'm not sending you back to your place without knowing exactly what the situation is there."

Her laugh was rueful. "I hope you can figure it out because I'm at a loss."

Considering everything she'd been through, she was holding up well, but she'd been operating on adrenaline. That high would wane, and the fall could be emotionally brutal as the reality of how close she'd come to being kidnapped, or worse, began to sink in. It was another reason he didn't want to let her out of his sight.

Ryan leaned back in his chair, rolling it back to give her more space to move the length of the office. "Have you made anyone mad lately? Had a business deal go south?"

"Shelton Hotels has been doing great since Nate and I took over and rebranded as an environmentally conscious chain," she said, pacing again, "but we are small potatoes in the hospitality industry. There's no reason for anyone to come after me."

Yet someone had. Twice in one day. He didn't believe for a second that her tumble into the street this morning was unrelated to the break-in at her apartment tonight. Both attacks were personal, if not well executed, which suggested someone close to her was behind them.

"But you can't think of anyone who might be angry with you or want to get back at you for some reason?" he said to Nadia's back.

She stilled, then turned to face him. "One of my exes came to see me today. Not about anything personal, but he definitely wasn't one of the guys chasing me."

"What's his name?"

"Mike Dexter. He's president of Aurora Hotels and Suites. He dropped by my office this morning, but I don't think he would do anything like this." Nadia shook her head in disbelief.

Ryan jotted the name down. He'd check Dexter out thoroughly because, while most people never thought someone they knew would target them, he'd been in the security business long enough to know how wrong they often were.

"Mike and I broke up over a year ago." She opened her eyes and looked at him head-on, considering what to say. "Since Nate's death, I've assumed sole responsibility for the company. I haven't had time for a personal life."

West Security had sent flowers when Nate died, and Ryan had gone to the memorial service. Nadia had been the picture of forbearance and graciousness, consoling Nate's many friends. But beneath it all he'd seen the unbridled grief, and his heart broke for her. He hadn't wanted to impose, so he'd signed the condolence book without adding to the throng of people surrounding her.

"I've noticed you've been putting your own stamp on the hotels. Leaning into the green initiative. Making some changes to the buildings. Have there been any employees unhappy with changes you've been making?"

Nadia smiled wryly. "Our employees loved Nate. Some of them preferred his—" she stopped as if searching for the right word "—looser management style to mine. But I can't see any of them attacking me or breaking into my apartment over it."

It was a long shot, but he'd seen people do a lot of irrational things. He wasn't ready to dismiss any potential suspects without an investigation. He asked Nadia for the names of the employees who'd shown unhappiness with her leadership. After a long moment's hesitation, Nadia gave him two names, both assistant managers at the hotel.

Taking over had to have been difficult for her, if only because she'd been thrust into the role of CEO. She'd had to work through the grief of losing Nate and at the same time keep the family business steady. And she'd done it, to all appearances, without breaking a sweat.

But he knew from experience, appearances could be deceiving.

"How are you coping with Nate's passing?"

Nadia plopped down on the couch, her eyes trained on the floor. "As best can be expected, I guess. It was a car accident, eleven months ago. Some days I forget he's even gone, and then it all comes crashing back."

They sat in silence for a long moment. He wanted to go to her, to pull her to him and promise he'd make everything all right. But she'd wrapped her arms around herself, her gaze still diverted from his.

He had the kitchen send a couple sandwiches back to his office, and he was glad to see some of the color returning to Nadia's face as she ate. Not long after they'd finished their dinner, Shawn and Gideon pushed the office door open, forgoing knocking this time. "We checked out the apartment. It was tossed, but I can't tell if they were just being destructive or if they were looking for something. Found this in the hall."

Shawn held her purse and keys out to her.

"Everything's here," Nadia said, relief clear in her voice. "Credit cards, ID and the little bit of cash I keep for emergencies."

Ryan's frown deepened. "So not a straight-up robbery."

Nadia's face paled, and the way she swayed made

Ryan glad she was sitting. He rose from his chair and moved to sit next to her on the couch.

"I've got this." Ryan nodded toward the door. It was a terse dismissal, but none of West's operatives were the type to get their feelings hurt easily. Shawn and Gideon shuffled through the door without a word.

Nadia held her head in her hands. "I don't understand why this is happening."

Ryan rubbed circles on her back. "I know. But until we figure it out, I don't think you should stay at your apartment."

She swiped away a tear. "I can take a room at Shelton Harlem for the night."

He wasn't sure that was a good idea either. Whoever was behind this knew who she was, and when she didn't come home, it wouldn't be much of a leap to deduce she might be at a Shelton hotel.

Every fiber of his being told him to take her to his home and not let her out until the threat had passed. The small part of his brain still functioning objectively countered that he was too emotionally involved. Still, his place was a lot safer than a hotel or her apartment. He could remain professional to keep an eye on Nadia.

"You can stay with me. If they know where you live, we have to assume they know where you work."

She examined him with wary eyes. "I don't know."

"I have a big place, and you can't get better security anywhere in the city."

A hint of a smile crossed her lips. "That I believe." Her shoulders relaxed, and a genuine smile transformed her face, making it even more gorgeous. "Okay. Thank you."

"Try not to worry. I promise I will keep you safe."

Chapter Four

Before heading to Ryan's apartment, they called the police and walked back to Nadia's condo to report the break-in. The officer taking the report wasn't nearly as concerned as Ryan would have liked. She seemed skeptical that the intruders had been chasing Nadia, preferring the theory that Nadia's sudden appearance caused burglars to flee the scene of the crime to avoid being caught. When Nadia pointed out that the men had followed her to Sentinel, the officer had brushed it off as little more than adrenaline-fueled hysteria.

They couldn't prove the guys that had come into Sentinel after Nadia were the same guys who'd broken into her apartment, so there was nothing else they could do except take the officer's card. Ryan didn't even bother to mention to the disbelieving officer that Nadia had been pushed into the street earlier that morning, and Nadia didn't appear to have connected the two events.

He typically used his ride-sharing app to get around the city on his personal time, but he wasn't taking any chances with Nadia's safety. He'd had a company car dropped off while he and Nadia spoke to the officer, and now he navigated the black SUV west to his Riverside Drive apartment building.

He glanced at Nadia in the seat beside him. Her head

leaned against the window of the SUV, her eyes closed. She looked tired and scared, but she was still the most beautiful woman he'd ever seen. She was luminous. Not for the first time, he considered breaking his rule about not dating Nadia.

WHEN HE LOOKED at her, he saw a curvy, luscious body, full and round in all the right places. A body he wasn't afraid to admit he'd dreamed about holding on more than one lonely night.

Get a grip.

His father, James West Sr., would have a fit if he knew what Ryan was thinking about a client. Shelton Hotels was one of West Security's oldest clients since Nadia's father had signed his first contract with West more than twenty years ago. Back then, his dad had focused primarily on alarms and security cameras for commercial businesses.

Ryan knew his father had hoped that all four of his sons would take over the firm, but James Jr. had decided to pursue a career in the military, and Brandon had earned his law degree. That left Ryan and Shawn, the youngest Wests, to follow in their father's footsteps.

In the years since joining the firm, Ryan and Shawn had expanded the business into a multifaceted, full-service security management firm that handled residential, commercial and personal security needs, as well as investigations of all types for some of the world's most prominent businesses and individuals. They'd also gotten their private investigator licenses and taken on fraud, cyber security and other investigations for their clients.

These days, James Sr. let his sons run the business, preferring the golf course to the office, but he stayed in the loop. More importantly, he held controlling interest and had made it clear that if he thought the boys were on the wrong track with the business, he wouldn't hesitate to take the company away from them. And there was no way their father would see dating the CEO of one of their best clients as anything other than a dumb business move.

Ryan glanced at Nadia again, her chest rising and falling in the steady rhythm of sleep.

He'd keep his hands to himself, but there was no way he'd leave her to deal with whatever this was on her own. Private, round-the-clock security started in the tens of thousands. Shelton Hotels was thriving under Nadia's leadership, but he doubted she'd be able to cover the tab for private security for long. He'd make it work. His brothers wouldn't like working for free, but they'd love having an IOU from him and something to hold over his head.

He turned the SUV into the parking garage under his apartment building. He only lived about a mile from Sentinel, but city traffic was such that even at midnight, a mile drive took longer than he'd like.

He backed the SUV into the space reserved for his unit and shut off the engine.

Nadia didn't stir.

He considered carrying her to his apartment, but after a moment, her eyelids fluttered, and she lifted her head. "I'm sorry. I'm usually better company."

"I'm sure your body needed the rest, with everything you've been through tonight. Come on. I'll show you to the guest room, and you can get some sleep."

He waved a small key fob over the plate built into the elevator control panel, and the button for the penthouse level lit up.

"The penthouse." Nadia's eyebrows ticked up as she smiled. "The security business must pay well."

Embarrassment ticked the back of his neck. West Security was doing well, but that had little to do with where he lived. He'd left the Army and moved back into his childhood bedroom at his father's place. He loved his dad, but that arrangement got old two weeks in. He hadn't cared about the apartment's aesthetics, just that it was his and walking distance from West's Upper West Side offices. He'd given Camille, his brother James's wife and a real estate agent, a budget and his meager must-haves and let her loose apartment shopping. He'd barely looked at the place before signing on the dotted line.

The elevator opened to a stark white hallway with an apartment on either side. Before moving in, he'd run a background check on his would-be neighbor. A pioneer in online gaming, richer than Caesar and a virtual recluse. In the five years he'd lived in the building, they hadn't said more than ten words. The perfect neighbor as far as Ryan was concerned.

The entrance to his apartment contained a small foyer with a long wall blocking the view of most of the apartment.

He tossed his keys into a basket on the table in front of the wall and led Nadia into the main living space. After months of prodding, he'd finally given in to Camille's pressure to let her decorate the living-room space. The outcome was sleek, contemporary furniture with sharp lines and lots of dark leather. Camille conceded to his tastes by artfully arranging a display of art history coffee-table books on the end tables. The overall effect landed nowhere near the rustic feel that he preferred. Since most of his time at home was spent sleeping or watching a game or movie on the big-screen television he'd had installed on the backside of the foyer wall, he hadn't seen the point in paying to have the space redecorated.

Nadia's eyes scanned the large space, and he couldn't help but wonder what the apartment would look like if she lived here. He shook off the thought before it took him to a dangerous place. She was staying with him until he knew she'd be safe, not moving in.

"I'll show you where you'll be sleeping."

He led her past the kitchen area and through the living room to the bedrooms. Despite the generously sized living room and kitchen, there were only two bedrooms, each with its own en suite bathroom and walk-in closet. A king-size mahogany sleigh bed with matching dresser and night tables anchored the room. The claw-foot tub was visible through the cracked bathroom door.

Nadia bit her lip, shifting her weight from one foot to the other. "I hate to bother you for anything else, but I didn't pack any clothes from my place. Can I borrow a T-shirt to sleep in?"

He shook his head, annoyed with himself for not thinking to have her pack a bag. Nadia wasn't the only one who needed to get some rest. "Of course."

Crossing the hall, he pulled a Knicks T-shirt from his bureau and a pair of socks. There was no way she'd fit into his sweats, but the shirt and socks should do for one night.

"We'll figure out the clothes situation tomorrow," he said, handing her the shirt.

"I'll be able to go back to my apartment by then, right?"

If he was right about the events of today being connected, Nadia's pursuers were persistent and determined. That didn't bode well for her being able to go back to life as usual anytime soon. He wouldn't lie to her, but it was late, and they both needed to rest if they wanted to deal with the situation with a clear head in the morning.

Before common sense could stop him, he ran his hand gently down the side of her face. "I don't know, sweetheart, but we'll do our best to get you back in your place as soon as it's safe."

He slid his arm around her waist and tugged her against him.

Nadia peered up at him with wide eyes. He could close the gap between them, just duck his head down and let his lips graze hers. Would she welcome him or think he was hitting on her?

Just the idea that she might think he was taking advantage had him stepping back, his hands falling to his side.

"If you need anything, I'll be right across the hall."

He strode to his bedroom, closing the door firmly behind him and leaning against it.

What was he thinking? She was a client, a client in danger no less. He'd brought her here to keep her safe, not to hit on her. Not only was his behavior totally unprofessional but he didn't take advantage of vulnerable women. He was not that guy.

He pushed off the door and crossed to the king-size poster bed that ate up most of the bedroom. He sat with his back against his headboard and opened his laptop. Shawn had forwarded the information on the owner of the stolen SUV Nadia's pursuers might be driving. The owner, a forty-three-year-old dentist and father of four, had no criminal record and no connection to Nadia or Shelton Hotels that Shawn could find.

He clicked to a second email, this one from Gideon. Still shots from the camera in Sentinel earlier that evening. They had a good shot of the man that had come in through the front door and a not-too-good one of the man that had come through the back. He'd get someone on upgrading those cameras. Gideon's email was one line. *Working on identifications.*

Good. The faster they found out who these guys were, the faster they'd sort this out.

Ryan opened a second email from Shawn. This one contained attachments with background on Nadia and Nathan Shelton.

West routinely conducted background checks on the principals of the companies they worked for. Even though he'd ordered thousands of reports over the years, for the first time he felt uncomfortable reading one, as though he was snooping into Nadia's life.

He pushed the feeling away and scanned the report.

Nadia's father, Calvin Shelton, had worked his way up from porter to general manager at a now-defunct downtown hotel. In the mid-1970s, Calvin purchased the Harlem property that would become the flagship of his small hotel chain.

A marriage in Calvin's fifties produced Nathan and Nadia before his much-younger wife succumbed to cancer. He ran the hotels until his death six years ago. After Calvin's death, Nadia and Nathan took over management of the company. Eleven months ago, at thirty-five years old, Nadia became the sole owner of Shelton Hotels when Nathan perished in a car accident while vacationing in Maine.

Nadia had graduated from State University with a degree in architecture, which explained the pictures of famous bridges gracing her office walls. She'd also received a certificate in business administration, confirming what he already knew. She was way too smart to be dating him.

His cell phone rang beside him.

"How's it going?" Shawn asked without preamble.

"All's quiet here. Nadia's gone to bed."

"You in there with her?"

"Don't be a jerk."

"Gimme a break, bro. You've had a thing for Nadia Shelton for, like, a year. Now, she's sleeping in your guest room, and you want to tell me you haven't thought about joining her?"

"I do not have a thing for Nadia Shelton." Ryan ignored the memories of almost kissing her that pushed their way into his head. "The woman is in trouble. I'm doing my job."

"Yeah, right." Shawn's guffaw was clear through the phone.

"Did you call to annoy me?"

"No, that was just for fun. Did you get my emails?"

"Looking at them now."

The clicking sound of keys being tapped sounded on Shawn's end of the line. "Sent you a video from Sentinel."

Ryan clicked on Shawn's email. A shot of a tall, well-muscled man, with dark facial hair covering the bottom of his face, filled the computer screen. He watched as the man scanned the crowd looking for someone.

"The second guy came in the back like she said, but it's not a good shot," Shawn said.

"We need to—"

"I know. Already got a man upgrading the camera. In any event, I didn't recognize the guy we can see clearly. I'll send the shot around the office tomorrow to see if anyone else can get us a name."

"Skip to the stuff about Nathan Shelton."

Ryan opened Nate's background check. Four years Nadia's senior, Nate had graduated from State with a business and finance degree. Despite never marrying,

Nate, a rich, good-looking hotelier, had been part of several high-profile, short-term relationships, although he appeared to be unattached at the time of his death. His background check showed a misdemeanor arrest for marijuana possession and an arrest for assault stemming from a bar fight, both from his early twenties. In both cases, the police dropped the charges before trial.

"A couple of arrests twenty years ago. But nothing that would explain what's happening now," Ryan said.

"Keep reading. Miss Shelton's brother liked to keep company with some bad dudes."

The report on Nate was thorough and included information on Nate's close associates, several of whom dabbled in drugs, guns and money laundering, although there was no indication Nate himself had been involved in illegal stuff.

"Notice who's in the picture I included in the report," Shawn said.

Ryan scanned the high-resolution pictures included in the report. Five men stood shoulder to shoulder outside what looked like a nightclub. The report identified each of the men, but Ryan was most interested in the man standing next to Nate. Brian Leroy.

"Nate and Brian Leroy look chummy," Ryan said.

Leroy styled himself as a small-business investor. In reality, the money he invested came from the mob. The owners of the companies that Leroy invested in soon found themselves with less and less control. The few that resisted retirement were met with unexplainable accidents, leaving them unable to work. Or worse.

"It's a place to start. If Shelton hung out with Leroy, there's no telling what he could have been involved in." Shawn paused. "There's no indication that Nadia knows Leroy, but you should find out if she recognizes him."

Ryan fought the urge to bite Shawn's head off. He didn't believe for a millisecond Nadia would get tangled up with the likes of Leroy. But he wouldn't be doing his job if he didn't follow up as Shawn suggested. Even if she wasn't doing business with Leroy, she may have seen him with Nate and know whether the two men had business dealings with each other.

"I'll take care of it," Ryan said. "In the meantime, can you dig up everything you can on Mike Dexter? And do you think you can work your magic and get me the police report on Nathan Shelton's death?"

"Anything else I can get for you while I'm waving my magic wand?" Shawn drawled.

"That's it for now," Ryan shot back.

"I'll see what I can do. No promises. Why do you want the police report, anyway?"

"Just covering all the bases."

Ryan ended the call and opened a browser window. West paid for several of the top-of-the-line background information programs, but it still paid to do a run-of-the-mill internet search. If people really understood how much of their personal information floated around on the World Wide Web, they'd never touch a computer again.

A search for Nathan's name produced more links than Ryan could read. He scrolled through the list reading the headlines announcing various charity functions and events Nathan had appeared at and donations from Shelton Hotels. It was obvious Nathan enjoyed being the face of Shelton Hotels. There were no hints of Nate being involved in criminality and no other pictures of him with Leroy. But there were a handful of articles about Nate's death. Ryan clicked on one.

While vacationing in Maine, Nathan Shelton's car had plunged off the side of a cliff. The police attributed the accident to driver error, but since the authorities believed Nate's body had washed out to sea, they hadn't been able to confirm. There was a string of related articles linked at the end, most of them about Nate's active social life.

One article caught Ryan's eye. Nadia's engagement announcement. Two and a half years ago Nadia had promised to marry Dr. Wallace Hardee.

A search for Hardee turned up the same engagement announcement and an article about Hardee's work at Mount Sinai's pediatric unit.

A doctor. He seemed like exactly the type of man a woman like Nadia should be with. So why had they split up?

He closed the laptop and tossed it on the bed before striding to the bathroom. He braced his hands on the granite vanity, staring at his reflection.

He'd been close to kissing Nadia, too close. She was a client, not to mention way out of the league of a junior-college dropout. He had to remember that and keep his hands to himself.

There was no question Nadia would be safe from the goons after her as long as she remained with him.

But would his heart be safe from her?

IT TOOK SOME time to fall asleep. When she finally drifted off, she was plagued with dreams of being chased by large, menacing men. A meaty hand had just wrapped itself around her arm when the distant sound of a phone ringing pulled her from the nightmare.

Nadia dragged herself out of bed and into the bathroom. Her reflection was a nightmare of a different sort. Without her sleeping bonnet to protect them, her curls had tangled into a rat's nest. Dark circles loitered under her eyes, and her mouth was as dry as cotton. There was

only so much she could do without her usual accoutre-
ments, but a hot shower would go a long way. A shelv-
ing unit built into the white-marble vanity held towels,
a basket of unopened toiletries and a comb that she used
to tame her wild mane.

She turned on the shower and shed her T-shirt. Multiple shower jets, including a rain showerhead, pummeled
her tired body.

By the time she finished, she felt human again. She
needed a cup of coffee and something to quell her growl-
ing stomach, but then she planned to put her mind to figuring out who was after her and why.

She put on her suit from the day before and padded
down the hallway. The scent of brewing coffee and cin-
namon hit her as she rounded the wall separating the
kitchen from the bedrooms.

Her stomach did a flip that had nothing to do with
hunger. Ryan stood over the stove, a tight black shirt ac-
centuating massive biceps and jeans cradling a behind
that could have been sculpted by Michelangelo.

Ryan looked up from the griddle where French toast
sizzled. His eyes stroked her from head to toe, heating every inch of her body. If she didn't know what she
looked like, she might have thought the look in his eyes
was desire.

"Coffee?" Ryan's husky timber shot through her.

"Yes, please." She ripped her gaze away and headed
for the coffee maker.

Coffee in hand, Nadia slid into a chair in the breakfast
nook next to the kitchen. She'd barely noticed the apartment the night before, but now she took in the stunning
view of the Hudson River from the large window. The
apartment was an open floor plan with a large island de-

lineating the kitchen from a sunken living room with its own equally stunning views of the city.

Ryan laid a plate in front of her with triangles of French toast sprinkled with powdered sugar and garnished with fresh melon. He went to the fridge and returned with a jar of maple syrup and his own plate.

She dug in.

"This is great. Where'd you learn to cook?"

Ryan sat across the table. "My mom passed when I was eighteen. My older brothers were off in the military and away at college. Dad worked a lot, so I left school to take care of my younger brother."

"I'm sorry about your mother. And that you had to leave school."

He chuckled. "I did more partying than learning, anyway."

Nadia laughed along with him. "What did you study?"

"Art history."

She raised an eyebrow. "Really."

"Really. When I was a kid, my class took a field trip to the Metropolitan Museum of Art. You know how people say you can go anywhere by reading a book?"

She nodded, taking a sip of her coffee.

"It's the same with art. After I dropped out of school, I got a part-time job with the security company that supplied the guards. Walking those halls sure is something. Almost like being transported to the past."

"I can tell how much you love it. But why choose to work for a security company that wasn't West?"

Ryan paused, his fork suspended halfway between his plate and his mouth. He frowned.

"Sorry. It's none of my business."

"My dad and I didn't always have the relationship we

have now. Losing my mother was…well, let's just say it was better that we didn't work together at the time."

"It must have been hard for you to lose your mother at such a young age."

He stared at her, sparking butterflies in her stomach. "It's always hard to lose a loved one."

A familiar pang sang in her heart. She waited until he finished chewing the bite of food he'd just put in his mouth. "I never thanked you for attending Nate's memorial."

Surprise registered on his face.

"You didn't think I noticed you there?" There was no way Ryan West could be in a room and not be noticed by every woman there, but it was endearing that he seemed to have no clue about his draw.

"There were so many people wanting to pay their respects. I didn't want to add to your load."

"You couldn't have."

Their gazes connected. His eyes held hers, not allowing her to look away. Not that she wanted to. Her heart pounded as if she'd just skied Whiteface Mountain, and there was no doubt in her mind that he knew the effect he had on her.

Ryan's phone beeped, and he pulled his eyes from hers.

She couldn't tell if the message was good or bad from his expression, but she was unprepared for his next question.

"What can you tell me about Dr. Wallace Hardee?"

"I… What?" She pressed a hand to her chest as much to quell the beating of her heart as in surprise. "Why are you asking about him?"

She hadn't spoken to Wallace in nearly two years—nor did she ever want to again.

"You were engaged to him?" Ryan's gaze searched hers.

"Yes, but that was a long time ago." She looked away.

She wasn't trying to hide anything from Ryan, but her relationship with Wallace was a source of humiliation she hadn't totally come to terms with yet. It wasn't as if she'd been a doe-eyed twentysomething when they'd dated. She should have seen the signs he was nothing more than a manipulative gold digger.

"Sometimes anger takes time to build to a place where it gives people the courage to act," Ryan said.

"You don't think Wallace…" She shook her head, her curls bouncing. "No way. I can say without a doubt Wallace doesn't care enough about me to do this."

The raw truth of the statement still stung.

"I want to check him out, anyway. Just to make sure," Ryan said.

Nadia exhaled. "I thought I was in love with Wallace when I accepted his proposal, and I thought he loved me." Bitterness imbued her words. "It took me longer than it should have to realize he only cared about the size of my bank account."

Wallace hadn't even cared enough to call or send his condolences when Nate died. In more than one way she was better off having broken up with him before they'd progressed down the aisle.

"He's an idiot."

She smiled wryly. "I agree."

Ryan's eyes locked into hers again. "You deserve a man so in love with you he burns with it. Who can't make it through a single day without seeing your face. Kissing your lips. Taking you to his bed. Dr. Wally was the luckiest man on earth and too stupid to know it."

Once again his gaze held hers as if it was magnetized. She was pretty sure she'd stopped breathing and would embarrass herself in front of him for the second time in as many days by passing out at any moment.

Thankfully, she was saved by a beep.

Ryan glanced at his phone and typed out a short message. "I need to clean up."

"Right," she said focusing on the remnants of her breakfast until her heart rate slowed. "If you don't mind, could you drop me off by my place? I need to change before I go to the hotel."

His body tensed. "I'll go with you."

"I really do appreciate your concern and letting me stay here, but I'm sure it's safe enough for me to go back to my apartment now." And she needed some time away from him.

Ryan lowered his phone to the table. "I put a couple of men on your apartment last night."

"What do you mean you put men on my apartment?" She sat her coffee cup back on the table with a thunk.

"I was concerned those guys might come back, so I had two of my operatives stake out the building. I wasn't wrong to be concerned."

Fear flowed through her. "They came back." The words were barely more than a whisper.

"They didn't go in. A police cruiser drove by and scared them off. Unfortunately, my men couldn't grab them."

Nadia wrapped shaky hands around her mug, grateful for the warm porcelain against her suddenly ice-cold palms.

"We can pick up some of your things, but I'm not sure it would be safe for you to stay at your apartment until we know more about who's after you. You should also consider avoiding the Shelton hotels."

Nadia shook her head. "I can't do that. We have a

conference booked next week at the Harlem property and three weddings this weekend at the Lower East Side property."

The lines on Ryan's forehead deepened along with the frown on his face. "Couldn't one of your managers handle it?"

She had a great team of people working with her, but she was the CEO of Shelton Hotels. "People depend on me. I have to go to work."

"I'm not suggesting you hide, just that you not take unnecessary risks. Anyone looking for you is going to start at your apartment and the Shelton hotels."

She couldn't hide away indefinitely. Still, she wouldn't dismiss the potential danger she faced.

She drained the last of her coffee. "I'll avoid my apartment and consider whatever you suggest to ensure my safety, within reason."

"*Within reason* meaning you need to go to work?"

She nodded. "Exactly."

Ryan let out a heavy breath and stood. "I can work with that. Let's finish up here and get to your place. I already cleared my day so I could stick with you."

Chapter Five

Ryan spent the ride to Nadia's condo on the phone arranging for increased security at the Shelton hotels, grateful to have something to do that would keep him from focusing on his almost kiss with Nadia. He'd been attracted to her for months. But hearing how strong she'd been in the face of Dr. Wally's betrayal and Nate's death had shown him a whole new side of her. One he liked. He could fall hard for her if he wasn't careful.

He shouldn't have said those things about kissing her, but he'd been dreaming about kissing her since the first time he'd laid eyes on her. As good as those dreams were, they didn't come close to the real thing. She'd felt so good in his arms. Better than good. It felt like she belonged in his arms.

He slowed the SUV to a stop in front of Nadia's apartment building. He'd had men waiting for them there, so Gideon slid up to the passenger door as soon as Ryan turned off the engine and helped Nadia out of the vehicle. He didn't think it would take too long for her to pack a bag, but he'd rather be safe than sorry.

Dale Jackson, another of West's operatives, slid into the driver's seat as Ryan hopped out, assuming the double duty of staying with the car and keeping an eye out for trouble outside the building. Ryan jogged to catch up to Gideon and Nadia as she unlocked the front door of the building.

Gideon stepped in first and conducted a quick sweep of the small lobby and mail alcove while Ryan and Nadia hung near the door. "All clear."

"This seems a bit excessive," Nadia grumbled as they strode to the elevator.

"Humor me."

Nadia lived in an older, renovated building with four apartments to each floor. The background check he'd pulled on Nadia last night showed she'd purchased the apartment four years ago.

They exited the elevator on the fourth floor.

Ryan grasped Nadia's shoulders, moving her to the side before she could unlock the door. "Let Gideon go in first."

She frowned but didn't argue.

Ryan took her keys from her hand and slid them in the lock. He glanced at Gideon, who held his gun out and at the ready. On Gideon's signal, Ryan pushed open the door. Gideon was inside for several moments before a sharp *Clear* sounded from inside.

Knickknacks, shattered glass and shredded stuffing from the sofa covered the wood flooring. Loose pages from a book scattered about. A general sense of destruction permeated the space.

Gideon stepped back into the hall as Nadia crossed the living room and picked up a picture frame from the floor. A quiet whimper escaped her lips.

Ryan stepped beside her. "Are you okay?"

She looked at him with glassy eyes. "I didn't expect it to look so bad."

Ryan wrapped his arm around her shoulders, and after

a brief hesitation, she leaned in to his side. "Why don't you go change and pack a bag."

"A bag? Why?" Nadia lifted her head from his shoulder and looked up at him.

"You can stay at my place until we figure this out."

Nadia eased from his grasp. "I don't know."

"You said you'd follow my lead." He quirked an eyebrow. "Staying at my place, in the guest room, is within reason."

She held his gaze for several long moments before nodding. "There's something else I remembered when we walked in here. I've been getting hang-up calls, and last week someone keyed my car."

"You have a car?"

"I keep it in the garage next door. I don't use it often, but it's useful if I want to get away for a few days." She shrugged. "That's not really the worst of it. Two nights ago I came home to find a mutilated rat on the fire escape outside my bedroom window. I tried convincing myself the neighbor's cat left it, but…"

"Now you're not so sure."

While she packed, he surveyed the damage. Nadia's apartment was an open floor plan, but on a smaller scale than his own home. The kitchen cabinets hung open, the cabinets, drawers and their contents strewn about the kitchen. Ryan lifted a dining chair only to realize one of its legs was broken. He walked through the space, trying to make sense of what they knew so far. Why push Nadia in front of traffic, then break into her apartment, seemingly in an attempt to kidnap her? Was she in possession of something someone wanted, or did they want Nadia herself?

"Ryan," Nadia called from down the hall.

He found her in a small second bedroom that doubled

as an office. It looked much like the rest of the house, with papers, books and files tossed haphazardly about the room.

"My computer is missing." Nadia pointed to the white architect-style desk. The power cord remained plugged into the wall behind the desk, but there was no computer at its other end.

"Have you noticed anything else missing?" He took her black travel bag from her hand and hooked it over his shoulder.

She shook her head, sending the loose curls at her shoulder bouncing. "It's hard to tell with all the destruction. If anything else is missing, it's not obvious."

"Anything on that computer worth attempted kidnapping or breaking-and-entering charges?"

"The company's files are kept on a secure server, and I use two-step authentication for all my personal information." She exhaled a sigh laced with exhaustion despite the time of day. "I'll change my passwords when I get to the office, but I doubt anyone could get much information."

Nadia's phone rang. She tugged it from her handbag and connected the call. The color drained from her face as the person on the other end of the line spoke. Nadia sprinted for the front door, the phone still at her ear.

Ryan followed, seizing her arm to stop her from barreling into the hallway. "What is it? What's wrong?"

Nadia pulled her arm from his hand, wrenching the door open with her free hand before turning back to him. "My hotel is on fire."

NADIA ENTERED THE hotel lobby at a run, Ryan at her side.

Olivia stepped away from the two men she'd been talking to when she spotted Nadia coming through the hotel entrance. "Everything's under control. The fire is out, and we evacuated the second floor just to be safe."

Nadia expelled a breath as the claw of tension gripping her neck and shoulders released. No one had been hurt. Insurance would cover any damages.

"Miss Shelton?" The taller of the two men stepped up. "I'm Detective John Parsmons. This is Gene Gould, Fire Inspector." Detective Parsmons gestured to the man that had walked over with him. "The fire has been extinguished, but we will need to cordon off the affected section of the second floor until we complete our investigation."

"Investigation?" Just like that, the claw gripped her shoulders again.

"Yes, ma'am. Unfortunately, it looks like the fire was purposely set in a trash can in the room."

Nadia gaped at the inspector.

"What about the people checked into that room?" Ryan asked.

Olivia shook her head. "That room is vacant."

"Vacant?" Nadia turned her attention to Olivia. "Then, how did anyone get in?"

"The log shows the door opened at 8:43 this morning," Olivia said.

"With whose key card?" Nadia asked, confused.

"No one's," Olivia answered. "That is, the door was opened with a guest key card, but our records don't show a card having been created for that room."

"We'll be investigating all that." Inspector Gould waved away Olivia's words, clearly irritated by the discussion. "Luckily, the people staying in the room next door smelled the smoke rather quickly, and you have a top-notch sprinkler system. The damage is mostly due to water and smoke and is contained to the one room."

Nadia knew the inspector meant well, but she wasn't feeling lucky at the moment. She was thankful no one was injured, but a fire in her hotel, one that may have been purposely started, was not good by any means.

Gould and Parsmons returned to the damaged hotel room. Nadia, Ryan and Olivia headed through the door behind the check-in desk. Nadia headed up the trio through a short hall leading to a small suite of offices where she, Olivia and the hotel department managers worked.

"How many rooms are in the section that the fire department has put off-limits?" Nadia asked.

Olivia sat behind the desk positioned in front of Nadia's closed office door. "Four, but only two were occupied. I've moved those guests to rooms on the fifth floor."

"Great." Nadia chewed her bottom lip. "The first guests for the photography conference will be checking in on Monday. They've pretty much booked every standard room we have. We'll have to move some guests to suites, assuming they aren't all booked too."

"I'll look into it." Olivia spun her chair, so she faced her computer monitor and began tapping away.

"I'll be back." Nadia headed back the way they'd come.

Ryan fell in step next to her. "Where are we going?"

"I need to see the damage."

Ryan put a hand on her arm, stopping her before she could enter the lobby. "It might not be safe yet."

She pressed her lips together, shaking free of Ryan's grip. "I'll be careful, but this is my hotel. I need to know what happened in that room." She was responsible for the hotel, its guests and her employees, and she would make sure they were safe.

He opened his mouth, but she didn't wait to hear what he would say.

Turning, she pushed through the door and into the hotel lobby. She picked up a master key from the front desk, then headed for the elevators, Ryan dogging her heels. With the fire contained to a single room on the opposite end of the floor from the elevator banks, there'd been no need to keep the elevators shut down.

As an enterprising businessman, her father had undertaken a major renovation of the hotel fifteen years prior. Each of the seven floors had been separated into five wings with fire doors between each wing. That, plus the fact that the affected room was at the back of the floor, would make it easier to keep nosy guests from sneaking a peek and getting hurt.

The scent of smoke and burned synthetic materials teased them as they exited the elevator, and it intensified as they neared room 232. Other than her heels squishing into the damp carpet, everything appeared normal from the hall.

She couldn't say the same when she opened the door to the room. "Oh, no."

The inspector said the fire had started in a trash can, but it had quickly claimed the once floor-length curtains which now hung unevenly from a nearby rod. Black marks climbed the wall to one side of the window, and the concrete flooring was exposed where the fire had eaten away at the carpeting.

Detective Parsmons's head snapped up. He pointed the pen he'd been using to scribble notes at them. "Hey, you aren't supposed to be up here."

Nadia squared her shoulders, ignoring the detective. "Have you found any sign of who could have done this?"

"Miss Shelton, we are just beginning the investigation." Detective Parsmons sighed. "Since you're here, are you sure no one checked into this room?"

She narrowed her eyes at the detective. "If Olivia said no one checked into this room, no one checked in."

Parsmons studied her without expression for a long moment. Guilt nibbled at her. The detective was just doing his job; she had no right to take her frustration out on him.

Softening her tone, she added, "I can double-check for you, though."

Parsmons gave her a brisk nod. "Please do."

"Why do you ask?" Ryan said.

Parsmons pointed toward the credenza in the room with the hand holding his small notebook. "There are ashes in a glass over there."

"It's illegal to smoke anywhere in the hotel," Nadia said, the words sounding inane to her ears as she said them. Guests did all sorts of things that weren't permitted by law or hotel policy, smoking the least of them.

"Someone didn't get that message. Look, it's probably just a maid sneaking a puff. Maybe they dropped some ashes in the trash and *poof.*" Parsmons raised his hands in demonstration of the fire igniting.

Nadia shook her head. "No Shelton employee would smoke in a guest room."

Parsmons shot her a dubious look but didn't press the matter.

"The fire isn't the only strange thing to have happened to Miss Shelton recently." Ryan eyed the detective.

"Oh?"

Nadia shot Ryan a look that he ignored as he continued to fill Parsmons in on the break-in at her apartment and her tumble into the street.

Parsmons scratched the back of his neck with the pen. "Well, I'll pull the report on the break-in, but I don't see how any of that is connected to the fire."

Ryan's lips twisted into a scowl. "You think it's a co-incidence Miss Shelton's apartment was broken into last night, and this morning a room in her hotel was set on fire?"

Parsmons shrugged. "You want me to tell you how many break-ins there were in this city last night? Coincidences do happen."

Ryan's scowl deepened. It was clear he didn't think much of the detective, and Nadia didn't disagree with his assessment. Parsmons seemed ready to blame her hotel staff for the fire, which would no doubt rebound negatively with guests, the media and her insurance company. An insurance company she still needed to inform about the fire, preferably before the detective could poison the well there.

Nadia massaged her temples. "I have work to do."

"We may need to speak with some of your employees," Detective Parsmons said as she and Ryan made for the door.

She turned back to face him. Making an effort to keep the annoyance out of her voice, she said, "Of course. The entire company stands ready to help with whatever you need to complete the investigation."

Olivia's desk was empty when they returned to the office suite. A manila envelope lay on the floor just beyond the door.

Nadia picked it up, her brow furrowing.

"What is it?" Ryan asked.

"Just mail. Olivia usually handles it, but she'll put anything I need to deal with in my inbox."

Ryan took the envelope from her using two fingers. "There's no return address or postage. And I'm guessing Olivia has a key to your office and doesn't need to shove mail under your door."

A weight landed on Nadia's chest at the concern etched across Ryan's face. "She has a key."

"Can I open this?" Ryan asked.

Nadia nodded, her gaze trained on the envelope as if it was a snake readying to strike. Stories about airborne toxins and letter bombs flitted through her mind, but she batted them away.

Ryan grabbed a letter opener and slit open the envelope. A single sheet of paper fluttered onto the desktop where they could both read it.

WHERE IS NATE?

Chapter Six

"This has to be a cruel joke." Nadia looked from the note to Ryan.

Cruel for sure, but his gut told him it was no joke.

"What's a cruel joke?" An older man with a paunch hanging over the waistline of his tailored suit trousers strode into the office.

Nadia turned, and after a beat, her mouth turned up into a tight smile. "Uncle Erik, what are you doing here?"

The man stopped in front of Nadia and raised an eyebrow. "Even though I had to hear about the fire through secondhand sources, I came to see if I could help."

Nadia stiffened. "Things have been hectic here, as you might expect."

Erik's gaze landed on Ryan. "Who are you?"

"This is Ryan West. He handles the hotels' security," Nadia said, her tone strained.

Recognition flickered in Erik's eyes. "West. Yes, I remember now."

"Uncle Erik's accounting firm handles the hotels' books."

Erik pointed to Nadia's desk. "What's that?"

Ryan's gaze flicked to Nadia in time to see her grit her teeth before responding to her uncle. "We're not sure. Probably a prank."

Erik reached for the letter.

"Sir, it's better if you don't touch it." Ryan seized the man's hand before he touched the paper.

Erik shook his hand loose with a glare. "Nate's gone. Why would anyone ask for him?"

Ryan wasn't sure it was a good idea for Nadia to share all that had happened to her over the last twenty-four hours, even with family. Whoever was behind these attacks had gotten into Nadia's home and an unoccupied room in the hotel without raising suspicions. That made everyone close to her a suspect.

Unfortunately, there wasn't time to convey his concerns to Nadia. Instead, he cataloged Erik's reaction as Nadia explained the events of the last day and a half to her uncle. It sounded like something out of a movie—she was pushed in front of the car, chased from her home, forced to face a fire at her workplace and received an ominous and confusing note all in less than thirty-six hours.

Her uncle's expression moved from shock to anger as Nadia finished her recitation.

"I knew this company was too much for you to handle alone," Erik sputtered before squaring off in front of Ryan. "What are you doing to ensure my niece's safety?"

Ryan eyed the older man. Had he been anyone other than Nadia's uncle, he'd have frog-marched him from her office, and they'd have had a long chat about how to speak to a lady.

Possibly sensing the potential for the conversation to head into dangerous territory, Nadia stepped between Ryan and her uncle. "West provides for the hotels' security system, not for my personal security."

"I'll be providing Nadia with personal security until we know what's going on," Ryan said.

Erik held Ryan's gaze, his eyes glittering with anger, along with something else Ryan couldn't name.

"Uncle Erik, do you have any idea why anyone would send me a letter asking for Nate almost a year after his death?"

Erik shuffled his feet and took a step backward. "Of course not. Why would I?"

Nadia took her uncle's hand. "You and Nate were always so close. I thought you might have an idea what all this is about. Was Nate involved in something I should know about?"

Erik's back straightened. He shook off Nadia's hand. "Nate was a brilliant businessman. He'd never be involved with thieves and arsonists. I can't believe you'd suggest otherwise."

Nadia stepped away from her uncle. "I'm not suggesting anything."

"Well, I will not stand here and listen to you disparage your brother." He turned and marched from the office.

"Uncle Erik!"

Erik didn't stop or respond to Nadia's call.

Nadia turned back to Ryan.

Ryan quirked an eyebrow. "Is he always so protective of Nate?"

She massaged her temple. He fought the sudden desire to replace her hands with his lips, soothing away the headache forming behind her eyes.

"Yes. Don't mind Uncle Erik. He's still grieving for Nate. We both are." Nadia eyed the letter on her desk, then moved to the small round conference table in the office's corner.

Ryan wasn't sure Erik's reaction was solely based on grief. Either way, someone believed Nathan Shelton was alive, and he was determined to find out who.

RYAN LEFT TO give the note to Detective Parsmons, but not before making a photocopy and making Nadia promise she wouldn't leave her office before he got back.

Moments after he left, Olivia entered and sat across from Nadia.

"I was able to move the conference-goers we'd planned to assign to these rooms on Monday to another part of the hotel. Can you believe this?" Olivia threw her hands in the air. "Even after the police release the room, it will take weeks before we can use it."

Nadia tapped the pen in her hand against the blotter on her desktop. "I know, but we'll manage. The fire isn't all we have to worry about."

She filled Olivia in on the break-in at her apartment the night before and the note asking about Nate.

Olivia stared, her hand covering her mouth, for several long moments. "This is wild. Is that why Ryan West is here?"

"Yes. He thinks the events are connected and I need protection."

"Does that include what happened yesterday morning?" Olivia said. "I overheard you say you were pushed into that street."

Nadia stilled. "I hadn't thought about it. Yesterday seems like a lifetime ago."

Olivia tilted her head. "It's nice of Ryan to see to your security himself."

Nadia narrowed her eyes at her assistant and friend. "He's just doing his job."

"But you stayed at his place last night?" Olivia shot her a devilish smile.

"Because mine wasn't safe," Nadia shot back. She kept her eyes cast down at the paperwork on her desk, but she could feel her friend smirking. "Don't we have some work to do?"

A knocked pulled their attention to the office door.

Mike stood in the doorway in a gray slim-cut suit that seemed to be in fashion these days. His eyes swept over Olivia from head to toe in blatant assessment.

Olivia's eyes narrowed to slits, her lips curving downward into a frown.

Mike finally turned to focus on Nadia. "I thought I'd drop by and see if you'd thought about my offer."

Olivia shot a questioning look at Nadia.

"And I thought I was clear. I will not sell Shelton Hotels."

"Come on, Nadia. I know your margins are razor-thin. Transforming yourself into an eco-friendly hotel was a good idea, but you don't have the financial heft to pull it off alone in the long run. You need Aurora's backing."

"I don't know what you think you know," Nadia said, "but Shelton is doing just fine. I neither need nor want Aurora's help."

"Fine?" Mike's tone was incredulous. "You can't even keep your staff from setting the place on fire."

Nadia's hands balled into fists at her side. "I don't know where you're getting your information, but the fire was not started by a Shelton employee."

"That's not the word on the street," Mike said.

"Well, I'm here running a business, so I don't have as much time to walk the streets as you obviously do," Nadia spat.

Olivia stifled a laugh.

Mike's eyes darkened. "I'd be very careful, Miss Bennett. I'll be your employer soon."

Olivia's mouth fell open.

Nadia's temper snapped. He'd made his offer, and

she'd rejected it. Even if Shelton was in trouble, there was no way on earth she'd sell to Aurora. She'd let her company go bankrupt before she'd let Mike get his hands on her father's legacy.

She stalked across her small office, squaring off in front of Mike. "Get out. And don't come back. Shelton's not for sale."

"You know I never thought you were particularly pretty, but you're actually pretty hot when you get worked up." Mike reached out and caressed Nadia's cheek with his thumb.

Nadia pushed his hand away. "Olivia, call security."

Olivia hurried from the office, leaving the office door wide-open.

If Mike worried about being physically ejected from the hotel, he didn't show it. His presence irritated her, but she couldn't let him know that. He'd use any perceived weakness against her.

Mike leaned in so there was nothing but a sliver of space between them.

She fought the instinct to lean away.

"You know, Nadia, I wouldn't mind seeing you worked up in other contexts. Just because we don't like each other doesn't mean we couldn't enjoy each other. It might even convince you to see reason on this sale."

Mike grabbed her arm and pulled her to him in a quick, practiced move. His lips crashed down on hers, demanding and without an ounce of seduction. He may be used to women who were okay with being manhandled, but she wasn't one of them.

Nadia bought the spike of her heel down on his foot while pushing on his chest with her free hand.

Mike jerked backward, his face twisted in pain, then morphing into surprise.

For a moment, Nadia thought her obvious unwillingness to participate in the kiss had caused Mike to back away. She stepped away from Mike in time to see Ryan spin him around and land a punch to his jaw that sent Mike careering into her desk.

Olivia yelped, moving from her place at the door as Mike pushed off the desk and stumbled toward the exit.

Ryan advanced on Mike with eyes darkened by the fury raging across his face.

"Ryan, no." Nadia grabbed his arm, stopping him from hitting Mike a second time, even though a large part of her supported the effort.

"Who is this barbarian?" Mike yelled. "I want him fired. Now!"

"That's not going to happen. I'm in charge here. I asked you to leave, and you not only didn't leave, you assaulted me. Now, get out before I have you arrested."

Mike swiped a handkerchief over his bleeding lip. "This isn't over, Nadia."

Ryan growled. "Get out of here."

"Not over by a long shot," Mike said, shooting a venomous look at Ryan and Nadia before heading out the door.

"Oh, my gosh. Are you okay?" Olivia rushed to Nadia's side.

The spot on her arm where Mike had grabbed her burned from the intensity of his grip. Ryan's temper looked to be on the edge of detonating, so she kept that information to herself. No permanent damage was done. At least not physically. Mike was not a man that liked to be challenged, especially by someone he didn't consider his equal. If he was determined to purchase Shelton Hotels before this, he'd be obsessive about it now.

"Are you okay?" Ryan's eyes probed hers.

"Yes, yes. I'm fine," Nadia said waving them both off.

"You should call the police and press charges for assault," Ryan said, refusing to be put off.

Nadia rubbed at the headache growing behind her temples. Any other time, she'd do just that, but there were other considerations. An allegation against Mike would bring the press to her door, and with everything else she had going on at the moment, that was the last thing she wanted.

Ryan's expression said he didn't believe it.

"What was all that stuff about? He's going to be my boss?" Olivia asked.

Nadia sighed. She hadn't planned to tell anyone about Aurora's offer. Since there was no way she'd accept it, there wasn't any need to worry the staff. Now, it seemed Mike's visit would make that impossible.

"Nothing. Aurora Hotels has made an offer, which I have rejected. Shelton is not for sale at any price, but Mike thinks he can change my mind." Nadia held up a hand to stop Olivia from speaking. "He's wrong. I will never sell Shelton. I don't want to start a panic among the staff, so Aurora's offer does not leave this office. Got it?"

Nadia looked from Ryan to Olivia. Both nodded their understanding. "Great. We have work to do. Let's get to it."

Olivia left, and Nadia moved behind her desk. Ryan sat at the table on the far side of the office, watching her with an unreadable expression.

"What?" Nadia finally asked on a sigh.

"How did an offer to buy Shelton Hotels end up with the president of Aurora Hotels forcing himself on you?" Ryan asked icily.

She wasn't surprised that Ryan knew who Mike was. There were good reasons West was one of the best. Still, the rancor in his tone shocked her. "That's a bit strong. Mike and I dated briefly. The fact that I broke up with him is probably the primary motivator for his interest in buying Shelton."

"He will not give up easily. Not on getting Shelton and not on getting you."

Nadia stared across the room at Ryan. "Mike doesn't want me."

His expression remained blank. "I wouldn't be so sure of that."

Chapter Seven

It was already nearing midday, well after the time Nadia usually checked in with her department managers, by the time she finally found the time to do so. She met with the general manager of the Harlem property to debrief the conference that had just ended and prepare for the upcoming one. They also discussed the fire and the workarounds they'd have to make to seamlessly host the events they had scheduled. The conference needed to go off without a hitch, and she had no doubt her team was up for the challenge.

She followed that meeting with conference calls with her general managers at the other two Shelton Hotel properties and a call with her insurance agent. So far the agent seemed nothing but sympathetic and helpful, but Nadia couldn't discount the horror stories she'd heard about insurance companies refusing to pay out claims. All she could do was hope that the police wrapped up their investigation quickly and their results unambiguously showed Shelton was not in any way responsible for the fire.

She and Ryan grabbed a quick lunch from the cafe in the hotel lobby, then she dived into reviewing invoices, preparing the monthly occupancy reports and planning a staff-training session. It was late afternoon before the crick in her neck forced her to take a break. She rolled her shoulders, tilting her head from left to right and back. Ryan worked dutifully on his laptop at the table in the corner of her office.

He'd dressed more low-key than usual today in dark slacks and a formfitting burgundy pullover that accentuated his broad shoulders, powerful biceps and flat abs. As flattering as yesterday's suit had been, she preferred the casual look.

"What are you reading so intensely?" Nadia asked.

Ryan looked up, spearing her with eyes that sent tingles rolling down her spine. "Confirmation on the current whereabouts on your ex-fiancé, Wallace. Seems he's living in Texas and engaged to an oil heiress."

"I guess he'll get his rich wife after all."

"I've also got the background report on Michael Dexter."

She rolled her eyes. "I don't even want to know what it says."

He shot her a crooked smile that added fireworks to the tingles. "It's nothing I wouldn't expect from a businessman that had risen to his position. Some hints regarding questionable ethics on various business deals, but nothing jumps out."

"Mike doesn't like to hear the word *no*, but I doubt he'd go to these lengths just to get me to sell Shelton."

Ryan hesitated before speaking again. "I've also been reading the police report on Nate's accident."

A mix of emotions churned in her stomach. She'd never seen the police report. She already knew more about how her brother had died than she wanted to remember.

"Why?"

Ryan crossed to Nadia and leaned a hip against her desk. "Just trying to get a feel for who your brother was."

Although Nate had been the CEO, Nadia had handled the day-to-day operations of the hotels. She wasn't sure if Nate had ever met Ryan or dealt with West Security, but if he had, his contact would have been minimal.

"That note makes it clear someone thinks Nate is alive," Ryan continued. "We need to know why. And if they're right."

Nadia rose, sending her chair rolling back into the wall behind her desk. She rounded the desk, stopping close enough to Ryan that she had to tip her head up to look him in the eye.

"Nate is dead."

Ryan cocked his head, his expression unreadable. "Someone doesn't believe it."

Nadia sighed. "If you really want to get to know what Nate was like, we should go to his apartment."

Ryan's eyebrows shot up. "I saw that his condo had been transferred to your name, but I'd assumed you'd rented it out. It's prime real estate."

Nadia reached for the picture of her and Nate on her desk, running a finger over her brother's smiling face. "I haven't been able to bring myself to get rid of his things. And it's convenient for Uncle Erik to have a place in the city to crash if he has a late meeting or doesn't feel like making the drive home to Connecticut." She looked at Ryan. "But that apartment was Nate's sanctuary. If there is something that might help us figure this mess out, it's there."

"I can go by myself."

"No. I want to be a part of this."

She stepped back behind her desk long enough to pull her purse from a drawer.

It was after five; the evening shift had already clocked in, and Olivia had headed home. Nadia locked her office, and they headed for the garage next door where Ryan had parked his SUV earlier that morning.

Ryan pointed them south to Nate's Upper East Side condo, fighting rush hour traffic the whole way.

Nate's building was architecturally more similar to Ryan's than hers. The thirty-three-floor high-rise possessed all the amenities a rich bachelor could want: onsite cleaners, concierge, maid service, spa and gym. Twenty-eight floors above the city, the condo boasted spectacular views, despite being relatively small. A galley kitchen jutted off to the right of the entrance and looked into a decent-sized dining–living room combo. A black bookshelf held a smattering of books and several framed pictures of Nate with prominent people. The mayor. A city councilman. Even a United States secretary of state.

A narrow hall opened up beyond the living space.

"Nate used the second bedroom as his office. I think we should start looking there for…" she threw her hands up "…whatever we're looking for."

Ryan followed her down the hall and into the bedroom the office. The room's sleek black-and-silver decor, minimalist and masculine, was all Nate. A sleek arched-legged desk occupied one corner, flanked on either end by more black bookshelves. A metal file cabinet stood in the adjacent corner.

"Do you mind if I see what's in here?" Ryan asked, pointing to the file cabinet.

Nadia's chest rose and fell with a shuddered breath. "I guess that is what we're here for."

She crossed the room to the desk while he turned to the cabinet. Sitting at Nate's desk, she let her gaze linger on a photo of the two of them at one of the rare charity functions where he'd felt they both needed to make an appearance. One of the last times she'd seen him.

She turned away from the photo and booted up Nate's computer. It was only the second time she'd been in Nate's apartment since his death but the first time she'd ventured into his office, a place Nate had rarely let anyone in. She could have sworn the space still smelled faintly of her brother's favorite cologne, though common sense told her that wasn't possible. An acute stab of grief rippled through her.

Shaking off as much of her melancholy as she could, she was for once thankful that he never listened to her about the danger of using a combination of their mother's name and their childhood address as his password. She scrolled through the files on the laptop not sure exactly what she was looking for. The file labeled *Bronx Project* both surprised and annoyed her.

She and Nate agreed never to keep company files on their personal computers. Having files spread over multiple devices not only made it difficult to keep track of them, but it also made it more likely sensitive company information could fall into the hands of a competitor.

"Humph."

Ryan turned at her exclamation. "Did you find anything?"

"Nothing that helps us. It looks like Nate was inquiring about buildings for sale in the Bronx. He never mentioned an interest in purchasing a new property to me." She didn't bother masking her irritation.

Ryan crossed the small room and looked over her shoulder at the computer screen. "Maybe he hadn't gotten around to talking to you about it."

"You're probably right." Nadia turned in her chair to look up at him. "Did you find anything?"

Ryan shook his head. "Just the usual personal papers—

copies of past tax returns, the deed to this place, insurance papers."

She sighed. "I probably should have known that. Uncle Erik was Nate's executor. He handled everything after Nate died. For a while, I could barely keep it together enough to handle the hotels."

Ryan laid a hand on her shoulder, which she covered with her own. "That's understandable."

When she'd come to the apartment with Uncle Erik, he'd been all business, hustling her in and out as quickly as possible. Maybe he thought it was the only way for them to get through being in Nate's space. But now new waves of grief for her brother washed over her, and she let herself feel them. Eventually, she'd have to get rid of Nate's things whether she rented the place or sold it, which would be yet another reminder that he was never coming back.

She leaned into his hand. He ran his thumb in soft circles over the swell of her cheek.

"Are we done? I've had enough memories for one day." She turned her back to Ryan, not wanting him to see the tears threatening to fall.

He stepped back, his hand falling from her shoulder. "I want to take a quick look in the bedroom."

She powered down Nate's computer, and they crossed the hall.

Nadia opened the bedroom door and screamed.

Ryan swore, reaching for the gun at his back, as he turned her away from the sight of the dead man on the floor, his sightless eyes staring at the ceiling.

Chapter Eight

The first officer to arrive took Nadia's and Ryan's statements, then ordered them to remain in the hall outside the apartment. They didn't wait long before Detective Parsmons arrived. He eyed them and went into the apartment without stopping to speak. Nearly an hour passed before Parsmons came back out with another man that he introduced as Detective Beard.

Detective Beard led Ryan to the opposite end of the hall to talk, while Parsmons asked Nadia to go over the events of the evening for him.

Exhaustion clutched at her despite the relatively early evening hour. Still, Nadia repeated the statement she'd given the officer when he'd arrived.

"Walk me through it again," Detective Parsmons said when she finished, peering at her over round-rimmed spectacles.

She sighed heavily, fighting the urge to slide down the wall and sit. Her legs felt ready to give out.

"I told you. We came by the apartment to see if we could discover who might be behind all the things that have happened to me."

"And you came straight here from the hotel?"

"Yes. I was at the hotel all day."

Detective Parsmons looked down at the notebook in

his hand. "And when you got here you went straight to the office? You didn't stop by the bedroom first?"

"No," Nadia said through gritted teeth. "The office seemed to be the most logical place to look first."

"Humph." Parsmons didn't look up from his notes. "Then what?"

For the second time, Nadia took him through the course of events, starting with finding nothing helpful in the office, then moving to the bedroom and discovering the dead man.

"Who has keys to the apartment?" Parsmons asked.

"My uncle and I. He stays here sometimes when he doesn't want to make the trek back to his house in Greenwich."

"But the place is in your name, right? So legally it's yours?"

Nadia rubbed her brow, warding off the headache growing there. "Yes, but this is the first time I've been here in months."

"Humph," Parsmons repeated.

"It's been a long day." Ryan's familiar deep voice came from behind Nadia, just before she felt his hand on her back. "If you're finished with your questioning, I'd like to take Nadia home."

Relief flowed through Nadia.

Detective Parsmons's eyes shifted to Ryan. "One more question. Either of you have any idea who the dead man is?"

"No," Ryan said.

At the same time, Nadia answered, "Yes."

Nadia shifted as Ryan and Parsmons looked at her with twin expressions of surprise.

"I don't actually know the man, but he looks like one of the guys that chased me into Sentinel last night."

"But you didn't recognize the dead guy?" Parsmons directed the question to Ryan.

Ryan frowned. "No, but I was focused on Nadia." Ryan tapped the screen on his phone. "I pulled the footage from Sentinel's cameras." He turned the phone so they could all look at the video. "He could be the dead guy."

Ryan pointed to the man that had come in through Sentinel's back door.

"Can you send me that video?" Parsmons asked, handing Ryan a business card.

Ryan tapped the phone screen a few more times, then tucked the phone into his pocket.

Parsmons snapped the leather cover on his notebook closed. "You know I find this all very peculiar, I have to say. There's a fire in your hotel, and a suspicious note is left in your office. And now the man you say broke into your home and attempted to kidnap you is found in an apartment you own."

Ryan's arm slipped around Nadia's shoulder, pulling her into his side. The warmth of his body radiated through her. "If you've got something to say, spit it out, Detective," Ryan growled.

Parsmons's eyes narrowed and swung from Nadia to Ryan and back. "Okay. You, Miss Shelton," Parsmons said, pointing to Nadia, "have access to all the relevant places in this story. Your apartment. This apartment. The hotel. You seem to be the common denominator. Why is that?"

Nadia stiffened but held Parsmons's gaze. "I don't know, Detective."

"Me either." Parsmons pointed his index finger at her. "But I'm going to find out."

SHE WAS MORE than ready to leave Nate's apartment once Parsmons released them. She didn't want her Uncle Erik to hear about the dead body found there from someone else and worry, so she called him as soon as she got back to Ryan's apartment.

"Are you okay? Tell me where you are. I'll be right there." Her Uncle Erik's voice boomed from the other end of the phone.

Nadia glanced around Ryan's guest room. She wasn't about to tell her uncle she stayed the night with a man she barely knew. He'd have a heart attack. She couldn't explain it, but despite only knowing Ryan through his security work with the hotel, she knew without a doubt she was safest with him.

"Don't come back into the city. You don't have to worry about me. I'm staying the night with a friend. I just wanted to warn you that the police will probably be in touch and Nate's apartment will be off-limits for a while."

"Well, for how long?"

Nadia clenched her teeth. "I don't know, but while the police are investigating, you can take a room at one of the hotels if you're going to stay in the city."

"It's not that. I was going to call you. I have to go out of town for a day or two."

"Something serious?"

"No, no. An issue with a client that has to be dealt with in person."

Nadia promised to keep him updated before ending their call and exhaling deeply. She fell back onto the bed, her legs dangling over the edge, and took a moment to simply feel the soft mattress at her back and enjoy the quiet. Uncle Erik was tightly wound by nature, and conversations with him were often energy sucks. Given where her energy meter had been when she'd initiated the call, she was now running on fumes.

She was debating whether to just call it a night and slide under the covers when the smell of onions and ginger snaked its way under the door, making her stomach grumble. She climbed off the bed and made her way to Ryan's kitchen.

Ryan spooned chicken stir-fry onto two plates. "I figured you'd be hungry."

"You were right," she said as Ryan brought their plates to the table. "This looks great. Thanks."

Ryan sat opposite her at the table but didn't begin eating. "It's not every day you find a body. How are you doing?"

She wasn't sure how to answer that. Finding a dead man's body in Nate's apartment had been a shock on top of all the other emotions that had swelled inside her from being back in her brother's personal space. Now, she just felt worn down, and she couldn't wait until she could fall asleep.

"As well as can be expected, I guess."

They ate in comfortable silence for several long moments.

"I have to take a day trip to Maine tomorrow. I've arranged for one of our best men to stick with you while I'm gone," Ryan said.

"What are you going to do in Maine?" she asked, although she thought she already knew the answer.

Ryan held her gaze. "I want to talk to the sheriff that investigated Nate's accident."

"Why? You read the report. What more do you need to know?"

Ryan hesitated before speaking. "The report is the official record, but it doesn't tell me anything about the investigating officer's opinions and gut feelings. I'm much more likely to get that out of the sheriff if I speak to her in person."

She shook her head. "I don't know what you think you'll find."

"Maybe nothing, but part of the reason I'm good at my job is that I'm thorough. I'll be back tonight."

"I'm going with you." Nadia wiped her hands on the cloth napkin next to her plate.

Ryan frowned. "That's not necessary."

"It absolutely is. You obviously think something Nate was into before his death could be the key to what's going on here. I don't know that I agree with that, but I trust you. And if you're right, I want to know what that is."

Nadia waited without breaking eye contact while Ryan silently assessed her. She was involved in this, whether she wanted to be or not. She would not sit back and play the damsel in distress, leaving Ryan and West Security to crack the case.

"Okay. We'll be leaving at six. It's a little over a three-hour drive to Northpath, Rhode Island. I'd like to talk to the sheriff and be back on the road to New York before the sun goes down," Ryan finally agreed.

They fell quiet once more as they finished their dinner. This time, Nadia broke the silence. "I love your view."

Through the floor-to-ceiling windows, she could see the lights of New Jersey across the Hudson River.

Ryan shifted his seat, putting his chair closer to Nadia at the same time. "I let my sister-in-law do most of the house hunting, sifting through all the condos on the market and all those viewings. I just chose from their top three, and the view out that window is what won me over."

"Wow. That's…efficient."

Ryan chuckled. "My needs are minimal. A large wall for the flat screen, a decent kitchen and a nice big tub are all it takes to make me happy."

Her stomach clenched as an image of Ryan in a tub lodged itself in her head. She wouldn't have pegged him as someone who'd prefer soaking over showering, but now that he'd mentioned it, she couldn't stop imagining him in the bath.

"It reminds me of this cabin in Maine my parents used to drag my brothers and me to every August," Ryan said, pulling out of her fantasies.

"You might be the only person to look out a New York City window and see Maine."

"It's the water and the lights. The cabin was on a hill next to this huge lake. It overlooked the town below, and at night I loved to sit out on the deck. I used to make up stories about what the people in all the houses below ours were doing. Always something cooler than daydreaming on the front porch."

"It sounds wonderful. My family used to go down South to my aunt's house in Atlanta for our family vacations. After my mom died, we stopped going. Kind of lost touch with that side of the family."

Aunt Celia had passed away when Nadia was a teenager, and now she had cousins she wouldn't even recognize. Since their father's passing, it had been her and Nate against the world. And now she was on her own.

She shook off the gloominess threatening to engulf her. She had Uncle Erik. They didn't see eye to eye on many things, but he was always there for her.

Nadia stole a glance at Ryan. When she'd needed him, he'd been there for her.

"You didn't take any vacations after your mother died?" Ryan asked, pulling her from her thoughts.

Nadia shrugged, swallowing the last of her dinner. "Dad worked a lot building the business, and once Nate and I were old enough, we also worked at the hotel. My father believed we should have a thorough understanding of the business we'd inherit someday, so I've pretty much worked every position we have at Shelton Hotels."

Ryan cocked his head to the side. "I'm trying to imagine you in a maid's outfit."

Heat flooded every inch of her body.

Ryan's face colored. "I'm sorry. I shouldn't have said that," he said, rising with his plate.

"It's fine." It was more than fine. The image stirred a desire in her that threatened to overwhelm her. And the knowledge that Ryan was attracted to her sent a surge of feminine confidence through her that she hadn't felt in a very long time.

"No, it's not. It was unprofessional." His plate clattered into the sink.

She followed him, carrying her plate. "It's not like I'm paying you," she said, attempting to lighten the moment.

When it didn't work, she moved on to something that bothered her.

"I know you said not to worry about it, but I want you to bill me for the personal security. I might need to work out a payment schedule, though." Nadia laughed, only half-kidding.

"Stop." Ryan faced her, his tone still sharp. "I told you not to worry about it, and I meant it."

She frowned, her annoyance growing. If he thought she would lose her head over one flirty comment, he could just get over himself. "Why? I know Shelton has been a client for years, but you barely know me. Why would you help me for free?"

"Why? Because every time I see you, it gets harder and harder to resist doing this."

He stepped forward, closing the space between them. Wrapping an arm around her waist, he pulled her tightly to his chest. The scent of his spicy cologne filled her senses. He dropped his lips to hers, and she gasped at the warmth of his mouth on hers.

She relaxed into the kiss, and he pulled her closer, his mouth moving against hers in a slow, seductive dance. His tongue stroked hers, sending heat spiraling through her body. She moaned and slid her hands over the coarse hair on his chest and around his neck, drawing their bodies closer, fixing her hips to his.

Ryan groaned deep in his chest and lifted her, sitting her on the countertop and stepping between her legs.

His cell phone vibrated, breaking the spell they'd been under.

He jerked away as if the touch of her lips had scalded him. His eyes were a storm of emotion as they held each other's gaze through two more rings before he tore away to look at his phone.

"I've got to take this." He answered the call, leaving the kitchen without looking back at her.

Nadia walked hurriedly to her bedroom. Hot tears stung her eyes. Ryan clearly thought their kiss was a mistake. She shouldn't let it bother her. They had a business relationship and nothing more. Adding a personal relationship to the mix right now was beyond unwise.

So why did she feel like she'd lost something she just realized she wanted?

Chapter Nine

Ryan stood in the kitchen at five fifteen the next morning. His cell jiggled on the countertop, and he looked down to see Shawn's face staring up at him from the phone's screen.

He pressed the button to start brewing coffee before connecting the call. "What's up?"

"Dead guy's name is Andrei Ledebev," Shawn began without preamble. "He and his brother, Taras, are new to the New York scene, but they're well-known in other illegal circles. They've been working with Brian Leroy."

"That's not good."

"No, but this is worse. Leroy appears to be working with Lincoln Smith."

The real mob families looked nothing like the one-note portrayals given in the movies with shakedowns at the neighborhood mom-and-pop stores. In reality, organized crime had stepped into the twenty-first century with everyone else. Today's gangsters had college degrees, wore three-thousand-dollar suits to the office and were more diverse and gender-balanced than the average state legislature. Greed knew no ethnicity, and mobsters like Lincoln Smith would work with anyone who could make them money.

New York organized-crime families, in particular, had

their hands in a wide variety of cookie jars, many of them quite legal, at least before the mobsters got their hands on them. Leroy was ostensibly a well-known small-business investor, but in reality, he was simply a well-educated and sophisticated loan shark. Aligning himself with Smith was a step up on the metaphorical crime ladder from the crew of misfits Leroy had run with in his youth.

"That is not good, but it is a link to Nate," Ryan said, putting four pieces of toast in the toaster.

"So Leroy or Smith could be behind the attacks on Nadia, but why?" Shawn asked.

"If we can figure out the relationship between Nate and Leroy we might answer that question. Has Eugene been able to get anything from the cameras at Shelton?"

He'd asked Eugene Paul, head of West's technology and communications department, to look at the security-camera footage from the hallway of the room where the fire had been started. He'd viewed the security tape himself, but whoever set the fire had kept his head down and face obscured. It hadn't helped that the cameras weren't the top of the range that West Security offered its customers. That was a problem Ryan had promptly fixed, ordering all the cameras in each of the three Shelton properties be upgraded and the bill directed to him. The IOUs he'd owe his brothers were adding up quickly, but as long as Nadia was safe, he'd happily pay them.

"He's working on it, but I wouldn't get my hopes up," Shawn responded.

"Tell him to keep at it and take a look at all the other footage of the hotel around the same time."

"Do you know how much time that could take?"

"I know, I know, but have Eugene do it, anyway. Something about that fire isn't right." Ryan rubbed the back of his neck.

"What do you mean, *isn't right*?"

"If I knew, I'd tell you. Just have Eugene do it as soon as he can." He looked over as Nadia entered the kitchen. "I gotta go."

Her forest green top grazed the top of the black jeans that hugged her hips. The outfit wasn't overtly sexy. Still, he couldn't tear his eyes from the way her hips swayed as she crossed the kitchen toward him, the steady rhythm of her low-heeled boots contrasting with the erratic beat of his heart.

She stopped at the edge of the counter, several arm lengths away from him. Her expression was blandly polite, revealing nothing of what she thought about the kiss they'd shared the night before.

"I made toast for the road. You can put your coffee in this and take it with us." He took a thermos from an upper cabinet and handed it to Nadia.

"Thanks." Nadia took the thermos and turned away from him.

He waited until she'd filled it and buttered her slices of toast. "You ready?"

"Sure." She turned for the front door without a backward glance.

A sigh escaped his lips. This was exactly why he'd sworn he wouldn't cross the professional line with Nadia. Then he'd not only crossed it, he'd leaped over it with abandon. If this road trip was uncomfortable, he had only himself to blame. Still, better that he endure an uncomfortable road trip than another broken heart.

Nadia's phone rang before she made it to the door. She glanced at the screen and groaned.

"What is it?" Ryan said.

"Uncle Erik. I left him a message telling him that we're going to Rhode Island." She silenced the phone and slipped it in her coat pocket. "I don't have to speak to him to know what he'll say. Let's go."

Dawn bloomed as they drove out of the city in silence. His GPS put the trip at three and a half hours. Nadia spent the first hour and a half studiously looking out of the passenger window.

He pulled into a rest area, more because he needed a break from the tension in the car than anything else.

"I'm going to grab a coffee and maybe a breakfast sandwich. Do you need anything?"

She studied the cars out the passenger window as if there'd be a quiz later. "No. I'll just wait here for you."

He pushed his door open, then slammed it shut again causing Nadia to start and face him for the first time since they'd gotten into the car. "Look, I'm sorry about last night. I shouldn't have kissed you."

"It's fine." Nadia twisted, so she looked out of the window once again.

He started to reach across the console for her hand, then thought better of the move. He wanted to repair the damage he'd done, not send mixed signals. "Nadia, please look at me."

She didn't react at all for several long moments. Finally, she faced him. "I get it. You made a mistake, and it won't happen again. You don't have to worry about me complaining to your father or suing or whatever."

His stomach clenched at the pain he saw in her eyes. "I'm not worried about you suing, and I don't think kissing you was a mistake. I've been thinking about kissing you for months."

Her expression read of disbelief, and he didn't blame her for her suspicion.

"It was unprofessional to have kissed you. Now is not a

good time for me to be distracted. Not when all my focus needs to be on keeping you safe."

The suspicion in her eyes turned to anger. "Well, I'm sorry I'm such a huge distraction." Nadia reached for the car door handle.

This time he did take her wrist, stopping her before she could exit from the car.

"That's not what I meant." He released her wrist and scrubbed his hands down his face. "Look, I'm attracted to you. I think you're attracted to me too, even though you look like you want to rip my head off. Right now you need someone focused on protecting you and figuring out who is behind all the things that have been happening to you lately. I can't be that person if I'm wondering when I'll get to kiss you again."

Nadia held his gaze for several long moments before her shoulders straightened and drew back. "You're right. We should keep things professional. Friends?"

She extended her hand.

Friends was the last thing he wanted to be, but he took her hand. Ignoring the electricity jolting through him at her touch, he said, "Friends."

They strode into the rest stop together. Nadia allowed him to pay for her breakfast, which he took as a good sign. They ate quickly and were back on the road to Rhode Island forty minutes after they'd stopped.

They hadn't made it far from the rest stop when his GPS alerted to a traffic accident backing up the interstate up ahead. He followed the mechanical voice directing him onto a two-lane state road. It would add a bit of time to their trip, but the road was lightly traveled.

"So West identified the dead man in Nate's apartment." Ryan shot a glance at her across the car. He hoped opening up about the state of the investigation would help to put them back on a sound footing.

"I overheard you on the phone this morning." She sipped the orange juice that had come with her breakfast sandwich.

"Have you ever heard the names Taras or Andrei Ledebev?"

Creases formed on her forehead. She considered his question for nearly half a minute before answering. "I don't think so. Is one of them the dead guy?"

"Andrei. But both worked for Brian Leroy."

Nadia scowled. "Leroy's construction company bid on one of our renovation projects a couple of years back. But Leroy wouldn't do all this just because we didn't use his company."

"No, but there's evidence that Nate and Leroy had a relationship that went beyond business. At least one event that they were both in attendance at and photographed together."

"That doesn't mean anything."

They'd just gotten back on speaking terms. He didn't want to rock their precarious boat, so he let the subject drop.

In the rearview mirror, he watched as a black pickup truck behind them accelerated. The road had narrowed into one lane in each direction, but they were the only two cars present at the moment.

The pickup rode their bumper. Despite the dangerous proximity, Ryan wasn't able to get a good look at the driver through the dark tint on the windshield.

Ryan sped up.

The SUV followed suit.

"Someone is tailgating us." He glanced at Nadia. "Make sure your seat belt is on and tight."

Nadia twisted so she could see the car behind them. "What is he doing?"

"Can you see who's in the car?" He pushed the accelerator to the floor, but the truck picked up speed along with them.

"No. The window is too dark."

The SUV rammed the back of their vehicle. Nadia jerked forward as the car slid, fishtailing, but Ryan kept them on the road. He guided the car out of the skid and revved the engine, sending them flying forward.

The SUV sped up, hitting them again and sending Nadia crashing into the dashboard.

"Nadia! Are you okay?"

She groaned. He risked a glance at her. Blood trickled from a gash on her forehead.

"I think so," she said.

The SUV hit them again, sending them into a tailspin.

Ryan fought to regain control of the car, but the tires slipped off the road and down an embankment.

Brush flew by as he pumped the brakes trying to slow the car. Several large oaks at the foot of the embankment loomed. He wrenched the wheel to the right moments before the sound of crumpling metal filled the air.

"Ryan!"

He swallowed a curse and reached across his torso, touching his hand to the site of the pain. A shard of glass from the shattered window left a deep gash above his hip. His fingertips were bloody when he pulled them away.

"I'm okay. How about you?"

"A bump on the head, but nothing to worry about." Nadia turned in her seat. "The back windshield is shattered. I don't see anyone."

"That doesn't mean they aren't there. We need to get out of this car." He reached for the seat belt release and groaned. He spent the next several moments concentrating on breathing through the searing pain in his side.

"You shouldn't move." Nadia pulled her phone from her purse at her feet and dialed 9-1-1.

She gave the operator their location and relayed a description of the car that had driven them off the road.

He fought through the pain and reached into the glove compartment, taking his gun from inside. They may not be able to get out of the car, but he would not let them be slaughtered like sitting ducks either. He rested the gun on his thigh, within arm's reach, as they waited for help to arrive.

The sound of sirens swelled nearly ten minutes after they'd landed in the ditch.

"Put this back in the glove box." He held the gun butt-first out to Nadia.

She recoiled as if the gun would bite. "I don't like guns."

He shot her a smile, twisted with amusement. "I'm not asking you to shoot it. Just put it back. This will go a lot smoother if it's locked away when the cops arrive."

The cops might still have questions for him, but since he had a license to carry, he doubted they'd give him trouble.

On the way down, in a car that refused to stop, it had seemed as if they were falling a hundred feet down a steep incline. Now, Ryan could see that they'd only slid about ten yards from the road, down a slight slope. He ignored the pain in his side and gave a statement to the deputy who followed them up the incline.

Two ambulances waited at the top of the incline.

Ryan lowered himself onto a stretcher with the help of the EMTs. "We need to ride to the hospital together."

The bleeding from the cut on his side had subsided,

but it still burned like the devil himself walked across his torso whenever he moved.

"Sorry, sir. Space won't allow two stretchers."

He didn't want to leave Nadia's side. Yet, he could barely sit up, and he wasn't going to take any chances that Nadia's bump on the head wasn't something more serious. He called out to the deputy that had taken his statement and explained that there had been several attempts to harm her. The deputy promised someone would stay with Nadia at all times.

It wasn't as good as having her by his side, but it was the best he could do at the moment. Still, if forcing them off the road was an attempt to separate him from Nadia, her assailant had just gotten exactly what he wanted.

The victims from the five-car pileup that caused him to turn off the interstate in the first place were also being seen at the hospital. Unfortunately, several people involved in that accident were in critical condition. The deputy kept his word, thankfully, and had an officer shadow Nadia while the doctors examined her head wound.

Ryan called Shawn and filled him in while he waited to be seen by the doctor. He wasn't surprised when a little over two hours later Shawn pulled back the curtain surrounding his hospital bed. He'd discouraged his brother from coming to the hospital, but he'd known the effort would be wasted breath.

Ryan scowled. "I told you not to come."

"The doctor has already discharged Nadia. Gideon is with her," Shawn said.

Ryan felt the tension in his body dissolve and with it the annoyance he felt at Shawn's presence. "I'm just waiting on my discharge papers."

Shawn sat in the metal chair next to the bed. "I got an

update from the deputies. They found the car that hit you. A rental. Name on the contract is a fake, but the identification was good enough to fool the clerk."

The nurse had offered painkillers, but Ryan had refused. Now the headache swelling behind his eyes had him rethinking his decision. "None of this makes sense. How did they know where to find us?"

"You sure you weren't followed?"

Ryan hit his brother with a scorching look. "We weren't followed."

"Well, somebody knew you were heading to Rhode Island today."

He trusted the employees of West Security implicitly, but he knew that Nadia had informed Olivia and the general managers of the hotels that she wouldn't be in the office today. He hadn't thought it necessary to keep where they were heading a secret. A number of people knew they were headed for Rhode Island: Olivia, Erik and several employees at West Security for starters. He'd told Shawn they hadn't been followed, but he couldn't be sure. He mentally kicked himself for having let his guard down.

"Hey." Shawn clapped a hand on Ryan's shoulder. "Don't worry about it. We'll figure it out."

"I could have gotten Nadia killed."

"But you didn't." Shawn withdrew his hand, running it over his bald head before crossing his arms. "Look, I knew you had a thing for Nadia Shelton, but it seems like there's more to your feelings than you just being hot for her. I don't have to tell you how bad that can end. For you."

Shawn had been there for him the last time—the only time—he'd thrown professionalism aside and fallen for a woman he'd been paid to protect. The chemistry was off the charts, and he'd fallen for her hard. But when the danger faded, so had her feelings for him.

"I've got it under control."

Shawn let out a weary sigh. "You may be further gone than I thought. Bro, Nadia is great. Smart, sophisticated, and has a body that—"

Ryan growled a warning at his brother.

Shawn raised his hands in surrender. "What I'm trying to say is right now you're her knight in shining armor, Black Panther and 007 all rolled into one guy. But when this is all over, you'll still be a glorified bodyguard, and she'll still be the heiress to a hotel chain. Never the twain shall meet. You know what I'm saying?"

Ryan understood what Shawn was getting at. He even understood his brother meant to protect him, and he loved Shawn for it. He'd said the same thing to himself a thousand times in the last two days. Nadia was out of his league.

Unfortunately, a little voice inside his head told him it was too late. He already cared about Nadia too deeply. The only thing he could do now was ensure the only heart broken when this was all over was his.

"I hear you. I'm not too involved," Ryan said.

Shawn's expression made his disbelief clear.

Ryan wasn't in the mood to continue the conversation, however. "Was Eugene able to find anything on the security tapes from the Harlem hotel that might help us identify our arsonist?"

"He cleaned the tapes up pretty good. There's still no way to get a positive identification on the guy, but I got to thinking about you finding Andrei Ledebev's body so soon after the fire, which made me wonder if maybe it could have been him," Shawn said.

"And?"

Shawn shook his head. "No way. Wrong body type and coloring for either of the Ledebevs."

Ryan scrubbed his hands over his face. "The fire feels different from this other stuff that's happened. If we assume Nadia being pushed into the street was intentional—and I believe in my gut it's a part of this—then all the attacks except for the fire have been personal and physical. The fire seems aimed more toward the hotel itself."

"Yeah, but Nadia is the hotel in a sense. She owns it. She runs it. She keeps her office there. The hotel could be seen as an extension of her."

Ryan didn't disagree with Shawn's logic, but his gut was still telling him something was off about the fire. The doctor chose that moment to return with the discharge papers, so he and Shawn would have to wait until later to discuss the situation further.

Ryan listened to the doctor's admonishment to take it easy and rest, a suggestion he didn't bother to pretend he'd be following, and headed out to meet up with Gideon and Nadia.

Nadia's head popped up as he exited the sliding glass doors separating the exam area from the waiting room. She hurried to him, Gideon following in her wake.

"How are you?" she asked, placing a hand on his bicep.

Concern for him darkened her brown eyes, and his heart fluttered at the sight of it. He tried for a smile, but the deepening creases in her forehead suggested it had come out as more a grimace. "Just needed a few stitches, and I'm as good as new. How about you?"

"I may have a headache for a day or so. A couple ibuprofens will take care of it."

"You were both lucky," Shawn said. "Things could

have been a lot worse. I'm guessing you still want to go to Rhode Island?"

Ryan nodded. He stole a glance at Nadia and found her doing the same.

"Okay. Northpath, here we come."

THE REMAINDER OF the drive to Rhode Island was, thankfully, uneventful. Nadia pretended to sleep for most of the trip. She understood the need for personal protection at the moment, but she desperately needed some time to process everything that had happened in the last couple of days. Ryan hadn't come right out and said it, but she got the feeling that things were going to get worse before they got better.

Nadia pretended to awake as Shawn pulled the car to a stop in front of a midsize hotel. A row of redbrick buildings with matching black awnings lined the cobblestone sidewalk as if they were the Queen's Guard. Antique lamp posts and the blue-purple sky cast shadows on those braving the chilly evening to spend cocktail hour outdoors.

Shawn returned from checking them in and announced he'd gotten them adjacent two-bedroom suites. They had just enough time for Shawn and Gideon to drop their bags in one of the suites before heading to the police station.

She'd overheard Ryan on the phone with Sheriff Charlotte Haley on the ride. The sheriff seemed understanding when Ryan explained that they'd been in a car accident. She'd been happy to push their meeting to six, meaning they now had a little over a half hour before they had to be at the sheriff's office.

The police hadn't allowed them to get their bags from the trunk of their totaled car. Shawn and Gideon offered to go to the big-box store outside of town to pick up basic toiletries and necessities while she and Ryan spoke with the sheriff. Since they were working with a single car, Shawn dropped Nadia and Ryan off in front of a sandstone building with imposing columns guarding the front entrance.

A deputy led them through a maze of desks and into Sheriff Charlotte Haley's spacious office.

"I'm glad you two made it in one piece." Sheriff Haley leaned back in her chair, her sharp eyes examining them.

Nadia sat beside Ryan on the other side of the sheriff's desk. A stout woman with red hair shot through with a generous dose of gray.

"We expected to be here hours ago. Unfortunately, as I said on the phone, we met with some trouble. Someone tried to run us off the road on the way here."

Ryan filled the sheriff in on the details of being forced off the road. As he spoke, Sheriff Haley's expression changed from one of alarm to concern.

"The driver didn't attempt to see if the crash killed you, though?" Haley asked when Ryan finished.

Lines formed on Ryan's forehead. "Not that we could tell."

"And no one approached you at the hospital, Miss Shelton?"

"No." Nadia looked from the sheriff to Ryan. They seemed to know something she didn't. "What am I missing?"

Sheriff Haley shot a look at Ryan.

"If the person who forced us off the road wanted to hurt you, they had the perfect opportunity to do so when we crashed," Ryan said.

"But they didn't take it," Nadia said.

"The crash could have been an attempt to separate you from your bodyguard here. That would make it a lot easier to kidnap you if that was the goal, especially in a busy hospital, but since no one approached you there..." Sheriff Haley shrugged.

"So what does that mean?" Nadia asked.

Ryan shifted awkwardly in his chair. The ER doctor had stitched his cut and prescribed a painkiller, which Ryan had declined to fill before leaving the hospital. Nadia knew he had to be in pain, but he hadn't complained once.

Neither Ryan nor the sheriff immediately answered her question. "Ryan?" she asked again.

"I don't know." Ryan shook his head. "But this incident feels different from the others. Whoever's doing this has been persistent from the start, so why did they walk away when we were in no position to fight back?"

"It is a conundrum, but you folks came up here to ask about Miss Shelton's brother's accident," Sheriff Haley said.

"We don't want to take up too much of your time, Sheriff. I've already reviewed your official report of the accident that killed Nate Shelton. What I'd really like is to hear your take."

Sheriff Haley narrowed her eyes at Ryan. "I won't ask how you got your hands on a copy of my file."

It was a question Nadia wouldn't mind an answer to, but Ryan remained silent and expressionless.

Sheriff Haley huffed. "If you read it, you know the important stuff."

"That depends on what you define as important. You noted the brake lines seemed worn," Ryan said.

"Yes." Haley's tone was cautious.

"*Seemed worn.* Those were the exact words you used in the report. Not *were worn*," Ryan pressed.

Nadia's gaze flicked between the two of them. They

were talking in code again. "Since I'm not fluent in what-ever coded language you two are speaking in, would you mind saying the unspoken parts out loud, please?"

"What did you see that made you think Nate's accident might not be an accident, Sheriff?" Ryan asked bluntly.

Nadia gasped, her mouth falling open at the implica-tion in Ryan's question.

Sheriff Haley seemed less surprised. "You're good."

The sheriff studied Ryan for a moment longer. "There was nothing I could prove, or you better believe I'd have chased it down to the end. I had an expert take a look at them, but the results were inconclusive. Still, the brake lines didn't look like any I'd ever seen worn. That doesn't mean it wasn't just regular wear and tear."

"But it got you thinking," Ryan pressed.

"Yeah. And when we couldn't find any reason for your brother to be in our little town..." Haley's voice trailed off, but she leaned forward, resting her arms on her desk, a questioning gaze focused on Nadia.

"I don't know why Nate was here. I assumed..." Even though he was gone, Nadia was hesitant to say anything casting Nate in a poor light. Her brother had his vices, but he was a good man.

She cleared her throat. "I assumed Nate came here with a woman. Those first days after Nate's death I was pretty out of it. Uncle Erik took care of all the paperwork and brought Nate's things back to New York."

"Erik Jackson. I interviewed him. He was quite torn up about your brother," Sheriff Haley said.

"Uncle Erik and Nate were close," Nadia replied. "Uncle Erik dodged all my questions about what Nate did in Northpath. I loved my brother, but I was well aware of his faults, including his penchant for dalliances with married women."

"Sheriff, there was something else in your report I wanted to ask you about," Ryan said, changing the subject. "You included a bunch of information about high and low tide and water flow in the sound. Why?"

"Well, you know our working theory was that Mr. Shelton's body was carried out to sea with the tide. It's possible, and hydrologists are expensive. In the absence of evidence of foul play, I couldn't justify spending the money for one." The sheriff's voice held more than a note of uncertainty.

Nadia's heart began galloping in her chest.

"But I've lived in this town all my life. I know the tide as well as I know the streets of this town. The tide that night was not strong enough to carry Mr. Shelton's body out to sea. I told your uncle all this when he was in town. I figured with your kind of money, you'd commission a hydrologist report."

Sheriff Haley tipped her head down, looking at Nadia over the top of her glasses. "To be honest, I expected to see you in my office months ago, Miss Shelton."

Chapter Ten

Shawn and Gideon were waiting in the car in front of the sheriff's office when Nadia and Ryan exited. It didn't escape Nadia's notice that cars appeared to be a difficult space for her and Ryan to navigate. At least one of them seemed to be annoyed with the other every time they were in one together. That or someone was trying to kill them.

If Shawn or Gideon noticed the tension, they didn't comment on it during the ride back to the hotel. Nadia hadn't felt comfortable asking Shawn to pick up clothes for her, but he'd done so, anyway. A modest nightshirt, a peach cardigan set and a pair of jeans that miraculously looked like they might actually fit were in the bags on the back seat when she and Ryan got into the car. He'd even picked out a camisole and a three pack of cotton underwear, a purchase that saved her from having to wash out her undergarments in the bathroom sink. She made a mental note to write a check to Shawn to cover the cost of the clothes.

The four of them agreed to meet for dinner in fifteen minutes and each pair retreated into their suite.

Nadia carried her bag of new clothes into the larger bedroom, not caring that she'd commandeered the room.

"You're angry with me."

She turned to find Ryan standing, arms crossed, in the door to the bedroom.

"Why would you ever think that?" She ripped the tag from the cardigan with enough force to leave a small hole and silently swore.

He crossed the room, pulling a key chain from his pocket as he did, and held a small Swiss Army knife out to her.

"I wasn't sure the sheriff had suspicions about the accident. It was more a feeling than anything concrete."

She turned to face him, full-on ignoring the offer. "Then, why didn't you tell me what you were thinking?"

He exhaled heavily. Lifting her hand, he dropped the key chain in it and sat on the edge of the bed, looking up at her. "Because you are Nate's sister. You're emotionally involved in this on so many levels. I didn't want to throw out theories that might be hurtful to you without evidence."

"So you thought it would be better to just spring it on me in the sheriff's office?" She didn't try to hide the incredulity in her voice.

Nadia sat beside him massaging her temples. Another headache threatened, but she didn't think this one had anything to do with the bump on her head.

"Are you okay? Do you want another painkiller?" Ryan asked.

"I should be asking you that." She raised her gaze to his. "I just don't understand any of this. Are you saying you and Sheriff Haley think Nate's accident could have been intentional? Like murder?"

"It's possible."

Fear pounded in her chest, even as her head rejected the notion. Even with everything she'd been through, it was hard to imagine Nate having been involved in something that would get him murdered.

She studied Ryan. "But you don't think so. If not murder, then what?"

His forehead creased. "Why do you think your uncle didn't tell you about Sheriff Haley's theory concerning Nate's death?"

Nadia clenched her teeth, biting back her initial response to him dodging her question. If he thought she would forget about it, he had another think coming. But she was curious enough about his line of questioning to play along for a bit.

"My guess? Just like you, he thinks he needs to protect me from information that might stun my weak female sensibilities."

Her chest rose and fell in time with her accelerated breathing, not all of which could be attributed to the anger and frustration she felt. Even at her most annoyed, heat crackled between them. Their position, sitting on the large king-size bed, didn't help to quell the fire building inside her.

Ryan exhaled slowly, an obvious attempt to rein in his temper. "I never called you weak."

"You treat me like I'm weak. Maybe Uncle Erik is right. I should have been more involved in the investigation of Nate's death." Regret gnawed at her. "If there was something questionable about his accident, I owed it to him to find out."

Ryan took her hand in his and squeezed. "You were grieving. You can't blame yourself."

Easier said than done. She blamed herself, and she had every intention of making things right as soon as she returned to New York. Starting with hiring the hydrologist. But first, she had to make one thing clear to Ryan.

"Look, I know where I am, Ryan. I wouldn't be here, in this hotel room with you, in this situation at all, if Nate was a fine, upstanding, aboveboard businessman and nothing else," she said. "I don't want you keeping things from me."

Ryan held her gaze for several long moments. "I'm sorry. I'll keep you in the loop from now on."

Their gazes held for a moment longer before Ryan rose and walked to the door.

Nadia followed him into the living room of the suite. "To answer your question for real, Uncle Erik could have been trying to protect me, but he also might not have believed the sheriff's theory."

She watched Ryan take a bottle of water from the minifridge, waving him off when he offered her a bottle. "You've seen how resistant Uncle Erik is to the tiniest bit of criticism of Nate."

Ryan's brows scrunched together. "Has he always been that way about Nate?"

She sat on the large beige couch while Ryan leaned against the television console, his Adam's apple bobbing as he took a long sip from the water bottle, her mind going to thoughts of what it would be like to rain kisses along his neck.

"Nadia?"

She tore her gaze from his neck in time to catch his amused gaze.

"You okay?"

"Yes, sorry. Um…" She cleared the frog from her throat and rewound to the conversation they'd been having before she'd gotten distracted. "Uncle Erik and Nate have always been close, almost like Nate was a surrogate son to him. Their bond became even tighter after my father passed away."

She hoped Ryan didn't notice the tinge of jealousy in her voice. Her uncle had never slighted her, but he'd never attempted to get close with her either, not like he'd done with Nate. Maybe it was just because he related better to Nate as a male, but she couldn't say that it didn't bother her just a little.

"I think you should hire that hydrologist," Ryan said.

"I'd already planned to do it as soon we get back to New York. I don't even know where to start looking for one. I guess you can search for anything on the internet."

Ryan smiled. "West can probably help you with finding a reputable hydrologist."

"You don't trust the internet." Her smile was full of mirth.

"The internet can be a great place for finding all kinds of information about things and people. Good and bad." His tone turned serious. "But we need someone good who can work fast. I have a feeling all this is going to come to a head soon, and it seems we're behind the eight ball."

"What else should we be doing?"

Ryan's eyebrow rose. "We should not be doing anything. We aren't in this together, Nadia. It's my job to protect you and find out who is attacking you."

Irritation erupted in Nadia. "We just had this discussion, and you said you'd keep me in the loop."

"And I will, but I will not put you in danger. You'll know of any significant information we find, but I can't have you out here playing Nancy Drew."

"Nancy… You know what? This isn't going to work." She stood. "You're already going back on our agreement, treating me like the weak link again. If you can't handle me being a part of this, then I'll find an agency that can. You're fired."

Ryan also rose, his hazel eyes blazing. "You no longer

want West to track down whoever is attacking you and provide your personal protection?"

Her hands found her hips. "That's what *you're fired* means."

"Fine." He closed the distance between them. "Then there's nothing stopping me from doing this."

He slid his hand around the back of her neck and brought his mouth within an inch of hers and stopped, waiting for her consent.

She didn't hesitate to close the remaining gap.

His mouth moved seductively over hers. It was a kiss that was both hungry and skillful. She reacquainted herself with the feel of his arms around her, sliding her arms up his chest and around his neck. She deepened their kiss, pulling him down into the couch cushions. His hand slipped under her shirt and up her torso to cup her breast, drawing a moan from deep within. She reached for the snap on his pants just as a knock sounded on the door.

"Ry? You in there? We going to dinner or what?" Shawn called from the hall.

Ryan drew back, his gaze a blaze of desire, his arms still locked around her.

"Hang on," Ryan called to his brother. "Am I still fired?" he asked Nadia.

His question hit her like a punch to the gut. She pulled from his arms. "Is that why you kissed me? To keep your job?"

"No, I…" He reached for her, but she took another step away. "Nadia."

"Ryan, what's going on in there?" Shawn called from the hall.

She held Ryan's gaze for a moment longer, unsure of what she saw in his eyes. Spinning, she went for the door to the suite, opening it to find Shawn's meaty fist raised for another knock.

"Everything okay?" Shawn's gaze flicked between her and Ryan.

"Fine." She forced her lips into a smile as she strode past Shawn and away from Ryan.

ALTHOUGH IT WAS the first time she'd ever been to Rhode Island, none of them were up for going any farther than the hotel restaurant for dinner. Ryan caught Gideon and Shawn up to speed on the information Sheriff Haley had relayed. Shawn lamented the fact that Nate's car had been destroyed. There was no way to have a look at the brake lines now, but he assured Nadia that he knew of a hydrologist that could help them. The foursome agreed to head back to New York at five the next morning.

Nadia's phone rang as she and Ryan entered their suite.

"Are you able to get New York news up there?" Olivia's harried voice carried through the phone.

"I don't know, but I'm sure I can stream it," Nadia said sitting on the couch and reaching for the laptop she'd left on the coffee table earlier. "Why?"

"There's a report on the fire at the hotel. The reporter is making it sound like a Shelton employee may have started it."

Nadia typed in the URL for the news station she regularly watched online. The station's website popped up almost immediately.

"*...the fire at Shelton's Harlem property was intentional. The NYPD would not comment, but sources tell WNYC News that police suspect it could have been an inside job.*"

NADIA WATCHED AS her picture came on-screen.

"Sources say CEO Nadia Shelton abruptly left town

the day after the fire. We have reached out to Miss Shelton for comment but have not been able to reach her."

Nadia paused the computer screen. "That reporter made it seem like I doused the room with gasoline and lit a match myself."

"What do you want me to do?" Olivia asked.

Nadia's stomach churned. She needed to squelch this rumor before it got out of hand. "Release a statement. The hotel is cooperating with the police investigation, and all Shelton properties are safe and open for business as usual."

"And if any of the guests ask questions?"

Nadia rubbed her temples. "Tell them that there was a small fire in an area that is closed off to the guests, and the hotel is one hundred percent safe. We're staying the night in Rhode Island, but I'll be in tomorrow morning."

"Great." Relief rolled palpably through Olivia's voice.

"And Olivia, thanks for holding down the fort while I deal with all this other stuff."

It didn't take much to imagine Olivia's ear-to-ear smile on the other end of the line. "No problem, boss."

Ryan had taken a seat next to her on the couch while she watched the news stream and spoke with Olivia. She turned to face him now.

"I don't know how much more of this I can take." She tossed her cell on the coffee table beside her laptop. "I'd always dreamed of taking over Shelton with Nate. He was so good at being the face of the company. Dealing with the press and marketing and all that. I'm just not sure I can be the one standing in front of cameras convincing people that all is well. I'm not even convinced all is well."

Ryan took her hand. "You can, and you will. I've seen firsthand how hard you work and how much you love this company. You've had a lot of stuff thrown at you in a short period, but you're still standing."

She slid her hand from his. The only thing she knew for certain at the moment was that she wasn't thinking clearly, and his touch only compounded that problem.

"Maybe I should sell to Aurora. Mike was right about our margins being tight. If we get a reputation for being unsafe, guests will stop coming and events will stop booking with us. We can't survive that, not even for a little while."

"Have you considered that that might be the reason behind tonight's broadcast?"

She shook her head in confusion. "What do you mean?"

"Mike Dexter was in your office yesterday implying that it would be detrimental if news of the fire being intentionally started by an employee got out."

She gaped at Ryan for a minute while the picture he'd started painting solidified in her mind.

"That slimy... Tipping off the press would be just like him."

"The information West collected on him suggests he's a ruthless and not always ethical businessman. That said, we don't know for sure he was the source of the information."

"He's the source. When I get back to Manhattan I'm going to..."

She let the thought trail off. There wasn't anything she could do, at least not to Mike. He'd never admit he was the source, and whatever damage he'd intended to do to Shelton was already done. The only thing she could do was mitigate it by showing the world that she was in control and on top of things at Shelton. And that was just what she planned to do as soon as she got back to the hotel tomorrow.

Ryan had fallen silent as her mind drifted. She looked down, surprised to see he'd reclaimed her hand and started drawing small circles on her palm with his thumb. The action was at once soothing and exciting. Her mind flitted back to their earlier kiss, and heat swelled in her.

Stop.

The last thing she needed was another man jerking her around. So they were attracted to each other. That wasn't something either of them could control, but they didn't have to act on it. He'd made it clear on the ride up that he wanted to keep their relationship professional.

And what about you? Do you want to keep things professional?

She shook the thought from her head. It didn't matter what she wanted. He'd made himself clear, and he was right about her needing his help.

"About what I said earlier…" Nadia began.

"I didn't kiss you to keep the job," Ryan said.

She wanted to believe him. "Can we just forget about it? All of it?"

"Nadia—"

She held up a hand. "Please?"

He frowned but nodded.

"I should head to bed. We have an early start tomorrow." She rose and headed for the bedroom.

"Sure."

She could feel his gaze on her, but she kept her eyes focused on her bedroom door.

"Nadia." Ryan spoke as she turned the handle.

She threw her shoulders back and turned, meeting his gaze.

He stood in front of the couch, his gaze unreadable. "Good night."

Chapter Eleven

Nadia waited until Shawn and Gideon joined them in their suite before coming out of her bedroom, foreclosing any chance Ryan might have had at discussing the events of the night before. Not that he had a clue what to say. Professional propriety, not to mention common sense, told him not to get involved with a client. He didn't want to make the same mistake twice. But his heart said something else entirely, and with each passing minute, he feared that he was already too far gone to change course now.

The drive back to New York the next morning was quiet but not uncomfortable. Ryan left Gideon and Shawn at West headquarters after Shawn assured Nadia he'd contact her soon with the name of the hydrologist. Ryan had promised to keep Nadia in the loop, and he intended to do so. But he wouldn't saddle her with the weight of more unproven theories. Getting a hydrologist to look at the water-flow patterns in the bay on the night of Nate's accident would go a long way in answering many of the questions about her brother's death. First and foremost, was Nate Shelton dead?

Ryan could understand Nadia's inability to see where the evidence pointed. Nate was her brother, and she loved and trusted him implicitly. But the absence of a body, the possible inability for the tide to have carried a body out to sea on the night of the accident and the fact that the brakes may have been tampered with were too many coincidences to ignore. Nate Shelton had the money to disappear and reinvent himself, and he knew people who could help him do it. The question was why? Why would a well-off businessman with familial ties chuck his entire life?

That was a question Ryan couldn't answer. Not yet.

After a quick stop at his place so they both could change before work, Ryan drove them to the hotel. He pulled the car to a stop in front of the Harlem hotel just after ten. The sliding door on the gray-paneled van parked three cars away slid open. A woman with a microphone in her hand bounded toward them as he opened the passenger door for Nadia.

"Miss Shelton? Alexandra Maloney, from WNYC News." A bearded cameraman trailed behind her.

Ryan positioned himself between Maloney and Nadia, but that didn't deter the reporter. "Care to comment on the fire at the hotel and the police investigation into whether someone working for you intentionally started it?" Maloney called out as they walked to the front of the hotel.

Nadia kept her head up but avoided looking at the reporter. Ryan kept one hand on her back, shepherding her into the hotel.

"I have sources that say the police are specifically looking at you, Miss Shelton."

The reporter's timing was terrible. Ryan had just opened the door to the hotel, and all eyes in the lobby turned to the scene occurring on the sidewalk.

He felt Nadia stiffen. She turned, taking a step away from the hotel's entrance toward Maloney.

"Your sources are mistaken, Ms. Maloney. There was

a small fire in a guest room. It was quickly extinguished, and no guests were ever in any danger. There is minimal damage to the room and no damage to any surrounding rooms. The hotel is perfectly safe, as are all Shelton hotels. We are open for business as usual."

Nadia shot the reporter a smile that could freeze water before turning and marching into the hotel.

Olivia met them in the lobby and walked with them to Nadia's office. "You did well. You were cool, calm and collected, and you made the fire sound like no big deal. Just one of those things that happens sometimes."

"Right, just one of those things that happens right after someone breaks into my home and right before I find a body in my brother's apartment."

Olivia cast her eyes down at the files she held.

Nadia sighed. "I'm sorry. Being snarky isn't going to solve this."

"I think you've earned a bit of snark." Olivia smiled. "Anyway, it's rare I see you anything less than the consummate professional in the office. Gives me hope that you aren't as perfect as you seem."

Nadia returned Olivia's smile. "Not anywhere near perfect." She sighed. "Well, we need to get serious. The local news running a story about the fire is one thing, but if they get wind of the attacks on me and the note implying Nate is alive, we'll be pulled into a maelstrom."

"Did you find out anything helpful in Rhode Island?"

Ryan stepped into the reception area for Nadia's office, leaving Nadia to fill Olivia in on their trip to Rhode Island. He called Shawn, getting the name and contact information for the hydrologist, a professor at a college upstate. She was more than happy to look over the police report and other information and provide her opinion, especially after the fee Ryan quoted.

He'd just ended the call with the professor when Detective Parsmons entered the office suite.

"Detective, any news on the fire investigation?" Ryan asked.

Nadia and Olivia exited the office and joined Ryan and Parsmons.

"The fire inspector is leaning toward arson, but it's not official yet. You probably know as well as I do that the camera footage was grainy and unhelpful. But I'm not here about the fire."

"No? Well, what brings you here, Detective?" Nadia asked.

Parsmons tipped his head in Ryan's direction. "I'm here to place Ryan West under arrest for assault."

A thin chuckle burst from Nadia, her eyes darting between the two men. "This must be a joke."

Ryan kept his eyes glued to Parsmons. The set of Parsmons's jaw left no doubt that his words were no joke.

"Who am I accused of assaulting?" he asked, even though he was sure he already knew the answer.

"Michael Dexter. You have the right to remain silent…"

He didn't listen to the rest of the Miranda warning. He didn't need to. He'd have liked to say this was the first time he'd been arrested, but that was far from the case.

"I'll hold off handcuffing you until we get outside in deference to Miss Shelton."

Nadia, who seemed to have been in a trance since Parsmons started reciting the Miranda warning, came alive. "This isn't right. Mike assaulted me. Ryan was just defending me."

Parsmons's eyes narrowed. "That's not how Mr. Dexter tells it. In any case, he filed assault charges, so my hands are tied."

"I'll be okay," Ryan said. "Call Shawn and tell him what's happened, please."

He wasn't even sure Nadia heard him.

Nadia's nostrils flared as she faced off with Parsmons. "Your hands may be tied, Detective Parsmons, but mine aren't."

NADIA MET SHAWN and another West brother, Brandon, at the police station. Brandon noted that having eschewed the security business in favor of the law had come in handy on multiple occasions. A few hours after he'd been arrested, Ryan had been arraigned and released on minimal bail.

Shawn gave them a ride back to Ryan's apartment and helped them carry in their bags before leaving them.

Nadia helped Ryan lower himself slowly onto the sofa, a groan slipping from his lips.

"How are you feeling? Should I get you a painkiller?"

"No, I'm fine."

"I can't believe Mike filed charges against you," Nadia called over her shoulder as she walked into the kitchen. She filled a glass with water and crossed back to Ryan. "I'm so sorry. You're in this mess because of me."

Ryan took the glass. "Don't apologize to me. I shouldn't have lost my temper. I embarrassed him, and guys like him lash out whatever way they can when they're embarrassed." He took a drink.

"Well, I won't let Mike get away with this."

He reached for her hand, pulling her down beside him. "Let's not discuss this right now."

She sat beside him and let her head fall to his shoulder. He reached his arm around her and pulled her closer. They'd discussed keeping things on a professional level just yesterday, but right now she didn't care. Life seemed to be lobbing hand grenades at her at every turn, and she needed to feel his warmth and ensure he knew she was there for him. And if they were truly being honest with themselves, they'd passed professional days ago. She was practically living with him, for goodness' sake. You couldn't get more unprofessional than that.

"You must be tired. You should go rest." Ryan ran his hand along her arm.

She laid her hand on his hard chest and felt the beat of his heart. She should be tired, but exhaustion was the furthest thing from her mind. Hyperaware of him next to her, arousal swept through her body.

"I'm not sure I can," she said.

"None of this is your fault," he replied, misunderstanding her comment.

"No, but in the last two days you've been hospitalized and arrested, all because you're helping me."

He pulled her closer. "You can't think like that. We'll figure this out soon. I promise."

"It's hard to think at all right now. Not when all I want to do is this."

She ran her hand over his stubbled jaw and covered his mouth with hers.

Heat crackled between them. She wanted more than just kisses. More than just making out like crazed sixteen-year-olds in his parents' basement. She wanted him, and his body hardening against her right now proved he wanted her just as much.

Ryan pulled away, but the lust in his eyes was clear.

"I want you. I know you're attracted to me." She wasn't usually this forward with a man, but she was tired of holding back.

"Of course, I am, but I don't want you to regret anything. Right now your emotions are heightened because of the situation, but when it's over, I'll still be a glorified security guard and you'll still be a hotel heiress."

"I've wanted you for six quarters."

"What?"

"Our first quarterly meeting about hotel security was six quarters ago. I knew I wanted you that first day. This drama I'm embroiled with now has only made me see how short life is and that I should go for what I want."

"And what do you want?"

"You."

She couldn't remember ever feeling more vulnerable. For a brief moment, she thought he'd pull away again. Then his hand curled around the back of her neck, and his mouth closed over hers.

The spicy scent of his cologne mingled with the minty taste of his mouth, igniting a passion inside her she'd never experienced before. She wanted to touch every inch of him. She threw one leg over his body, straddling him.

She wasn't usually the aggressor when it came to sex, but she wanted to leave no doubt in Ryan's mind that she wanted to be with him in this way, at this moment.

She tore at the buttons on his shirt, her mouth never leaving his. He met her urgent fumbling with equal desperation, dragging her shirt over her head.

There'll be time for a slower exploration later.

That this was just the first time of many they'd be together excited her even more. When he closed his mouth over one hard nipple, his hand skimming under the lace edges of her panties, she moaned her encouragement.

"You are so perfect." He trailed kisses across her chest, lavishing her second breast with the same attention he'd paid to the first. "You don't know how many nights I've dreamed of doing this. Of touching you. Making love to you."

"As many nights as I've dreamed of being with you."

He slid a finger inside her, and she lost the ability to say anything further. Lost the ability to think about anything other than wanting him inside of her.

She drew him into a long, deep kiss that sent them both into overdrive.

She rose to chuck off her jeans and underwear, and he did the same, pulling protection from his wallet before letting his pants fall to the floor. She took the condom from him, rolling it over his arousal slowly before straddling him again.

He took her face between his hands. "Are you sure?"

She lowered herself in answer, taking him inside, bearing down until he was completely within her.

He moaned, bringing a smile to her face. She rotated, and he grasped her hips, thrusting upward. She set the pace, slowing things down with long, slow movements. He skimmed his lips over her neck, to her jaw and back, sending her arousal soaring. Her back arched with the pleasure, and he used the opportunity to capture a nipple between his teeth, stroking it with his tongue.

"Ryan," she cried out as raging hot need exploded within her. She moved her hips faster, frantically racing toward the release they both craved.

Ryan pulled her closer, even as his thrusts grew more hurried, uncontrollable. He claimed her mouth as they climaxed together.

They stayed locked that way for several minutes, coming down from their explosive lovemaking. It wasn't until she finally rolled away that she remembered the gash on his side.

"Oh, I forgot about your injury. I didn't hurt you, did I?" She ran her hand over his bandage.

He caught her hand, brought it to his lips and kissed her palm. "Baby, nothing about what we just did hurt."

She felt her cheeks heat.

Ryan pulled her back into his side but angled them so they could look at each other. "Are you okay?"

She knew what he really asked. Did she regret what they'd done?

She pressed her body closer to his, her bare breasts pressing against his chest. His arousal swelled, and she fought the desire to touch him.

"I am so much better than okay." She smiled a flirty smile. "Want me to show you?"

His smile was laced with desire. "How about I show you a thing or two," he said, rising over her and forcing her to lie back on the couch.

She laughed, then lay back and enjoyed the show.

Chapter Twelve

Nadia awoke with a start. It took her a moment to place where she was. Ryan's bedroom. They'd retreated to his bed after ordering in dinner from the Chinese restaurant on the corner. They made love twice more, exploring each other more fully each time before falling into a sated sleep. But he wasn't in bed beside her now.

Shadows danced over the room. She wasn't sure what had awoken her, but a creak from outside the bedroom set her heart pounding. Something was very wrong.

A shadow moved at the side of the bed. A hand came down over her mouth before she could scream.

Her eyes adjusted to the darkness in the room, and Ryan's face came into focus hovering over the bed.

"Shh. Roll off the bed, and stay down."

She did as he said, her heart thumping in her chest. She wedged herself into the space between the bed and night table.

Ryan rose and put his back to the wall. She caught a flash of silver in his hand. A gun.

She barely had time to process what was happening before the door to the bedroom swung open slowly.

Ryan raised his gun. "Freeze."

The figure at the door swung toward Ryan, his gun outstretched.

Two pops sounded in quick succession.

She did scream this time, unable to stop the sound from bursting from her throat.

The man at the door swore. His gun clattered to the floor, and his right hand flew to his left shoulder. He ran from the room.

Ryan sprinted for the bedroom door. "Don't move."

She didn't know if she could move even if she'd wanted to. Fear paralyzed her.

A crash sounded from the other room.

She couldn't stay cowering in the corner. Ryan could need help.

Nadia eyed the gun the intruder had dropped. She didn't know the first thing about guns—she'd never even touched one before the previous day—but she couldn't leave Ryan to fend for himself. She grabbed the gun from the floor and raced from the room.

Ryan and the intruder grappled in the living room. The intruder landed a punch to Ryan's stomach, sending him doubling over. The man grabbed the Guggenheim book from the table next to the sofa and swung it at Ryan, catching him on the side of the head. Ryan fell onto the sofa, stunned.

"Stop!" She pointed the gun at the intruder.

Blue eyes held her in a sinister gaze. The man took a step in her direction.

She kept the gun outstretched, but the quiver in her hands increased to a tremor.

The intruder paused, his gaze traveling to her shaky hands. That he questioned the wisdom of attempting to take the gun from her was written all over his face.

Ryan pushed up from the sofa, and the intruder turned, dashing toward the apartment entrance. He was out the door before Ryan made it onto steady feet.

Ryan's eyes landed on her. "Are you okay?"

"I think so. Yes."

Ryan stepped next to her, wrapping his steady hands around hers and taking the gun from her. He set it on a nearby table and guided her to the sofa. "Sit. I've got to secure the apartment and call the cops."

She grasped Ryan's arm before he could walk away. "Why is this happening?"

His eyes flashed in anger, but his touch was gentle as he ran his thumb over her cheek. "I don't know, honey. But I promise you, I will find out and make it stop."

DETECTIVE PARSMONS WAS not happy that Nadia and Ryan were involved in yet another *incident*, as he referred to it. He'd declared Ryan's apartment a crime scene.

They were quickly running out of places to stay, but Ryan ensconced them in one of West Security's safe houses about an hour outside the city.

Numb from exhaustion, Nadia barely made it through her nighttime routine before falling into bed.

Morning came sooner than she'd have liked. Ryan tried to talk her into taking the day off. Hanging around the safe house wondering what would happen next held no appeal, and as long as Ryan was by her side there didn't seem to be any reason to avoid going to work.

Ryan kept a go bag in his car for himself, but they headed to Nadia's apartment so she could change before heading to the hotel.

Just as before, Gideon met them at the apartment, but this time Shawn was with him. Gideon again stood guard in the hall while Shawn stayed in the lobby keeping an eye out for trouble. Nadia had no idea what her neighbors thought about the cadre of big scary men traipsing through the building the last several days, but since they were New Yorkers it may not have raised any eyebrows at all.

Ryan followed Nadia into the apartment, but he remained just outside her bedroom when she went in to change. Taking a breath, she yelled through the door, "It's obvious the guy that broke into your apartment last night is connected to the dead guy we found in Nate's apartment."

She grabbed her favorite blush-red suit, tossing it on her bed before diving back into her closet for the black silk blouse she always wore with it. Her power suit, she thought, because she never lacked for confidence when she rocked it.

They'd kept the conversation light and to a minimum on the drive into the city from the safe house. But with the closed door between them, she felt more comfortable broaching the subject.

"I think that's a safe bet," Ryan answered.

She pulled the blouse over her head before speaking again. "Since all the other attacks were clearly aimed at me, it's also safe to assume that the guy last night was coming after me too."

The thought of what could have happened if Ryan hadn't been there sent a shiver down her spine.

Wiggling the skirt over her hips, she zipped it in the front before spinning it around her hips.

"Also a safe bet."

She could hear the tension in Ryan's tone.

She grabbed her black kitten heels and suit jacket.

"So how did he know I was at your place?" Nadia said, pulling the door open simultaneously.

Ryan leaned against the door frame, his arms crossed over his chest, his biceps bulging.

She pulled up short, just inches from smacking into his hard body.

He didn't flinch. Ryan had several inches on her. His head dipped in a slow, appreciative gaze that heated every inch of her as it passed over her body.

"I like the suit," he said, his voice husky.

Nadia wasn't sure she could breathe, much less speak. After a too-long moment, she swallowed hard and forced words from her throat. "Thank you."

Ryan's mouth turned up in a sexy smile, and he took a step back.

Nadia slid past him, her eyes cast down at her feet.

She made it to the couch and sat, putting on her shoes.

"To answer your question, it wouldn't have been that hard to figure out you were staying at my place."

It took a moment for her to remember she'd asked a question.

"If they've monitored your apartment, they know you aren't staying there. And I've been sticking to you like..." Ryan's eyes flashed with an emotion she couldn't name but that sent a zing of excitement through her. "Well, I've been staying close. I never thought anyone would be stupid or reckless enough to breach my home. These guys are more desperate than I thought."

"Desperate isn't good, is it?" Nadia stood, donning her suit jacket.

"No, it isn't. Which is why I don't want to stay here any longer than necessary." Ryan grabbed the handle of the bag she'd packed before changing and led her to the door.

Having completed their duty, Gideon and Shawn headed back to West's headquarters while Ryan drove Nadia to the hotel. It was after ten when they arrived, and although check-out wasn't for another hour and Olivia was helping the clerk, there was a line at the reception desk.

Nadia hurried through the lobby to the door leading to her offices, Ryan on her heels.

As a boutique chain, they didn't have the same hiring luxury as larger hotel chains. Calvin Shelton had been adamant that employees of his hotels knew how to do more than one job, and it was a rule that applied doubly to his kids. Pitching in as a desk clerk for a few hours was just part of the job, even for the CEO.

Nadia unlocked the door to her office, intending to drop her briefcase and purse on her desk before heading back out.

The man sitting behind her desk brought that plan to a sudden halt.

In one swift motion, Ryan shifted Nadia behind him and reached for the gun under his shirt.

"I'd rather you not." The man nodded toward the door Nadia and Ryan had just entered through, and they turned.

A second man, almost as wide as the door frame, stood gun in hand.

"I would just like a few moments of Miss Shelton's valuable time. Of course, I expect you want to stay, Mr. West. Please have a seat," the man directed with an authoritarian benevolence.

They sat in the chairs facing her desk.

"Do you know who I am?" the man asked.

Ryan answered, "The authorities haven't been able to get many pictures, but I'm guessing you are Lincoln Smith."

Smith bowed his head. "A pleasure to meet you both."

Ryan seemed to know who Lincoln Smith was, but the man in front of her was a complete stranger to Nadia.

"I apologize, but your name doesn't ring any bells for me."

Smith looked surprised that she'd spoken. Nadia speared Smith with a cool stare, despite his menacing demeanor. He was in her office, sitting behind her desk, and if he thought she would play the silent woman in this drama, he could think again.

Smith's smile was slick as oil and just as cold. "It's always humbling to realize one is not as well-known as one believes. You may not know me, but I believe you have met my associate, Mr. Brian Leroy."

Nadia frowned. "I have."

"I found it unfortunate that Mr. Leroy's company was not awarded the contract for the work on your last hotel." The iciness in his tone had her tensing. Ryan also tensed.

Smith raised a hand. "It is what it is, in this business. One can't expect to get every contract." But his tone made it clear that is exactly what he would have liked.

"In any case, your brother made a much more interesting business proposition." Smith pinned Nadia with his stare. "One which I took him up on."

Nadia's brain clouded with confusion. "I don't understand. What business proposition?"

Smith cocked his head. "It's best you know as little about that as possible. But you can be of help to me. I need to know where your brother is."

Anger and frustration broke through the other emotions coursing through her. "Serenity Valley Cemetery."

Ryan sent her a cautioning look, which she ignored.

Smith's eyes darkened. "I'm not a man to be played with."

"Neither am I," Ryan intoned.

Smith's attention swung from Nadia to Ryan.

She felt the man standing behind her shift.

The tension in the room cut through her anger. "I assume you are responsible for the note asking about Nate, as well as all the other incidents that have happened to me and my hotel in the last few days?"

Smith's forehead wrinkled. "I don't know what happened at your hotel. I directed a few employees to locate your brother. They used you to draw him out."

"Nadia has nothing to do with your business with Nate Shelton." Ryan glared at Smith.

Smith shrugged. "They are contractors. I don't question their methods as long as they do the job."

Ryan shot daggers at Smith.

"Fortunately for you, you are very resourceful, Miss Shelton." Smith shot a glance at Ryan. "And my men very inept." Smith frowned. "I'd hoped a few warnings—the calls, the damage to your car—would scare you enough that you'd reach out to your brother, giving my men a chance to locate him. However, whoever attacked Mr. West's home yesterday in an attempt to get retribution for Andrei Ledebev was not authorized or condoned by me."

Nadia glanced at Ryan. "We had nothing to do with that man's death."

Smith waved away her comment. "It's of no concern to me if you were. Hazards of the job. Taras is bereft over the death of his brother and acted rashly. I will deal with him."

Another jolt of fear ran through Nadia's body. She didn't want to know what Smith intended.

"An internet search would have given you my brother's location. He died almost a year ago."

Smith locked on to Nadia's face. After a long moment, the hostility in his eyes morphed into disbelief. "You really don't know?"

Nadia looked at Ryan, wondering if he understood what Smith was saying, because she certainly didn't.

Ryan reached for her hands, which she clutched so tightly in her lap her knuckles had gone white.

Smith motioned to the man standing behind them. The man stepped around the desk, pulling a letter-size envelope from the inside breast pocket of his jacket.

Smith handed a five-by-seven photograph across the desk.

Ryan and Nadia both scooted forward in their chairs, Ryan's hand still covering hers.

The picture showed a man with a shaved head and full beard but still recognizable as Nate.

Nadia's heart shuddered, an audible gasp slipping from her lips. "It's Nate."

Ryan squeezed her hand. "That does not prove Nate's alive."

"The date-time stamp," Smith said simply.

The picture had a date and time stamp in the bottom right corner. It had been snapped a month ago.

"Time stamps can be faked," Ryan said.

Smith spread his hands in front of him in a gesture of innocence. "What reason would I have to falsify the photo?"

Ryan didn't have a good answer for that question, but he knew enough not to trust Smith.

"It can't be," Nadia whispered, despite everything in her screaming that it was Nate. Nate was alive a month ago. If what Smith said was the truth, Nate was alive at this very moment.

"I'm sorry." Smith's eyes held sympathy. "I figured you knew. My men almost had him, but…well, I obviously need to improve my hiring practices."

Smith looked away for a moment, seemingly lost in

thought. When his gaze returned to Nadia, any trace of sympathy was gone. "However much of a shock this is to you, the fact remains that your brother stole from me."

Smith's words were a second punch to her gut. "What? How?"

"As I said before, it's best you not know the details. Since it is obvious you know nothing about my business with your brother or his deception, I will leave you out of this, as long as you produce Nathan within forty-eight hours."

That didn't sound at all like he was leaving her out of it, but she didn't have time to say so.

"And if she doesn't produce Nate?" Ryan scowled at Smith.

Smith's gaze dropped the temperature in the room ten degrees.

"I'm sure neither of you want to find out the answer to that question."

Chapter Thirteen

Smith left the same way he'd appeared to have arrived, without being captured by the supposedly upgraded security in the hotel.

Ryan made a mental note to order a full review of the hotel's security and find out how Smith had gotten in. He called Dale, the West Security member stationed in the hotel lobby, the moment Smith stepped foot out of Nadia's office.

Dale arrived in Nadia's office ten minutes later. He'd done a sweep of the lobby and exterior of the hotel but there was no sign of Smith. Dale explained that a guest had approached him and reported seeing a strange man entering her room as she'd gotten off the elevator. Given the circumstances, he'd gone to check out the room and, finding it empty, had proceeded to the security room to check the tapes for the man. That's where he'd been when Ryan called.

Ryan sent Dale back to the control room to pull the video showing how Smith got into Nadia's office. Even having distracted Dale, Smith would have needed a key card to access the area. This was the second time someone had accessed an area of the hotel with a key they shouldn't have had, and Ryan wanted to close this security loophole ASAP.

"I can't believe Nate is alive." They were the first words Nadia had spoken since Smith had left.

"If he is. We can't just trust Smith. This could be some kind of trick."

As soon as he could, he'd have the technology whizzes at West examine the photograph to determine if it was genuine.

"He is. That picture." Nadia pointed to the picture that Smith had left behind. "It's Nate. And when I saw it I knew. How could he do this?"

If Nate really had stolen from Smith, he had a very good reason to want to disappear. Smith may not be the boss. Still, he had to pay the bosses just like all the other midlevel mobsters, and when it came to getting their cut, they wouldn't care that Smith had been ripped off. In fact, if the bosses found out Nate had stolen from him, it would have made Smith's position within the organization precarious. Smith had several reasons, personal, financial and political, to want to make an example out of Nate. Or someone close to Nate.

A vise closed round his heart.

Ryan pushed down the rising fear. It wouldn't help him keep Nadia safe, and that was the only goal at the moment. The best way to keep her safe was to find Nate.

He called Gideon and Shawn and relayed the conversation with Smith. After a copious amount of swearing, Gideon got started on a deep search of Nate's and Nadia's lives to turn up any leads on where Nate might be.

No matter how motivated, it was difficult to disappear completely. Humans are creatures of habit with a deeply rooted instinct to gravitate toward things, areas and people familiar to them on some level. Even if he'd moved to a new city and assumed a new name and career, it was likely that Nate still listened to the same music and frequented the same kind of restaurants. Those were all threads West Security could follow to find him. Of course, they usually had more than two days to pull those threads.

"Do you have a scanner? I want to get those pictures to my tech guy. Maybe we can see some detail that will tell us where they were taken."

Nadia showed him the machine, and he made quick work of scanning the pictures and sending them. He mentally kicked himself for not asking Smith where the photographs had been taken. Hopefully, they could get something helpful from the photos.

While he spoke to Eugene Paul, he kept an eye on Nadia. She stared quietly across the room, lost in thought.

Ryan ended the call.

"The listings." Nadia looked at him with glassy un-focused eyes.

"What?"

"Smith said Nate and he were involved in a business deal. And Nate had those listings for the buildings for sale in the Bronx."

"You think Nate and Smith's business deal involved buying those buildings?" Ryan turned the possibility around in his head. "It's a place to start, but I'm not sure I remember the addresses, and Parsmons hasn't released Nate's apartment yet."

"One was 1437 Ambrose Avenue." Nadia rose and moved behind her desk. She logged in and typed the address into the search bar.

The listing popped up on-screen.

She reached for the phone on her desk. "I'm going to call the realtor. See what information I can get about the property."

Ryan skimmed the listing. It gave the name Carol Alvarez as the realtor.

Miss Alvarez picked up on the second ring.

"My name is Nadia Shelton. I'm interested in one of the properties you have for sale. 1437 Ambrose Avenue."

"Are you representing a buyer?" Through the speaker, Alvarez's voice dripped with suspicion.

"No, I'm not a realtor." A sucking sound came from the other end of the line. Ryan imagined Alvarez readying to end the call. Nadia spoke quickly. "I'm the CEO of Shelton Hotels. I'm always looking for opportunities, and this property came to my attention."

"It's a great property." Enthusiasm laced Alverez's tone now. "A lot of potential. The entire block is for sale."

Ryan searched Alvarez's brokerage website for any properties for sale on the same street. Listings for four adjacent properties appeared.

"Although the properties are listed separately, the sellers have a strong preference for selling the buildings together. I realize you may not be interested in all four," Alvarez blurted, obviously anticipating that most buyers are not in the market to purchase an entire city block. "But there was another potential buyer not long ago, and they may be interested in forming a partnership with an interested party such as yourself."

"Another buyer?" Nadia asked.

"Yes, the buyer had an exclusive option to purchase the properties last year. Unfortunately, they weren't able to get financing."

"Do you mind me asking how much the buyer paid for the option?"

"Ten million." Nadia turned to Ryan, her eyes wide. He motioned for her to keep talking.

"Yes, well, and what is the seller asking for the combined properties?"

"One hundred ten million."

Under different circumstances, Nadia's stunned expression might have been comical.

"Miss Shelton? Are you still there?"

"Yes, I'm here. Well, we are in the beginning stages of scouting properties. I'll be in touch if I decide to pursue one or more of the properties."

"Of course." Alvarez's palpable disappointment carried over the phone line.

Nadia moved to replace the receiver, then stopped. "Miss Alvarez?"

"Yes?" The other woman's voice rang over the line hopefully.

"Would you mind telling me the name of the buyer who had the option?"

Alvarez hesitated.

"If I am going to consider a partnership, I'd like to know who I'd be working with," Nadia added, glancing at Ryan.

"I guess it wouldn't hurt. It was an LLC. Abebe Holdings."

Nadia's back stiffened.

"Do you have the name of a contact person for the LLC?"

Sounds of paper shuffling came from the other side of the line. "Here it is. Erik Jackson."

RYAN DIDN'T TRY to talk Nadia out of going with him to confront Erik with the information Carol Alvarez had given them. Without knowing exactly how deep in this mess Erik was, it would have been safer for Ryan to speak with Erik alone, but he understood Nadia's need to confront the man she trusted.

Having Nadia along also made it easier to get past the security in the lobby of the law firm. The guard on duty merely sent Nadia a cheery smile and waved them both through the gate.

They took the elevator to the forty-second floor. Nadia had said very little since they'd left her office. Now she almost radiated with anger.

Nadia stepped from the elevator before the doors had completely opened and stormed down the brightly lit corridor toward an office at the far corner. An older lady with a gray bob sat at a cubicle off to the side of the door. She looked up from her computer screen, her welcoming expression changing to one of surprise as Nadia blew past, flinging the door open hard enough that it slammed into the wall.

Ryan caught it before it bounced back, but Nadia was already across the large office, stopping in front of her uncle's desk, her hands fisted on her hips.

"Where is Nate? I know he's alive. I know he was involved in some business deal with Lincoln Smith that went wrong."

Erik hurriedly replaced the phone receiver he'd been speaking into and rose. "Nadia, you need to calm down. I don't know what you think you know."

Ryan's eyes narrowed in on the butterfly bandage covering Erik's right cheek and the brace on his left wrist. He caught Erik's gaze, and the guilt swimming in the man's eyes was unmistakable.

"I know," Nadia yelled. "I spoke to the realtor, Carol Alvarez. I know about the buildings in the Bronx, Abebe Holdings and the ten-million-dollar option. You're listed as the contact person on the documents, Uncle Erik."

Ryan laid a hand on Nadia's shoulder, concerned she might launch herself over her uncle's desk and physically attack him.

Not that Erik looked like he would put up much of a fight. He visibly shrank with each word from Nadia's mouth. Erik fell back into his chair.

There was a long moment's pause. "How did you find out?"

"Does it matter?" Nadia answered incredulously.

Anger boiled in Ryan's stomach. Erik didn't seem to grasp the seriousness of the situation. "Lincoln Smith dropped by Nadia's office this morning for an impromptu meeting."

Erik's face went ashen.

Maybe he was coming to understand the danger his and Nate's lie had put Nadia in. Lincoln Smith was a killer, and he'd been within feet of Nadia. If that didn't make this situation real for Erik, nothing would.

"He showed me pictures of Nate. Pictures taken a month ago. Why, Uncle Erik? Why did you and Nate do this?" Nadia's voice cracked.

Ryan's heart pinched. Nadia didn't deserve to be put in this situation by the people she trusted the most.

Erik sighed heavily. "We didn't have any other choice. Nate wanted to make a name for himself, outside of what Calvin had built. He saw this project as a way to do that. You can't understand a man's need to prove himself to the world." Erik straightened in his chair.

Nadia felt anger flare in her gut. "Lots of people, men *and women*, want to prove themselves, Uncle Erik. They don't throw in with the mob, though."

Erik's gaze dropped to his desk. "I don't know if Nate realized who he was doing business with, not at first. His friend Brian Leroy brought him the deal initially."

Ryan resisted the urge to call Erik a liar. They had most of the story, but Ryan had no doubt that Erik either knew where Nate was or how to get in contact with him. Since they needed that information, he reined in his temper.

"By the time Nate came to realize his partner wasn't the businessman he'd thought, it was too late. And then the financing fell through, and things spiraled."

Nadia sank into the visitor's chair in the office. Ryan stood behind her. "How did Nate get ten million dollars to buy the option?"

Erik sighed. "Smith put up the money for the option, with Nate acting as the front man due to Smith's reputation. Nate was supposed to come up with half the hundred-ten-million-dollar purchase price, and Smith would supply the other half."

"Fifty-five million? How did Nate expect to raise that?" Nadia asked, her voice rising.

Erik leaned forward, locking gazes with Nadia. "You have to know Nate was adamant about not using any of Shelton Hotels' assets for this deal. He wanted to do it all himself."

Ryan pressed his lips together. That Erik would justify his nephew's stupid decision to get involved with mobsters, even after everything that had happened, boggled the mind. But he and Nadia still needed Erik to tell them where Nate was, so Ryan would keep his mouth shut, for now.

"You think I should, what, give him a prize for that?" Nadia said.

Erik's eyes turned hard.

Ryan interjected before the man could respond. "Could we get back to my question? How did Nate plan to raise the twenty million?"

"Nate is a Shelton. He has friends. Connections. Only, it was more difficult than he could have expected. The option was about to expire, and he didn't have anywhere near what he needed.

"And Smith would lose ten million dollars. A loss like that was not something Smith and the people he answered to would just write off."

"So Nate faked his death and went into hiding." Ryan cut to the end of the story.

Erik nodded. "Nate figured if he died in an everyday car accident, Smith wouldn't have cause to be suspicious." Erik shrugged. "Car accidents happen every day."

"But Smith didn't buy it?" Ryan said.

"It seemed like he had. But then Nadia told me about the men at her apartment and the fire at the hotel. Even then I wasn't sure if any of this had to do with Smith until…" Erik's voice trailed off.

Ryan could guess where this part of the story was headed.

"Until what?" Nadia looked from her uncle to Ryan, confusion clouding her eyes.

"Until Andrei Ledebev showed up at Nate's apartment while your uncle was there," Ryan answered for Erik. It was a shot in the dark, but it made sense that Erik could have been staying over at the apartment on the night Andrei broke in.

Erik's gaze pleaded. "It was self-defense. He attacked me. I had no choice."

Nate's apartment was probably one of the worst places for Erik to have used for his overnight stays in New York under the circumstances. As soon as Smith realized Nate was alive, he'd have scoured the city real-estate records for other properties in Nadia's or Erik's name looking for Nate.

Nadia covered her mouth with her hand, the color fading from her face.

He hoped she wasn't about to be sick. He needed her to hold on for a little while longer. Then he'd get her somewhere safe and bring Nate in. After that, he wasn't sure what would happen. The best thing for Nadia would be if he turned Nate over to Smith, but Ryan was sure Nadia would object, and it would sign the man's death warrant. No matter what Nate had done, Ryan wouldn't aid cold-blooded murder. But first things first.

Ryan locked eyes with Erik. "Where's Nate?"

The older man looked ready to argue for a moment before all the fight seemed to be expelled right out of him like air from a balloon.

"I don't know." Erik's gaze listed left.

Nadia surged to her feet. "Enough lies, Uncle Erik," she said, slamming her hand on his desk. Ryan rose to stand beside her.

Erik started, his chair rolling away from his desk. "I don't know for sure. But he calls me weekly, just so I know he's okay."

"What's the number?"

Erik shook his head. "It's always a different number."

"So you never call him?" Ryan asked.

"I've called him a few times. Always on the last number he used to call me. Sometimes it works, sometimes it doesn't. I called Nate yesterday to tell him about the note Nadia received at her office asking about him."

"Give me the number you used to call him." Ryan took a pen from a holder and tossed it on the desk in front of the man.

Erik puckered his lips but picked up his phone, scrolled for a moment, then scribbled a number on a sticky note.

"What else can you tell us?" Ryan asked.

"Nothing." Erik held up his hands. "Nate has to be careful. I get the feeling he moves around a lot. The phone numbers he calls from usually have different area codes."

That meant very little these days, with easily acquired burner phones and numbers, but he didn't mention that to Erik.

"Nate's never said anything about his location?" Nadia asked.

Erik hesitated.

"Uncle Erik, Smith knows Nate is alive. The only chance he has is if we find him and he goes to the police."

"I really don't know where Nate is. Not for sure. But a while back he complained about his boss. Some disagreement, I can't remember over what, but it doesn't matter. His boss shut him down and said something like 'It's the way it's always been done at the Delaney, and it's the way it always will be done'."

Nadia gripped Ryan's arm. "The Delaney Hotel? In Atlanta?" Her voice rose in excitement.

Erik looked as if he'd aged a decade since they'd walked into his office. "I don't know. I don't even know if he referred to a hotel, but that's what I assumed."

Ryan pulled up the website for the Delaney Hotel on his phone. "It's a place to start. One more thing before we leave. How did you get those injuries?"

Erik hesitated. "I was in a car accident."

Erik didn't meet Ryan's eyes when he spoke, but Ryan didn't let his gaze leave the man's face. He was already sure he knew the answer, but he wanted to see the older man's reaction to the question. "It won't be difficult to find out where you were yesterday."

Silence hung in the room for several long minutes.

"Uncle Erik?"

Erik raised his head, his eyes watering as he looked at his niece. "I just wanted to keep you from going to Northpath."

Nadia gasped and reached for Ryan. "You forced us off the road."

"When you left that message saying you were going to Northpath to talk to the sheriff, I panicked. The sheriff was suspicious from the beginning. I couldn't let her put those ideas in your head."

Tears rolled down Nadia's cheeks as she stood up. She speared her uncle with a look of contempt before turning her back to him and starting for the door.

Ryan followed suit.

"You may not believe this," Erik called out, "but your brother and I love you. We did this to protect you."

Nadia turned back to her uncle. "No, he didn't. His ego got him into this mess, and now his cowardice could get me killed."

Nadia didn't wait for her uncle's response before striding from the room.

Ryan followed, unclenching his fists. He would have liked to have had a private chat with Erik, but he didn't have the time to make the man understand how foolish it was to have tried to fake Nate's death. Or how deeply he and Nate had hurt Nadia in doing so.

"I need to head to my office to put together a game plan for bringing Nate back to New York," Ryan said once they were back in the car.

Nadia nodded. "Whatever you think is best."

"I'm glad you said that, because I think you should stay here while I go to Atlanta."

Nadia shook her head. "I told you I didn't want to be left out."

"I'm not leaving you out. But we don't know what

we're walking into. We can't call Nate and tell him we're coming. He's bound to be on edge since he's on the run. It's too dangerous to take you."

She pushed her shoulders back. "I. Am. Going. With you."

He shook his head, his jaw clenching.

"Nate won't know you're coming. Who knows how he'll react? If I'm there, he'll know you aren't working for Smith."

He could see her point, but his every instinct told him she should stay in New York.

"Nate's safety isn't my primary concern. Yours is."

Nadia's gaze was unreadable. "I'm concerned about Nate's safety."

After everything her brother had put her through, she still put him before herself. It was why he loved her.

He loved her.

Despite all the reasons he shouldn't, didn't even want to, he did.

"Please." Nadia's voice broke through his thoughts.

They still had most of the forty-eight hours Smith had given them to find Nate. But they couldn't be sure Nate was still in Atlanta or if he had even truly been there in the first place. Flying down there could end up being wasted time, but they had nothing else to go on.

Ryan navigated them through city traffic. "Okay. But you do what I say. I'm not taking any chances with your safety."

Nadia reached over the console between them and took his free hand. "Thank you."

While he drove them to the safe house, she called Olivia to let her know that they wouldn't be back to the hotel today.

When they arrived, he ran his usual check of the premises, making sure the windows and doors were locked.

Then he did what he'd been aching to do since they'd left Erik Jackson's office. He pulled Nadia into his arms.

She stiffened for a millisecond before sliding her arms around his waist and burying her face in his neck. They stood that way for several minutes, her hot tears soaking his collar before Nadia stepped back out of his arms.

"I'm sorry." A rueful laugh slipped from her lips. "I've been pushed into oncoming traffic, chased by madmen and shot at all within a week, and then I fall apart when I get good news. Nate's alive. I should be ecstatic."

He kissed her forehead before placing a light kiss on her lips. "You've had a lot thrown at you. It will take some time to process it all. Until then, you feel how you feel."

"I'm going to lie down." She turned away, but stopped and turned back before disappearing down the hall. "When will we leave for Atlanta?"

"I've got to coordinate some things with Shawn, but this evening."

She nodded. "I'll be ready." Nadia headed to the bedroom before facing him again. "Thank you."

The bedroom door clicked shut.

He didn't want to go chasing after Nate. He wanted to wrap Nadia in his arms and spirit her away from all this madness for good.

That wasn't an option right now, but soon. He'd do his best to get her brother out of the mess he'd gotten himself into, but getting Nate back to New York was only one piece of the puzzle. Getting him clear of Smith would be infinitely harder.

And when this was all over and Nadia was safe, he'd tell her how he felt. Because he knew now that this wasn't just a passing infatuation spurred by the intensity of their situation.

It was the real deal.

Chapter Fourteen

Ryan tried the number Erik gave him for Nate, but the call went directly to voice mail. Nate Shelton wasn't a stupid man. Even burners had GPS nowadays so their users could use mapping and directional apps. That meant that the phones could be tracked, even though it was much more difficult to track burners than standard phones since they weren't associated with contracted carriers. Lucky for them, West Security did the impossible every day.

He made reservations for them at the Delaney. They'd probably get there too late to talk to many of the staff, but he'd booked a suite for two nights so they'd have a legitimate reason to be at the hotel all day tomorrow. Given the time crunch, he hoped they wouldn't need to stay the second night.

Ryan let Nadia sleep for as long as he could, waking her when there was a little more than an hour to get to the airport. She'd showered, packed and was ready to go fifty minutes later. He drove them to a private airstrip in the Bronx.

A dark blue sky hung overhead as he drove into the airport, though the tarmac was amply lit. Nadia's eyes grew wide as Ryan pulled to a stop beside a sleek white jet idling in front of one of the hangars, its steps already lowered.

They got out of the car and moved to the trunk.

Nadia looked from the plane to Ryan. "Does every security firm have a private jet on standby?"

He smiled, lifting his bag onto his shoulder. "The plane is a loan. A while back we rescued a wealthy client's son from a group of kidnappers. The client was appreciative and offered his plane if we ever needed it."

"You called in a favor for me?"

If he counted the IOUs he owed his brothers, he'd already traded several favors helping her find Nate. He'd call in a hundred more if it would keep her safe, but now wasn't the time to get into that. He simply answered "Yes."

Nadia touched his arm, sending a tingle through him. "Thank you."

His eyes locked on hers, and despite the time and place, the urge to tell her how he felt overwhelmed him. "Nadia, I'd do—"

"Mr. West?" A thin woman in a dark blue suit, white shirt and practical pumps approached from the hangar. "We're ready to board you and your guest now."

The woman made a sweeping gesture toward the plane, her practiced smile fixed in place.

He held Nadia's gaze for several seconds then swung her bag from the trunk and followed her to the plane.

It wasn't the first time West Security had borrowed a plane from this particular client, but since the client owned at least three private jets that Ryan knew of, he wasn't surprised to realize he'd never flown on this plane before. Custom cherry woodwork and beige leather seats as soft as butter greeted them along with the flight attendant. Traveling the world by private plane was a life many people dreamed of having. Ryan thought back to the crisis that had brought his client to West Security. The maxim *Be careful what you wish for* sprang to mind.

He and Nadia settled in, and the pilot had them in the air quickly.

Once they reached their cruising altitude and the attendant deemed it safe, he tried calling the number that Erik had given them for Nate again. The call went straight to voice mail, and Ryan hung up without leaving a message.

He leaned his head back on the seat, intending to take a moment or two just relax. He awoke with a start as the plane bounced along a patch of turbulence. A glance at his watch told him he'd slept for nearly an hour and a half. He'd intended to work for most of the three-hour flight, but he'd obviously needed the sleep more.

Ryan looked across the aisle to where Nadia sat on the leather couch across from his seat, looking out of the window at the passing clouds.

"You're awake." She turned to him, a half smile on her face.

"Yeah. Sorry about that."

"Don't be sorry. You must be exhausted."

"I'd planned to work on the flight, but I did research the Delaney Hotel before we left. Given your industry experience, you could probably tell me more about the place than I learned, though. It's an icon, according to the internet."

Nadia's half smile turned full. "It is. It was built in the 1920s—I can't remember the exact year—and for a long time, if you were somebody and visiting Atlanta, you stayed at the Delaney."

"And now?"

"Times changed. The family that owned it sold, and the brand lost its luster. And then the Great Depression hit." Nadia shrugged.

"But the hotel survived."

"It did. One of the big international chains eventually purchased it."

Ryan raised a brow. "Aurora?"

His heart buoyed at her laugh. "Mike wishes." She named one of the other well-known hotel chains.

"I'm sure you'll find the building fascinating with your background in art. It's on the historic register, and the brand's been repositioned to appeal to guests who'll pay a premium for the architecture and historic charm."

A premium was an understatement. The room he'd booked had not been cheap.

"You know, we can't be sure that Nate is still at the Delaney or if he ever was. Uncle Erik could have heard him wrong, or it could be another hotel named Delaney."

Ryan studied her. He saw a woman conflicted. She wanted to find Nate, but finding him wouldn't solve her problems. In some ways, it made them even worse. Smith had forced her into a position where she had to choose her brother's safety or her own. Could she do to Nate what he'd, however unintentionally, done to her? If it came down to it, could she sacrifice Nate to save herself?

"We don't, but it makes some sense that Nate would start over in Atlanta," Ryan said. "There's a family tie, even if he can't reach out to the family, and he's somewhat familiar with the city from your childhood trips. It's also a big enough city that he can blend right in. And with his knowledge of the hospitality industry, it makes sense he'd get a job at a hotel."

Nadia didn't look convinced.

He unbuckled his seat belt and moved to the couch where Nadia sat. "Hey." He took her hand in his. "We'll check in, get a good night's sleep and hit the ground running. Who knows, by this time tomorrow we could be back in New York with Nate."

Nadia's eyes locked with his. "Then what?"

He didn't have an answer for that, at least not one she'd want to hear. He pulled her close, and she laid her head on his shoulder.

"I don't know if I've said it before, but thank you." She didn't lift her head as she spoke. "I don't think I could have made it through all this without you and Shawn and West helping me."

He dropped a kiss on the top of her head. "You're the strongest woman I've ever met. You'd have done fine if you'd had to go it alone, but you should know that you never have to. I'll always be here for you."

They sat that way, with Nadia's head on his shoulder and his arms around her, until they landed.

IT WAS LATE by the time they arrived and checked in at the Delaney. Ryan had booked a suite, but this one didn't have two separate bedrooms like the suite in Richmond. Not wanting to be presumptuous or place any pressure on Nadia, he'd intended to bunk on the couch. Not that he'd planned to get much sleep at all. He wanted to do more research before morning and maybe take a tour of the hotel to see if he couldn't find a staff member or two willing to talk to him.

But by the time he and Nadia had eaten their room-service dinner, they were both exhausted. Nadia quickly disabused him of the notion of sleeping on the couch, and they fell into bed, wrapped around each other.

A beam of sunlight shot through the space between the closed curtains and illuminated Nadia's sleeping form. Her soft body snug against his, loose curls falling across his hard chest. Touching her creamy skin set his blood racing to his groin. Another morning, when they had more time and were free of the mess Nate had created, he'd make good on the thoughts running through his head. For now, he had work to do.

He rose from the bed and quietly made his way into the common area of the suite.

If Nate was in Atlanta, Ryan wanted to find him fast. He could almost hear the forty-eight-hour deadline ticking away like a detonator counting down the seconds before an explosion. Smith didn't issue idle threats. If they didn't turn over Nate, the dynamics of the situation would take a drastic turn for the worse.

He opened his laptop and scoured the background report on Nate for clues to help them figure out where he might be. He also researched the Delaney Hotel and its employees, giving thanks for the public penchant for oversharing on social media.

Water ran in the bathroom on the other side of the bedroom's door, calling his attention to the time. He'd spent the last hour and twenty minutes researching and had gotten a good start, although no concrete leads on Nate's whereabouts.

He called down to room service, hanging up the phone just as the bedroom door opened.

"I ordered breakfast."

"Great," she said, lingering near the bedroom as if she wasn't sure whether she wanted to come out into the living area.

"If you're done with the bathroom, I'll get washed up before the food gets here." Ryan strode toward the bedroom. There was only one bathroom in the suite, and it was through the bedroom door.

"Oh, yes, sorry." She moved into the living room and took a seat on the couch.

He ran through his morning routine, quickly showering, shaving and putting on fresh clothes. He reentered the living room just as Nadia closed the door to the suite.

A rolling table covered with a white tablecloth sat in the middle of the room with silver plate covers over the food and the morning paper perched at its edge. Nadia had moved the vase of flowers that decorated the round dining table in the room to the credenza behind the couch and set the table for breakfast.

"I should have waited until after the food arrived to shower," he said, pushing away the irritation he felt with himself. "I don't want you opening the door to anyone. We can't be sure who's on the other side."

Nadia froze with the plate cover she'd just lifted in her hand. "You think we could be in danger here?"

He took the cover from her, putting it aside and removing the covers from the other three plates on the tray. "I think I'm not taking any chances with your safety, so please don't open the door without me, okay?"

She nodded and sat, her expression pensive.

They ate in silence for several minutes.

"You know way more about how hotels run than I do. If Nate works or worked here, what kind of job would he have?" Ryan asked.

Nadia swallowed the piece of toast she'd been chewing. "Well, he's qualified for almost any job. Remember I told you my father made sure we could do just about every possible job at a hotel. But I'm assuming he couldn't produce references, at least not good enough ones for managerial positions since he can't use his real name—"

"A safe assumption."

"Then, entry-level positions. Clerk, housekeeping, janitorial."

"He'd probably want to stay behind the scenes as much

as possible," Ryan added. At least that's what he'd do if he was on the run. No telling who could walk up to check-in and recognize the clerk behind the desk as Nathan Shelton. Better not to take that chance, even if he was hundreds of miles away from Manhattan.

"Um…then janitorial, laundry or maintenance would be the most likely. Also, if the hotel runs the restaurant in the lobby, he might try for a kitchen job like dishwasher."

"Okay, then we'll target staff from those departments," Ryan said as he finished his omelet.

Nadia had eaten very little, mostly pushing pieces of egg around on her plate. "That's not going to be easy. The nature of those jobs has them behind the scenes."

Ryan stood. "We'll play it by ear. First, though, I want to walk around the hotel. Get the lay of the land."

They each grabbed a key and headed out the door.

The articles he'd read describing the Delaney hadn't done it justice. Much of the first floor had been given over to retail establishments, including four restaurants of varying cuisines. The lobby soared four stories and boasted cut glass skylights he hadn't noticed checking in after dark last night. They walked the hotel for nearly an hour, eventually finding their way to the lower level where half a dozen large conference rooms and twice as many smaller meeting rooms were situated. None of the rooms appeared to be occupied at the moment. Two oversize white doors showcasing the words *Staff Only Beyond This Point* stenciled in bold red font stood out among the sea of yellow on the walls.

"Laundry, janitorial services, housekeeping—pretty much the business end of the hotel—are probably behind those doors," Nadia said, heading for the doors.

"Hang on." Ryan grabbed her arm. "Let's just wait for a bit. See what we see."

She gave him a curious look but let him lead her to a sitting area at the other end of the hall where they could still monitor the staff door.

Hotel employees in black polyester skirts and pants with matching vests came and went through the staff door.

After ten minutes, Nadia slid to the edge of her seat, her hands twisting in her lap. "What are we waiting for?"

"If we're right that Nate would prefer a job that's out of sight, he'd most likely befriend similar workers. The people going in and out of this door aren't dishwashers, launderers or janitors—not dressed like that."

"You're right. There's probably a service hall and elevator on the other side of the doors. They'd use that to get around as much as possible."

He studied the doors. "Then, we're not going to find the people we want to talk to here."

Nadia snapped her fingers. "How about the employees' entrance? I should have thought of that sooner." Nadia glanced at the watch on her arm. "It's not quite nine. We could still catch someone coming in."

"It's worth a shot." Ryan stood, offering Nadia his hand. He pulled her to her feet. They took the elevator to the lobby level and exited the hotel through the main doors.

The hotel spanned the entire city block, but halfway along the length of the building, a service alley cut the building in two. A gray steel door with an assortment of dings opened into the alley. A black square keypad was mounted next to the door.

Ryan nodded toward the coffee shop across the street. "Let's have a cup of coffee."

Nadia squinted at him. "We just had a cup of coffee."

Ryan took her hand, pulling her across the street. "Let's have another."

He bought their coffee and steered them to a table on the outdoor patio that gave an unobstructed view of the alley and the door. The day was already starting to heat up, so they weren't the only patrons choosing to take their refreshments on the patio.

Nadia followed Ryan's gaze. "Ah, I see. More watching."

Ryan shot her an amused glance. "A lot of a private investigator's work is sitting and watching."

She laughed. "I'd be horrible at that."

They didn't have to watch long before the steel door opened. An employee clad in white trousers and a long-sleeved white shirt stepped into the alley and lit a cigarette.

"Bingo." Ryan rose, leaving his coffee on the table.

He and Nadia crossed back to the hotel side of the street. They skirted around a row of dumpsters emitting a vaguely noxious odor despite the closed covers.

The man blew a ring of smoke into the air and watched as Nadia and Ryan approached. "You're not supposed to be back here." The nameplate pinned to the man's chest read *Brian*.

Ryan smiled. "We'll only be a minute. We'd like to ask you a couple of questions."

Brian blew another ring of smoke. "What questions?"

"We're looking for someone who might work here or have worked here in the last couple months."

Brian threw his cigarette on the ground and snubbed it out with the toe of a scuffed red Adidas sneaker. "I don't want to get involved."

"Please." Ryan frowned when Nadia stepped in front

of him toward Brian. "I'm trying to find my brother. He's in trouble, and I just want to help."

Brian's eyes roamed Nadia's body from head to toe, lingering on her breasts. Ryan cleared his throat and fixed the man with a warning glare.

Brian's eyes snapped to Ryan's, a guilty smile twisting his lips.

"Please," Nadia said, drawing the man's attention back to her. "If you could just look at this picture and tell me if he works here?" Nadia held her phone out.

Brian sighed. He studied the picture on Nadia's phone for several seconds. "It looks like it could be Jamal. His head was shaved, and he had one of them skinny beards right here." Brian tapped the cleft in his chin. "But yeah, I think it's Jamal. He don't work here no more."

The familiar rush flowed through Ryan; the surge of adrenaline that hit whenever he was on the right track in a case.

"What's Jamal's last name?"

Brian tilted his head back, eyes turned to the sky in thought. "Fredricks, I think."

"Do you know where Jamal works now?" Ryan asked.

"Nah, man. He left, like, four, five months ago. We weren't friends or nothing. I just knew him from around."

"Was Jamal friends with anyone in particular?" Nadia followed up.

Brian hesitated, obviously reluctant to share the names of his coworkers.

"We won't say how we got the name," Nadia said.

Brian hesitated for a moment longer, then shrugged. "I guess it don't matter since I didn't give you my name, anyway. Jamal hooked up with one of the girls in housekeeping. Karen Vernon. I don't think she's on the schedule to work today."

His excitement waned. They didn't have a lot of time for tracking down people. Hopefully, there weren't a lot of Karen Vernons in Atlanta.

"Thanks, man." Ryan offered his hand, a twenty discreetly palmed.

Brian grasped Ryan's hand, taking the twenty without blinking an eye. He swiped a plastic square over the black box on the wall. The locks clicked open, and he pulled the door open.

Ryan and Nadia turned.

"Hey," Brian called before they'd taken more than five steps.

They turned back, Ryan angling himself in front of Nadia.

"I think she lives with her mother out in Myers Grove." Brian went inside without waiting for a response.

Nadia glanced at Ryan. "To Myers Grove?"

"To Myers Grove."

Chapter Fifteen

Myers Grove was a working-class neighborhood approximately thirty minutes outside of the city. The homes were small and neatly kept. Ryan had called Shawn on the drive and had him run a basic check on Karen Vernon. He'd also passed on the fake name Nate had been using in Atlanta.

Thirty-two years old, Karen had worked at the hotel for the past seven years, rising to the rank of assistant manager of housekeeping services. With one ex-husband and no run-ins with the law, Karen was the model of an upstanding citizen.

Ryan knocked on the door of the white clapboard house Karen shared with her mother and ten-year-old son.

A woman in her midthirties with shoulder-length chestnut hair opened the main door but left the screen door firmly shut. "Can I help you?"

"Ms. Vernon? My name is Ryan West. I'm a private investigator, and this is Nadia Shelton. We'd like to ask you a few questions about Jamal Fredricks."

Karen took a step back, her eyes clouded with suspicion. "Why are you asking about Jamal?"

"I'm his sister. I need to find him. It's very important." Nadia took a step forward, assuming control of the conversation. Ryan let her. He'd interviewed enough people to know when one was close to slamming the door in his face. If tapping into the woman's sentimental side would help them get answers faster, it was worth taking a back seat.

"I can't help you. I'm sorry." Karen took another step back and began to close the door.

"Please. The man you know as Jamal is my brother, Nathan Shelton. He's in trouble."

Karen tilted her head and studied Nadia for several moments. "You look like him." She sighed and unlocked the screen door, pushing it open.

Ryan and Nadia stepped into the living room. The space was compact but tidy. Karen waved Nadia and Ryan to the couch, where they waited while she made coffee.

Karen returned with a tray holding three mugs. She set the tray on an ottoman and passed a cup to Nadia then Ryan before settling in the easy chair opposite them with her cup.

"You don't seem surprised to learn that the man you knew as Jamal is not who he said he was." Ryan started the conversation with the obvious observation.

Karen sighed. "I guess you already know Jamal and I dated for a while or you wouldn't be here." Karen placed her mug back on the tray and lowered her fingers. "The minute we met, Jamal—Nate and I connected. My mother thought we were moving too fast, but sometimes the attraction, not just physical stuff but something deeper, it just hits you."

Ryan caught Nadia's eye. A current of electricity sizzled between them.

Karen's gaze bounced from Ryan to Nadia, her mouth turned up in a half smile. "So you two do know what I mean." Karen's smile fell. "A few weeks after we started seeing each other, Jamal told me the truth about who he was and why he was in Atlanta."

"And you stayed with him?" Nadia said with surprise.

"Everyone makes mistakes and deserves a second chance." Karen shrugged. "And we love each other."

Ryan set his coffee aside and pushed to the edge of the sofa. "Do you know where Nate is now?"

Karen's eyes drifted up and to the left. "No."

"It's important we find Nate as soon as possible. The men he told you about know he's alive," Ryan said.

Concern coursed across Karen's face. "He thought someone was watching him, following him. That's why he left Atlanta."

"When was this?" Ryan asked.

"About a month ago."

That matched up with the dates on the photographs Smith had given them. Nate's instincts had probably saved his life, but his luck wouldn't hold out forever.

"Please, if you know where Nate is, tell us so we can help him," Nadia implored.

Karen sighed. "I don't know for sure. He calls at least once a week, but he's careful not to give any specifics. We use burner phones."

He read between the lines. "You don't know for sure, but you have an idea where he is."

Karen sighed again. "I drove him to the bus station and purchased his ticket for him. The bus lines only ask for identification when you purchase the ticket."

"So even if someone got a passenger list his name wouldn't appear." Ryan was glad to see that Nate wasn't completely oblivious about how to fly under the radar. Hopefully, it would be enough to keep him safe until they could get to him.

"Where was the ticket to?" Nadia asked.

"DC."

Another big city where the addition of one more person wouldn't be noticed by many.

Ryan rose and pulled out his phone to call Shawn and get him started on tracking down any Jamal Fredrickses in DC or the surrounding areas. They couldn't be sure he was still using the name Jamal, as doing so would be a huge risk, but good fake identification was expensive. Since Nate wasn't sure he was being followed, he might have considered it worth the risk. They couldn't even be sure he'd taken the bus all the way to DC, but it was a place to start.

The hum of adrenaline he'd felt after talking to Brian earlier had risen to a drumbeat. They were getting close to finding Nate. Their luck just needed to hold for a little longer.

THEY THANKED KAREN for her help and promised to let her know when they found Nate. Ryan drove them back to the Delaney while Nadia thought about what Karen had said. Had her brother really been in love? It seemed impossible that her confirmed bachelor of a brother had found love in the midst of the chaos that was his current life, but stranger things had happened. That he'd told Karen the truth about who he was and what he'd done went a long way to showing that maybe he had found love. She just hoped they could figure out a way for him to live long enough to enjoy it.

Ryan's phone rang as they entered the hotel lobby. "Shawn, what's up?"

He pulled Nadia into an alcove off the busy lobby and held the phone so they could both hear.

"No Jamal Fredricks in DC, but I checked the next biggest city on the bus route, Richmond, Virginia, and found three. Only one recently applied for a Virginia driver's license, though," Shawn said.

"I'm not even going to ask how you got that information so fast," Ryan replied.

"I'll shoot you what I have and keep digging. Are you guys going to head to Richmond?" Shawn asked.

Nadia glanced at her watch. It was still early in the afternoon, and Richmond was only an hour and a half flight.

"Yes. I'll let you know if that changes." He ended the call and turned to Nadia.

"So we're headed to Richmond now."

Ryan nodded. "I'm going to call the pilot now, and then I'll let the front desk know we won't need the room another night."

"Okay. I think I'll head upstairs and start packing."

"Make sure to lock the door, and don't open it for anyone," he reminded her.

"Got it."

She took the elevator to their room, her mind on packing and the possibility that they'd find Nate before the end of the day. She didn't notice the movement from behind her until she'd already inserted her key card.

The locks on the door beeped open at the same time a large palm landed between her shoulder blades and shoved her forward.

She stumbled into the room, landing on one knee hard enough to make her teeth chatter.

It took a moment before she was able to push from the floor and turn to face her attacker.

When she did, she looked into the face of Taras Ledebev, the man who'd attacked her and Ryan in Ryan's apartment.

"Where's your boyfriend?"

"He'll be here any minute, so I'd run now if I was you."

Taras sneered. "Not running, girlie. I'm going to pay you and your boyfriend back for killing my brother."

Nadia glanced around the suite looking for a weapon within reach. Their breakfast dishes had been removed while they'd been out, dashing any hope of using a knife in self-defense. The only things within arm's reach were the newspaper that had been delivered with their breakfast and the vase of yellow roses, both of which were on the credenza behind the couch.

"We had nothing to do with your brother's death." She hoped keeping him talking would give her time to come up with an idea.

"He just happened to die in your brother's apartment," Taras growled. "I'm not that stupid."

"You're plenty stupid if you think I killed your brother. Or that you can get away with killing me and Ryan in a hotel full of people."

Someone pounded on the door. "Room service," a voice boomed from the hall.

Taras turned.

The door burst open, and Ryan barreled into the room. He rammed his shoulder into Taras's stomach. The two men crashed into the armoire. Ryan threw a punch, catching Taras in the jaw, momentarily stunning him.

Taras pulled a switchblade from his pocket. The blade snapped out.

Taras stepped forward, slashing out with the knife and missing before the two men tumbled to the ground. Taras straddled Ryan's legs and swung the knife down toward Ryan's face. Ryan rolled to his side, throwing Taras off-kilter. But not for long. Taras raised the knife again. Ryan gripped Taras's wrist with both hands, the two men struggling for control.

She couldn't just stand there and watch Ryan get stabbed.

Nadia grabbed the glass vase behind the couch. She rushed toward the struggling men and brought the vase down on the top of Taras's head.

Taras rolled off of Ryan, dazed but conscious, and ran for the door. He sprinted into the hall as Ryan pushed up from the floor.

"Stay here," Ryan called out as he followed Taras from the room.

Nadia stayed on the couch and rubbed her sore knee, coming down from the adrenaline high of the moments before.

Ryan was back in less than five minutes, but it seemed eons longer as she waited and wondered if Taras has gotten the jump on him again.

"He got away." Ryan locked the door to the suite.

"Should we call the police?"

Ryan hesitated. The police would ask a lot of questions he didn't want to answer at the moment. Reporting the intrusion would also eat up time they didn't have. "Let's report it to the hotel management as a simple break-in. Since nothing was taken, they'll probably be happy to go along when we decline to make a police report. I'll let Parsmons know when we get back to New York."

Nadia crossed to where Ryan stood, a slight limp in her gait.

"You're hurt." He slid his arm around her waist.

"It's nothing. I can walk it off. How did Taras know we were in Atlanta?" Nadia asked more to herself than him.

Lines formed in Ryan's forehead. "He must have followed us to the airport in New York. I didn't see anyone tailing us, but that doesn't mean no one did."

"What now?"

"I'll call the front desk, and you pack. We have a plane to catch."

It took the hotel management nearly two hours to take their statements and document the damage to the room, but they were more than happy to handle the situation in-house. The plane was fueled and ready to fly by the time Nadia and Ryan arrived at the small private airport where they'd landed the night before. Thankfully, the flight from Atlanta to Richmond was short, but it was still late afternoon by the time they arrived.

Ryan gave his name at the check-in counter at the chain hotel where he'd had Shawn make them reservations.

The clerk punched several keys on the computer in front of him.

"Mr. West, welcome." The clerk beamed. "Your room is ready, and your companions have already checked in."

"Companions?"

The clerk's smile dimmed but held. "Yes. Mr. Shawn West and another gentleman. Mr. West asked me to tell you he is in room 4123 just a couple doors down from you."

Ryan barely stopped long enough to drop their bags off in their suite before he hustled them to Shawn's room.

Shawn opened the door with a grin.

"What are you doing here?" Ryan frowned across the threshold at his brother.

"Hello to you too. You want to come in so you can lay into me out of earshot of the whole hotel?"

Shawn stepped back, opening the door to the room wider.

Nadia smiled as she walked past him into the room. "Hi, Shawn. Hi, Gideon."

Gideon nodded from his seat at the table in the hotel room.

Shawn strode back to the table and sat, leaving Ryan

to close the door to the suite. "So what are you two doing here?"

Shawn's brows lowered. "Helping you. I got an address for Jamal Fredricks. A PI I've worked with before is there now with eyes on the place. He hasn't spotted Nate, but if he's got a job, he may not be home yet," Shawn said.

"What's this?" Nadia asked, pointing to the map spread out on the table in front of Gideon and Shawn.

"An aerial map of Nate's neighborhood," Shawn answered.

"Good." Ryan's tone was grudging. "We're on a tight timeline, but I want to know as much as possible about what we are going into. If Nate is smart, he's got himself some protection. I don't want any of our guys getting shot trying to bring him home."

"Nate wouldn't have a gun," Nadia said, drawing the men's attention to her. Their parents had kept a close eye on them, but both she and Nate had lost friends to the epidemic of gun violence plaguing New York in the 1980s and '90s. "He hates guns." A tremor slivered through her at the memory of holding a gun on the intruder in Ryan's apartment. "We both do."

Shawn met her gaze. "People do things they'd never think of doing when they're in the kind of trouble your brother is in."

Shawn's statement hung in the air for a long moment. Nadia glared, but Shawn held her gaze, seemingly unaffected.

"Let's focus here." Ryan sat at the table next to Gideon, while Shawn went back to studying the map of Nate's neighborhood and planning how to approach Nate.

Nadia joined the three men but held her tongue as Ryan, Shawn and Gideon talked through possible scenarios for getting Nate to return to the city, from Nate

willingly coming back with them to the need to remove
him forcibly. She didn't like the idea of physically making Nate return to New York. It wasn't lost on her that
some of the plan Bs they discussed technically amounted
to kidnapping her brother, but there didn't seem to be
much else she could do if Nate wouldn't come willingly.

And then what?

"What happens once we get Nate back to New York?"

Getting Nate back to New York wouldn't end this
nightmare. They'd still have to deal with Smith, and she
wasn't about to just hand Nate over like a lamb to slaugh-
ter.

One gigantic problem at a time.

Ryan shared a look with the men at the table.

"The safest thing for you would be for us to turn him
over to Smith," Gideon said emotionlessly.

Nadia pushed her palms against the table. "No."

"The alternatives?" Ryan said, sending Gideon a look
that would have made other men shrink.

Gideon's expression didn't change. "We can try to
work out a deal with Smith that ensures your and Nate's
safety. Or go to the cops and set up a sting."

"I don't see Smith being willing to negotiate, not that
we could trust his word, anyway," Shawn said. "But Nate
has made him look bad, not to mention cost him millions
of dollars. Smith needs to make an example of him."

"Okay, so we take option two." Nadia speared Ryan
with a look.

"Going to the cops won't be easy either." Ryan shook
his head. "Parsmons isn't sold on all the incidents being
connected, and we haven't exactly kept him in the loop.
We'd lose a lot of time just bringing him up to date and
getting him on board."

"Not to mention completely lose control of the situation after we bring in the cops," Shawn chimed in.

"The NYPD can't mount an operation like this as fast as we can, and there's the little matter of them leaking like that strainer to the press." Gideon studied the documents on the table. "I've got a friend at the FBI's New York office. I've worked with her before, and I'm sure I could convince her to let us in on the op."

Gideon looked up when his statement was met with silence. "What?"

"I'm shocked to hear you refer to someone as a friend," Ryan teased.

"I'm shocked his friend is a woman. The perpetual scowling and grunting usually scares them off," Shawn said.

Nadia concentrated on the map on the table so Gideon couldn't see her smile. Despite the serious nature of the conversation, it was nice to have a moment of levity.

Gideon didn't appear to share her sentiment. His scowl deepened. "Do you want me to call her or not?"

"Yes," Nadia answered quickly before Ryan or Shawn could say something that might jeopardize her best chance for getting Nate out of this mess safely. "Thank you, Gideon."

She thought she saw Gideon's scowl soften for a fraction of a second, but before she could be sure, he grunted and ducked his head.

Ryan and the guys packed up the map and other documents they'd been studying.

"Everyone ready?" Ryan looked at each of them.

Shawn and Gideon nodded and grunted respectively.

Nadia swiped sweaty hands over her thighs. "Ready."

Shawn and Gideon started for the door.

Ryan stepped in front of Nadia and ran his hands up

and down her forearms. "You sure you want to go along? Even if everything goes as best it could, it's bound to be emotional for you."

She went up on her toes and laid a soft kiss on his lips. "I have to do this. I'll be okay."

Ryan pulled her closer, his kiss hard and demanding. After a minute, the conspicuous throat clearing from the hall had them pulling apart, but not before they were both breathless. "This is all going to be over soon. Don't worry."

Chapter Sixteen

It was dark when Ryan parked the rental they'd picked up at the airport behind a black Nissan Sentra. Ryan and Shawn got out of the car, leaving Gideon to watch over Nadia.

A tall African American man with wraparound aviators unfolded himself from the driver's side of the Sentra as Shawn and Ryan approached.

Shawn had given them all the lowdown on Jeremiah Griffin on the flight to Richmond. The ex-cop turned private investigator was selective about which cases he took but owed Shawn a favor. For several hours, he'd been watching the small bungalow that Nate rented.

"A man matching your subject's description went into the house at 6:28. Looks to be watching television in the front room just off the door," Jeremiah said without preamble.

Ryan glanced at his watch. It was 8:57. Nate had been home for almost two and a half hours, long enough to settle in and relax.

"How do you want to play this?" Shawn asked.

Two pairs of eyes turned to Ryan. "We don't have a phone number for him, so we'll have to knock."

"And if he doesn't open the door?" Jeremiah said.

Ryan raised an eyebrow. "You're not a cop anymore, right?"

Jeremiah smiled wryly. "That's what they tell me."

Ryan sent Jeremiah and Shawn to cover the back while he climbed the front steps of the house. He had his gun out of its holster, but he held it down by his side so any nosy neighbors wouldn't notice it.

He knocked on the door. "Nate, it's Ryan West. Nadia sent me. Open up."

The curtain at the front window fluttered. Several moments passed with no further movement.

"I'm not very inconspicuous out here on your porch," Ryan called out. "Why don't you let me in? We can talk."

"How do I know Nadia really sent you?" Nate called from the other side of the door.

Ryan shook his head. If he'd been one of Smith's men, Nate would be dead by now, his voice giving away his location within the house.

He pulled his phone from his pocket and sent a text to Gideon. Moments later, Nadia and Gideon stepped from the car.

"Look out your window," Ryan called.

The curtain fluttered again.

"This could be a trick. You could have kidnapped her. How do I know you aren't using her to get me to open the door? Then you'll kill us both."

The vein in Ryan's neck pulsated. There was no doubt Nate Shelton was a coward, but the man stomped on Ryan's last nerve. "If I'd wanted to kill you, you'd be dead, and I'd be on a plane back to New York already. Now, open the door."

Another minute passed before the door slowly opened. Ryan raised his gun.

Nate peeked around the door, his eyes going wide at the sight of the gun pointed at him.

"Is anyone inside with you?" Ryan asked.

"No."

Ryan motioned to the threadbare sofa in the small living room. "Sit and don't move."

He moved down the hall, clearing the other rooms in the house and letting Shawn and Jeremiah in through the back door.

Ryan sat in the chair across from the couch while Shawn and Jeremiah took up strategic positions throughout the room. "Did Nadia really send you?" Nate asked.

"Yes. She's anxious about you," Ryan said, taking out his phone once again and texting Gideon.

Less than a minute later, the front door swung open. Nadia stepped into the house, her eyes falling on Nate the moment she entered the house.

"Nate." His name came out on a sob.

She crossed the room, sweeping her brother into a hug before he rose from the sofa. Her shoulders shook, and she held on to him as if he might disappear if she let go.

A big part of Ryan wanted to turn away from the intimate moment between brother and sister, to give them privacy, but they didn't have the time for the Shelton siblings to work through their relationship. They needed to convince Nate that the only solution to this mess he'd gotten himself and Nadia into was for him to come back to New York and work with the authorities to take Smith down.

Ryan rose. "I'm sorry to interrupt this moment, but we have some things to talk about."

Nadia stepped out of Nate's arms and surprised them all by hauling off and punching her brother in the jaw.

Ryan stepped over the small ottoman between his

chair and the sofa and grabbed Nadia's arm before she could land a second punch to Nate's face.

"How could you do this?" she hissed. "How could you be so stupid and selfish?"

Nate rubbed his jaw. "I'm sorry. I didn't mean for any of this to happen. Things just got out of control so fast."

"Let's all have a seat," Ryan said, leading Nadia to the chair he'd been sitting in.

Ryan noticed she cradled the hand she'd hit Nate with.

"I'll see if there's ice in the fridge," Jeremiah offered, noticing Nadia's injury as well.

Once Nadia and Nate sat, Ryan spoke. "We got most of the story from your uncle, but I think you owe your sister an explanation."

Nadia glared at her brother. "He owes everyone in this room an explanation. Both Ryan and I landed in the hospital because of the secrets you and Uncle Erik have been keeping."

"Uncle Erik told me about the stuff that's been happening. I didn't know things would go this far." Nate's eyes held a plea for understanding.

Ryan examined the man in front of him. Gone was the confident, fit hotel executive that appeared in the pages of background information Ryan had on Nate. This Nate was thin, his skin sallow and saggy. The last eleven months had worn on him. Ryan couldn't bring himself to feel sorry for the man.

"Well, they have. How did you get mixed up with Lincoln Smith?" Nadia said.

Nate swallowed hard. "You talked to Smith?"

Jeremiah returned with ice in a dishrag. Nadia took it from him with a nod of thanks.

"Smith ambushed Nadia in her office and demanded

that she hand you over in forty-eight hours or else," Ryan said.

Nate turned to his sister with wide eyes. "And you're going to let these guys take me to him."

The anger in Nadia's eyes gave way to hurt. "Of course not."

Nate dropped his head. "It was just supposed to be a small real-estate venture. But the plan just kept growing bigger. I thought I could handle it. I wanted to prove that I wasn't just my father's son, a small-time hotelier. But I couldn't raise my half of the funds, not before the option expired. But I also didn't have ten million to pay Smith back what he'd put up for the option." Nate looked at Ryan, fear swimming in his eyes. "I know who Lincoln Smith is, and I knew he wasn't going to just write off ten million dollars."

Ryan fought the urge to knock some sense into the man. Smith might be a criminal, but he wasn't stupid. The fake-death gambit never had a chance of working. Nate was lucky he'd survived as long as he had.

"We are here to take you back to New York. Nadia is adamant that we not turn you over to Smith, even though it's what would be safest for her. And it's no more than you deserve."

Nate's head snapped up. "You don't think I know that? I know what a coward I am. I don't need you to remind me."

"We can try to get you out of this mess, but you need to come back to New York with us." Ryan paused for a second, letting his words sink in. "So what are you going to do, Nate? Are you coming with us, or are you going to leave your sister to face Smith on her own?" Ryan challenged.

It didn't matter that Nate didn't have a choice. He was

going back with them one way or the other. But maybe hearing how much Nadia was willing to sacrifice for him would compel Nate to man up.

Nate stared at the floor for several long minutes.

"Nate?" Nadia said.

Nate raised his head, locking gazes with Nadia. "I'll go with you. I'll go home."

Chapter Seventeen

The time neared two in the morning when they arrived back at the safe house in New Jersey. Nadia couldn't remember ever being more emotionally exhausted. Nate hadn't spoken to her at all on the flight, and a part of her welcomed his silence. There was so much distance and anger between them, and she wasn't sure they'd ever get back to where they used to be. The relief she felt at Nate being alive would have to be enough for now.

Until they sorted everything out, Nate would stay with Ryan and Nadia at the safe house. Given the late hour, Shawn decided to stay with them as well.

Nadia slid into bed and stared up at the ceiling. As tired as she was, sleep wouldn't come. Too much worry and…anticipation.

The soft click of her bedroom door opening finally came.

"Are you awake?" Ryan whispered.

She pushed herself up on the pillows. "Yes. I hoped you'd come."

Ryan snapped the door closed and slid into bed, drawing her to him.

"How are you doing with all this? Really?"

His hand trailed up and down her side, sending zaps of electricity running through her.

"It's almost surreal. I'd just started getting used to Nate being gone, and now he's back."

She pressed her hand to Ryan's chest and felt his heart rate pick up when she threw one of her legs on top of his and pressed in closer to his side.

"I'm glad he's alive, but…"

Ryan pressed a kiss to her forehead. "It will take some time for you and Nate to sort this all out. Don't rush yourself."

She tilted her head back so she could look into his eyes. "I don't want to talk about Nate or mobsters or either of us getting hurt right now. I just want to forget." She skimmed her hand down his bare chest to the waistband of his pajama pants. "Make me forget everything but you, Ryan."

His lips took hers softly, exploring slowly. She had been the initiator their first time together, but this time Ryan took control. His hands trailed over her body, stripping her of her nightgown before doing away with his own bottoms. He pressed his mouth to every inch of her flesh, learning what she liked, teasing and tantalizing her with every swipe of his lips or sweep of his tongue.

That they were attempting to be quiet so they didn't wake their brothers only heightened their passion.

"Ryan, please," she whispered his name, reaching for him.

He caught her hand, raising it above her head. "Unh unh unh, Miss Shelton. I'm in charge of this gorgeous body right now. I want to know every part of you tonight."

He continued to caress and tease until she was sure she couldn't take a moment more. And then he rose above her, his eyes locking on hers as he pushed himself inside her so exquisitely slowly that she was on the verge of breaking apart by the time he'd seated himself completely.

They stayed frozen that way for a moment. Then Ryan's breath hitched. Their eyes stayed locked as they moved in time with each other, slowly at first, and then faster until they reached a fever pitch.

He covered her mouth with his own as her climax hit. He followed her over the crest moments later.

They held each other afterward, whispering honeyed words of affection that led to a second round of lovemaking.

She awoke some time later, the room still too dark, even with the curtains pulled, for dawn to have broken.

She'd been too consumed with need earlier to consider whether their lovemaking might not be wise considering the injury to his side. She touched the unbandaged wound now, happy to see that it didn't appear that they'd done any more damage.

"It's fine," his sleepy voice rumbled.

"I'm just making sure. I don't need another thing to feel guilty about."

Ryan rolled, so he was on top of her. "You definitely should not feel guilty. I'd suffer through a lot more than a little cut for you."

As corny as the line was, it still brought a smile to her lips.

He kissed her, pulling away much too soon.

"Maybe I should head back to my room."

She stiffened beneath him.

"I just mean, I don't know if you want Shawn and Nate to know that I spent the night in your bed."

Nadia relaxed, a chuckle rushing through her. "It's a little late to be concerned about my virtue, don't you think?"

"Make fun if you want, but it'll be awkward walking

out of this room together, half-dressed since I don't have a shirt, I might add, with our brothers out there."

She wrapped her arms tighter around him. "I don't care if your brother or my brother or anyone else knows I spent the night with you. I…care about you."

She more than cared about him. She loved him. But she suspected he'd pull away again if she told him that now. "I think we could have something real, here. If you want to try for it."

Ryan pushed a lock of hair from her forehead.

She didn't think last night was just about them letting off steam, but she wouldn't beg him to be with her either. He had to be in this as much as she was or it would never work.

He dropped his lips to hers, brushing a soft kiss over her lips. "I want to try."

That was all she needed to hear. She knew she wanted Ryan, and if they tried, they could have something incredible.

The next time she awoke, the sun peeked around the edges of the curtains, and the other side of her bed was empty. She glanced at the clock and pushed back the irritation she felt at finding Ryan gone. It was after eight in the morning, and as much as she didn't want to, they had to get up sometime.

As soon as we settle this chaos, we'll pick a day to stay in bed all day.

A tremor of excitement shot up her spine.

Unlike Ryan's apartment, the four bedrooms in this house shared a single bathroom.

She opened the bedroom door, and voices drifted toward her from the front of the house.

"You're the best strategist we have. We need you. Dale can cover the hotel today."

"I can coordinate with you from the hotel. We'll brief the team via video conference if we have to."

They both fell silent as Nadia stepped into the kitchen.

"Don't stop your arguing on my account," she said, grabbing a mug and pouring herself a cup of coffee.

"We're not arguing. We're just making a plan for the day," Ryan said.

Shawn frowned at his brother. "We are arguing, because your plan is stupid and won't work."

Nadia took another sip of coffee, hiding a smile. "What is—"

"My plan is not stupid." Ryan crossed his arms over his chest.

Nadia tried again. "What—"

"You are the best man we have when it comes to planning ops," Shawn said.

Irritation brewed inside her. She set her coffee mug down and turned to the sink.

Ryan and Shawn continued to argue.

Nadia gathered a bit of water in her cupped hand and flung it at the brothers.

"Hey!"

"What the—"

They broke off their staring contest to glare at her.

"Don't ignore me. Why is it a problem for Ryan to do the planning for dealing with Smith?"

"I need the team and the resources we have in our office, so I couldn't be at the hotel with you."

"I didn't come all this way to screw it all up because the best man on the team was playing babysitter instead of doing his job."

"Hold it, now. I didn't say he was the best man on the team," Shawn interjected.

Both she and Ryan rolled their eyes and ignored Shawn.

"If you need to be in the office, that's where you need to be." Nadia threw her hands in the air. "Smith gave us forty-eight hours. I'll be safe until they are up, but we have less than a day left."

"What is going on out here?" Nate appeared at the kitchen entrance, his T-shirt and mesh shorts bedraggled, his feet bare.

Shawn strode across the kitchen and cupped his shoulder. "Come on in the living room. I think this conversation is headed for a place no sibling wants to witness."

Ryan growled at Shawn's back as he and Nate left the kitchen. "Jerk."

Nadia smiled. "He loves you, and you love him. Be grateful for every day you have together."

Ryan faced her, contrition painted across his handsome face. "I don't want to leave you alone."

Nadia rolled her eyes. "I'll hardly be alone at the hotel. And Dale will be there, right?"

"Yes," he muttered.

She kissed him, a smile on her lips. "I'll be fine."

"Promise?"

"Promise."

Chapter Eighteen

Gideon arrived at the safe house to stay with Nate while Ryan escorted Nadia to work, making sure she was safely under Dale's watch before he left. Being with Ryan had been good for chasing away thoughts of mobsters, real-estate options and the millions of dollars she and Nate didn't have to pay back Smith. But now, all those worries came flooding back. What if the plan to hand Smith over to the authorities didn't work? What if it did? There would still be the problem of Nate faking his death. He'd almost certainly broken some laws. She hadn't touched the money she'd collected as the beneficiary on his insurance policy, so that wasn't an issue. Still, she wasn't sure whether there was legal liability for having accepted it. She'd have to consult a lawyer. Under normal circumstances that would be her Uncle Erik, but she wasn't ready to speak to him.

That fear and worry stayed with Nadia all morning, through her usual meetings with her managers and into the early afternoon when she would have bombed a conference call with the bank's loan officer if not for Olivia's presence.

"Why don't you go home? Take the rest of the day off?" Olivia said after Nadia had disconnected the call.

Concern stabbed Nadia. "You think it went that badly?"

"No, it's not that. You just seem so distracted. Your mind isn't here, and that's understandable."

"I'm sorry, Olivia. I've been leaving you to deal with the hotel for the last several days, and even when I'm here I'm not."

"It's fine. I can handle it."

"No, it's not fine. And yes, you are handling it well, which is why I wanted to talk to you about taking on more responsibility if you're interested."

Olivia scooted to the edge of her chair. "I'm interested."

"I've been handling most of the tasks Nate used to do with the general managers' help, but that's not a long-term answer. I need another executive, someone who can look across all the properties and help me grow the business. I thought that could be you."

"Yes!"

Nadia laughed. "You've more than proved you can handle it, even before this last week. Does the title of VP of Hotel Operations have a nice ring to it?"

Olivia squealed and bounded around the desk, catching Nadia in a hug. "Thank you. Thank you. Thank you."

"Thank you. Honestly, I wouldn't have made it through the last eleven months without you, much less this week. You deserve the position."

Olivia returned to her seat. "You've been through a lot."

Nadia exhaled deeply. "You can say that again."

She hated keeping a secret from Olivia, but it was for the best at the moment. It wasn't clear exactly what Nate had gotten himself into, and until they knew, it was safer if no one knew he was alive. She hadn't even told Olivia about the man that attacked her and Ryan in his home, not wanting to give her friend another thing to worry about.

As if she could read Nadia's mind, Olivia asked, "Where is Ryan? He's been sticking to you like glue lately. Did something happen between you two?"

Nadia felt her cheeks heat with the memory of exactly what had happened between them.

"Oh, my goodness. Something did happen. Did the two of you—" Olivia made a gesture.

"Olivia!" Nadia thanked her lucky stars that Dale preferred to station himself outside the door to the outer office rather than sit in the office suite as Ryan did. Although, Dale's presence may have tempered Olivia's more inquisitive inclinations.

Olivia sprang out of her chair. "You did! I knew it. It's about time. You two have been circling each other like wolves for over a year. I'd begun to think it would never happen with you two."

Nadia felt her blush spread to the back of her neck. "I have not been circling anyone."

"You have. So, give me all the details." Olivia reclaimed her seat, an avid expression on her face.

"I will not. This is a place of business."

"Okay, let's go out for drinks after work tonight." Olivia held up a hand, warding off Nadia's refusal before it came. "You have to. We need to celebrate my promotion, anyway."

Nadia hesitated. "Okay, but we are celebrating your promotion. Nothing else."

"Got it. But just tell me if Ryan's a good kisser. He looks like an amazing kisser."

He'd kissed her more thoroughly than any man before him ever had, but Nadia wasn't about to confirm or deny that to Olivia. At least not without several cocktails first.

"Olivia."

"Okay, okay. I'll bug you when we're out later. But seriously, where is he? Is everything okay?"

Nadia wasn't ready to tell Olivia everything, but she wouldn't lie to Olivia either. "He's in Richmond tracking down a lead. He'll be back in the offices tomorrow."

"Oh, good. That means he's making progress. I've been so worried about you these last few days. That's part of the reason why I've wanted to do whatever I could to take some of the burden off your shoulders."

"And I'm so grateful for it." Nadia sat back. "I'm worried about Ryan. Not only did he get hurt because of this mess I'm in he also got arrested because of me."

Olivia grimaced. "Mike Dexter is such a jerk. I can't believe he wanted you to be some fawning bubbleheaded woman when you dated. And now to manhandle you the way he did."

"Ryan and West are doing all this stuff for me—protecting me and investigating to figure out who's behind everything that's been happening. I just feel like I should do something to get Mike off of Ryan's back."

"Why don't you go talk to him? I know Mike isn't known for his compassion, but he has to have a heart in there somewhere." Olivia shrugged. "You've got nothing to lose, at least."

"I'm not as sure as you are that he has a heart, but…" An idea formed in her head.

Appealing to Mike's heartstrings would get her nowhere, but he was all about business. And she not only had something he wanted, the more she thought about it, she realized she also held his career in her hands.

"I've got an errand to run. I'll be gone for a few hours." Nadia grabbed her purse and headed for the office door.

Olivia laughed. "You're going to enjoy having a second-in-command, aren't you?"

Nadia laughed along with her. "I think I am."

FORTY-FIVE MINUTES later Nadia stood at the receptionist's desk at Aurora Hotels' headquarters in Tribeca, Dale standing a discreet distance behind her. Upon hearing that Nadia did not have an appointment, the brunette's smile had fallen, and she'd lost interest in feigning politeness.

"As I've explained, Mr. Dexter does not take meetings from just anyone walking off the street."

Nadia's breathing quickened, and she glared at the receptionist, fighting to keep her temper in check.

"And as I have explained, I am not just anyone off the street. My name is Nadia Shelton. I am CEO of Shelton Hotels, and Mr. Dexter and I are in the middle of a business negotiation. While I don't have an appointment, he will want to see me."

The woman's gaze slowly traveled from Nadia's head to her toes, as if she couldn't believe the woman standing in front of her was CEO of anything. The receptionist took another hard look at the business card Nadia had given her before sliding it back across the top of her desk. "Be that as it may, Mr. Dexter does not take unscheduled meetings."

Nadia didn't have the time or the patience for this little power trip.

"Tell Mr. Dexter if I'm not in his office in the next two minutes, the police will be here hauling him out in handcuffs in twenty."

The receptionist shot her a dubious look, but Nadia held the gaze. "Try me."

Apparently, it wasn't a call the receptionist was willing

to make on her own. She pressed a button on her phone and then turned her back to Nadia. Her voice was a murmur, but the word *handcuffs* rang loud and clear. After several moments of silence, the receptionist swung her chair back around, replacing the handset on its cradle.

"Mr. Dexter will see you. Just around to the right and down the hall. His assistant will meet you and escort you to Mr. Dexter's office."

Dale moved to walk with her, stopping when Nadia held up a hand. "You need to stay here. I'll be fine."

Dale shook his head. "I don't know. Ryan wouldn't want me to leave you alone."

"There are dozens of people working on this floor." At his still less-than-convinced expression, she added, "If I'm not out in fifteen minutes, you have my permission to snowplow through whoever may be foolish enough to try and stop you and come find me, okay?"

He wasn't happy about it, but he took a seat in the reception area.

Nadia followed the receptionist's instructions. A lithe blonde met Nadia halfway down the hall, her pretty face marred by lips pursed as if she'd just sucked on a lemon.

"Mr. Dexter is a very busy and important man. He can only spare a few minutes."

Nadia marched toward the corner office, its large wooden door adorned with a plaque marking it as Mike's. "I won't need more than a few minutes for the business I have to take care of."

Nadia reached for the door handle, turning it and pushing into Mike's office without waiting for the assistant to announce her. The assistant bounded in behind her, apologizing for Nadia having barged in.

"It's all right, Portia. Miss Shelton and I go way back."

Portia shot one long glare at Nadia before backing from the room, closing the door as she left.

"I guess I can hardly complain, seeing as how I've made more than one unannounced trip to your office. What can I do for you, Nadia? You ready to sign on the dotted line?"

"I've been busy running a successful hotel chain, so maybe I missed the news. Has hell frozen over?"

Mike frowned. "If you aren't here for business, why are you here?"

"I'm here for business, but it has nothing to do with the hotels. I want you to drop the assault charges against Ryan West."

Mike laughed. "Now, why would I do that?"

"Because you assaulted me first. Ryan was protecting me."

"Oh, come now," Mike leaned back in his chair, his mouth drawing to one side.

"You may fancy yourself Don Draper, but it isn't 1950, and grabbing a woman and kissing her is a crime. I've already let Detective Parsmons know I'd be stopping by this afternoon."

Mike blew a raspberry. "You can't prove anything. Nobody will believe your jailbird bodyguard. But, look, I'm a reasonable man. Sell Shelton Hotels to Aurora, and I'll drop the charges. I'll even throw in the VP position for you like I offered." He flashed a cocksure grin.

Nadia placed both hands on his desk and leaned forward. "They don't have to believe him. My brand-new security system caught it all on tape. I wonder what the board will think about their president being arrested for assaulting the CEO of the company they're trying to acquire?"

Mike's grin morphed into a scowl. "I don't believe you."

Nadia smiled, stepping back from his desk. "Fine." She shrugged, pulling her cell phone from her purse and turning to leave the office. "I'll just give Detective Parsmons a call on my way out. Let him know I'm on my way to the police station."

Nadia reached for the door with one hand and lifted the phone to her ear with the other.

"Wait," Mike called out before she crossed the threshold.

Nadia held up her index finger. "One second, Mike. I'm on a call."

"Hang up the phone," he ground out between clenched teeth.

Nadia disconnected the call, not moving from the doorway. "We have a deal?"

Mike glowered, but she just waited, doing her best to remain expressionless. After a long moment, he spoke. "We have a deal."

"Great. Let's go. We have an appointment with Detective Parsmons, and I don't want to keep him waiting."

NADIA PRACTICALLY BOUNCED back into her office, with Dale trailing her.

Olivia looked up from the file she read. "Hey, you're back. I thought your errand would take longer."

"I got Mike to drop the charges against Ryan."

Olivia's eyes went wide. "You did? How?"

"I used his own dirty tactics against him. I threatened to press charges against him for grabbing me in my office the other day. No matter how much Mike's made for Aurora, the board isn't going to look the other way if I decide to press charges for his assault on me."

"So a bit of blackmail?"

Nadia narrowed her eyes at Olivia, but a smile played at her mouth.

Olivia raised her hands. "Hey, I'm here for it. I never liked Mike anyway."

"Did I miss anything?"

"No, but I'm glad you're back. There's some kind of problem in the kitchen, and a guest demanding to speak with you."

Nadia noticed Dale's eyes sharpen at Olivia's words.

"Mrs. O'Sullivan in 137. She's been a hassle since her arrival last night."

"A hassle how?" Dale asked, standing.

"The usual persnickety guest. The room we put her in last night was on too high a floor and not near an exit. The remote was missing in the room we moved her to this morning, and the temperature wouldn't set correctly. Now there's something wrong with the bathroom." Olivia rolled her eyes.

Dale relaxed.

"Why does she want to see me?" Nadia asked.

"Well, she requested to see the manager, but I can't find Stephen."

Nadia frowned. "Maybe he stepped out for a smoke."

Smoking wasn't allowed inside, obviously, and although she couldn't ban employees from smoking altogether, she'd stressed that employees who smoked should not return to work with cigarette smell lingering on their clothes. Most of the smokers hung out outside for a bit after finishing their cigarette to allow the smell to dissipate.

Nadia sighed. "I'll talk to her."

Olivia smiled. "Great. Maybe getting a private audience with the owner will get her to chill out."

"Ha. We should be so lucky." Dealing with crabby,

demanding and even rude guests was just part of being in the hospitality business. Nadia had learned how to deal with them without letting them get to her long ago.

Nadia stowed her purse, and Dale followed her out of the office suite.

The hotel had a handful of rooms on the first floor, tucked away from the noise of the conference rooms and the lobby.

Room 137 was the last room in the hall and next to an emergency exit leading out into a small alleyway.

Moments after Nadia's knock, a petite woman with gray hair pulled back into a chignon opened the door.

Nadia smiled down at the woman, extending her hand. "Mrs. O'Sullivan, I'm Nadia Shelton. I understand you haven't been having the most pleasant stay, and I wanted to see what I could do to change that."

The woman took Nadia's hand and frowned at Dale. "That's an understatement. I'd always heard good things about this hotel chain, but obviously those reviews can't be trusted," Mrs. O'Sullivan complained in a high-pitched voice.

Nadia pushed down her annoyance with the woman. "I understand we've already switched your rooms once. Is this room not more to your liking?"

"It most certainly is not. The sink is broken. How am I expected to get a good night's sleep with an incessant drip, drip, drip? Come see."

Mrs. O'Sullivan stepped away from the door and disappeared into the bathroom. Nadia hesitated for a moment, shooting a glance at Dale before stepping into the room. The bathroom was to the right of the room's door, across from the closet, its wood-slatted doors closed.

Mrs. O'Sullivan stood at the center of the bathroom, prattling on about the dripping sink. Dale followed Nadia into the room, letting the door close behind him but stopping outside the bathroom.

Nadia reached for the faucet, seeing the problem immediately. She pushed the handle backward a fraction, and the dripping ceased.

Annoyance swelled within her, but Mrs. O'Sullivan hadn't stopped complaining long enough to allow anyone else to get a word in.

Nadia glanced over her shoulder at Dale, catching his exasperated expression before keying in on the now-open closet door and the black-clad man stepping from it.

Dale must have noticed the change in her expression. He turned, but not before the man's hand shot out. A cracking sound rang through the room as the large black stick in the man's hand made contact with the side of Dale's head.

Dale dropped to the ground, blood seeping from his wound.

Nadia stepped back as something hard was shoved in her side.

"Keep your mouth shut, and you'll be just fine." The high pitch was gone, replaced by a far more menacing tone.

The man from the closet stuck his head out into the hall. "It's clear. Let's go."

The woman dug the gun into Nadia's side. "Move."

Nadia followed the man into the hall, Mrs. O'Sullivan—or whoever the woman was—falling in step behind. Nadia glanced down the hall, hoping someone would glimpse what was going on.

As if reading her mind, the woman spoke. "I'd hurry if I was you. Having a guest shot in your hotel would probably be bad for business."

The man pushed the emergency door open. The alarm that should have sounded was mute.

A black SUV waited in the alley.

The man opened the back door. "Get in."

Nadia hesitated, calculating the likelihood of getting past her two abductors and making it to the end of the alley. The odds were not with her.

The man stepped toward her. "Get. In. Now."

Nadia turned, lifting herself into the back seat. As she did, an excruciating pain burst at the back of her head and radiated forward. Then everything went black.

Chapter Nineteen

The small conference room at West was crowded when Ryan entered. He'd dispatched an operative to the safe house to babysit Nate. Now, Shawn sat at the rectangular conference table talking to Eugene. On the other side of the room, Gideon and a dark-skinned beauty with closely cropped natural hair appeared to be facing off. Gideon, his arms crossed over his large chest, stood silently stoic, as the woman, no doubt Gideon's FBI-agent friend, read him the riot act in whispered tones. Gideon's unaffected countenance seemed to increase the woman's annoyance.

Ryan raised an eyebrow, making a mental note to delve into that relationship when things settled down.

"You want to tell me what the Sam Hill you think you're doing?"

Ryan turned toward the conference door.

Detective Parsmons stood, hands on his hips, his mouth curled into a snarl.

"Why don't you have a seat, Detective, and we'll get started." Ryan waived Parsmons to the table.

Gideon and the woman with him took the hint and headed for chairs next to Shawn. Gideon pulled out a chair for the woman, earning another eyebrow raise from Ryan.

"Get started on what?" Parsmons snarled, moving to

the table and sitting heavily in a chair. Ryan took the chair next to Parsmons. "You call me and say Nathan Shelton is alive and well, and then insist I beat it down to your offices. If Shelton is alive, where is he?" Parsmons pointed across the table. "And what is the fed doing here?"

"Agent Johnson is here to help." Gideon's face showed no emotion, but his voice carried a clear warning.

Detective Parsmons narrowed his eyes at Gideon, but he wisely shut up.

Ryan made introductions around the table before getting down to the business at hand. "As you all know now, Nathan Shelton is alive." He quickly summarized how he and Nadia discovered Nate's duplicity, Erik Jackson's part in the scheme, and their trip to Richmond to pick up Nate.

"Where is Shelton now?" Parsmons asked.

"We've got him in one of our safe houses." Ryan cut Parsmons off when the detective started to object. "We've got a man with him. He's not going anywhere."

"I hate to agree with Detective Parsmons," Agent Johnson said, "but why not just hand Shelton over to the cops?"

"Because we work for Nadia Shelton," Shawn said, jumping into the conversation. "And our client is worried that her brother won't be safe in custody."

"Maybe she'll feel differently after I have her locked up for aiding and abetting fraud, harboring a fugitive and anything else I can get the district attorney to throw at her. How about that?" Parsmons said, rising.

Ryan ignored the anger bubbling in his stomach. "Sit down, Detective. Miss Shelton isn't trying to keep her brother from you. She's trying to keep him from Lincoln Smith."

Ryan explained that the reason Nathan Shelton faked

his death was to get clear of a business deal he'd been involved in with the mobster that had gone south.

"We asked you here, Detective Parsmons, because we have a plan. But we'll need the NYPD to buy in. And the FBI," Ryan said.

Parsmons crossed his arms over his chest. "I can't promise anything, but let's hear it."

Ryan looked across the table at Agent Johnson. "It's well-known that the FBI has been trying to track down Smith for a while."

Agent Johnson nodded.

"Smith has given Nadia forty-eight hours to turn over Nate." Ryan looked from Agent Johnson to Detective Parsmons. "We're proposing a sting operation. We let Smith think we're turning over Nate—"

"But the feds are there for him," Parsmons interrupted. "What does the NYPD get out of this?"

"Nate Shelton," Ryan replied. "Miss Shelton understands that her brother broke the law and won't be able to just walk away from that without suffering the consequences. She simply doesn't think the consequences should include being brutally murdered by a mobster."

Parsmons seemed to consider what Ryan said. "And how do you envision this going down?"

Shawn leaned forward, steepling his hands on the table. "That's still up in the air somewhat. Actually, a lot."

"As the FBI knows well, Smith is elusive. We don't have a way to contact him, so we have to wait for him to reach out. It's doubtful he'll go for any plan we suggest."

"He definitely won't." Agent Johnson shook her head. "Smith hasn't evaded capture this long by being careless. He'll want to control all aspects of Shelton's handoff."

"We know, and we'll just have to go with that. Eugene is the best at communications. Since we have to be flexible if this has a chance of working, I wanted him in on the plans from the start. We'll need to be in constant contact with each other."

Eugene flipped the cover open on the tablet in front of him and began tapping the screen. "That's not a problem. We've got everything we need here, and I can run a centralized command center remotely if we need to."

Detective Parsmons threw up a hand. "Hang on. The NYPD hasn't agreed to anything yet."

"You have a better idea?" Ryan asked.

Parsmons glared for a long moment before turning to Agent Johnson. "Is the FBI on board with this?"

Agent Johnson shrugged. "Officially, no. I'm not here. Unofficially, we want Smith."

"In other words, the FBI is happy to take the credit, but if this whole thing goes south, you know nothing about it," Parsmons spat.

Agent Johnson touched her nose before pointing at Parsmons.

"I'll ask again. Any of you have a better idea? Because I just don't see it." Ryan looked at each of the faces around the table.

"You could just hand Shelton over to the NYPD. Let the feds worry about Smith," Parsmons offered.

"I don't think that would be in the NYPD's best interests, Detective," Agent Johnson interjected. "This is the best chance the FBI has had at getting its hands on Smith, and I think my superiors will agree that it's worth a shot. If the NYPD doesn't agree, I'm sure we can find a few federal crimes Nate Shelton's escapade violated."

Agent Johnson's implication was clear; the NYPD would get on board or be pushed out of the way.

Detective Parsmons glowered.

Ryan held up his hands to quell the interagency war

threatening to break out. "Okay, I'm sure Agent Johnson and Detective Parsmons have to run this plan up their chains of command. Why don't you two do that? Gideon can show you to empty offices if you need privacy, and we'll reconvene shortly."

They all rose, and Gideon led the agent and the detective from the room. Eugene left after them to amass the equipment he thought they'd need for the operation.

Shawn circled the table, stopping beside Ryan. "What are the chances of this working?"

Ryan shook his head. "I don't know. Not great. There's too much we can't plan for. But our first priority is protecting Nadia." Ryan held his brother's gaze. "No matter what."

Shawn paused a moment, then nodded. "No matter what."

"Good. I'll call her now. I want her back at the safe house before all this goes down." Ryan punched the speed dial number for Nadia. "Who knows what Smith will do."

The phone rang four times before connecting to voice mail. He left a short message for Nadia to call him as soon as possible.

"She might be in a meeting or something. I'll try Dale," Shawn offered.

Shawn put the call on speaker, but the call once again went to voice mail.

The hair on the back of Ryan's neck rose. Nadia might be in a meeting, but Dale would have taken a call from Shawn. Unless he couldn't.

Shawn tried to call Dale a second time with the same result. He ended the call without leaving a message and dialed another number. Kevon, the operative that had taken Dale's spot manning the hotel lobby answered on the first ring.

"I need you to find out where Dale and Miss Shelton are right now," Shawn barked.

Ryan didn't hear Kevon's reply because his phone rang at that moment.

Nadia.

Relief flooded through him. He punched the button to accept the call.

"Nadia."

But it wasn't Nadia's voice that came from the other end of the line.

"Sorry to disappoint you." Smith's voice flowed over the line.

A moment passed before fear gave way to rage and Ryan regained the ability to speak. "Where is Nadia? If you've hurt her, I swear—"

"Calm down, Mr. West. Miss Shelton is fine. And she will remain so as long as you convey Nate Shelton to me," Smith responded.

"It hasn't been forty-eight hours."

"And yet my sources tell me you have already located Nate. I knew you were good, but I am impressed."

"Let Nadia go."

"Of course. Miss Shelton is just…a little insurance. As soon as you turn Nathan Shelton over to me, I will release her."

A knot tightened in Ryan's stomach. He knew better than to trust Smith. He should have moved faster, should never have let Nadia leave the safe house this morning.

As if he could hear his brother's thoughts, Shawn dropped a hand on Ryan's shoulder, steadying him.

"Where?" Ryan asked.

Smith gave an address.

"One hour, Mr. West. Be ready to trade."

Chapter Twenty

Nadia opened her eyes, blinking until her glassy vision came into focus. She was lying on a cot, a flat tin roof high above her. Rolling her head to the side, she saw large windows running in a horizontal line along the midpoint of the four surrounding walls. Through their dirty panes, she could see nothing but night. She slowly pushed up to a sitting position and waited for the room to stop spinning. Her head ached, and her stomach roiled. A sound from the far side of the room drew her attention. Lincoln Smith.

"There is aspirin and water on the table next to you." Smith sat at a card table a couple dozen feet away. "My sincere apologies for my friend's heavy-handedness." Smith shot a glare at the man from the hotel room. "Rest assured we have discussed how a lady should be treated."

The same man who'd struck Dale, and presumably her, hung his head, chastised. But when Smith looked away, the man's gaze returned to Smith once more, his expression morphing into a glower that sent a chill running down Nadia's spine.

She swallowed two aspirin, washing them down with water. "Where are we?"

Smith waved away her question. "No need to worry yourself with trivial details."

"Why have you brought me here?"

"Although I like to leave innocent family members out of my business dealings, I am not a patient man. Unfortunately, you are the best motivation to get both your brother and Mr. West to do what I desire."

Icy fear raced through her veins. "Nate."

Smith shook his head. "I know this must be distressing for you."

"I have money. It will take some time, but I can come up with six million. Six million, and Nate is free of all this."

Smith looked at her with a mixture of pity and sympathy. "Making promises he could not keep is how your brother got himself into trouble. Don't make the same mistake."

Nadia glared. "That's more than half of what Nate owes you."

Smith stood and moved closer to where she still sat on the cot, forcing her to tilt her head back to maintain eye contact. "It's not about money at this point. I won't let anyone get away with humiliating me. Ripping me off. Where I come from, it would be seen as an intolerable weakness."

"So you would kill a man to allay your insecurities." Nadia didn't hide her revulsion.

Fury, dark and malicious, lit Smith's eyes. "Be careful, Miss Shelton."

The cell phone on the card table rang. Smith stepped back, snatching the phone from the table. He listened for less than ten seconds, then returned the phone to the table.

Headlights swept across the windows at the front of the warehouse.

"They're here. Get her into the office there." Smith

pointed to the row of windowless offices lining the side wall of the warehouse.

The goon grabbed her arm and all but carried her to the middle office. He shoved her into the office. The door snapped shut before she'd righted herself and turned around. The lights in the room were on, probably controlled by a switch outside the door, illuminating a space with bare white walls and not much else. The office had been stripped of everything except a metal desk pushed against the wall, one of its legs propped up with a brick.

Nadia tried the handle on the door and, unsurprisingly, found it wouldn't turn. The lock looked to be nothing more than the cheap interior kind found at every hardware store in the country. It seemed of little use to break it, with Smith right outside the door, but she couldn't sit here and let Ryan and Nate walk into a trap. And she had no illusions that a trap was exactly what Smith had planned.

Voices sounded from outside the office.

"Where is Nadia?"

Ryan!

"Now, now, Mr. West. I promise you no harm has come to Miss Shelton. I am a man of my word."

"If you were a man of your word, Smith, Nadia wouldn't be here at all." Rage poured from Ryan's words. "Where is she?"

"Miss Shelton, would you be so kind as to let Mr. West know you are perfectly content."

Content wasn't exactly how she'd define her current emotional state, but Ryan sounded as if he was hanging on to his temper by a thread. The last thing the situation needed was for him to think she was hurt.

"I'm fine. I'm locked in one of the offices."

"Hang on. I'm going to get you out of here."

Not if she got out of here first. She focused on doing just that, blocking out Ryan's and Smith's angry words coming from the other side of the door. Ryan didn't want to hand Nate over to Smith before she was out of danger. Smith was not in agreement with that plan.

Nadia looked up. If the office door wasn't an option…

White pockmarked drop panels formed the ceiling. She doubted the panels would hold her weight, but maybe she could crawl along the top of the wall.

And go where?

Dropping into the middle of the warehouse floor onto a group of men who undoubtedly carried more weapons than she'd ever laid eyes on did not seem a good idea. Yet, staying in this room left her a sitting duck. Even if she was only able to shift over an office or two she'd have the element of surprise on her side.

She hauled herself onto the desk and teetered for a moment before finding her balance like a surfer catching a wave. Once she was sure the desk wouldn't throw her off, she pushed the panel closest to her up and away from the metal frame.

Taking a deep breath, she jumped, grabbed the top of the wall and pulled herself onto its narrow width.

She exhaled exhilaration and fear and began crawling along the wall.

"This is getting tiresome," Smith's agitated voice carried into the ceiling. "Produce Mr. Shelton, or I'll have my man here put a bullet in your pretty little girlfriend. I'm sure you don't think you can dispatch me and get to her before a bullet does."

She didn't wait for Ryan's response.

The ceiling of the office next to the one she'd been in was missing several tiles. It wasn't as far as she'd hoped to get, but from what she'd heard, she didn't have long before someone came looking for her.

She crawled to the adjacent office. Thankfully, the setup here was the same as in the office she'd left, with the desk pushed against the wall. Unlike the office she'd come from, this one did have a small window near the door.

She dropped down onto the desk, careful to stay out of view. She froze at the thud of her feet meeting the desktop. Seconds passed, and no one rushed through the door.

A pile of crumpled clothes near the desk caught her eye. It took a moment for her to realize that someone wore the clothes.

It looked like Smith had caught up with his rogue employee. Taras Ledebev lay on the floor, his face a bloody patchwork of bruises. His chest fell in slow, shallow breaths that made it clear he was in serious trouble.

The whine of a metal door opening filled the warehouse.

"Mr. Shelton. I'm glad you could finally join us."

She chanced a peek through the window.

Ryan stood beside Nate, steps inside the warehouse's open door, his gun held outstretched toward Smith. Smith had adopted a similar posture with his stance and gun.

She wouldn't let Nate turn himself over to a killer to save her.

"I'm here. Now let my sister go."

Nadia heard the door in the next room open.

A beat past. "She's gone."

Anger hardened Ryan's face. "What game are you playing, Smith?"

"She must be in one of those rooms. Find her," Smith barked.

Nadia scanned the room for something to defend herself with. This office had been stripped similar to the other, but a broom and bucket had been left in a corner. It wasn't much of a plan, but if she could incapacitate Smith's helper, it would increase the odds in their favor.

She grasped the broom in a batter's stance and waited to the side of the door.

The door swung open, and Smith's goon stomped in, gun in hand.

Nadia swung the broom handle, connecting with the man's hard stomach with enough force to send vibrations up her arm.

He bent at the waist, his large frame blocking the door. He'd had the wind knocked out of him, but he was rallying fast.

She raised the broom again, preparing to bring it down across the back of his neck.

The man raised his gun. "I wouldn't do that if I was you. Drop it."

Nadia opened her hands and let the broom fall to the floor.

"Move." The man waved his gun toward the door, stepping away from it to give her room to exit.

She took pride in the fact that he was still hunched a bit as he followed her out of the office.

Smith smiled without looking at her. "You are a fighter, I'll give you that, Miss Shelton. But I tire of these games." His smile dropped. "An even exchange, Mr. West? Miss Shelton will walk toward you at the same time Mr. Shelton makes his way to me, yes?"

"No!" Nadia called out.

"Shut up." The man behind her pushed her forward, farther from the office.

Ryan's eyes narrowed, never leaving Smith's face. He nodded assent.

"Okay. Move." Smith waved her toward Ryan and Nate with his gun. "But not too fast."

Nadia took a step, and Nate did the same.

Another step forward. Nate stepped forward too.

She felt as if she was involved in a weird mirror-image wedding march, but this was no happy occasion. Nate was effectively walking to his death. She couldn't let that happen.

Nadia stopped walking halfway between Smith and Ryan.

"I'm sorry I got you mixed up in this. I'm sorry for everything," Nate said, his eyes glassy with unshed tears.

"Nate, don't do this. You can't trade yourself for me." Nadia didn't try to stop her tears from falling.

"Don't worry, sis. Everything will be all right. Just keep walking." Nate stepped away from her, toward Smith.

She turned, a hand outstretched to reach for Nate.

"Nadia, come on. Let me get you out of here, sweetheart."

Ryan still held his gun pointed at Smith, but his gaze flicked to hers for a moment. She wasn't sure whether he was trying to communicate something to her or if it was just unbridled hope that this was part of a plan to get them all out of this unscathed, but she dropped her hand and moved forward.

It felt like hours, but she finally made it to Ryan's side.

"Keep going, sweetheart. I'll be right behind you."

"No. Not without Nate." The words barely escaped her mouth before a pair of large arms thrust through the open warehouse doors, grabbing her and yanking her into the dark night.

Behind her, glass shattered, and men shouted incomprehensible words. Three thunderous booms preceded a flash and the rapidly repeated bangs that could only be gunfire.

Nadia felt herself being lifted, and then the world turned upside down. Her torso made contact with a broad shoulder, knocking the wind from her for a moment. The ground sped by beneath her.

Moments later, she was placed on her feet and looked up into Shawn West's eyes.

The fear-fueled temper she'd been ready to unleash died at the sight of the warehouse.

Smoke billowed out of the shattered windows, and flames licked the roof. The blue door Shawn pulled her through was gone, a gaping hole where it had been.

"Ryan!"

A beefy arm wrapped around her waist, keeping her from running back toward the warehouse.

"No. You need to get checked out by the medics," Shawn said, showing no signs of strain against her struggling.

"But Nate and Ryan are still in there!"

"Ryan is good at what he does. If anyone can get himself and your brother out of there, it's him. And the first thing both of them will want to know is that you are okay."

Nadia let Shawn lead her to the back of an ambulance. He was right. There was nothing she could do but get out of the way.

There were people everywhere, many wearing windbreakers embossed with *FBI*, others clad in black and wearing bulletproof vests.

Please let Ryan and Nate have on bulletproof vests.

She knew what gunfire sounded like, and there had been more than enough bullets fired to take down both men.

She stared at the warehouse, trying to identify Ryan

and Nate among the people moving in and around the building. The frantic pace of her rescuers slowed, and three fire trucks moved in to begin dealing with the flames.

Still, there was no sign of Ryan or Nate.

"Nadia." Nate's weary voice sounded seconds before he rounded the open ambulance doors, leaning heavily on Ryan.

She wasn't sure which man to hug first, so she threw her arms around them both, dragging them into a three-person hug.

Nate groaned, and Nadia pulled back, the relief that had soared through her at seeing Nate and Ryan in one piece replaced by concern.

"Nate took two in the chest. He had a vest on," Ryan added quickly, "but he'll still need to go get checked out, and he'll be sore for a while."

Ryan helped Nate lower himself into the back of the ambulance, then stepped away so the EMTs would have room.

Nadia stepped into Ryan's arms, carefully this time in case he too had been injured. She tilted her head back so she could look into his eyes. "Thank you."

"Mr. Shelton, I'm Agent Kenzi Johnson with the Federal Bureau of Investigation. I'll be accompanying you to the hospital."

Nadia tensed, and Ryan ran a hand up and down her back. It was too much to hope that Nate would get out of the mess he'd made completely unscathed. She didn't know what the penalty was for faking one's death, but whatever it was, they'd deal with it. Nate and Ryan were alive, and that was what she wanted to concentrate on now.

A throat cleared behind them. "I'll pick you up at the

hospital," Gideon said, the statement obviously meant for Agent Johnson.

The agent narrowed her eyes at Gideon. "That won't be necessary."

"I'll stop by the coffee shop you like on the way," Gideon continued as if Agent Johnson hadn't spoken. "Mocha caramel latte, right?"

A low growl sounded in Agent Johnson's throat. "Fine. Do what you like. I don't have time to argue with you. I have to interview a witness."

Agent Johnson hoisted herself into the back of the ambulance with Ryan.

Ryan's, Shawn's and even Nadia's mouths fell open at the sight of Gideon's mouth curling into a smile.

The ambulance doors closed, and moments later it raced away from the scene.

"I can't believe it," Shawn said, his voice full of awe as he watched Gideon stroll away, a definite skip in his step. "You and Gideon have women, and I'm single. How is that even possible?"

Ryan dropped a hand on his brother's shoulder and pulled Nadia closer to his side. "You know what they say, bro. Love comes at you when you least expect it."

Chapter Twenty-One

Ryan had shot Smith and the man who'd kidnapped Nadia. Smith's wound would heal, but the other man hadn't been as lucky. Neither was Taras. Both men had succumbed to their wounds on the way to the hospital. Nadia wasn't sure how she felt about the men's deaths. On the one hand, they were the criminals who'd kidnapped her. On the other hand, they'd been killed so she could be saved. It was something she'd have to deal with in the coming days.

One thing she wouldn't have to worry about was Smith. He was somewhere in the hospital in FBI custody, under whose mandate he'd likely stay for the rest of his natural life, based on the information Agent Johnson had shared.

"The FBI aren't the only ones with good news," Detective Parsmons stated once Agent Johnson finished. "We caught a man attempting to set fire to a business in Lower Manhattan. An arsonist for hire. He was quick to give up his many contractors, one of whom was Mike Dexter."

Parsmons's words hit Nadia with a force similar to a knock to the head. "What! Why?"

Parsmons rocked back on his heels, happy to be the center of attention. "Mr. Dexter lawyered up, but his arsonist kept detailed notes and recordings for just such an occasion. It was all part of Mr. Dexter's campaign to get you to sell Shelton Hotels."

Even with all that she'd just been through, it was hard to believe Mike would go so far in his quest to get Shelton. And she planned to do everything she could to make sure he didn't weasel out of the consequences.

Parsmons and Agent Johnson said their goodbyes and headed for the exit. Nadia watched as the federal agent left the hospital through the ER entrance and strolled toward the black SUV Gideon leaned against. Gideon opened the passenger door for the agent. She paused at the open door, saying something that made Gideon throw back his head in laughter before getting in.

Nadia glanced at Ryan, whose mouth hung open like the clown at a carnival ball-toss game, just waiting for someone to toss a ball in.

It was a nice, if short, break from wondering whether Nate was okay.

She'd insisted Ryan drive her straight to the ER, but the doctors hadn't allowed her to see Nate. Ryan assured her Nate would be okay, that the bulletproof vest had caught the worst of it, but she wouldn't stop worrying until she saw for herself that Nate was fine.

As worried as she was about Nate, she couldn't help replaying in her mind something Ryan had said.

Love comes at you when you least expect it.

Love. Did he mean that he loved her? Because she knew without a doubt that she loved him. Had loved him since the day, over a year ago, when he'd first walked into her office. Whether it was propriety, professionalism or just simple fear that had been keeping her from admitting it, it wouldn't stop her from going after what she wanted now. And what she wanted was Ryan West in her life. Forever.

She glanced at him, and he squeezed her hand. "Nate's tough. He'll be okay."

The doors marked *Authorized Personnel* slid open, and a doctor strolled into the waiting room. "Miss Shelton?"

"That's me." She hurried toward the doctor, Ryan on her heels.

"Your brother will be fine. He's bruised, but none of the bullets penetrated his skin. We're going to keep him here for observation overnight, just as a precaution. He inhaled quite a bit of smoke, and we want to make sure there's no damage to his lungs."

She exhaled heavily. "Thank goodness."

"The police said it would be okay for you to go in and see him, if you'd like," the doctor said.

Her relief flagged at the reminder that even when Nate left the hospital, it might not be for home. Nadia and Ryan passed through the doors the doctor had come through, still holding hands. It wasn't difficult to discern which cubicle Nate was in. A uniformed NYPD officer stood at attention in front of only one of the curtained areas that lined either side of the ER.

The officer nodded at them, obviously having been told that they were okay to enter.

Ryan stopped outside the curtain. "I'll wait for you here."

She bussed a kiss on his cheek. She was ready to share her life with Ryan, but her relationship with Nate was in a precarious place. She preferred that these opening salvos into whatever relationship they might have going forward be made in private.

Nate's eyes were closed when Nadia pushed through the curtain.

His face was gray, and the strain of the last year showed in the lines that marred his face.

"Nate."

His eyes opened, and his lips turned up into a trembling smile. "I wasn't sure you'd want to see me ever again."

Nadia reached for her brother's hand, surprised to feel hot tears on her cheeks. "I just spent eleven months thinking you were dead. Of course I want to see you."

"I'm so sorry, Nadia." Nate's voice broke. "I just didn't know what else to do."

"We've got a lot to talk about. But you, me and Uncle Erik, we're all the family each other has, and we'll work through it."

She stayed with Nate a few more minutes before promising to be in touch the next day.

Ryan waited on the other side of the curtain. "You ready?"

She nodded, falling in step next to him.

They were silent on the walk from the hospital to the car.

Ryan held the passenger door to his SUV open for her just as Gideon had for Agent Johnson, and just like the agent, Nadia paused before getting in the car.

"You can drop me off at my apartment."

Ryan's mouth turned down in a frown. "Is that what you want?"

Her gaze swept the ground. "I can't keep imposing on you. Smith isn't a threat anymore."

"No, he isn't. And he's not why I want you to stay with me tonight either."

Nadia looked into Ryan's eyes. "You want me to stay."

"I do. I know I said I wanted to keep things professional between us, but I lied. It's never just been a working relationship with us, least of all these last few days."

Nadia felt heat rise on the back of her neck at the

thought of just how unprofessional they'd acted several times over the last few days. Still, she wouldn't have changed a thing.

She smiled. "No, it hasn't been. I want to see where this goes. I haven't exactly had great luck in the relationship department, but I think you just might be the man to change that, Ryan West."

She moved around the open door and slid her arms around his waist.

His arms came around her, drawing her close. "You know, I have been told I am the best at what I do."

His mouth met hers, proving that he was, in fact, the best at one thing.

* * * * *

COMING SOON!

We really hope you enjoyed reading this book.
If you're looking for more romance, be sure to
head to the shops when new books are
available on

Thursday 4th February

LET'S TALK
Romance

For exclusive extracts, competitions
and special offers, find us online:

f facebook.com/millsandboon

🐦 @MillsandBoon

📷 @MillsandBoonUK

Get in touch on 01413 063232

For all the latest titles coming soon, visit
millsandboon.co.uk/nextmonth

MILLS & BOON

THE HEART OF ROMANCE

A ROMANCE FOR EVERY KIND OF READER

MODERN

Prepare to be swept off your feet by sophisticated, sexy and seductive heroes, in some of the world's most glamourous and romantic locations, where power and passion collide.
8 stories per month.

HISTORICAL

Escape with historical heroes from time gone by. Whether your passion is for wicked Regency Rakes, muscled Vikings or rugged Highlanders, awaken the romance of the past.
6 stories per month.

MEDICAL

Set your pulse racing with dedicated, delectable doctors in the high-pressure world of medicine, where emotions run high and passion, comfort and love are the best medicine.
6 stories per month.

True Love

Celebrate true love with tender stories of heartfelt romance, from the rush of falling in love to the joy a new baby can bring, and a focus on the emotional heart of a relationship.
8 stories per month.

Desire

Indulge in secrets and scandal, intense drama and plenty of sizzling hot action with powerful and passionate heroes who have it all: wealth, status, good looks…everything but the right woman.
6 stories per month.

HEROES

Experience all the excitement of a gripping thriller, with an intense romance at its heart. Resourceful, true-to-life women and strong, fearless men face danger and desire - a killer combination!
8 stories per month.

DARE

Sensual love stories featuring smart, sassy heroines you'd want as a best friend, and compelling intense heroes who are worthy of them.
4 stories per month.

To see which titles are coming soon, please visit

millsandboon.co.uk/nextmonth

GET YOUR ROMANCE FIX!

MILLS & BOON
— blog —

Get the latest romance news, exclusive author
interviews, story extracts and much more!

MILLS & BOON
MODERN
Power and Passion

Prepare to be swept off your feet by sophisticated, sexy and seductive heroes, in some of the world's most glamourous and romantic locations, where power and passion collide.

MILLS & BOON
True Love
Romance from the Heart

Celebrate true love with tender stories of
heartfelt romance, from the rush of falling
in love to the joy a new baby can bring,
and a focus on the emotional
heart of a relationship.

MILLS & BOON
MEDICAL
Pulse-Racing Passion

Set your pulse racing with dedicated, delectable doctors in the high-pressure world of medicine, where emotions run high and passion, comfort and love are the best medicine.